TEMPEST RISING

Book One of the Jane True novels

NICOLE PEELER

www.orbitbooks.net

ORBIT

First published in the United States in 2009 by Orbit
First published in Great Britain in 2010 by Orbit

A CIP catalogue record for this book
is available from the British Library.

ISBN 978-1-84149-966-6

Typeset in Times by Palimpsest Book Production Limited, Falkirk, Stirlingshire
Printed and bound in Great Britain by CPI Mackays, Chatham ME5 8TD

Papers used by Orbit are natural, renewable and recyclable
products sourced from well-managed forests and certified
in accordance with the rules of the Forest Stewardship Council.

Mixed Sources
Product group from well-managed
forests and other controlled sources
www.fsc.org Cert no. SGS-COC-004081
© 1996 Forest Stewardship Council

FSC

Orbit
An imprint of
Little, Brown Book Group
100 Victoria Embankment
London EC4Y 0DY

An Hachette UK Company
www.hachette.co.uk

www.orbitbooks.net

To my family, for giving me every opportunity

CHAPTER ONE

I eyeballed the freezer, trying to decide what to cook for dinner that night. Such a decision was no mean feat, since a visiting stranger might assume that Martha Stewart not only lived with us but was preparing for the apocalypse. Frozen lasagnas, casseroles, pot pies, and the like filled our icebox nearly to the brim. Finally deciding on fish chowder, I took out some haddock and mussels. After a brief, internal struggle, I grabbed some salmon to make extra soup to – you guessed it – freeze. Yeah, the stockpiling was more than a little OCD, but it made me feel better. It also meant that when I actually had something to do for the entire evening, I could leave my dad by himself without feeling too guilty about it.

My dad wasn't an invalid – not exactly. But he had a bad heart and needed help taking care of things, especially with my mother gone. So I took up the slack, which I was happy to do. It's not like I had much else on my plate, what with being the village pariah and all.

It's amazing how being a pariah gives you ample amounts of free time.

After putting in the laundry and cleaning the downstairs bathroom, I went upstairs to take a shower. I would have loved to walk around all day with the sea salt on my skin, but not even in Rockabill was Eau de Brine an acceptable perfume. Like many twentysomethings, I'd woken up early that day to go exercise. Unlike most twentysomethings, however, my morning exercise took the form of an hour or so long swim in the freezing ocean. And in one of America's deadliest whirlpools. Which is why I am so careful to keep the swimming on the DL. It might be a great cardio workout, but it probably would get me burned at the stake. This is New England, after all.

As I got dressed in my work clothes – khaki chinos and a long-sleeved, pink polo-style shirt with *Read It and Weep* embroidered in navy blue over the breast pocket – I heard my father emerge from his bedroom and clomp down the stairs. His job in the morning was to make the coffee, so I took a moment to apply a little mascara, blush, and some lip gloss, before brushing out my damp black hair. I kept it cut in a much longer – and admittedly more unkempt – version of Cleopatra's style because I liked to hide my dark eyes under my long bangs. Most recently, my nemesis, Stuart Gray, had referred to them as 'demon eyes.' They're not as Marilyn Manson as that, thank you very much, but even I had to admit to difficulty determining where my pupil ended and my iris began.

I went back downstairs to join my dad in the kitchen, and I felt that pang in my heart that I get sometimes when I'm struck by how he's changed. He'd been a fisherman, but he'd had to retire about ten years ago, on disability, when his heart condition worsened. Once a handsome, confident, and brawny man whose presence filled any space he entered, his long illness and my mother's disappearance had diminished him in every possible way. He looked so small and gray in his faded old bathrobe, his hands trembling from the anti-arrhythmics he takes for his screwed-up heart, that it took every ounce of self-control I had not to make him sit down and rest. Even if his body didn't agree, he still felt himself to be the man he had been, and I knew I already walked a thin line between caring for him and treading on his dignity. So I put on my widest smile and bustled into the kitchen, as if we were a father and daughter in some sitcom set in the 1950s.

'Good morning, Daddy!' I beamed.

'Morning, honey. Want some coffee?' He asked me that question every morning, even though the answer had been yes since I was fifteen.

'Sure, thanks. Did you sleep all right?'

'Oh, yes. And you? How was your morning?' My dad never asked me directly about the swimming. It's a question that lay under the auspices of the 'don't ask, don't tell' policy that ruled our household. For example, he didn't ask me about my swimming, I didn't ask him about my mother. He didn't ask me about Jason, I didn't ask him about my mother. He didn't ask me whether or not I was happy in Rockabill, I didn't ask him about my mother . . .

'Oh, I slept fine, Dad. Thanks.' Of course I hadn't, really, as I only needed about four hours of sleep a night. But that's another thing we never talked about.

He asked me about my plans for the day, while I made us a breakfast of scrambled eggs on whole wheat toast. I told him that I'd be working till six, then I'd go to the grocery store on the way home. So, as usual for a Monday, I'd take the car to work. We performed pretty much the exact same routine every week, but it was nice of him to act like it was possible I might have new and exciting plans. On Mondays, I didn't have to worry about him eating lunch, as Trevor McKinley picked him up to go play a few hours of cheeky lunchtime poker with George Varga, Louis Finch, and Joe Covelli. They're all natives of Rockabill and friends since childhood, except for Joe, who moved here to Maine about twenty years ago to open up our local garage. That's how things were around Rockabill. For the winter, when the tourists were mostly absent, the town was populated by natives who grew up together and were more intimately acquainted with each other's dirty laundry than their own hampers. Some people enjoyed that intimacy. But when you were more usually the object of the whispers than the subject, intimacy had a tendency to feel like persecution.

We ate while we shared our local paper, *The Light House News*. But because the paper mostly functioned as a vehicle for advertising things to tourists, and the tourists were gone for the season, the pickings were scarce. Yet we went through the motions anyway. For all of our sins, no one could say that the True family wasn't good at going through the motions. After breakfast, I doled out my father's copious pills and set them next to his orange juice. He flashed me his charming smile, which was the only thing left unchanged after the ravages to his health and his heart.

'Thank you, Jane,' he said. And I knew he meant it, despite the fact that I'd set his pills down next to his orange juice every single morning for the past twelve years.

I gulped down a knot in my throat, since I knew that no small share of his worry and grief was due to me, and kissed him on the cheek. Then I bustled around clearing away breakfast, and bustled around getting my stuff together, and bustled out the door to get to work. In my experience, bustling is always a great way to keep from crying.

Tracy Gregory, the owner of Read It and Weep, was already hard at work when I walked in the front door. The Gregorys were an old fishing family from Rockabill, and Tracy was their prodigal daughter. She had left to work in Los Angeles, where she had apparently been a successful movie stylist. I say apparently because she never told us the names of any of the movies she'd worked on. She'd only moved back to Rockabill about five years ago to open Read It and Weep, which was our local bookstore, café, and all-round tourist trap. Since tourism replaced fishing as our major industry, Rockabill can just about support an all-year-round enterprise like Read It and Weep. But other things, like the nicer restaurant – rather unfortunately named The Pig Out Bar and Grill – close for the winter.

'Hey girl,' she said, gruffly, as I locked the door behind me. We didn't open for another half hour.

'Hey Tracy. Grizelda back?'

Grizelda was Tracy's girlfriend, and they'd caused quite a stir when they first appeared in Rockabill together. Not only were they lesbians, but they were as fabulously lesbionic as the inhabitants of a tiny village in Maine could ever imagine. Tracy carried herself like a rugby player, and dressed like one, too. But she had an easygoing charisma that got her through the initial gender panic triggered by her re-entry into Rockabill society.

And if Tracy made heads turn, Grizelda practically made them spin *Exorcist* style. Grizelda was not Grizelda's real name. Nor was Dusty Nethers, the name she used when she'd been a porn star. As Dusty Nethers, Grizelda had been fiery haired and as boobilicious as a *Baywatch* beauty. But in her current incarnation, as Grizelda Montague, she sported a sort of Gothic-hipster look – albeit one that was still very boobilicious. A few times a year Grizelda disappeared for weeks or a month, and upon her return home she and Tracy would complete some big project they'd been discussing, like redecorating the store or adding a sunroom onto their little house. Lord knows what she got up to on her profit-venture vacations. But whatever it was, it didn't affect her relationship with Tracy. The pair were as close as any husband and wife in Rockabill, if not closer, and seeing how much they loved each other drove home to me my own loneliness.

'Yeah, Grizzie's back. She'll be here soon. She has something for you . . . something scandalous, knowing my lady love.'

I grinned. 'Awesome. I love her gifts.'

Because of Grizzie, I had a drawer full of naughty underwear, sex toys, and dirty books. Grizzie gave such presents for *every* occasion; it didn't matter if it was your high school graduation, your fiftieth wedding anniversary, or your baby's baptism. This particular predilection meant she was a prominent figure on wedding shower guest lists from Rockabill to Eastport, but made her dangerous for children's parties. Most parents didn't appreciate an 'every day of the week' pack of thongs for their eleven-year-old daughter. Once she'd given me a gift certificate for a 'Hollywood' bikini wax and I had to Google the term. What I discovered made me way too scared to use it, so it sat in my 'dirty drawer', as I called it, as a talking point. Not that anyone ever went into my dirty drawer with me, but I talked to myself a lot, and it certainly provided amusing fodder for my own conversations.

It was also rather handy – no pun intended – to have access to one's own personal sex shop during long periods of enforced abstinence . . . such as the last eight years of my life.

'And,' Tracy responded with a rueful shake of her head, 'her gifts love you. Often quite literally.'

'That's all right, somebody has to,' I answered back, horrified at the bitter inflection that had crept into my voice.

But Tracy, bless her, just stroked a gentle hand over my hair that turned into a tiny one-armed hug, saying nothing.

'Hands off my woman!' crowed a hard-edged voice from the front door. Grizelda!

'Oh, sorry,' I apologized, backing away from Tracy.

'I meant for Tracy to get off *you*,' Grizzie said, swooping toward me to pick me up in a bodily hug, my own well-endowed chest clashing with her enormous fake bosoms. I hated being short at times like these. Even though I loved all five feet and eleven inches of Grizzie, and had more than my fair share of affection for her ta-ta-riddled hugs, I loathed being manhandled.

She set me down and grasped my hands in hers, backing away to look me over appreciatively while holding my fingers at arm's length. 'Mmm, mmm,' she said, shaking her head. 'Girl, I could sop you up with a biscuit.'

I laughed, as Tracy rolled her eyes.

'Quit sexually harassing the staff, Grizzly Bear,' was her only comment.

'I'll get back to sexually harassing you in a minute, passion flower, but right now I want to appreciate our Jane.' Grizelda winked at me with her florid violet eyes – she wore colored lenses – and I couldn't help but giggle like a school girl.

'I've brought you a little something,' she said, her voice sly.

I clapped my hands in excitement and hopped up and down in a little happy dance.

I really did love Grizzie's gifts, even if they challenged the tenuous grasp of human anatomy imparted to me by Mrs Renault in her high school biology class.

'Happy belated birthday!' she cried as she handed me a beautifully wrapped package she pulled from her enormous handbag. I admired the shiny black paper and the sumptuous red velvet ribbon tied up into a decadent bow – Grizzie did everything with style – before tearing into it with glee. After slitting open the tape holding the box closed with my thumbnail, I was soon holding in my hands the most beautiful red satin nightgown I'd ever seen. It was a deep, bloody, blue-based red, the perfect red for my skin tone. And it was, of course, the perfect length, with a slit up the side that would rise almost to my hip. Grizzie had this magic ability to always buy people clothes that fit. The top was generously cut for its small dress size, the bodice gathered into a sort of clamshell-like tailoring that I knew would cup my boobs like those hands in that famous Janet Jackson picture. The straps were slightly thicker, to give support, and crossed over the *very* low-cut back. It was absolutely gorgeous – very adult and sophisticated – and I couldn't stop stroking the deliciously watery satin.

'Grizzie,' I breathed. 'It's gorgeous . . . but too much! This must have cost a fortune.'

'You are worth a fortune, little Jane. Besides, I figured you might need something nice . . . since Mark's "special deliveries" should have culminated in a date by now.'

Grizzie's words trailed off as my face fell and Tracy, behind her, made a noise like Xena, Warrior Princess, charging into battle.

Before Tracy could launch into just how many ways she wanted to eviscerate our new letter carrier, I said, very calmly, 'I won't be going on any dates with Mark.'

'What happened?' Grizzie asked, as Tracy made another grunting declaration of war behind us.

'Well . . .' I started, but where should I begin? Mark was new to Rockabill, a widowed employee of the U.S. Postal Service, who had recently moved to our little corner of Maine with his two young daughters. He'd kept forgetting to deliver letters and packages, necessitating second, and sometimes third, trips to our bookstore, daily. I'd thought he was sweet, but rather dumb, until Tracy had pointed out that he only forgot stuff when I was working.

So we'd flirted and flirted and flirted over the course of a month. Until, just a few days ago, he'd asked me out. I was thrilled. He was cute; he was *new*; he'd lost someone he was close to, as well. And he 'obviously' didn't judge me on my past.

You know what they say about assuming . . .

'We had a date set up, but he cancelled. I guess he asked me out before he knew about . . . everything. Then someone must have told him. He's got kids, you know.'

'So?' Grizzie growled, her smoky voice already furious.

'So, he said that he didn't think I'd be a good influence. On his girls.'

'That's fucking ridiculous,' Grizzie snarled, just as Tracy made a series of inarticulate chittering noises behind us. She was normally the sedate, equable half of her and Grizzie's partnership, but Tracy had nearly blown a gasket when I'd called her crying after Mark bailed on me. I think she would have torn off his head, but then we wouldn't have gotten our inventory anymore.

I lowered my head and shrugged. Grizzie moved forward, having realized that Tracy already had the anger market cornered.

'I'm sorry, honey,' she said, wrapping her long arms around me. 'That's . . . such a shame.'

And it was a shame. My friends wanted me to move on, my dad wanted me to move on. Hell, except for that tiny sliver of me that was still frozen in guilt, *I* wanted to move on. But the rest of Rockabill, it seems, didn't agree.

Grizzie brushed the bangs back from my eyes, and when she saw tears glittering she intervened, Grizelda-style.

Dipping me like a tango dancer, she growled sexily, 'Baby, I'm gonna butter yo' bread . . .' before burying her face in my exposed belly and giving me a resounding zerbert.

That did just the trick. I was laughing again, thanking my stars for about the zillionth time that they had brought Grizzie and Tracy back to Rockabill because I didn't know what I would have done without them. I gave Tracy her own hug for the present, and then took it to the back room with my stuff. I opened the box to give the red satin one last parting caress, and then closed it with a contented sigh.

It would look absolutely gorgeous in my dirty drawer.

We only had a few things to do to get the store ready for opening, which left much time for chitchat. About a half hour of intense gossip later, we had pretty much exhausted 'what happened when you were gone' as a subject of conversation and had started in on plans for the coming week, when the little bell above the door tinkled. My heart sank when I saw it was Linda Allen, self-selected female delegate for my own personal persecution squad. She wasn't quite as bad as Stuart Gray, who hated me even more than Linda did, but she did her best to keep up with him.

Speaking of the rest of Rockabill, I thought, as Linda headed toward romance.

She didn't bother to speak to me, of course. She just gave me one of her loaded looks that she could fire off like a World War II gunship. The looks always said the same things. They spoke of the fact that I was the girl whose crazy mother had shown up in the center of town out of nowhere, *naked*, in the middle of a storm. The fact that she'd *stolen* one of the most eligible Rockabill bachelors and *ruined him for life*. The fact that she'd given birth to a baby *without being married*. The fact that I insisted on being *that child* and upping the ante by being *just as weird as my mother*. That was only the tip of the vituperative iceberg that Linda hauled into my presence whenever she had the chance.

Unfortunately, Linda read nearly as compulsively as I did, so I saw her at least twice a month when she'd come in for a new stack of romance novels. She liked a very particular kind of plot: the sort where the pirate kidnaps some virgin damsel, rapes her into loving him, and then dispatches lots of seamen while she polishes his cutlass. Or where the Highland clan leader kidnaps some virginal English Rose, rapes her into loving him, and then kills entire armies of Sassenachs while she stuffs his haggis. Or where the Native American warrior kidnaps a virginal white settler, rapes her into loving him, and then kills a bunch of colonists while she whets his tomahawk. I hated to get Freudian on Linda, but her reading patterns suggested some interesting insights into why she was such a complete bitch.

Tracy had received a phone call while Linda was picking out her books, and Grizelda was sitting on a stool far behind the counter in a way that clearly said 'I'm not actually working, thanks', But Linda pointedly ignored the fact that I was free to help her, choosing, instead, to stand in front of Tracy. Tracy gave that little eye gesture where she looked at Linda, then looked at me, as if to say, 'She can help you,' but Linda insisted on being oblivious to my presence. Tracy sighed and cut her telephone conversation short. I knew that Tracy would love to tell Linda to stick her attitude where the sun don't shine, but Read It and Weep couldn't afford to lose a customer who was as good at buying books as she was at being a snarky snake face. So Tracy rang up Linda's purchases and bagged them for her as politely as one can without actually being friendly and handed the bag over to Linda.

Who, right on cue, gave me her parting shot, the look I knew was coming but was never quite able to deflect.

The look that said, *There's the freak who killed her own boyfriend.*

She was wrong, of course. I hadn't actually killed Jason. I was just the reason he was dead.

CHAPTER TWO

I was already stripping off my clothes by the time I got to the secret cove that is my little sanctuary. I was way too pissed off to bother with the wetsuit.

Fuck Linda, I thought, as I tore off my shirt and bra.

Fuck Rockabill helped propel me out of my jeans and panties.

And fuck me accompanied my shoes and socks, and then it was a short sprint into the ocean, whose waves reared up and enveloped me the way my mother's arms had when I was a little girl. In fact, swimming was all I had left of my mother, really. Her real face, the face in my memories, had begun to fade years ago, leaving behind only details I'd memorized from photographs. But I would never forget our clandestine nightly swims. The little secret that bound us together when I was a child.

And which, I suspected, had driven my family apart.

My mother, Mari, had turned up naked as a jaybird one night right before an awful storm hit. My father and the other young men of the town had been racing around for the preceding few hours, helping people board up the windows of the shops and houses that lined our small main street and central square. Then, out of nowhere, his buddy Trevor had let out a low whistle of surprise at the same time that Louis said, 'Holy shit,' in the awestruck voice he used when they went to the big Fourth of July celebration in Bangor to see a real fireworks display. My father, along with just about everybody else who lived in Rockabill at the time, had looked up to see a naked young woman, black hair swirling down to her waist, sauntering down the street as if she had an invitation that specifically requested 'stark naked, only, please'. No one moved, except my big brave father, who took off his coat and went and put it around the young woman's shoulders. She smiled up at him, and that's the moment he says that he knew he loved her and couldn't live without her.

For propriety's sake, he'd taken her to the Grays', Rockabill's only bed and breakfast at the time. That it was strategically so close to our house was never mentioned in the official story. Nick and Nan were still alive and in charge, not Stuart's nasty parents, Sheila and Herbert. Nick and Nan gave her a bed for the night but weren't all that surprised when they woke up to find it empty. Nor were they surprised when they found the girl and my dad at the local diner that morning, sharing a big breakfast of bacon and eggs and pancakes. I came around about a year later into an ideal family. My parents adored one another; Nick and Nan served as the perfect surrogate grandparents (my father's parents had passed away before I was born), and soon Jason joined his grandparents, Nick and Nan, to take his place as my best friend and soul mate. For six years I lived as happily as a child could live. Until the night another big storm struck, one almost as bad as the one that was raging the night my parents first shared a bed together. That morning, my mom was gone as suddenly and inexplicably as she had appeared.

Then I learned the truth about our family: that the cozy nest of happiness in which I'd enjoyed growing up was a sham. Rockabill, except for Nick, Nan, and Jason, had never accepted my mother. Many in the village considered her dangerously different and were happy to have their worst suspicions confirmed by her abandonment of her husband and young daughter. That a young girl whose mother had deserted her deserved any sympathy was trumped by the fact that I looked almost exactly like her: the same dark hair and eyes, the same pale skin, and, as I grew older, the same dangerous curves. Rockabill wasn't an overtly religious community, but our Puritan ancestors must have channeled Melanie Griffith down through the generations. *Like her mother*, they whispered, *that girl has a bod for sin*. The whispers had stuck, growing into shouts as the years went by and other worse things happened.

Angrily, I swam and swam, letting the powerful currents and riptides of the Old Sow and her piglets jostle me back and forth. I wanted to lose myself in the whirlpool, and she was always happy to oblige.

The Old Sow used to be the bane of Rockabill's fishermen and had killed more than her fair share of our men. Now, however, she was our livelihood: the tourist attraction that we depended on for sustenance. She was one of the five biggest whirlpools on earth, and boats had to be careful to avoid her. But there I was, plunging along her outermost boundaries like a naked little seal.

I didn't know why I was such a powerful swimmer, since I was so small, or why I loved it so much. And yet I was never happier than when I was in the water. If I was honest with myself, there was more to it than that. I really *had* to swim. It was as much of an addiction as it was a desire. Not that I understood the implications of that need. I knew my swimming was the key to something, but it was that annoying, anonymous key that hung on every inherited key ring. The key that didn't fit any door in the house, or any drawer in the office, or any suitcase in the attic. Swimming was my mystery key that constantly nagged me with its presence. But, no matter how many locks I tried, it never revealed anything about what it concealed.

I tried to push away my negative thoughts and focus on my delight as the thunder clapped and the rain poured down, causing the ocean to buck in response. The storm that was percolating when I drove home from the grocery store had struck while my father and I were eating dinner. It was all I could do to get through the meal without banging down my fork and running off into the night like some maenad. I was still so angry from my biweekly run-in with Linda that I was short-tempered with my father. Which made me feel guilty, which made me feel frustrated, which made me feel even more angry . . .

When I got like that only a swim helped.

And if any old swim was therapeutic, a swim during a storm was better than Prozac. Maybe it was because my mother had appeared, and disappeared, during a storm that made me so obsessed with them. But I was never happier than when the sea was wild and thrusting and angry and I was roiling around in it as powerless and riveted as one of Linda's paperback heroines confronted with her first unbuckled swashbuckler.

A particularly strong wave dunked me, and I realized I was getting dangerously close to the Old Sow. Who, in her bounteous unpredictability, was happily swirling away despite the fact that she should really be quiet at this time of night. But I was so pissed off that only really rough water was going to do for me tonight. Whenever I had a run-in with Stuart or

Linda, I couldn't help but think about my mom. Her disappearance was like a sore tooth demanding to be prodded.

I used the riptide caused by one of the Sow's piglets to help shoot me up into the air so I could dive back down, like a porpoise. I landed more heavily than I'd anticipated, the piglet forcing me into a strong current that wanted to carry me to her mother. I fought hard to free myself, but the current had me in its vicelike grip. The Old Sow was nowhere near the most powerful of the earth's whirlpools, but she was far too strong even for my freakish swimming abilities. I had gotten way too close, and it was taking everything I had to extricate myself from the current.

I was fighting and fighting, but not going anywhere, when I felt the panic start to rise. If I did drown, I'd be so pissed off. It would prove that everything they'd said about me after Jason's death was true, even though it was a total pack of lies.

But then, as if by magic, the current around me slacked off, just for a second. With an almighty effort I was free, backing respectfully away from the Old Sow and her progeny. I treaded water, still feeling the adrenaline surging through my veins. I couldn't believe I'd been dumb enough to get that close. I was cursing my own stupidity as my heart thudded in my chest, partially from exertion and partially from fear.

Then everything froze: my heart felt like a cold hand had shot out of the water and wrapped around it, stopping it midbeat. My brain ceased all coherent function. Only my hands and feet continued treading water as if on autopilot, keeping me afloat.

I'd gotten out of the Old Sow unscathed, but somebody else hadn't.

I could see a shape bobbing in the grasp of the main whirlpool like some nightmarish buoy. And I knew from terrible experience that it had to be a human. If I thought I'd been afraid before, I nearly Roadrunnered it to shore as my fight-or-flight response kicked in. Every fiber of my being told me to get the fuck out of the water and not face whatever was out there.

It's not that I thought it was some kind of monster. I assumed it was somebody I loved: dead and drowned, because of me.

Who could have seen me come to the cove? I'd come from my house, through the back door, and out through our woods. Nobody lived by us except the Grays, and Sheila and Herbert wouldn't be hanging around outside on a cold night like this. That left Stuart, but if Stuart *had* thought I was drowning he certainly wouldn't attempt a rescue. He'd sit down and light up a cigar to celebrate my demise.

That left my father. At that thought my heart, which had tentatively begun beating again, seized right back up.

But then my brain kicked in. My father knew I swam even if he didn't talk about it, and he wouldn't attempt a 'rescue'. So the only way I was going to find out if, once again, I'd gone and killed somebody was to get that body out of the Sow.

The real whirlpool, whose little, eddying piglet had just about drowned me a minute ago. Shit.

I swam a wide circuit of the Old Sow, trying to figure out how the hell I was going to get out there. But it was impossible, there was absolutely no way to get any closer. Nevertheless, the body was doing an obscene dance, caught as it was in the whirlpool's currents. I couldn't leave it like that. It had been a person up until quite recently and probably a person I knew. Panic rose, and I told myself not to go there.

I backed away, treading water. *Think, Jane.*

But nothing was coming to me. There was no way I could get any closer than I was, and watching as the body was sucked under the waves and then forced back up to the surface made my anxiety and fear all the more acute.

My emotions were roiling inside of me. I tried to suppress the memories but seeing the body caught up in the whirlpool was like watching a video recording of that other horrible night. But I closed off my mind to those memories. I wasn't going there; nothing could make me go there. As I struggled to get my fear under control another emotion rose to the fore – anger. I was totally pissed off. What the hell was *another* body doing in my whirlpool? How many times did I have to find a body? Shouldn't bodies be like lightning and avoid striking the same person twice?

I gritted my teeth and willed myself to focus on the here and now, on the tiny bobbing speck at the mercy of the Old Sow. The body was caught in the strong currents circling the whirlpool's epicenter, but she must have been losing power for it seemed as if the body's circles had gotten larger and looser. *Of course it is*, I thought, honing in on my anger to help keep my fear at bay. *I am Jane True: corpse whisperer.*

The body was definitely coming free of the Sow. She didn't appear to be quieting, but her internal coil must be loosening imperceptibly, sending outward what she once drew near.

Come on, I thought impatiently, ignoring my fear and purposely stoking my bad temper. I preferred anger to memories, any day. *Come to Jane . . .*

The bobbing figure was getting closer, but one of the piglets had it now. In my frustration I nearly screamed. I could now see the body was that of a man, and I didn't think I recognized him as one of Rockabill's residents. *Who are you?* I thought, before turning my attention to the hungry piglet. 'You let go!' I shouted, even though my voice didn't make a dent in the cacophony created by the storm and the roiling ocean.

But as if it had heard me, the piglet spat out its gruesome plaything. The man was finally free of the Sow, and a helpful current was carrying it straight toward me. I shuddered, not only because of the approaching corpse but also because of the uncanny resemblance of this night to that other night. *You will* not *think about that!* I thought, shutting that door in my mind before it could fully open.

Besides, here in the present, the unknown body was nearly at arm's length—

Gotcha!

I now had hold of the corpse, and I started towing it to shore. The sea was rough and it was a long swim to get me and my heavy burden back to land. But I was nowhere near as exhausted as I'd been that other night, so the swim went quickly and soon I was close enough to the shore that I'd have to stop swimming and get my legs under me to walk without letting go of the body. Whoever he was, he was fully clothed and getting more and more awkward to handle. And I still hadn't gotten a good enough look at his face; the sea was too rough for me to stop and turn him so I could see.

I managed to haul myself up to a standing position and drag my burden onto the public beach. I collapsed next to it, trying to get my breath back. The swimming hadn't been so bad, but lugging him that short walk had nearly killed me.

I was also getting a bad case of the heebie-jeebies. As the adrenaline faded, and with the struggle to get the body onshore over, I was now contemplating the fact that I had been clutching a corpse.

I had to touch him again, too, if I was going to see who the hell it was.

The body was facedown in the sand. When I went to turn him, I got a good look at the back of his head and my gorge rose.

There was a big flap of scalp hanging off the back of his head, showing an expanse of very white skull that was obviously smashed. The sea water had washed away the blood, but that made it worse. It was not often we got such a stark reminder that underneath our own fleshy little faces was one of those leering white skeletons that symbolized death and decay in every culture. I thought I saw a little bit of brain peeping out from a particularly bad crack, which really made me want to puke.

I sat down heavily, my back to the body, trying to breathe as I fought the waves of nausea battering my stomach. Whoever this was, he hadn't died by drowning. There weren't any rocky outcroppings around the Old Sow on which he could have bashed his head like that. I felt a flash of relief: Whoever had died here tonight, it wasn't my fault. That didn't make the guy any less dead, but I couldn't help but feel relief.

Then the penny dropped: bodies with bashed-in heads didn't walk themselves down to the beach.

He'd been murdered.

And to find out who he was, I was going to have to touch him again to turn him over.

So I did what any brave warrior would do when confronted with an awful task: I squeezed my eyes shut and squealed, 'Ew, ew, ew, ew, ew, ewwwww,' as I groped for where I knew the cadaver's arm should be and hauled with all my strength to propel him sunny-side up as quickly as possible.

Then I sat back down, shuddering and murmuring 'ew' until the vomit receded back down my throat.

I steeled myself to look at him, but couldn't work up the nerve.

C'mon Jane, I told myself. *It might not even be anybody from Rockabill. He's probably a stranger.*

I actually had to use my fingers to peel my eyelids up.

My body was saying, 'Oh, hell no,' even as my mind was scolding it for being a complete pansy.

When I finally peered down at the dead man's face, I nearly sobbed with a combination of relief and guilt. I was relieved because although I knew who the body was, it wasn't someone I knew well or had any connection to. It was Peter, who was renting one of the Allens' rental cottages for the winter. I didn't even know his last name. He said he was writing a book and had come during the off-season for the quiet. He shopped at the bookstore often, and always seemed interested in speaking with me, but his interest didn't seem creepy. Peter was just a rather average, middle-aged man who was friendly to everyone and a little lonely in his tiny cabin all by himself. He did ask some rather intrusive questions sometimes, but when he realized he'd crossed the line he'd back off, apologizing that he forgot that real people weren't characters in books waiting to reveal their secrets.

Which is why I felt really guilty about feeling relieved. Peter had been a nice man, and he'd stayed nice even after he'd been in Rockabill long enough to learn my 'real' story. He certainly didn't deserve to be murdered and dumped like some sack of garbage.

And on that note . . .

What the hell am I going to do with this body?

There was no way I could call the police. How was I going to explain my presence? Or the murder victim? *You're 'crazy', remember*, my brain very helpfully reminded me. *They'll probably think you killed him.*

My calling the police was *entirely* out of the question. I'd never live it down. Things were finally okay for me in Rockabill. Not exactly pleasant, but no one, with the notable exceptions of Linda and Stuart, was actively trying to drive me away anymore. If I did anything weird – and finding a murdered body was definitely weird – it would all start back up again.

An anonymous phone call was also out of the question. There are a few hundred people tops in the Rockabill area during low season. Anonymity was never an option where I was concerned, not least because the sheriff who the phone call would go to was George Varga, one of my dad's best friends and my 'godfather' for the pseudopagan naming ceremony Nick and Nan had given me when I was born.

But if I left Peter on this stretch of beach, anybody could find him. I didn't want some nice L.L. Bean family to come strolling along with their obligatory blond-haired twins and Labrador retriever, only to stumble across a man whose scalp resembled a cat flap.

Or worse yet, *nobody* could find him and he could lie here for days. Even L.L. Bean catalog people didn't go out strolling through storms. Leaving Peter dead on the beach to be pecked at by seagulls and gnawed on by crabs was out of the question.

Then I remembered old Mr Flutie and his arthritic dachshund, Russ. Mr Flutie was a retired fireman from Eastport, so he could handle seeing a dead body. And he used the same little path every day to 'walk' his dog. I say 'walk' because he actually carried Russ for most of the way in one of those fancy baby slings that trendy Trustafarian mothers in big cities use. He only set Russ down to do his little doggie business and then back the dog went into the sling.

I liked Mr Flutie a lot, but even I had to admit that the baby sling did interfere with his dignity.

Anyway, Mr Flutie was the perfect body-finder. Come rain or shine, he got up at the butt crack and walked the otherwise seldom-used path that was right off the main beach. And finding Peter's corpse wouldn't scar him for life.

It was nearly one in the morning by this point, so I had to move fast if I was going to get any rest before work the next day. It took me nearly half an hour to drag the body the short way up to the path, since I had to sit down panting just about every ten steps. People are *heavy* when they're dead. I also nearly ralphed every time I caught a glimpse of the skin flap flapping, and I'd seen enough *CSI* to know that my stomach contents could be used to link me to the site.

Despite my exhaustion and nausea, we made it up to Mr Flutie's path. I tried arranging Peter so he looked natural until I realized how absurd that was. Then I felt that it was wrong just to walk away. So I bowed my head and gave as good a prayer as I could give, never having been in any place of worship in my life. I told Peter I was sorry he died and that I hoped he could find peace. I also told him I was sorry for leaving him and hoped that, as a writer, he could understand my dilemma and my reasons for not calling the police. As I started to tell him how efficient Mr Flutie would be in getting the authorities involved, I had a mental vision of myself, starkers as I was, having a serious conversation with a cadaver. So I cut my prayer short and ended with a moment's silence. Then I walked back to the beach, making sure that I erased any signs of our trail that the storm hadn't gotten to first.

I made a beeline back to the ocean. I was filthy. The rain had melted the last of our most recent snowfall and I was covered in a thick coating of dirt overlaid with sand. I scrubbed myself down in the shallows and then swam out a ways both to rinse off and to get back to my secret cove where my clothes were.

Getting dressed, I knew that I wasn't going to get any sleep that night. And that if I did, it would be full of visions of drowned bodies bobbing in my head.

CHAPTER THREE

The sharp notes of my alarm clock burst through my brain, setting the dreams that had haunted my night's brief sleep to flee. There was an awful taste in my mouth: my stomach's revenge for the panic and nausea it had endured the night before. Speaking of which . . .

I had found a murdered man.

I lay in bed, immobile, trying to get to grips with what I'd done. In the light of the weak November sun leaking through my curtains, my actions were nowhere near as logical as they'd seemed under cover of darkness.

First of all, I had no guarantee that the body was any more likely to be found where I'd put it than wherever the Old Sow would eventually have deposited it. What if Russ had decided he'd rather be taken down a different trail? What if Mr Flutie had decided to skip his morning constitutional and instead gone to Vegas to blow his retirement savings on black-jack and lap dances? What if, gods forbid, I'd overestimated his intestinal fortitude and now there were two bodies lying across that path: Peter dead of foul play and Mr Flutie dead of a coronary?

Second, I must have annihilated any evidence that might

have been on Peter's body. If there had been any clues as to who had killed him left intact after his time in the sea, they'd doubtlessly been totally erased by the long drag up the beach. Not to mention there would be confusion over the fact that it would appear as if his killer had left him on the beach after apparently dipping him in the ocean just for kicks . . .

In turn, this led me to my third reason for why I should never have touched Peter. If a murdered body wasn't bizarre enough for Rockabill, the police would now have a body that had either dragged itself up out of the ocean or whose killer had had second thoughts about dumping it and decided to use his victim to decorate the local nature trail, instead.

I pulled my pillow out from under my head and smothered my face with it. How could I have been so stupid? Why didn't I just leave well enough alone?

Then I thought of Peter's poor dead face as well as the polite kindness he'd shown me when he was alive, and I knew I couldn't have left him out there, abandoned to the elements.

I pushed the pillow away and willed myself to move. I had to get down to the village and face the music if there was any music to be faced.

Alternatively, came the sly voice in my head, *you could just bury your head under the covers and never come out, no matter who came knocking.*

But my hospital experience had taught me that bedclothes never protected you from anything. So I got up and got ready for work, and then went downstairs to make breakfast and perform my Tuesday chores as normally as possible. It's not like my method of cleaning the upstairs bathroom would give away the fact that I'd spent the previous evening dredging a body out of the Old Sow, but I was still jumpy.

I started to relax when dad and I got through breakfast without Sheriff Varga stopping by in his official capacity. It was only when I walked into town that I realized a smallish circle of hell had broken loose.

A goodly portion of Rockabill's permanent residents were milling about, sipping coffee from Thermoses and talking in hushed tones. Rockabill was still decidedly more shabby than chic, although it did have a naturally cutesy aspect that we'd tried to ham up for the tourists. And we did achieve a pretty homey feel, especially when the square was crowded with people, as it was today. Not that we often gathered to discuss the murder of a vacationing stranger.

I braced myself to weave through the small crowd, but I relaxed as I realized no one was paying me any undue attention. I could see Grizelda's tall form – she was extra conspicuous in a fuchsia satin capelet – flitting from group to group, and I gave a little internal cheer. Grizzie was a gossip sponge. She'd have every single drop of delicious rumor soaked up in no time. I just had to wait for her to come spill.

Tracy was already opening up the store when I got there, and her normally cheerful face looked grim. My heart missed a beat. Was Varga waiting for me at work?

But she was just reflecting the town's mood, and her greeting was normal enough until she added, 'Did you hear about the body?'

I tried to make my face look confused.

'No, what happened? What body?'

'Peter Jakes,' she replied, frowning. 'His body was found by Mr Flutie this morning on that nature trail on the back side of the beach.'

So, I thought, *his last name was Jakes.*

Tracy continued, 'The police won't say anything official, but apparently Jakes was murdered.'

'No way,' I said, trying to channel a little bit of last night's shock into my words. 'Are you serious?'

'Yup. Grizzie's getting the rest of the story now. Knowing her, she'll have copies of the police reports by the time she's done.'

Tracy's speculations weren't far off. Grizzie came in about an hour later looking flushed. She was practically bursting with information, but she had to wait until we finished serving the last few customers from our unexpected morning rush before she could empty out her gossip sack.

And empty she did.

Before the door had even shut on the last customer's heels Grizelda was facing Tracy and me, her hands on a shoulder each, as if linking us in her holy trinity of rumor, conjecture, and innuendo.

'Peter Jakes,' she said, with the voice of a narrator from some true crime docudrama, 'was murdered.'

Tracy just rolled her eyes in exasperation and I made a sort of 'get on with it' rolling-hands gesture.

Grizzie ignored our impatience, continuing at the same dramatic pace.

'He was killed in his own driveway,' she intoned. 'He'd been to market for groceries and was unloading them from his car when, *bam,* somebody hit him on the back of his head with a stone from his own garden's decorative border.'

She looked at each of us in turn, letting her words soak in before continuing.

'They know because that young bag boy at McKinley's helped Peter load his trunk and his groceries are still spilled all over his driveway. And the stone was just lying there, all covered in blood, next to his Cream of Wheat.' She paused for effect before gleefully plunging back in.

'Old Mrs Patterson says that she saw a black Mercedes drive up toward his place around five-thirty, and then drive away again at, like, four in the morning.' Grizzie shook her head. 'That old gossipmonger never sleeps.' Tracy and I met each other's eyes and tried not to scoff too openly. 'Anyway, the police think that whoever was driving the car might be the murderer. If so, that means it was somebody from outside Rockabill, 'cause nobody here owns a Benz.'

I felt a wave of relief wash over me, but the sensation was short-lived.

'There is one thing that doesn't make any sense, however . . .'

Uh-oh, I thought. *Here it comes.*

'Apparently, the man we know as Peter Jakes barely existed.'

I schooled my face into blandness, as Tracy grunted. 'What does that mean?'

'It means,' Grizzie said, impatiently, 'that Jakes had a credit card and a Canadian passport, but nothing else. No home address, no records in the U.S. or in Canada. Nothing. It's like he didn't exist. He just had some P.O. box out near Québec, somewhere.'

'That is a mystery,' I murmured, but Grizzie wasn't through. Dammit.

'Oh, duh, that reminds me of the *big* mystery . . . Jakes's body was definitely in the ocean, which makes the police think that whoever killed him tried to dump him. But he somehow ended up on that trail, instead.'

I furrowed my brow, narrowing my eyes into their best 'Wow, how interesting, I wonder why that could be?' look, and focused my gaze somewhere above Grizzie's head. If I could have whistled innocently I would have.

'So they don't know how he got there, or who did it. There aren't any fingerprints anywhere. Nothing was taken except for that file where he kept his notes for his book, which wasn't valuable at all. Oh, wait, his car *is* missing. But it was a beater, so why would somebody kill him for that? Plus, if it was the person in the Mercedes who killed Peter, they obviously didn't drive off in his car. The police think that the killer must have used Peter's car to dump the body, and then abandoned it. They're organizing a small search party to find it, but it could be anywhere.'

She looked from one to the other of us for effect. 'So it can't have been a robbery or some kind of an accident. Whoever killed Peter Jakes came to Rockabill expressly with the intent to commit murder.'

Tracy sighed. 'He seemed like such a quiet man,' she said ruefully. 'But I guess we all have our secrets.'

The veracity of Tracy's words was demonstrated by how, standing in our little circle, we avoided each other's eyes. We three knew all about secrets.

Work went by quickly. Lots of people stopped by Read It and Weep ostensibly for a coffee or a newspaper but really to take advantage of Grizzie's well-known capacity for gossip. Then a busload of oceanographers on a day trip from a conference at the University of Maine came to see the Old Sow, and we let them drink their takeaway coffee at our café tables while the rest bought souvenirs and stuff. One of the tourists was pretty creepy and kept staring at me. He was a little greasy for an academic, but otherwise fit the bill: big, geeky plastic-framed glasses, chinos, and a button-up Polo shirt. His lank brown hair fell in his face and he stared like I had sprouted horns. I shivered, checking the front door. It was shut, but a cold draft from somewhere had raised goose pimples on my flesh. When I looked back, Creepy McCreeperson was still staring at me. Of course, I knew better than to think he was admiring my effervescent personality or understated beauty: he probably remembered me from the papers. I hope I lived up to my headlines.

By the time the oceanographers left and I'd put the café back to rights, it was nearly four. Nothing more had developed regarding Peter's murder: the car was still missing and the small search party had called it quits, as it was getting dark.

We were all pretty beat from our unexpectedly busy day, so we went ahead and closed a half hour early. I faked bundling up against the cold, hating the fact that I felt I needed to be circumspect even around Tracy and Grizzie, then said my goodbyes and started off home.

My daily commute was about an hour on foot, but I despised driving. Plus, it's not like I had much of a social life, so walking helped fill my time. I only took the car when I had to pick up groceries; otherwise, I left it at home so Dad could go out if he wanted to do something.

There were still more people around town than usual, and the Trough was packed. *Nothing like a grisly murder to bring people together*, I reflected bitterly. I knew all too well how otherwise decent people got off on the tragedy of others.

My anger subsided once I got to the end of our little main street. I took a few deep breaths and unwound my scarf, then unzipped my coat and stuffed my mittens in my pockets. I knew the air must be cold; my breath steamed away from me so thick it appeared solid. But my body told me it was comfortable, and if I'd had more courage I would have taken my coat off altogether.

After all the stress of the afternoon and the night before, I was happy to let my mind wander and enjoy the walk home. I loved this time of year. The sea was actually slightly warmer than usual – although still bone-chilling – as it took longer to cool down from summer than did the earth itself. But because the outside temperature was so cold and the tourists were almost entirely gone, I didn't have to be so paranoid.

It's not like I could ever really be comfortable in Rockabill, but walking home every day without seeing a single soul, tourist or native, went a long way toward helping me relax. That said, sometimes the long walk home in the darkness could be creepy – especially when somebody had just been murdered and I'd been the one to find the body.

I couldn't help but shudder, remembering poor Peter's clammy skin and staring eyes. And the wound on the back of his head . . .

I had unconsciously picked up my pace, but I forced myself to slow down. *Don't be ridiculous*, I told myself. *This is Rockabill. Whoever Peter really was, he must have brought the trouble with him, and sent it packing with his death. Little villages in Maine are not apt to become the site of serial killings. Unless that village is Cabot Cove, of course.*

I couldn't help but smile, imagining Angela Lansbury down at Rockabill's tiny Sheriff's office: George Varga shaking his head and saying, 'Gee, Mrs Fletcher, I had no idea that the butler did it!'

I realized that I was mixing up my genres, and that butlers were about as likely to be in Rockabill as were serial killers or fictional murder-mystery characters, when I heard a resounding *snap*.

I froze. The forest surrounding me on either side of the road was deathly quiet, which was not at all normal. Rockabill was out in the middle of nowhere, really, and my dad and I lived as far out as we could and still be considered living in the village. Our woods were replete with all sorts of wildlife and birdlife at any time of year.

When had it gone quiet?

I was listening as hard as I could, when from my right

there was the slightest sound of movement. But it wasn't the random scurrying of little feet. Whatever made that noise was coming toward me at a steady pace.

I turned toward the sound, desperately peering into the dark woods. The moon was but a crescent sickle hanging in the sky and I couldn't see a thing.

Suddenly, my heart lurched as my peripheral vision registered something large dart across the road about twenty feet behind me. Then I started to run.

Panic sent a flood of adrenaline rushing through my system, and I was running like I'd never run before. I wasn't thinking about anything except pumping my little legs and trying not to fall over my flapping scarf. I somehow managed to wrench it from my neck and let it fall on the roadside when a shadow darted across the road again, this time in front of me.

Shit! I thought, and veered off the road. Part of my brain acknowledged that leaving the road was a very bad idea, but the rest of my brain was just trying to put as much distance between myself and that menacing shadow as possible.

I also knew I was going in the direction of the beach and that if I could get in the water I'd be safe. My running took on a new purpose with that thought. Nothing could follow me into the water, but if I brought the trouble home with me, what could my dad do to protect us? We didn't own a gun, and he was too sick to take somebody on. So I had to get to the beach. That was better than leading whatever was behind me to my only family.

I tripped, cursing, just barely managing to keep my feet. Loud rustling from the forest behind me meant I was still being followed. But my pursuer wasn't getting any closer, and that actually worried me. With the exception of when I was swimming, I was definitely built for comfort rather than speed. I could possibly outrun a three-year-old, but anything else?

I started to swerve left, the shortest route to the sea and escape. I could smell the ocean beckoning, guiding me to the safety of her waters.

But once again a flash of darkness darted on my left, forcing me to veer back to the right. For a second, I caught a glimpse of the whites of eyes and the flash of teeth. Whatever was chasing me was some kind of animal.

Under the circumstances, I certainly wasn't capable of being glad of that fact, but some part of my brain recognized that whatever was following me couldn't have killed Peter. Large-toothed beasties don't club their victims over the head with decorative stones and then stuff them in a car for convenient disposal.

That part of my brain, however, was quickly being hedged out by exhaustion. The first burst of adrenaline had faded, and my lungs and legs were aching. I may have had tons of stamina in the water, but on land I was about as nimble as your average guinea pig. Whatever it was could easily have caught me. If it didn't want to catch me, what *did* it want to do with me?

I tried again to veer left. The beach was close this way, the salt air whispering to me of safety. But once again, the dark outline of my pursuer steered me to the right, and my fears were confirmed.

I was being herded.

Whatever this thing was, it was moving me where it wanted me to go, like I was some damned sheep.

My legs were aching so bad that I don't know how I kept going. Only those little glimpses of moving darkness kept my feet churning. I was really starting to slow, my energy almost totally spent. And I was starting to think my best bet was to stop in my tracks and confront whatever was behind me.

But then I realized where I was: right at the back of my secret cove. It was only accessible through the forests to the side of my property or by the sea. Except for its slender strip of beach and a narrow breach on the cove's far side from the sea, it was surrounded by natural rock walls. If only I could make it to the cove . . .

I pulled on my last dregs of energy in order to get to that breach. Hopefully, whatever was chasing me thought it was driving me into a trap, unaware that I knew about the break in the cove walls. And once through that gap, it was a straight shot into the ocean and away.

I wasn't running now so much as stumbling quickly, panting like a geriatric lion. Every step was torture. Pain shot through my calves and my lungs felt like they were going to burst. But I knew I couldn't let up so I steamed ahead. I was swinging toward the right, heading for the break, which my shepherd was allowing. It must not think I could get out that way. Little did it know . . .

When I hit the break I plunged through, shouting in triumph, only for my voice to be cut short with a painful 'Oof.' My damned coat had caught on something as I tried to squeeze through the narrow opening at too high a speed. My own momentum slammed me painfully into the rough wall of the cove, and I felt a gash open up above my eyelid. I'd had the wind knocked out of me, and I barely managed to stay upright. I heard an ominous rustle behind me, and I peered frantically into the forest as blood dripped down into my eye, stinging horribly. Something was emerging from the undergrowth, and I really didn't want to be wedged here when it came out to introduce itself.

I made a bizarre strangled sound, like a wounded hare, and scrabbled at my snared coat liner. It wouldn't budge. Then my brain reminded me I was an idiot and I shrugged out of my jacket, leaving it hanging from the rock. Turning around I dashed into the cove, to get my second profound shock in as many days.

Sitting on a little rocking chair that stood on a colorful quilt draped over the pristine sand of my cove sat a little woman. She couldn't have been more than two feet tall when standing. Dressed in rustic-looking clothes of blue and green, with long gray hair pinned up into a preposterously large bun, she was smiling at me with as kindly an expression as one could imagine.

'Hello, child,' she said, as behind me I heard a series of low pants and a funny little whine.

I didn't want to look away from the kindly old lady, convinced she would pull a knife the minute my back was turned. Nor did I particularly want to see the true face of whatever had been chasing me. And yet I couldn't let it take me down while my back was turned; I had to face my enemy.

Very, very slowly I swiveled, clenching my hands into fists, ready to fight. Not that I'd ever been in a real fight in my life. Although they'd caused their fair share of damage, my antagonists had always used words as their weapons.

In front of me stood the biggest dog I'd ever seen. It didn't look like a wolf; it looked more like some sort of black-furred saber-toothed hellhound. My stunned gaze traveled up from its enormous clawed paws, over its powerful shoulders, and to its oversized jaws – which were filled with the largest fangs I'd ever seen outside of a prehistoric-mammal exhibit.

Its slavering mouth opened wider as a low whine emerged out of its belly. Its ears pricked up at me, as if to fix me in its sights. I felt a wave of absolute terror rise up from the pit of my being and threaten to overwhelm me.

But the Trues were made of tougher stuff than that, and I behaved with as much bravery and resolve as I'd shown the night before when turning over Peter's body.

I fainted dead away.

CHAPTER FOUR

I woke up to the sensation of something warm and wet lapping
at my face and I was overwhelmed by the smell of fresh
toothpaste. My eyes weren't quite functioning and all I could
see was a large, fuzzy shape looming above my head. As my
pupils slowly started to focus, I figured out that something
was licking my cut clean. It felt incredibly soothing, until my
brain restarted and I realized that the tongue in question was
attached to the fanged mouth of the black hound of hell that
had just been chasing me through the woods. I moaned with
fear, trying to sit up and scramble backward at the same time.
All I succeeded in doing was to bring my face closer to the
dog's enormous teeth and to make my head bleed again.

Good strategy, Jane, I thought as my world spun and I
collapsed back down with a thump.

Another face swam into my vision. This wasn't the dog,
or the kindly old lady with the bun. This face had mud-brown
eyes and thick tendrils of green hair, like seaweed. Her skin –
for I thought it was a her – was a luminous pearl gray and
she had a strange, flat nose that barely rose off the surface
of her face.

Whatever she was, she wasn't human.

But she was talking.

'Let him heal your wound,' she said, in an oily, unpleasant voice that did little to quell my fears.

The sound made me freeze, even if I didn't really want to follow her instructions, and I again felt the rough tongue of the big black dog lapping at my eyebrow.

I lay there, feeling as uncomfortable and on edge as I've ever felt, while the dog gently continued to lick. The gray-faced being was making a strange, leering expression at me, and then she reached out and patted my hand.

That isn't a leer, I realized. *That is a smile.* The strange girl was trying to comfort me, which was about as effective as a bear hug from the steely arms of an iron maiden.

The dog had stopped licking my brow, which, I had to admit, felt much better. But it was now licking off the blood that had streamed down my face, and then it leaned in to lick the blood that had dripped over my neck and into the top of my shirt.

'Okay,' I said, in what I hoped was a commanding voice. 'Off.'

I raised my arms and pushed weakly. The big dog did back away slightly, wagging its tail in what I assumed was hell-hound for 'Don't worry, I'm satiated by your delicious blood and therefore won't eat you . . . tonight.'

The gray girl took a firm hold of one of my upraised hands and helped me to sit up. *Hel-lo Dolly*, I thought, as I got a gander of her. She was very naked, and very obviously female. And that strange gray skin continued the whole way down to her webbed feet with their thick black toenails.

She *definitely* wasn't human.

'Can you sit up?' came that oily voice, again; she didn't release her grip.

'Yes, I think so.' I'd say anything to get my hand back.

She leered – no, smiled at me again – and trotted over to

the little old lady sitting on her chair. Where, with no modesty whatsoever, she plopped down beside her, Indian-style, airing her bits for the world to see.

She has seaweed pubes, observed my brain, unhelpfully, as I blinked and looked around at my little cove.

My secret strip of beach that had once been as familiar as my own childhood bedroom had become an alien realm. If the enormous devil-dog, the eensy cartoon grandmother, and old barnacle crotch weren't enough, there was a large globe of light suspended about eight feet above the old lady's head. There were no wires that I could see, but it hung like a chandelier, bathing my little cove in an eerie luminescence.

I felt a chill run down my spine, and I looked at the plump old woman.

She smiled beatifically, which didn't make me feel one bit better.

'It's so nice finally to meet you, Jane,' she said. 'Anyan has told us so much about you.'

The dog whined and lay down uncomfortably close to me while the old lady kept on smiling, clearly waiting for a response.

'It's nice to meet you, too?' I queried, not really sure of my role here. Were we going to have tea and chicken salad sandwiches like ladies who lunch or were they going to sacrifice me to their dark god of chaos? If they'd been banking on me being a virgin, they were plumb out of luck . . .

'I realize you are at a disadvantage here, and that you are unsure of what is happening, but you are perfectly safe. I am Nell and this,' she gestured toward the gray girl, 'is Trill.' Trill gave me that horrible grin again, but now that the grin had a name, it wasn't quite as scarifying.

'You've already met Anyan,' she said, indicating the giant dog.

She again seemed to be waiting for some sort of response. 'He's got very fresh breath,' I said, the first thing that popped into my mind. 'For a dog,' I clarified.

'Yes,' she smiled even wider, if that were possible. 'He's very hygienic. And he's done a good job on your head.'

I raised my hand to my brow and felt absolutely nothing. There was no cut at all, and only the slightest tenderness when I pressed down on where my hurt had been. *What the fuck?* I thought, shooting a sharp glance at the canine. In response, Anyan wagged his tail and stretched his back paws out behind him so he was lying with his stomach embedded in the sand. It was such a doggy thing to do, for a hellhound, that I nearly smiled. He looked over at me and for a second I could have sworn he winked. But I guess I just hit my head harder than I thought. Speaking of which . . .

'Why did he chase me?' I said, remembering the awful run through the woods. If they were so friendly, why scare the shit out of me and make me nearly brain myself in the process?

'We're sorry about that,' came Trill's slippery voice. 'It's just that first contact is always difficult, even when it doesn't have to be rushed like this. We couldn't wait; we had to get you here tonight. And there were all sorts wandering the woods today so we had to meet you under a glamour.'

She was looking at me like I was supposed to understand what she'd said. So I just stared right back, beginning to tire of this game.

'Look, I have no idea what you're talking about. You've gotta throw me a bone, here. What's first contact? And I assume you're not talking about a fashion magazine when you say glamour.' Now that I was asking questions, the most obvious one popped into my head. 'And what the hell are you people, anyway?'

Nell and Trill exchanged looks, and Nell said, 'How much did your mother tell you about her . . . family?'

I was taken aback. The last direction I thought this conversation would go was toward my mystery mother and her unknown origins.

'Her family? Nothing at all. She was apparently too busy planning her abandonment of me to bother filling in a family tree.' Okay, fine, I'm bitter.

Nell sighed. 'This always makes it harder.' She got that same look of concentration on her face that my college professors had when we couldn't grasp a particularly difficult concept and they knew they were going to have to reduce it down all the way to idiot speak.

'Your mother, like us, wasn't really . . . human,' Nell said, finally. 'She was . . . more like Trill here.'

I made a face. I'd been six when my mother disappeared, but I could remember she wasn't gray and clammy and seaweedy. She'd been beautiful. And what did they mean, not human? Fine, Trill was obviously not human, but my mom was obviously not like her, ergo my mom was *not* not human. Yes, I minored in rhetoric.

'Well, not really,' Trill interrupted. 'I'm a kelpie. Your mom's a selkie. We're pretty different.'

Oh, I thought, frustrated to the point of screaming. *Of course!* I finally met people who claimed to know something about my mother and they insisted on speaking in riddles.

'From the beginning, *please*,' I said through gritted teeth.

Nell took over, the voice of reason. 'Kelpies,' she explained, in her professorial manner, 'are two-formed, as are selkies. They have a human, or in the case of kelpies, a humanoid form and an animal form. Trill, here, changes into a sort of sea-pony. Your mother was a selkie; her other form is that of a seal.'

Oh shit, I thought. I'd seen *The Secret of Roan Inish. If what this little person is saying is true, so much would be explained . . .*

The thought that I'd finally have my mother's desertion made understandable pulled at my heart, but then the weight of reality crushed my hopes. How could I have been such an idiot to get sucked into this shit?

'Okay, that's enough,' I said. 'I'm sure that Linda, or Stuart, or whoever, paid you good money to come down here and make me look like an idiot. I'm sure they gave you a great excuse for hurting me by telling you what a monster I am, and how I deserve this sort of treatment. And they're right. But I can't be hurt anymore. I've been hurt as bad as I'm gonna get, and nothing you or they can do will ever be as painful to me as losing Jason. So, just take your fake fangs off your dog, wash off the makeup, and go back to your circus. And don't forget your big light. I'd like my cove put back the way it was, not that I'll ever use it again.'

I started to get up, my already-cramping legs wobbly, but I registered with more than a little pride the stunned expressions that 'Trill' and 'Nell' were exchanging.

My momma may have walked out on us, but she didn't nearly halfway raise no fools, I thought smugly.

But that thought, along with my very slow upward momentum, was cut short as the air around Trill began to shimmer. An iridescent bubble the same color as her skin but more transparent encircled her. It looked like it was made of energy and it pulsated slightly, just like the light above Nell's head. Underneath the surface of the ball something was happening that looked like the shadowy development of a fetus played in fast-forward.

When the bubble popped, there stood a weird gray pony, with a seaweed mane and tail. Its small black hooves were the same color as Trill's toenails, and Trill's muddy-brown eyes were staring out at me from the pony's face. I could see the faintest hint of gills ribbing the beast's short neck.

I'd never fainted before today, but I had the distinct impression I was going to make it a two-for-one deal here in the hysterical woman department.

Anyan had crept closer, maybe to keep me from running if I had actually made it upright or maybe to break my fall if I fainted again. Whatever the reason, I was grateful when the hand I put out to steady myself met with a solidly muscled, very furry, and surprisingly high shoulder. The dog's broad back came up to well over my waist. I was only five foot one, but that was still a whole lotta dog.

I sat back down, heavily, and Anyan parked himself next to me, propping me up. I watched, deliriously, as the bubble once more extended out from Trill and, with another pop, she was humanish again.

Unless Stuart's or Linda's plot involved slipping me hallucinogens or plugging me into some *Matrix*-style virtual reality computer program, what was happening before me was *real*. I felt a chill of fear work its way down my spine as I took more than my fair share of deep breaths.

Okay, Jane, I told myself firmly, *get a grip. Whatever these things are, hellhound here could have killed you at any point and he hasn't, so you have to assume they want you alive. And you may not like what they have to say, but they're going to tell you about your mother*. This thought seemed to fortify me, and so I honed in on it. *For the first time in your life, someone is going to tell you the truth about your own mother*. I got my breathing under control, and if I didn't feel fantastic, I did feel like I could face what was happening.

Anyan's soft tongue grazed my cheek and I couldn't help but smile at him. It's funny how sensitive dogs are to people's moods. You'd think he understood how hard this was for me.

'All right,' I said, looking Nell in the eye and trying to avoid looking at Trill. After her little performance, if I looked at Trill I'd need more than just a few deep breaths. Maybe a few deep breaths alongside a few shots of Jack Daniels. 'You've made your point. You're not . . . human. And you weren't sent by anybody to fool me. So what are you, and why are you here? What do you have to do with me and my family?'

My voice sounded strong. I was proud of myself.

Nell, damn her, was still beaming away like the figure on a syrup bottle. 'You're taking this very well, Jane,' she said, and I only just managed to keep from giving her the finger. 'As I was saying, your mother is a selkie: a two-formed who can take either the shape of a seal or of a human. But she's not really human *or* seal; she is, for want of a better human word, supernatural.'

I grunted. It wasn't particularly erudite, but it was all I could manage to summarize the maelstrom of emotions flooding through me. On the one hand, I wanted to scream that none of this was true. That my mother wasn't some monster from legends. Despite that loud, angry voice, there was another whispering echo, more profound for its restraint, that acknowledged that what Nell said made *sense*.

My memories of my mother – the swimming, her happiness in the water, the way she plunged me into the ocean as if she were taking me home – weren't normal memories. They weren't natural, at least not by human standards.

Supernatural, I thought, letting my mind sink into the curves of the word. I was surprised to discover it felt good. Or, maybe it just felt like *something* where once there had been nothing.

'Supernatural creatures are all around you, and have been throughout history, as you can tell from the impact we've had on human myths and legends. You know us, all of us, but not necessarily in our true forms. For example, I'm a gnome. Humans have made us into little clay sculptures that protect their gardens. That's not entirely false. We gnomes are earth-bound and we protect our territories to the death – usually the death of the intruder. Selkies, like your mother, are known in stories throughout the world. But they don't shed their skin, nor are they the captive of whoever steals their skin. They come of their own free will to mortal men and women, usually with the intention of begetting a child.' Here, Nell paused, and I could see she spoke her next few sentences with some discomfort despite the fact that she never stopped smiling. 'We supernaturals find it difficult to . . . procreate successfully with each other, but we seem to have fewer problems when we liaise with humans. You, Jane, are the result of one such union.'

I was trying not to look too scornful of her words, but this was ridiculous. I was Jane True from Rockabill, Maine. I was not the half-supernatural love child of a seal woman and a mortal man. If I was, surely I'd be taller . . . more statuesque.

Eyeballing Nell, however, I realized that was an entirely illogical train of thought.

I also thought about how my mother had appeared, out of the middle of nowhere, and how she'd disappeared as mysteriously. I again thought about my swimming, and my tolerance for cold. I shivered, a knot in my throat, as my still-resistant brain slowly started to accept that this woman might be telling the truth.

'We've been watching over you since your mother left. She had to return to the sea, and you did not inherit her two-formed nature, so she was forced to leave you behind. If you had been almost entirely human, we would have let you live out your life without revealing ourselves to you. But your power is strong, and we would have come to you when you were more mature. Your actions the other night, however, made our meeting more precipitate.'

My power? I thought, confused. 'What did I do?'

Nell's smile faltered. 'The body you found in the sea was a halfling, like yourself. Part supernatural and part human. Peter Jakes was apparently in the service of . . . of some very powerful beings. His presence here in these parts appears to have been on their orders. His murder needs to be investigated by our community and, as the person who found the body, you must be interviewed as part of that investigation.'

This was far more prosaic a reason for 'first contact' than I had expected, and also rather galling.

My irritation came through in my voice. 'So, if I hadn't been the one to find Peter's body, you guys would have just let me bumble along for a few more years, not knowing who – or what – I was? I'm twenty-six years old; would you have told me before or after I was retirement age?'

Nell's smile returned, full blast. 'Child, and you are yet a child to me, human years mean nothing to us. Nor will they mean much to you. Your manipulation of the elements is strong; although you are not two-formed, your mother's powers are as potent in you as if you were. Age will not affect you as it does humans. You have only lived for the briefest moment of the life stretching before you.'

I could tell Nell thought this was supposed to be good news, but my whole being rebelled at what she was saying.

'Look, you're crazy. I've been in the hospital. And I mean I've *really* been in the hospital. I've had about every test done to me that can be done, and nothing ever came out saying, "Oh, good heart and lungs coupled with seal blood means she'll live forever." This is crazy. I can't live forever; I don't want to live forever. My life sucks enough as it is . . .' In saying these last words the true horror of what Nell had so blithely told me began to descend upon me. Would entire generations of Rockabillians know me as Crazy Jane?

At least you'll get your chance to dance on Stuart's and Linda's graves, my brain chipped in, unhelpfully.

Nell interrupted my malicious fantasies. 'Don't worry, child,' she said. 'You won't live forever. Just a long time. And you're certainly not immortal; you can be killed. But human concerns – such as years, age, birthdays, and the like – will cease to mean much to you after a few centuries.'

'Oh, great. I'm sure they will,' I said, sarcastically. 'Right around the time I go mental with loneliness from living in my recluse shack where no one can find the lady who doesn't die. That's going to be a great life. Maybe I should invest in the property market now, while it's on the downturn? I wonder what a hermit's cave is going for these days. I'll obviously only need the one bedroom.'

Nell shook her head. 'You won't be alone, child.' With these words she looked me full in the face, all traces of her smile gone. 'Your life has only just begun.'

I didn't know whether her words were a promise or a warning. Or both.

I watched, mute, as she climbed down from her rocking chair. She wrapped it up inside the quilt and laid her little bundle over Trill's back. Disconcertingly, the kelpie had turned back into a pony and I hadn't even noticed.

'Take a swim, Jane,' she said. 'You need it. Recharge your batteries. Tomorrow, an investigator will be in touch. Jakes was important, although I don't know why, and events are moving quickly. I don't know who they will send, but expect someone. And don't worry, we will be here to

answer your questions. There is no hurry. You are in my
territory.'

As Nell said those final words the air crackled around her
with energy, and I suspect she had granted me the merest
glimpse of the power that lay within her plump little form.

Before I could protest, she was trundling along beside the
pearly gray pony as they walked toward the solid face of the
rock wall . . . and disappeared. Nell took her light with her,
and it took my eyes a minute to adjust to the soft glimmering
of the night's sky.

I sat in silence, absently scratching at a furry belly. With
a start I realized that at some point during Nell's Revelation
Hour I'd thrown an arm around Anyan and was scratching
away at his densely haired hide distractedly. For his part, he
didn't look like he minded.

I couldn't begin to wrap my head around everything I had
learned tonight. It made no sense, yet it made every sense.
And Nell's words, if I was honest, scared the shit out of me.
I may have hated the fact that I had been so defined by the
events of my life; how I was trapped in a place that never let
me be anything but one version of what they wanted to see.
But I also knew my role, my place. There were no questions
or insecurities about what I'd do, day to day. Suddenly, everything had changed. And I couldn't begin to understand how.

Part of me, however, was quite certain that I'd wake up
tomorrow and realize it had been a dream. But for right now,
Nell was right. I needed a swim the way Joel Irving, our town
drunk, needed that first shot of vodka in his morning coffee.

I stood up, stretching my still-aching legs. I was going to
feel tonight's run something awful tomorrow morning. I
kicked off my shoes and pulled off my jeans and socks. I
was just starting to pull my shirt over my head when I realized that Anyan had slipped away. I let my shirt fall and

turned around to find him looking back at me as he headed toward the breach in the cove walls.

No teleporting for the pooch, I thought, smiling, as I pulled my shirt over my head. Anyan jerked his head around so quickly he smacked his muzzle against the break's rough walls. My head throbbed in sympathy.

That is one odd dog, I thought, as I pulled off my bra and panties and ran toward the ocean, plunging in gratefully.

And what exactly *had* Nell meant when she said he'd told her all about me?

CHAPTER FIVE

My walk back into town the next morning was a strangely surreal experience. Surprisingly, I'd slept well that night, which meant I hadn't really had time to process what I'd seen. But throughout breakfast I kept going over the previous evening's events. I'd gotten a glimpse into a whole other reality and I had no idea what it all meant. The thing that most caught my imagination was when Nell had said that her kind were all around us. Granted, Nell or Trill would stand out in a crowd, but my mother had looked totally normal. Were there other supernatural creatures running around Rockabill?

And why was I accepting all of this so calmly? I'd just met a talking garden gnome and the nightmare version of My Little Pony. Oh, and I mustn't forget my little race with the saber-toothed canine. Why wasn't I more alarmed at what I'd seen?

Because, the little evil voice I tried to suppress chimed, *you always knew you were more of a freak than anyone – even Linda or Stuart – could guess.*

Of course, I considered, *the doctors could just be correct and you've finally gone off the deep end. Maybe you really are Crazy Jane True.*

My blood ran cold at that thought. There had been more

than a few times during my hospital stay when I'd genuinely feared that I was losing my mind. When I felt there was more than just grief shrouding my thoughts in darkness. I'd had the most vivid dreams about a stranger who held my hand and told me stories, all through the night. They'd seemed so real, and yet they could not have happened. *Maybe I am mad*, I thought. *Maybe madness is what drove Mom away, and she left it for me, in my blood, as her parting gift.*

Whatever, Jane, my brain admonished. *Either some 'investigator' shows up today, like Nell said would happen, and you know you're okay. Or, nobody appears and you check yourself back into the funny farm. In the meantime, get over yourself and go with the idea it's all real.*

I imagined the whole day spent analyzing Read It and Weep's customers, searching for some clue as to their true identity. In other words, I'd play the supernatural version of *Sesame Street*'s 'one of these things is not like the others'.

Grizzie presented me with my first challenge. She looked resplendent, as always. Over shiny black leggings she sported purple, thigh-high, patent-leather boots with enormous stacks that made her about six-foot-four. On top, she wore a fuzzy, purple angora sweater that fitted snugly down over her hips. The sweater was cinched tight over her waspish waist by a wide patent-leather belt that had an enormous silver lightning bolt for a buckle. For a bra, she'd chosen a very fifties 'lift and separate' number that made it look like she was wearing traffic cones under her sweater. She'd done her long ebony hair up into a giant coiffure from which a fake ponytail streamed down to the small of her back. Her makeup was minimal. After all, it was bad taste to wear purple thigh-high stacks *and* overdone eye shadow. She had only two wings of black liquid eyeliner accentuating her vivid violet eyes, and the barest hint of pink blush and lip gloss.

'You look hot, Griz,' I greeted her, eyeballing her appraisingly.

'Thanks, darling.' She grinned, giving me a little twirl so I could appreciate the outfit in full. 'You look edible, as always,' she said as she stooped to give me a peck on the cheek.

If anybody is supernatural here in Rockabill, it has to be Grizzie, I thought. But then again, magical, nearly immortal beings probably didn't star in such films as *The Ass-prentice: You're Nailed!* Not that I didn't appreciate Grizzie's oeuvre.

Tracy had the day off, so the first few hours of work went extra quickly. It's not that Tracy was dull by any means, but neither did she use her spare time to expound upon the difference between a clitoral, versus an anal, orgasm. I spent half the morning on the floor laughing and the other half with my hands over my ears trying to drone Grizzie out by humming ABBA's greatest hits. But just when I thought Grizzie would succeed in her attempt to prove embarrassment could be fatal, a silver Porsche Boxster came snarling into the bookstore's line of vision. To our mutual surprise, it whipped into a parking spot right in front of our door.

Well, that didn't happen often, even during tourist season.

The car's top was down, another surprise for this time of year. Grizzie and I exchanged looks. It was cold, at least for everybody but me.

As the driver opened his door and stepped out, Grizzie made a lascivious meowing sound. I seconded that meow, silently. We had a very clear view of the man as he stretched luxuriantly. He wasn't extremely tall, probably about five foot nine. But he was *very* well put together. His shoulders were broad in his crisp white shirt and his waist tapered invitingly to his brown leather belt holding up his brown tweed trousers.

For shoes, he had on a pair of what I can only assume were brogues, as I'd never actually seen brogues before. But whatever they were, they looked expensive. As did his gold-rimmed aviator sunglasses. He oozed money and confidence, and I felt a pang of disappointment. *Too bad you're probably a twat*, I thought, snarkily. *'Cause you are one fine piece of man-meat.*

Jane, don't be a bitch to the tourists, I admonished myself. *Not least because they're the only people who treat you like a real person, and not a ticking time bomb.*

As if to drive home my point, behind the mysterious stranger I saw Mark, in his postal uniform with his satchel over his shoulder, head into the Trough to deliver their mail and grab a cup of coffee. For obvious reasons, Mark no longer lingered over a latte here at Read It and Weep. On cue, I felt that familiar little burn of humiliation I now associated with the man I'd so nearly dated.

So, be nice to the hot stranger, I thought, forcing my eyes back to the guy with the Porsche. To my disappointment, he'd finished stretching. *You missed the whole show*, my libido grumbled at me. I apologized profusely and dutifully paid close attention as he checked that he had his wallet before running a hand through his short-cropped, thick brown hair.

'Bonjour, Brick Shithouse,' Grizzie drooled as, to her evident delight, he walked toward our bookstore.

He pushed open the door and, just as our annoying little chimey thing heralded his presence, his eyes met mine. I felt a jolt, and not only because his almond eyes were gorgeous, but also because those pretty eyes crinkled in a combination of recognition and interest. I knew I didn't know this man, and there shouldn't be anything of interest to one such as he in the utterly prosaic Jane True.

He approached the counter and, up close, his face didn't

break with his body's precedent. He had high cheekbones that tapered down to a narrow and shapely chin. His mouth was small but full-lipped, which gave him an extremely sensual expression, as if he were just about to pucker up to kiss his way down your belly—

Woah, Jane, I thought, trying to get a handle on my suddenly raging hormones. My dirty drawer might be well stocked, but it seemed I missed the real thing even more than I realized. That fact, however, did not give me the right to rape random tourists. *And before you get your hopes up, people who are climbing whatever ladder he is evidently climbing don't date crazy women*, I reminded myself. *He wouldn't want his girl-friend to start gibbering at his CEO over cocktails.*

The sharp sting of my own mental self-flagellation explained why I was more than a little surprised when the beautiful man grabbed my hand from over the counter and pulled me toward him. I was so surprised, in fact, that I let myself get swept up into what must have looked like the most natural of hugs.

'Jane True,' he said, pressing me close. The awkward angle – with both of us leaning over the counter – meant that our hug mostly consisted of me wedging my bazongas into his chest. I meeped, in surprise, as he continued.

'I told you I'd surprise you here in Rockabill, and here I am!'

He released me and I took a dazed step back. Not missing a beat, he turned to Grizzie and was pumping her hand as if he were absolutely thrilled to meet her.

'You must be Grizelda. I'm absolutely thrilled to meet you,' he said, putting his actions into words.

'Jane here has told me so much about you.' He let go of Grizzie's hand but kept his eyes locked on hers. 'I'm Ryu, Jane's friend from college. I hope she told you about me. She certainly talked enough about you and Tracy.' Only then did his eyes break from Grizzie's and meet mine. He gave me a roguish wink.

I was waiting for Grizzie to inform him that, no, actually, I had never mentioned an incredibly handsome male school friend named Ryu. And that from my reaction when he got out of the car and walked into the store I'd obviously never seen him before.

Instead, she smiled down at him and said, 'Oh, of course! Yes! That's great you could make it to Rockabill. We've heard so much about Jane's friend Ryu!'

I swung around toward her, unable to believe what I was hearing. But she just beamed at me. A look of genuine pleasure washed over her features. What the hell? I had no idea who this guy was, and I'd certainly not attended college with him. I'd have remembered – and I'd have the fantasies to prove it.

'Why don't you go into the back, Grizzie, while Jane and I talk?' Ryu was once again staring into Grizzie's eyes, and I nearly fell over when instead of saying, 'Why don't you go fuck yourself,' she just maintained her huge smile. Then, with a swish of her shiny hips, she headed back into our stockroom. Gritting my teeth, I rounded on the stranger.

'Who the hell are you and what did you do to Grizelda?' I demanded.

The smile he gave me was no less handsome than the one he'd presented to Grizzie. But it was more natural, less eerily animated. 'My name really is Ryu,' he replied, his eyes flicking down surreptitiously to rove the top half of my body that was not hidden by the counter. I forced myself to desist from squirming as his gaze lingered on my breasts for a split second. 'But rather than a college reunion, I'm actually here to ask you about your involvement in the murder of Peter Jakes.'

It took me a second to cotton on to what he was saying,
as I couldn't imagine a policeman zipping around in a Porsche
and I couldn't work out how the authorities had figured out
my role in finding Peter's body.

'Ohhh,' I said, as the other shoe dropped. 'You're the one
Nell said I should expect. You're *that* investigator.'

'Quite,' he said. 'I'm *that* investigator.'

This time I went ahead and returned his slow once-over,
so we could each weigh the other up.

'You don't look right,' I blurted out, before I realized I'd
depressed my EDIT button. Then I about turned purple.

'I don't look *right*?' he inquired, raising an elegant eyebrow
at me.

'You're too . . . too . . .' My brain scrambled to finish my
sentence. All I could think of was teeny-tiny Nell, in her rustic
clothes, and the kelpie with her gray skin and oily voice.

'Normal,' I finished, only to regret, instantly, my word
choice.

'Normal,' the beautiful man repeated, his voice flat.

'Well, not normal,' I stammered. 'Obviously. I mean, you're
really good-looking. But you know that, already.' I watched,
horrified, as his other eyebrow swept up to join the first.
Mentally, my brain scrambled to get my EDIT function back
online, but it had very evidently gone haywire. 'I mean, you're
totally hot, and obviously super-successful, and I just saw
you work some . . . magic? Do you call it magic?' He
shrugged, neither agreeing nor disagreeing. 'Well, so you're
magical, which is not normal. And you're hot—'

Stop telling the hot man he's hot! my brain commanded,
even as my mouth went right ahead ejaculating embarrassment.

'I mean, really hot, but, like, you're not weird.'

'Not weird?'

'Not . . . different.'

His lips parted in a feral grin, and for a split second I swear he'd grown fangs. When he opened his mouth to speak, however, they were gone. Which meant I was now babbling like a maniac *and* seeing things. *Rock on.*

'I can assure you, Jane True, that I am very different.' He said those words as if they were a promise, and I felt a shiver at the base of my spine. I realized, after a stunned minute, that it was a shiver of unmitigated lust. *Haven't felt that in a while*, I thought, marveling. But Ryu wasn't through playing his little verbal tap dance on my libido.

'Something I'm now very much looking forward to proving to you,' he said, his eyebrows striking a come-hither pose. I nearly took an obliging step forward. 'But not here, in your place of work, with your friend lurking.'

My brain schismed at that. One half dissolved into a sputtering goo that belched *gagagagagaga* over and over. The other half latched onto the idea of 'friend' in order to save my fragile sanity.

'So what the hell *did* you do to Grizzie?' I managed to ask, finally.

'Oh, nothing really. Just a little glamour to help her believe what I was telling her.'

There was that bloody word again, *glamour*.

'Look,' I said. 'I just found out about you guys last night. You really gotta quit with the supernatural jargon, because none of it makes any sense to me whatsoever.'

He grinned and threw back his head to let loose a funny barking laugh that was *not* what I expected. He was so smooth I would have imagined his laugh to be more 'smoky chuckle' than 'tickled coyote'. I smiled back at him. The laugh made him less corporate bloodsucker and more nerdy chic.

'Right,' he said. 'Let's start over. A glamour is a little technique that we all use. It's kind of like a Jedi mind trick.

Basically, we nudge people's perception a bit, so they see or hear what we want them to.'

'So, when you told Grizzie that she had heard of you, she believed you.'

'Exactly. All we have to do is back up the suggestion, and the human does the rest. It's the nature of the human mind to fill in gaps in its perception. If it sees something that doesn't make sense or learns something that can't actually be true, instead of doubting what it's seen or heard, it will fill in a story to make everything reasonable.'

'So, can you guys glamour one another?' I asked, intrigued.

He paused, considering his response. 'In rare circumstances, yes. Normally we can easily feel a glamour. But sometimes we don't.' He gave me a wily little grin. 'We like to think of ourselves as far superior to humans, but there are times when even our highly evolved brains want to fill in gaps as well.'

I mulled over Ryu's words, giving my bottom lip a little chew as I concentrated. He didn't interrupt me, just waited patiently, which I appreciated.

'So, what do you need from me?' I asked.

'Oh, just some information. We know you didn't have anything to do with Jakes's murder, but I need to ask you about the circumstances surrounding your finding the body. Also, I was thinking that since you're a native you can tell me what the humans are doing about the murder. Like, what they think happened and what information they have. Finally, I want to hear about the time Jakes spent living here. What he was doing, that sort of thing. Or if anything strange happened in that time. Were there other unfamiliar people or beings around, besides Peter?'

'Oh, okay,' I said, figuring he would want to get out of Rockabill as soon as possible. So, once again, I ignored my poor, repressed libido – which was currently clamoring for me to lure Ryu behind the counter and knock him out with an unabridged dictionary in order to make him mine – and went ahead and started in on what he wanted to know. 'Well, as for finding the body, there isn't really much—'

Ryu held up his hands, interrupting me. He tried to look professional, but there was a quirk to his lips suggesting things that could only be filed, in a professional sense, under sexual harassment. 'Do you mind if we do this later? I'm not at my best during the daytime, and I'm tired from the drive. I've rented one of those little cottages, by where Peter stayed, for a few days. I'd like to get settled and clean up before we get to work.'

I couldn't really imagine him getting any cleaner, nor did I really want to contemplate how much better his 'best' was. I shrugged my assent, hoping that whatever kind of supernatural being he was, he couldn't sense my libido planning things that might have made even Grizelda blush.

Unfortunately, Ryu gave me a smile that told me (a) he knew exactly what I was thinking and (b) he would see whatever my libido ponied up and raise it, fivefold.

'Great. I'll pick you up at six tonight. We can get something to eat and chat over dinner.'

'Um, okay,' I said, externally quite calm.

Shit, shit, shit, was my internal line of thought. *What the fuck am I going to wear?*

'Wait.' I had just remembered something. 'You don't know where I live.'

'Sure I do,' he said, slyly.

I thought about this for a minute. 'How do you know so much about me?'

'I've been briefed on the essentials by Nell.'

'Um, okay,' I murmured, suddenly terrified he didn't know *everything*, and that our dinner would turn into a hasty phone conversation once he knew my real story.

He smiled at me and took my hand. His was very warm and very strong. 'It really is a pleasure to meet you, Jane. I look forward to tonight.'

His eyes are almost golden, I thought. 'It's, um, nice to meet you, too,' I managed to respond.

He let go of my hand after a moment and looked toward the back of the store. 'Grizzie? You can come back.'

Grizzie emerged from the stockroom, still smiling happily away.

'I'm leaving now. It was very nice to meet you. Don't tell Tracy I came in. Let me surprise her.'

'Oh, that's a fantastic idea,' Grizzie cooed. 'It was great meeting you, too.'

Ryu gave me a parting wink, and then he was out the door and back in his car. Grizzie and I watched in silence as he sped off down the road.

'He's as gorgeous as you said he was,' she purred.

'Er, yes. He is, isn't he?' I couldn't help but feel guilty about lying to Grizzie like this, but I didn't see any other option. How could I begin to explain the truth of what had just happened?

'Are you seeing him tonight?' she said, turning toward me with a calculating look on her face.

'Yes, actually, I am. He's taking me to dinner.' I could feel the blood running to my cheeks and I was horrified. *Why am I blushing like a schoolgirl? I'm sure it's not a date. He's investigating a murder, fercrissakes!*

Grizzie frowned, and looked me up and down. I dreaded what I knew was coming next.

I blanched as she said, 'What *are* you going to wear?'

CHAPTER SIX

I opened the doors of my closet with trepidation. I was hoping that Nell might have secret aspirations of becoming a fairy godmother, and not just a garden gnome, and had filled it with beautiful things. But all that greeted me was my usual wardrobe of about six different Read It and Weep shirts, a few pairs of jeans and trousers, and a smattering of old shirts.

Grizzie was right to be worried. I sighed. *I dress like I'm homeless. Or about seven years old.*

I had only one option that was remotely dressy: a lovely red wrap dress that I'd found in my parents' closet. My father – always hoping that mother would return – had never packed away her things. Their bedroom remained as she'd left it. But he had allowed me to 'borrow' her red dress, even though I suspected that I'd never need to return it.

I took it out of my closet and held it in front of me while looking at myself in the mirror. It was, like all wrap dresses, incredibly flattering. Wedging the hanger underneath my chin, I pulled the dress tight around my waist, wondering what shoes I could wear. I didn't really have anything that went with it, as I'd only worn it once . . .

To a high school dance with Jason.

I sat down, heavily, upon my bed, guilt racing through my brain. *What the hell do you think you're doing?* I interrogated myself, angrily. *First of all, this isn't a date; you're being investigated. Second, even if it was a date, you've lost your chance for dates. People who kill the love of their life don't get* dates. *Third, Ryu, whatever he is, will probably just use his supernatural powers to run for the hills even faster than other men have once he learns the truth about you. So don't make an ass of yourself, Jane, and dress up like you're in some episode of* Sex and the City. *There's a reason they didn't have 'certifiably crazy' as a fifth character. There's not much scope for love interests.*

I replaced the dress in the back of my closet and went to take a shower. I scrubbed my body as if I could imbue myself with self-confidence through exfoliation, and then pulled on my newest pair of jeans and, after a minute's debate, a long-sleeved navy T that had three little buttons decorating its V-neck. It passed for fancy in my wardrobe, so it was a good compromise for the dress. Instead of my usual canvas sneakers, I pulled on my black, low-heeled, ankle-length boots. They were more serviceable than glamorous but at least they were proper shoes. To make up for the boots, I wore a minimum of makeup. Part of me recognized that my give-and-take game with my shame was ridiculous, but I couldn't help it.

I gave my damp hair one last brushing and hoped it would dry nicely . . . but not too nicely.

Grizzie had forced me to leave work an hour early, presciently doubting my ability to make myself presentable, so I'd come home to find my dad still gone. He'd taken the car to Covelli's to get it serviced, which I knew entailed him and Joe sitting around for a few hours shooting the shit.

I had taken lasagna out of the freezer that morning and had put it in the oven to bake for my dad's supper when I'd gotten home. I had just gone downstairs to check on it when I heard our rattling old car pull up our long drive. Dad came in through the back door and gave me a kiss on the cheek.

'You're home early,' he said, noticing my lack of work uniform. 'And you look very nice.'

'Yeah, Grizzie let me go at four,' I said, busying myself by fussing with the lasagna, checking to see if it was cooked through. It needed about another fifteen minutes so I put it back in the oven.

'Someone I know from college came into Read It and Weep, today. We're going to dinner. To catch up,' I finished, lamely.

'Oh, how nice,' my dad responded, slightly confused. I'd done a part-time undergraduate English degree at the University of Maine in Machias, which was about an hour and a half away. I'd commuted two days a week because I couldn't afford to live on campus. Not that I would have wanted to, anyway. For about two weeks I'd been anonymous, until someone had made the connection and the whispers and pointing had started. Of course, it was nowhere near as bad as it had been in Rockabill for the years after my little 'accident', but it still wasn't pleasant. I felt labeled, and as such I never really tried to make any friends. My professors had been great – despite the fact that my file had a warning on it, something like 'keep an eye on this one to make sure she doesn't show signs of going postal' – and there'd been a few girls with whom I didn't mind going for coffee or lunch. But I had to be careful not to get close enough that they were comfortable asking about what had happened to me. I certainly couldn't tell them the truth, and I refused to lie, so I had to keep my distance. Therefore I never made any *real* friends at the university – the story of my life.

So, no wonder my dad was slightly taken aback.

'Well, I'm glad that you have plans this evening, and that you're seeing a friend from school. That's really great,' he said, nodding his agreement with himself. 'You should go out more.'

I busied myself washing up a few stray glasses that had found their way into the sink, unable to look at my dad. I couldn't believe he didn't think it odd that I'd never talked about anyone from school, and yet I was claiming that somebody had shown up in Rockabill, of all places? I wondered if I had some sort of unconscious glamour power, but then I thought about my dad's reaction and what Ryu had said about human minds filling in gaps. I didn't need a glamour to make my dad want to see me happy. *I've made such a mess of things*, I thought, angrily scrubbing at an already clean glass.

I realized what I was doing and forced myself to rinse and release the glass back onto the draining board. I got myself together and had managed a smile when I turned around to face my dad again. He was sitting at the kitchen table, watching me quietly.

'Yes, well, you're probably right,' I answered him. 'I should go out more.'

He knew better than to push the subject. 'So, who's your friend?'

'His name is Ryu,' I said.

'Oh, it's a man,' my dad replied, almost gleefully. I blushed.

'Yes, a man. From school.'

'And his name is Ryu?'

'Yup, Ryu.'

'Like kanga-roo?'

'Yeah, I guess. I'm not sure how it's spelled, actually.'

'Neat. Is it a family name?'

'I'm not sure, but I'm assuming it is.' If by 'family' my dad meant the genus *things-that-go-bump-in-the-nighticus*.

Speaking of family, I thought. *What* is *Ryu, anyway?*

'What does he do?' said my dad, bringing me back to earth.

'Um . . . he's an investigator.'

'Oh, okay. With the police?'

'I'm not really sure. I think he might be private. A private investigator,' I finished, lamely.

'Ah, a gumshoe. Well, that must be exciting.'

'I think it must be, yes.'

The timer on the stove *pinged* and I nearly leapt over to the oven door. Our conversation was getting decidedly awkward. I knew suspiciously little about this good friend of mine.

I made a big production of taking the foil off of the top of the lasagna and turning up the oven to let it brown. I set the timer for another ten minutes. 'How was Joe?' I asked, using the opportunity to change the subject.

'Oh, fine,' my dad said, and then he rattled off to me what he and Joe had talked about that afternoon, and what Joe had said about our old car.

I set my dad a place at the table after making him a small salad. Then the lasagna was done, and I served him an oozing hunk – I make a mean lasagna – and sat at the table with him while he ate. As usual, I told him about Grizzie's outfit that day. He thought of her as some sort of exotic bird and he loved to hear about her ever-changing plumage.

My dad was just finishing dinner when our doorbell rang.

I leapt up, nearly knocking my chair over. My dad gave me a funny look, and I managed to smile. 'Guess I'm a little nervous,' I said, weakly.

Luckily, he let it go, and I forced myself to walk calmly out into the hallway and to our front door.

Ryu was wearing gray trousers and another crisp button-up with two-toned gray stripes, one stripe the exact color of his trousers and the other almost black. His belt and shoes were black. *No coat*, my mind whispered approvingly. *And you're underdressed*, it chastised.

He grinned at me and I noticed he was carrying a large rectangular box. He handed it to me and I took it gingerly by its handle. 'I couldn't find a florist,' he explained.

'Oh, okay. Thanks. What is it?'

'A lobster.'

'A lobster?'

'A lobster.'

'Right. Well, thanks again. C'mon in.' I held the door open and told my stomach to quit it with the butterflies as he edged past me. He smelled *good* – like freshly scrubbed man with a hint of balsam and something darker. Maybe cumin . . .

My father was standing in the doorway between our kitchen and family room, wiping his hands on a towel.

'Ryu, this is my father. Dad, this is Ryu.' I used the lobster box to gesture awkwardly between the two. Something rattled inside and I silently apologized for my rough handling, lowering the box gently to my side. The two men shook hands, exchanging pleasantries.

'Well, Ryu, it's nice to meet someone from my daughter's school days.' If my dad was surprised at just how posh Ryu was, he did a good job of hiding it.

'And it's a pleasure to meet you, sir. Your daughter often talks about you.'

'Well, she's really something special,' my dad said, and I blushed.

'Yes, she certainly is,' Ryu said, slipping me that naughty wink of his. If I was blushing before, I now thought my cheeks would burst with the blood surging through them.

'What's that you've got there, Jane?' my dad asked, noticing my embarrassment.

'Ryu brought us a lobster,' I said, hoping Ryu had *not* noticed my embarrassment.

'A lobster?'

'A lobster.' *Déjà vu*, my brain cackled, slightly hysterically.

'Well,' my dad said. 'Isn't that nice. Let me take that for you.'

I handed him the box with relief. I had a funny feeling that the lobster was going to end up back in the ocean as soon as I left with Ryu. Both my dad and I loved seafood but neither of us could abide the squealing of a lobster being boiled alive.

The three of us stood there in awkward silence until, as if on cue, we all started to speak at once. Ryu and I quickly ceded the floor to my father.

'You kids have fun, tonight. And be careful. See you in the morning, Jane.' He kissed me on the cheek and shook Ryu's hand, and then retreated to his recliner to watch the Food Network.

Ryu turned to face me. 'You look very nice, Jane. Do you need a coat?' he asked.

'No,' I said, without thinking. 'Oh wait, yes. And thank you.'

He looked at me curiously, but I ignored him and got my jacket.

We walked out into the crisp November night, and I noticed he still had the top down on his Porsche. He opened the passenger door for me, and I sank into my little seat. I'd never been in a car this fancy in my life, and I had to admit that I was a little excited.

He got in and started the car. 'I'll put the top up for you,' he said as I belted myself in.

'No, don't,' I blurted, blushing again as his curious

look returned. 'I don't really get cold,' I tried to explain. 'But I have to wear a coat so I won't stand out. Anymore than I already do.' I had no idea if he could understand my need to fit in, but I hoped he did. 'I'd really like to ride with the top down, but if we could put it up before we get to town, I'd appreciate it.' It sounded lame, I realized, and he would probably be disappointed with my stupid human concerns.

'Of course,' he said immediately. 'Don't worry, I understand. I'll put the top up when you say so. And if anybody sees us before that, I'll take care of it.' He smiled at me, and then reached forward to straighten out my seat belt where it was twisted over my chest. I froze at his touch, my heart racing.

I turned to face forward, my expression a blank mask. I hadn't done this – whatever this was – in a very long time and I had no idea how to act. So I followed my favorite attention-diffusing mantra: when in doubt, act fossilized.

He pulled out of our winding drive in silence, the car's powerful engine purring like a tiger. I relaxed as the night wind blew through my hair, and I closed my eyes and took a deep breath of pure anticipation. This ride was going to be *fun* . . .

For at least five minutes we enjoyed the peace and quiet, the darkness of the night only barely interrupted by the car's low headlights. When he finally spoke, he did so gently, as if not to disturb the mood. 'Where would you like to eat?' he asked.

I smiled. 'Well, there's not much choice in Rockabill. We have one diner open at this time of year, and then there's a place where you can get delicious burgers that seal shut your arteries.'

Ryu didn't have to think long about that one. 'Rockabill's only diner it is, then,' he decided. He barked his funny laugh again. 'What's it called?'

'The Trough. It's right on the main square, catty-corner from my work. You can't miss it.'

'"The *Trough*"?' he asked, skeptically. 'What's with the name?'

'Well,' I explained, a little embarrassed. 'Rockabill used to be a fishing village, but now we've tried to move toward tourism and our tourist attraction is the Old Sow.' Ryu looked puzzled, so I continued. 'The Old Sow is a giant whirlpool, one of the biggest in the world. She's very powerful and very unpredictable, and she creates all these really rare tidal phenomena. Like thunder holes,' I clarified. 'And standing waves.'

'Huh,' was his only response. Some people were more impressed by tidal phenomena than others.

'Anyway, the town did a sort of big revamp a few years back and the community thought it would be a good idea to make the Old Sow a recognizable brand that could be associated with Rockabill. Hence all the pig connections.'

Ryu chuckled, shaking his head. 'That's hilarious. I get the logic, but it's a terrible idea. Why would anyone want to eat at a restaurant called the Trough?'

I couldn't help but laugh, too. 'At least the Trough is just a diner,' I told him. 'We have what passes for a fancy restaurant here in Rockabill. It's only open in the summer, and it's called the Pig Out Bar and Grill.'

Ryu could only groan. 'That's awful!'

I grinned. 'Well, the owners are pretty awful, so I guess it fits.'

We were getting near town, and I asked if he would put up the convertible top. He assented without comment and we rode into Rockabill in silence.

Our entrance, even with the top up, received a fair amount of attention from the few people in our main square. It was rare to see such an expensive and impractical vehicle on the streets of Rockabill at this time of year. When we pulled into a parking space right in front of the Trough, it took a moment for me to work up the courage to get out. Everybody in the diner was already peering at us from their tables, and I felt distinctly uncomfortable at the thought of letting them see it was me in the fancy car.

In the meantime, Ryu had come over to the passenger side and opened my door, offering me a hand out of the low seat. I took it, grateful for the support even if he didn't know why I really needed it. He shut my door without letting go of my hand. Examining my face, he asked, 'Are you all right?'

I tried my best to smile, despite the fact that I'd seen the looks exchanged between some of the diners when they'd realized I was the mystery vehicle's passenger.

'I'm fine,' I said. Unsatisfied with my response, Ryu didn't let go of my hand nor did he unlock his eyes from mine. 'It's just that I'm not entirely . . . popular, here in Rockabill.' I chose my words carefully. 'I have a reputation for being . . . unstable. There's a lot of stuff that happened, in my past. It's been years, and I'm fine now, but people here haven't really moved on. So I don't like to attract attention.' I looked down at my feet, embarrassed by my outburst and terrified that now Ryu would ask me what had happened, and that he'd change toward me once I told him the truth.

Ryu placed his free hand under my chin, forcing my head up so that I met his eyes. 'But we both know it's bullshit,' he said, his voice low and serious. 'I know everything that happened to you, Jane. And I know you're not unstable. The humans fear you because they sense you're different. And you *are* different. You reek of power and otherness. Look, my kind knows all about living among humans and I can tell you this: they're like wild animals. If you let them sense you've a weakness, they'll take advantage of it to hurt you.'

I mulled over Ryu's words. The part of me that was pure girl whined that he'd said I 'reeked', but I ignored her. For hearing he knew about my past and that he didn't care *floored* me. The breath I hadn't realized I'd been holding whooshed out of my body and, to my horror, I felt the telltale pinprick of forming tears. I blinked fiercely. I would *not* cry in front of this man just because he deigned to speak with me despite my history.

As Ryu stepped forward, his eyes locked on mine, and I was overwhelmed by his physical proximity. His warm hand still cupped my jaw, and his face was way too close for comfort. *His eyes are flecked with green*, I noted. *I think they're actually hazel. I don't know if I've ever seen real hazel eyes before . . .*

Ryu let his hand drop from my chin as he took a small step backward, and then he brushed my hair away from my face. My skin thrilled at his touch but his movement also broke the spell of the previous moment. I took a deep breath as he offered me his arm like a gallant Victorian gentleman.

'My lady?' he queried, with a slight bow.

I took his arm. 'Regulators, mount up,' I muttered, channeling Warren G to fortify myself for our entrance into Rockabill society.

If I'd walked into the Trough singing the national anthem at the top of my lungs Ryu and I couldn't have attracted any more curiosity. The whole restaurant was staring at us, silently, as the door chimes tinkled a sarcastic little welcome.

But then Louis Finch, my dad's childhood friend and the owner of the Trough, bustled over to give me a hug. He had been a tall skinny teenager nicknamed 'Beanpole', a moniker that had stuck despite the fact that he was now incredibly fat.

He was also incredibly kind, and I still had the teddy bear
he and his wife, Gracie, had sent me while I was in the
hospital.

He showed us to a seat in Amy Bellow's section. Besides
Grizzie and Tracy, I considered Amy one of my few friends
here in Rockabill, and my dad and I always sat in her section
when we came into the Trough. Louis handed us menus and
made a funny little congratulatory face at me as Ryu opened
his, and I couldn't help but laugh. Ryu looked up and I think
he caught the exchange, which made me blush again. If I
wasn't careful I was going to turn red permanently.

'So, what do you usually order?' he asked, scanning the
menu.

'I always get the tuna melt. I like tuna.' *Be careful, Jane*,
I thought, blanching internally. *You don't want to overwhelm
him with your cool sophistication.*

'I prefer red meat,' he replied, conversationally. 'I'll get
the rib-eye.'

He looked around the diner. 'Nice place, very homey.'

'Yes,' I said. 'It should be.' I leaned over the table, conspiratorially. 'Louis and Gracie – they're the owners; he's the guy
that greeted us – spent a fortune on an interior decorator to
give the place a "country diner" feel. Which the decorator
did. Only it looks exactly the same as when she started, except
for there's more peach involved. Gracie swears it's all in the
little touches, but nobody else can see any difference.'

Ryu barked his absurd laugh, causing old Mrs Patterson
to glare at him from over her clam chowder, and I giggled
at both of them.

At that moment, Amy came over with her pad and pencil.
Her dishwater-blond hair, complete with dark roots, was cut
in a shaggy surfer 'do, and she was dressed more like she
was headed for a bonfire on a beach in California than a

Northeastern winter. She also had the habitually lazy eyes and perma-friendliness of someone who smoked loads of pot. So I was more than a little surprised when, after seeing who I was sitting with, her expression changed from friendly and open to closed and threatening.

'Jane,' she greeted me with a nod before turning her attention to Ryu. 'And who might you be?' she questioned, coldly. All traces of friendly stoner were gone; Amy suddenly crackled with energy and malice. Whatever was going on here was beyond me.

Ryu introduced himself amicably enough, and Amy seemed to back down a little bit. But they both still had the air of two dogs circling each other. If they started sniffing each other's butts, I was out.

'Did you check in with Nell?' she asked, still on guard.

That crafty little minx, I thought, as I realized what was happening. *She's one of them . . . she owes me fried cheese for keeping secrets.* In my world, fried cheese is the gold standard.

'Of course,' Ryu responded. 'Nell knows of my presence here. I'm investigating Jakes's murder.'

I looked around, astonished. He'd said that really loud, and Amy's out-of-character animosity toward him must have attracted attention. But no one in the Trough was paying us any mind; in fact, it was like we weren't even there at that moment.

While Amy sized him up, Ryu smiled at me. He'd obviously noticed my shocked expression.

'No worries, Jane. They won't pay us any attention if I don't want them to. And right now, I don't want them to.' I was about to ask him more questions when Amy finally finished her assessment.

'Okay, then.' Her attitude went back to normal and she was, once again, in surfer-waitress mode. 'What'll you have?'

I ordered lemonade with my tuna melt, and Ryu ordered a Coke when he was told there was no booze available.

When he ordered his steak, Amy responded by asking, 'Let me guess, you want it very rare? Maybe even bloody?' He grinned at her and she rolled her eyes. 'I'll be right back with your drinks, dudes,' she said, giving me a friendly bop on the head with the menus as she walked away.

'So,' I said, as soon as Amy was out of earshot. 'What do you mean they can't see you? And what is Amy?' Then I thought for a moment. 'Matter of fact, what are you? And how did she recognize you?'

Ryu leaned back in his chair. He was smiling at me like the cat who'd stolen the cream. I got the feeling he was enjoying his role as tour guide through the world of the supernatural.

'She recognized me because I'm doing a sort of reverse glamour. I'm here on official business, so I'm broadcasting my presence, my credentials, to the natives. But in a way that only other supernaturals can sense. Otherwise we can't really recognize each other, although, obviously, some of us stand out. It's hard to miss a satyr, for example. What with the horns. And the lack of pants.'

At Ryu's joke I gave a very unladylike snort, nearly died of embarrassment, and then somehow managed to knock my napkin-wrapped cutlery off the table. He caught it before it hit the ground.

'And glamouring answers why people can't see us when I don't want them to,' he said, setting my cutlery down a safe distance away from me. 'My particular kind live closely with humans. Not all kinds of supes do, and, for some of our various factions, human life is a complete mystery. But I live a significant amount of time as a human. I have a human surname, albeit one that changes every twenty years or so. I own a house; I have a social security number; I pay taxes.

Which is probably why you think I appear more normal than someone like Nell, or her kelpie.' As he said the last bit, his lips curved, just slightly, and I remembered the promise he'd made about proving how different he actually was. My breathing hitched, and he smiled as if he could hear me. 'Anyway, the point is that I am used to humans. So throwing up glamours when humans might see something fishy is pretty much reflex. I bet you can feel it, if you pay attention. Shut your eyes.'

I did as he asked, and I suddenly did feel something. It was like the slightest of cool winds blowing across my exposed skin, raising the hair on my forearms.

'Wow,' I breathed, opening my eyes to find Ryu smiling at me.

'Get ready for a lot of "wow" from here on in, Jane.'

I gulped, not sure if I was supposed to be reading anything more into that statement.

'Amy?' I prompted, nervously changing the subject. Ryu smiled, knowingly, and I cursed my clumsiness.

'As for Amy, she's a nahual: a shapeshifter,' he explained. 'They're not like the two-formed; they can shift into anything they wish. But otherwise they have less access to the elements than two-formeds.'

'And that translates as . . .' I prompted him, gently.

'Right. That translates as: nahuals are shape-shifters but that's pretty much all they can do. Obviously, they're stronger and faster-healing than humans, and they live longer. But they can't do much of what humans would call magic. Selkies and other two-formeds can shift only into the one alternative shape, but they have more power. Like you do when you swim, they can manipulate the elements.'

What he said knocked me for six. It should have been obvious, but it wasn't until he'd said it.

'So, you're telling me that when I swim, I'm manipulating the ocean?' He nodded.

Ryu's casually telling me I used some kind of magic when I swam was completely crazy at the same time that it struck me as completely logical. It answered so many of my questions. Why I didn't drown, or freeze. Why I was so strong in the water. My brain went deeper. Why I *needed* to swim. I flashed back to Nell telling me to go 'recharge my batteries'. Then my brain went too deep. 'The bodies,' I whispered. 'The Sow didn't just let them go, did she?'

'No,' he answered, calmly sipping his Coke. Amy must have brought us our drinks while I was in my little trance. I stared down at my lemonade, unseeing.

'That's how we knew something was up the night you found Jakes. Your release of power was loud; almost as loud as the night with your . . . friend.' Here, Ryu finally looked uncomfortable. 'Nell knew something had happened, but she felt you go back to normal swimming so she assumed you were okay. When she bothered to investigate, it was already too late and Jakes was in the hands of the humans.'

I blinked back tears, trying to steady myself. This wasn't the time or the place.

'So,' I changed subjects, helped along by Amy bringing us our dinners. Ryu's steak looked almost raw it was so rare. 'If Amy here is a nahual,' Amy gave me a little smile and bobbed her head, 'then what are you?' Amy snorted with amusement as she walked away, shooting Ryu a look that said, 'Have fun.'

Ryu thought about that one, taking the time to cut off a piece of bloody steak and pop it into his mouth. He chewed slowly before swallowing. 'Well,' he said. 'How should I put this . . .' He appeared to be at a loss. 'You've been told how we are the origins for many different myths and legends, yes?'

I nodded, and he continued. 'Well, some myths hold more truth than others. For those of us who live most intimately with humans, there has been a tendency to understand us less . . . accurately.'

I swirled a French fry in some ketchup, rather enjoying his discomfiture. *It's about time you had a turn feeling out of your depth*, I thought smugly as I raised the fry to my mouth.

'I'm what is known to my people as a baobhan sith,' Ryu said, pronouncing it baa'-van shee. 'Like I said, we live closely with humans, so we're pretty famous. We've inspired tons of humans myths. Like strigoi, nosferatu . . .' I stopped chewing as my eyes widened in alarm. *Holy shit,* I thought. *He's a goddamned—*

'In short, you would probably call me a vampire.'

I nearly choked, bits of fried potato going down the wrong pipe. I was coughing like crazy, my eyes watering while Ryu whacked me on the back, urging me to drink my lemonade.

I could feel the whirl of Ryu's power around us, so no one else in the diner noticed my near-death experience. Except for Amy, who shot me a sympathetic look as she disappeared into the kitchen.

When my coughing fit subsided, and I was able to breathe normally again, Ryu returned to his chair. He looked both concerned and amused, and I wanted to kick his shins under the table. I sat and sipped my lemonade until I could talk again.

'So,' I finally managed to get out, 'you're a vampire.'

'Yes, and no.' He smiled. 'As you know, I can move about during the day, although it is true that our strengths are diminished in the daytime. And we are certainly not dead humans. We are very much alive and very much *in*human.'

'It's great that you're alive and all, but what about the

bloodsucking? And the killing? And the fangs?'

He ran one hand through his brown hair, giving his head a good scratch. His hair was so thick that if it weren't short it might look like a toupee. It glistened like melted milk chocolate in the diner's bright lights. Then I realized he was watching me stare at him. He smiled as I looked down, hastily. 'It's true we drink blood, but not for food. Food we get like you do.' He gestured at his plate with a little flourish. 'From blood we get what we call essence, which is to the elements what energy is to matter in your human science. Basically, we feed off human emotions. The most potent emotions are love and hate, but it's nearly impossible to stimulate such powerful emotions quickly. So mostly we feed off fear or lust. Sometimes a little of both.'

I thought about what he had just said while I ate a bite of my tuna melt. I swallowed carefully and said, 'So, you can scare somebody, and then feed off of them, and that tops up your . . . essence tank. From which you derive power, like I guess I do from the sea.' He nodded. 'I get how fear works,' I continued, 'but lust?' He looked at me like I was a bit slow, and I reflected for a moment. 'Oh, of course,' I said, blushing. I was *very* slow.

'So, we don't need much blood, and certainly not enough to exsanguinate somebody. But we do need to be around humans. Most other supernatural beings don't generate the right caliber of emotional essence.'

'And can the humans you bite, can they . . . catch it?' I knew I was being vague, and Ryu looked annoyingly amused.

'It?' he queried, his lovely lips curling in a smirk.

I sighed. I could tell he was one of those people who liked to make things difficult. 'You know, vampirism. Like in the movies.'

He shook his head. 'Forget everything you've seen in the

movies,' he said. 'They are – for the most part – based on misconceptions, half-truths, or out and out fantasy. I don't carry a virus or a pathogen or a curse. What I am is another species, or race, to you. If I bit you,' he explained, 'you could no more get "vampire" than you could give me "human" or "female" or "Caucasian" by biting me.'

I kept eating, trying to take in everything he was saying.

'Does it hurt?' I asked eventually, curiosity getting the better of me.

'It can, if we'd like it to.' Ryu's voice was low, his eyes suddenly hot on mine. 'But it can also feel very good indeed. And we can heal a bite, no problem. Which feels quite nice as well.'

Those words, coupled with the heat of his gaze, made various bits of my anatomy, which had been dormant for the past eight years, rocket to life. In order to cover my confusion, and to keep the whimper that was hovering just at the back of my throat from escaping, I bit into my pickle.

'As for the fangs,' he continued, 'they only come out when we're . . . excited.'

I tried to keep my face noncommittal as I took a sip of my lemonade.

'Told you I was different.' He smirked, and I nearly choked, again. *Note to self*, I thought. *Stop eating around this man. He will be the death of you.*

'Does that answer your questions?' he asked, taking my hand and giving it a squeeze. 'I know this has to be a lot of information coming too quickly. You halflings don't have it easy when you've been raised human. But it *will* begin to make sense, eventually. And you've got a long time to get used to it.'

He let my hand go with a stomach-churning caress and started back in on his steak. We finished what was left of our meals in silence, for which I was happy. I didn't know how much more my poor brain could take in one night.

After dinner we ordered pie and coffee, and only then did Ryu ask me about Jakes. I told him about finding the body and I told him everything that Grizzie had told me about the investigation. Ryu was most interested in the stuff about Peter's car. I told him that I didn't think there'd been anything strange happening during Peter's stay here in Rockabill, but I wouldn't have known what to look for anyway.

We finished our desserts and Ryu asked for the bill. I tried to pay for my share, but he just rolled his eyes at me. 'It's on the company,' he said. 'Don't worry about it.' I didn't know whether to be pleased or displeased at that information. When he'd insisted on paying, it had felt like a date, but I didn't know if I should be on a date. So I settled on feeling ambivalent, and let it go at that.

He had a faraway look in his eyes as he helped me into my coat, and then turned me around so he could zip me up. I felt like a child standing there, but I don't think he was even aware of what he was doing. He took my hand and we walked out into the parking lot. I waved at Amy through the window, still feeling slightly superfluous as we walked to Ryu's car. He opened my door and then went around and got into the driver's seat.

Starting the engine, he turned to me. 'The obvious course of action is to find Jakes's car,' he said, decisively. 'But tonight's not the right time. A night like this is too good to waste.' There was that cheeky wink again. 'Let's go out. Do you want to go out?'

'Yes, please,' I answered, my voice strangely small.

'Excellent.' He grinned, adjusting my seat belt again. My heart palpitated, right on cue.

'So what passes for a watering hole here in Rockabill, Maine?'

I hated to tell him. 'It's called the Pig Sty.'

His yipping laugh echoed through the car as we peeled out from our parking space and into the night.

CHAPTER SEVEN

From the parking lot, Ryu eyed the Sty skeptically. The Pig Sty was your average country watering hole: big and airy, a little shabby, and with a large quantity of very little selection. There were no rare micro-brewery pilsners, nor were there any pinot grigios or un-oaked chardonnays. The Sty had 'red wine' or 'white wine', a few different, inevitably domestic species of beer and light beer, and the standard selection of hard liquor. That said, the owners, Marcus and Sarah Vernon, had always been really nice to me, going out of their way to be inviting. And the Vernons made sure everyone behaved.

Legend has it that Marcus had chucked Stuart, my nemesis, into the Dumpster the first night the Sty opened. Stu had been throwing his weight around, as usual, and had grabbed some tourist's ass and said something filthy in her ear when out of nowhere Marcus struck. Marcus was decidedly smaller than Stu, but Stu hadn't had a chance. One minute he was standing there looking surprised, the next he had disappeared into the filthy Dumpster out back. Marcus hadn't even broken a sweat.

I would have paid good money to have seen the look on Stu's face that night.

The best part is that Stu, in the end, had to humble himself

and ask Marcus for forgiveness. The Pig Sty was the only
bar for miles and Stu was *already* barred from half the places
between here and Eastport. So, he'd sucked it up and apologized, and I guess Marcus had felt that he'd made his point
and allowed Stuart to come back.

More's the pity, I thought, recognizing Stuart's enormous
SUV in the parking lot. I stifled a groan. But the Sty was a
big place and the parking lot was pretty full. Hopefully Stuart
would overlook my presence.

Ryu parked close to the main entrance and, once again,
took my hand as we walked into the bar. *He's making a habit
of the hand-holding*, I thought, unsure how I felt about that
fact. No, check that. I knew I felt pretty damned good about
holding his hand, but I was also pretty sure that I shouldn't.

Not least because he just admitted to being a vampire, I
reminded myself.

Whatever, my libido purred. *You don't get to judge him for
having fangs when he hasn't judged you for going bonkers.
Not to mention, vampires are hot.*

You're not helping, the more virtuous aspect of my personality scolded.

The gods help those who help themselves, my libido
smirked, taking control of my hand long enough to give Ryu's
a little squeeze. He smiled at me, pleasure suffusing his
features.

Jane True, get a grip! I threatened, my face coloring for
about the fiftieth time that evening.

Behind the large bar were Sarah and Marcus. Both about
the same size, they looked like brother and sister except for
their skin tones. She was very pale and he was very dark,
although they had the same boyish haircuts. Sarah spiked hers
up, as if to match her husband's afro. They were each about
five foot six and muscular, but in a really attractive way –

they looked like acrobats rather than weight lifters. They'd always gone out of their way to speak to me in the village and I enjoyed coming into the Sty because of them. That said, I rarely made an appearance, as Stuart often lurked in the vicinity.

Sarah and Marcus both looked up sharply as Ryu and I entered. *Hmm*, I thought. *I know that look.* So I was both surprised and not surprised when I felt Ryu's power begin swirling, presumably making us invisible, and Marcus stalked forward demanding to know if Ryu had checked in with Nell.

Well, now I know why they were so nice to me.

Ryu assured Marcus his presence was legitimate, and then Marcus turned to face me.

'Welcome, Jane,' he said, wrapping me up in a hug as if I were his long lost sister. When he let me go, Sarah was right there to replace him. She hugged me so tight my vertebrae crunched, murmuring, 'I'm so glad you finally *know*,' in my ear.

They both stood there beaming at me for an uncomfortable moment, before escorting us to the left-hand side of the bar.

Sitting there were Gus Little, Miss Carol, and a man I didn't recognize. Gus worked as a bag boy at McKinley's grocery store, even though he appeared to be middle-aged. Rumor had it that Gus was 'special', but in the short bus, rather than the supernatural, way. He was a small man, and very chubby, with a huge round face and these funny eyes that swam alarmingly behind enormous, Coke-bottle glasses. He was also bald as an egg.

Miss Carol was one of my favorite Rockabill characters, next to Grizzie. She had to be at least seventy and she'd been living in Rockabill, and had been old, for as long as anybody could remember. She had a thick Southern accent for absolutely no discernible reason, and she wore hideous pastel-colored suits, with matching gloves, shoes, and hat every day of the year. I would *never* have pictured her hanging out in the Sty.

The unknown man was very slender and strangely elongated, like he'd been stretched on a rack. He gave me a watery smile, his slightly bleary eyes rather unfocused. He had the air of someone elderly, even though he didn't look to be more than fifty-five.

All three were greeting me like an old friend when I heard the *pop* of a champagne cork, an incongruous sound for the Sty. Marcus and Sarah were pouring out glasses and handing them around our little group. I wondered what they were celebrating, when Sarah held up her glass and announced, 'To Jane! Welcome to the family!' They all clinked glasses while I sat stunned. Ryu clinked his glass to mine and leaned over to whisper, 'You should say something.' His lips brushed my ear and I started.

'Thank you,' I said, holding up my glass. 'I wasn't expecting this. I, um, really appreciate it.' I clumsily saluted them with my champagne flute and raised the bubbly to my lips. It was delicious. I'd never tasted champagne before.

They all drank with me, and then Miss Carol gave a little cheer and hollered, 'Does this mean I get a discount?' I laughed so hard I nearly snorted champagne out of my nose. Miss Carol was one of our best customers, but she read the filthiest books imaginable. She special ordered them and we had to keep them wrapped up and behind the counter till she picked them up, they were so dirty.

Everyone laughed with me, and Sarah and Marcus went back to work, each giving me another warm smile before attending to the other customers. None of whom, I noticed, had paid the slightest bit of attention to our little party in the corner.

Ryu refilled my glass and I took the opportunity to whisper, 'So, what is everybody?'

He refilled his own while he answered. 'Marcus and Sarah are nahuals, like Amy. They're the most prevalent type of supernatural being at the moment, for complicated reasons. Miss Carol is actually Nell's niece; she's a gnome.'

'Wait,' I interrupted. 'She doesn't *look* like a gnome. And she's lived in Rockabill all of her life.'

'She's young for a gnome,' he explained. 'When she gets to full power, she'll wizen right up like Nell. And then she'll have to find her own land; two mature gnomes can't share the same territory. But for right now Nell protects her while she gathers her strength. And as for her residency in the village, I bet nobody ever remembers a time when "Miss Carol" was young?'

'Ah,' I said, taking the hint. 'She's glamoured.'

'All the time,' he concurred.

'And what about Gus?' I asked. 'Everybody in Rockabill says he's, er, slow.'

Ryu grinned. 'Gus isn't slow,' he responded. 'He's a rock.'

I got the feeling he wasn't making a cruel joke, so I waited for him to explain.

'Gus is a stone spirit. Somewhere around Rockabill is a boulder that Gus is attached to. He'll spend most of his life as part of the stone, but for a few decades every couple of hundred years, he'll emerge to try to find a mate. Stone spirits are incredibly rare, so his chances are almost nil. But he'll give it a go.'

'And in the meantime he bags groceries?' I asked incredulously.

'Why not?' Ryu asked. 'It gets him out, gets him interacting with people in a way that he can handle. We all enjoy being around humans. They're like . . . fireworks. They're brilliant and they dazzle and then they fade and die. Gus's nature is to be a stone. He's not going to turn around and become a race-car driver. But he can bag groceries and soak up some human vitality, so he does.'

I mulled this over before I pointed discreetly at the elastic-man. 'And who's he? He seems to know me but I don't recognize him.'

Ryu's grin was so big it nearly split his face. 'That . . . is Russ.'

I blinked. 'Mr Flutie's *dachshund*?'

'Yup.' He laughed. 'Nahuals aren't as long-living as others of us since they don't have as much contact with the elements. Russ is about four hundred years old, which is ancient in nahual terms. Sometimes, when they're that age, they retire as pets. It's a good life, I guess. All the food you can eat and somebody to scratch your belly.' He arched his expressive brows at me and my spine tingled. 'There are worse ways to spend your golden years.'

'Huh,' was all I could say, trying to still my butterflies while mulling over what Ryu had just told me. *And I thought I had secrets . . .*

'It's all fun and games till the vet tries to put you to sleep,' I said, finally. Ryu barked like a seal.

When he'd regained his composure, I asked, 'How do you know so much about everybody?'

'It's the job, remember?' He smiled at me.

'Yeah, yeah . . . the job.' *Smug little shit*, I thought. *Very hot smug little shit*, I corrected myself.

Right then Miss Carol laid a hand on Ryu's arm and asked him about his presence in Rockabill, giving me a chance to look around the Sty. There were a fair few of Rockabill's great and good sitting around the place. Those who were just drinking were mostly sitting around the actual bar. Joel Irving was propped up in what I imagined was his usual place. He was nursing a shot and a beer.

Other patrons were eating dinner at tables. The Sty was basically an enormous rectangle. Two-thirds were made up of a huge bar, the kitchens – which served the aforementioned incredibly tasty but artery-clogging burgers and brats and things – and a little dance floor around the jukebox. The other third held tables for eating, the washrooms, and a small stage for karaoke or whatever entertainment the Vernons managed to entice out to Rockabill.

Next to me, the supernatural folk were talking about the murder. They were asking about its implications, I think, for whatever power structure existed in their world. I hadn't the faintest clue what any of it meant.

I was distracted when I spotted Stuart and his thuggish band of brothers sitting at a table in the very far corner of the eating area, partially hidden by a couple of one-armed bandits that the Sty has 'for entertainment purposes only'. I hoped he hadn't spotted me. Or, better yet, that we were still glamoured as we must have been for what had turned out to be our rather dramatic entrance.

Sarah had come back over to hear what Ryu was saying to Miss Carol, and I watched the little group as if from a very great distance.

All this time, I thought, *and right under my nose* . . . The thought of having been surrounded by all these different creatures, and not having realized it, was overwhelming. I thought of all the humans sitting in this room, some of whom had been quite happy to brand me a freak. *If they only knew what was really going on*, I thought, watching as the stone spirit nodded assent at something the dachshund was saying. The young gnome, who looked like an elderly lady, flirted with the handsome vampire and I grinned.

I'm practically normal, I thought, feeling hope well up in that deep, dark place within me that was lonely and tired of feeling outside of my own life. *Hell, to them I'm probably so normal I'm boring—*

Someone touched my hand. It was Marcus, holding out a five-dollar bill toward me. 'Why don't you pick out some tunes on the jukebox?' he said.

I smiled back, taking the money. I didn't feel like Marcus was getting rid of me, I just assumed he knew how lost I was by the neighboring conversation.

'Tunes it is,' I said. 'Thank you.'

He returned my smile and I hopped down from my bar stool. The jukebox was on the wall behind where we were sitting, and I knew from past experience how well it was stocked, at least by my standards. It had all the classic bar anthem-type artists, like Aerosmith and AC/DC, as well as popular selections that were playing on the radio right now. But it also had a bunch of artists that were less well known whom I absolutely loved.

Five dollars bought ten songs here at the Pig Sty, and I nearly quailed at the pressure. That was a lot of songs; whatever I picked was going to be the bar's soundtrack for well over an hour.

Lay on, Macduff, my brain intoned, solemnly accepting the challenge.

I tried to pick out a selection that included every genre and that alternated between fast and slow songs. *Just like a good mix tape*, I thought. Not that anyone made mix tapes anymore. I did sneak some of my favorite songs by the Indigo Girls, David Gray, and REM into the mix.

It took me about ten minutes to complete my selection, and when I got back to the bar the others were winding down their conversation. Ryu put a hand on my waist to help me up onto my bar stool, which was completely unnecessary and totally sexy. At that exact second, my first selection ripped out of the speakers: Great White's 'Once Bitten Twice Shy'.

'You did *not* choose this song,' he said, laughing.

'It's one of my all-time favorites and I thought it was fairly appropriate, given the circumstances,' I said. 'And if I have much more of this,' I held up my champagne glass, 'you might get the chance to see my best one-legged hopping, air-guitaring, spontaneous riff.'

Ryu was grinning like the Cheshire cat. 'Garçon!' he cried, holding up a single finger. Marcus obligingly fetched another bottle of bubbly.

I started to protest, but Ryu shook his head decisively. 'It's a good night,' he said. 'And you need a good night. Anybody can see that you're wound tight as a guitar string.'

I accepted another glass without complaint, and we clinked another toast. 'To the Pig Sty,' he said, giving me that damned wink. 'To the Sty,' I echoed, as we drank together.

We sat, not speaking, for a moment. I was enjoying the music and the taste of my third-ever glass of champagne. I don't know what Ryu was thinking. Then Miss Carol started talking to me about the bookstore, and we talked about how great Grizzie and Tracy were, and different books she wanted to order. She recommended to me a few things that were already lurking in my dirty drawer – presents from Grizzie. I promised her I'd read them, but kept my fingers crossed. Ryu chatted with Marcus, while Sarah took over from him for a bit, and I think they were talking about me because they kept glancing over to make sure Miss Carol had my attention.

Another favorite song of mine, the Killers' cover of 'Romeo and Juliet', came on the jukebox when Russ stood up and held out a hand. 'Will you dance with an old dog?' he offered, very politely.

I didn't know how to react, so I just said yes. He limped out on to the dance floor with me, and we took a very formal waltz position. The song wasn't really right for slow dancing, but I didn't have the heart to tell him. As we moved awkwardly around the floor, him gimping so badly I felt like I was more his crutch than his dance partner, we talked about the morning he found Peter's body. He told me that he'd tried to distract Mr Flutie, but there was only so much a dog in a sling could do when his master had spotted a dead body on the path. I apologized for making things difficult. I'd gotten the distinct impression they'd rather the authorities not become involved. He shrugged, and told me not to worry – such things were always handled with the minimum of fuss.

I had thought of something while we were dancing, and I said so.

'Fire away, child.' Russ smiled benevolently at me.

'Rockabill isn't a very big place, but there seems to be a fair proportion of, um, your kind of folk living here. Are there that many of you, or is Rockabill special or something?' I was thinking about Buffy's Sunnydale, and wondering if Rockabill was a Hellmouth. *Which would explain Stuart and Linda.*

'Oh, no, Rockabill is just Rockabill,' the dachshund-man replied. 'And there are proportionally very few of us left anymore. But those of us who live among humans usually prefer either large cities or places like Rockabill that have small native populations but busy tourist seasons. In the former, you are another anonymous city-dweller; in the latter, you have a lot of contact with people at different times of the year and yet you have fewer locals to deal with. Many of our kind are rather territorial, as well, so we have to spread out. But Nell is very generous in sharing her territory and her protection, so we've got a fairly large congregation here in Rockabill. Does that make sense?'

I thought it over, and yes, it did make sense. *So much for Linda and Stuart being demon spawn*, I thought, regretfully.

When the song was over, Russ gave me a gentlemanly bow and thanked me for the dance. 'Thank you, Mister, er . . . Mister Russ,' I finished uncertainly.

Sarah interrupted our awkward exchange as Pink's 'U & Ur Hand' blared forth. 'Can you swing dance?' she asked as she took my hands in hers.

'No, sorry.' I shook my head.

'Too bad,' she said. 'Just try to follow and hold on to your hat!'

With that she swirled me around in a perfect twirl. Sarah was incredibly strong. Which was good, since I was doing my best to fall on my face. But between her patient tutelage, and her being able to lift me up and set me down wherever she wanted, pretty soon we were doing what was, for me at least, a pretty good approximation of a swing dance.

I couldn't remember the last time I'd had this much *fun*. I loved the song we were dancing to and I couldn't think of anything better than the feeling of moving my body to one of my favorite songs playing over a jukebox so loudly that the speakers rattled. It was made even better by the fact that Sarah was such a strong partner. I felt like I was dancing well enough not to be embarrassed, so it was just unmitigated pleasure. I was panting and aching by the time we were done, but I didn't want the song to end. When it finally finished I couldn't help it, I threw my arms around her and said, 'Thank you,' like she'd just saved my life.

She pinched my cheek. 'Thank *you*,' she said. 'We've been waiting to have you in our bar like this for a long time. It feels good.' She gave me another little hug.

'Well, I need to get back to work,' she said, pulling back. 'And it looks like there's someone trying to cut in.'

I turned around to find Ryu waiting behind me, holding my champagne flute. I took a grateful gulp, having discovered that swing dancing was thirsty work. He took my glass and set it down on the bar, and then extended his hand.

'Am I on your dance card?' he asked.

'Hmm, let me check,' I teased. I think I was slightly drunk, as flirting was suddenly coming a lot easier.

'Well?' A dark eyebrow arched questioningly over a golden eye and my heart skipped a beat.

'I guess I can squeeze you in. For a quick one.'

He glided toward me and suddenly I was in his arms. *Just like that*, I wondered, shocked by the ease of it all. Then I realized that the champagne probably had my inhibitions in a head lock.

The song that was playing was one of the sexiest I could think of: David Gray's 'Debauchery' from his album *A Century Ends*. It's about a rather inebriated couple who meet on a ferry, go to his house for more drink, and have sex in front of his gas fire. It sounds awful, but it's both funny and really erotic at the same time. Plus David growls like an animal at one point, and my knees go weak every time I hear it.

Ryu and I danced like kids at a school prom: my arms over his shoulders and his around my waist. I could feel every inch of his body against mine as if it were electrified.

One thing I couldn't feel, however, was his power. He wasn't glamouring us. Instead, he was dancing with me, in public, and letting everyone see. I was so flattered that he wouldn't mind being associated with the town crazy that I didn't warn him it probably wasn't the best idea, considering Stuart lurked.

Ryu raised his eyebrows as David Gray sang of stripping his new ladyfriend. Then Ryu laughed as David sang of encouraging her with that classic enticement: copious amounts of vino.

'Nice choice,' he said, holding me a little tighter.

'Yes. I like it. A lot.' *Oh, sweet baby Jesus. I certainly do like it . . .*

I pressed my cheek against his chest so I didn't have to look at his face. His beautiful, beautiful face.

But when I heard his heartbeat pounding just as hard as mine, I raised my head again. The sound of his heart hadn't helped to calm my hormones one bit.

I sought frantically for something to talk about. There was one thing that had been bothering me . . .

'Ryu?'

'Yes?' he murmured, his lips brushing my ear.

'You said that you . . . that vampires, that baobhan sith, I mean, feed off either fear or lust. Does that mean that you prey, like really *prey* on humans, even if you don't kill them?'

Take that, hormones! I thought, exultantly. Imagining Ryu pursuing terrified women through dark city streets was better than a cold shower.

'Some of us do,' he admitted. 'But emotions flavor the blood. So it becomes a matter of preference, like preferring red or white wine. I don't enjoy the taste of fear.'

I mulled over the implications of what he'd just said, feeling my knees weaken. And David Gray hadn't even growled yet. *Lust it is, then*, my libido exulted.

One of Ryu's hands moved lower, gently stroking the small of my back. He was sort of massaging me, sort of bringing my hips closer to him.

The song helped him along, as David Gray urged his own lover closer in the song. And then David growled. David's growl always got to me.

Ryu's other hand was brushing my hair away from my

face, and then stroking over my cheek. Then he was supporting the back of my neck as he tilted my face up toward his . . .

For a second I wondered if I should resist, if I was doing the right thing. But he was funny, and beautiful, and so *different*, and he knew my secrets and didn't care . . . I studied Ryu's face, looking for an answer to a question I couldn't even articulate.

Which is when I noticed, with the tiny portion of my brain that wasn't entirely *vaklempt*, that the pointy tips of two very sharp-looking fangs had just begun to peep out from under his top lip. *Holy shit!* thought the part of me that was trying to remember where I kept our Band-Aids. Meanwhile, the part of me that was really attracted to Ryu was wondering, *Does that mean he likes me?*

Every last one of my conflicted feelings went entirely silent, however, as Ryu's lips brushed my own: just the faintest touch like that of a feather. *He likes me!* I thrilled. And, if I was honest, I liked him right back . . . so I braced myself for what was coming.

But before Ryu's lips could again touch mine, we were interrupted by a voice choked with anger and contempt.

'Nice display, slut.' It was Stuart, of course.

Ryu's arms turned to steel around me, but I managed to extricate myself from his grasp and turn around. Stuart was standing behind me, his gang spread out behind him like some Wild West posse. He looked at me as if he would like to hit me, which he probably did.

'Look, man,' he said to Ryu. 'I don't know what this bitch told you, but I hope you have good life insurance. She kills her boyfriends.'

I got a glimpse of Ryu's face as he took a step toward Stuart, and I couldn't believe Stuart was so dumb as to challenge him. Ryu didn't look scary, he looked *terrifying*.

He really is a vampire, after all, I marveled.

One of Stuart's few good points is that he's consistent. And in this case, he was consistently stupid. Instead of backing away, as his friends were doing, he didn't notice the warning signs.

Stuart looked back at me, staring me full in the face. His voice dripped with vituperation as he said, 'It should have been you who died that night, you stupid cunt.'

He'd only just articulated the *t* in 'cunt' when he was on the floor, knocked out cold by a single punch from Ryu. All but two of Stuart's friends fled.

'Get him up, and get him out of here,' Ryu growled. Something told me he didn't need to use a glamour to make them obey. 'And if you hang around waiting for us, I'll break your legs.'

Stuart's friends each grabbed an arm and dragged him out of there as fast as they could. The bar was silent for another second, as Ryu watched their progress out the door, and then everybody went back to their private conversations. People were used to Stuart acting like a dick.

'Are you all right?' Ryu asked, taking my hand and peering into my eyes.

'Yes,' I lied. It had been such a nice night, and Stuart had ruined it.

'Can I get you anything?' he asked.

'No. Can you just take me home? I'm sorry.' I suddenly wanted very much to have a good cry. Then a good swim. And then maybe another cry.

What were you thinking? Rockabill will never let you forget . . .

'Of course,' Ryu said, although he didn't look happy about it.

I went to stand by the door while he settled the bill and collected my things. I merely waved goodbye to my new friends. I didn't want to go over and have them apologize for Stuart. It was too embarrassing, and too depressing, and it made me fear that this taste of freedom, this opportunity to escape my past, that I thought I had glimpsed tonight was just an illusion.

Ryu made me walk out ten seconds after he did, so he could make sure Stu and his gang hadn't waited to wreak vengeance in the parking lot. While I was standing at the door, I noticed that the greasy academic from yesterday morning was sitting at a little table tucked away in a corner, behind the big table where Stuart had been sitting. Creepy must have liked the Sow enough to stay the night in Rockabill. The light reflected off his glasses with an eerie flash, but I could tell he was watching me. I felt the bitterness churn inside my belly. *I hope we gave you a good show, jerk.*

I pushed open the Sty's door to join Ryu, figuring there would be no trace of Stu or his buddies. Stuart's friends, at least, were smarter than him.

Ryu and I drove the short way from the Sty to my house in silence. When we arrived, he got out of the car to walk me to my door.

'Thanks,' I said. 'I had a really good time. I'm sorry that Stuart ruined everything . . .' I felt tears hovering and I lowered my head to try and hide them.

But Ryu put his finger under my chin, again forcing me to meet his gaze. 'I feel like you're trapped here,' he said. 'And I hate it.'

I shook my head, blinking back the wetness in my eyes. 'I'm not trapped,' I lied. 'There's my dad, and Grizzie and Tracy, and now I know about Amy and Nell . . .' My voice trailed off. I realized I was protesting too much.

Ryu took my hand and raised it to his mouth. I felt his lips press against my palm.

'You deserve more,' he told me. 'Much more. More life, more happiness.'

'Maybe I don't,' I whispered. And then the tears came.

He used his thumbs to brush them away and then he cupped my face in his hands and I felt his lips against mine. When I didn't respond, he backed away.

He straightened my coat and gave me a sad smile.

'Good night, Jane. I'll see you tomorrow, after work. I'll pick you up from the bookstore.'

I nodded, too weary to reply.

When he'd gotten into his car and pulled away, I let myself into the house. My dad was already asleep, and all was quiet. I walked in through the front door and then right out through the back.

I needed a swim.

At work the next day, all I could think about was the night before. Even my dreams had consisted entirely of stylized revisions of my 'date', if that's what it had been. My sleeping mind would flash from abstract image to abstract image: Ryu and I wearing fancy dress clothes – tux for him, puffy princess dress for me – in the Trough, eating a lobster that kept asking me 'why' and weeping into a lettuce leaf. Then we'd be in his car, dressed in PVC unitards like warriors from some sci-fi movie, motoring to the moon while we discussed rescuing Peter from an enemy known only as the Sow. Then we'd be back in the Sty, and Ryu would be fighting a duel with Stuart, using *Star Wars* lightsabers. Then Ryu and I were naked, in a sea of red velvet, and I was falling into his arms . . .

And then my damned alarm clock went off . . . the story of my life.

Tracy was working with me that day, and she didn't mention Ryu. I understood what Ryu had done, glamouring Grizzie not to mention his appearance at Read It and Weep. After all, if Grizzie had gone home to announce the arrival of my great friend from college, that one I always talked about, Tracy would think Grizzie had lost her mind.

But it also made things difficult. I had so many secrets rattling around in my empty little life that I hated adding any more. Plus, I really would have appreciated being able to talk to Tracy about the whole situation. In the warm light of day, my evening with Ryu was far less ruined by Stuart's outburst than it had felt like at the time. Instead, I was mostly thinking about the good stuff. Like dancing with Ryu. And holding Ryu's hand. And being in Ryu's arms. And Ryu whispering in my ear. And the brush of Ryu's lips against mine.

Not to mention my tuna melt had been particularly tasty.

It didn't help that a few of the customers coming in for their newspaper and morning coffee were giving me the stink eye, having heard about – or witnessed for themselves – my dinner with Ryu or the little spat between Stuart and me in the Sty. Villages like Rockabill have long memories. Jason may have died eight years ago, but in the collective unconscious of the town it had happened just recently.

Luckily, that morning we'd gotten nearly our entire inventory for that month delivered in one fell swoop, so we had a lot to keep us busy. Tracy and I took turns taking care of customers and stocking shelves, making the day go by quickly. I bunked off at a quarter till closing, to change my clothes, at which Tracy only raised an eyebrow. I never bothered to change at work unless I was going out with them after. But I'd just go ahead and let Ryu explain everything.

When I emerged from the bathroom, freshly deodorized and changed and variously brushed and touched up, Ryu was at the counter, already whammying Tracy with our fake backstory. She was nodding her head agreeably, although, being less omnivorous than her life partner, Tracy wasn't nearly as impressed by Ryu's good looks as Grizzie had been.

I watched the exchange, shivering at the touch of his power. It felt like someone had turned on a fan somewhere in an already chilly room.

It's so easy for him, I thought. *He manipulates us so effortlessly. His kind must find it easy to hold humans in contempt . . .*

The idea was disturbing. Equally disturbing was that I had just used 'us' and 'humans' as synonymous but I wasn't sure what I was anymore. Was I human, or supernatural, or both, or neither? I had heard myself called a halfling by the supes, but that seemed a rather loaded term, like the words 'mulatto' or 'quadroon' from the slave days.

The more I find out about this world, the more questions I have . . .

My reverie was interrupted by two sets of eyes staring at me inquisitively. Tracy and Ryu were waiting for an answer to a question I hadn't even heard. 'Sorry, off in my own world,' I apologized.

'I was just asking where you two were off to tonight. You've already experienced our one and only diner and our lone bar, so will you head over to Eastport or just repeat yourselves?'

I hadn't even thought about tonight beyond remembering to bring to work the stuff I needed in order to get ready. I knew Ryu wanted to look for Peter's car, but obviously I couldn't tell that to Tracy. So I mumbled something about 'playing it by ear', which seemed to satisfy her.

'Well, you two go ahead and have a good time. I'll close up here.' Tracy looked so obviously pleased I had a date that it bordered on humiliating. I knew I was fairly pathetic, but was I really *so* pathetic?

Probably, replied my inner voice, snarkily.

Bite me, I thought. Followed quickly by, *I really gotta stop talking to myself.*

Ryu waited to greet me properly until we got out to his car. With one hand on my door's handle he used the other to brush my bangs from my eyes. 'Hey there,' he said, gently. 'You feeling okay today?'

'Oh, yeah,' I said, blushing. 'I'm sorry I freaked out last night. Stuart and I go way back and he knows exactly how to get under my skin.'

Ryu smiled. 'No need to apologize, I figured as much. But I hate to think that idiot wrecked our evening.'

'He didn't,' I assured Ryu, blushing even harder. 'I had so much fun last night.' I wanted to tell him it had been one of the best nights I'd had in the last eight years but I knew how pitiful that sounded.

'Good.' He grinned, opening my door for me. He looked decidedly pleased with himself. After he'd settled himself in his seat and we were pulling away from the bookstore, I realized I had no idea where we were going.

'Everything got rather exciting this morning and so today's plans have changed slightly,' he said, as if he'd read my mind. 'Anyan already found the car; somebody set it on fire late last night. But now there's a protective spell over the whole thing so we can go investigate at our leisure.'

I gave a murmur of assent. I wasn't at all opposed to spending another evening in Ryu's company, but I wasn't sure why he was bringing me with him on his search.

'So,' he continued blithely, 'I figured we would check out the car, see if there are any clues there as to what happened to Jakes. Then we can just take it from there. We'll have to eat at some point, obviously, so dinner can be your payment for being my sidekick, if you like.'

'Oh, I'm your sidekick, am I?' *That's the worst excuse I've ever heard*, I thought, smugly.

'Of course,' he said, grinning cheekily. 'It's hard work, but somebody has to do it.'

'What's my job description?' I asked, enjoying our easy repartee.

'Well, you have to write down everything I say,' he said with a nod to the glove compartment. 'There's pen and paper in there. And you have to underline anything you think is particularly clever, so that you can congratulate me on my quick thinking when the appropriate moment arises. That's usually when my theories are proved correct, which of course they will be. You also have to question anything I say that might need an explanation, so that I get the chance to provide one in order to highlight my own genius. Oh, and if you could leave the pithy one-liners to me, I'd appreciate it. Pithy one-liners are not for sidekicks, I'm afraid.'

'Do vampires watch too many television mysteries?' I asked.

'Hey,' he said, acting affronted. 'It's research!'

I laughed, and our homicide-drama banter continued until we pulled off the main road onto a tiny winding dirt track that must lead somewhere toward the ocean. I could feel it pulsing in front of me, beckoning.

As we drove farther, I finally recognized where we were: right near the Rockabill Bluffs, an area of small cliffs adjoining our public beach. In the summer months, they were where the local boys took their seasonal girlfriends for a little heavy petting.

They were also a very good place from which to launch a body.

Right before we got to the bluffs, we turned off onto a small track that couldn't even be called a road. I didn't think a Boxster was really the best vehicle for such terrain, but at least it was small and couldn't get stuck on anything. Also, the temperature had dropped precipitously after the storm the other night, so although the ground was muddy the mud was frozen solid.

Good. I wouldn't want to ruin my shoes, I ironized, looking down at my already filthy, kelly-green, high-top Converse.

We stopped after just a little ways: Ryu must have been equally concerned about getting his car back out. 'It's right up ahead,' he said, as we got out. 'Go on, if you'd like, while I secure the car. The others are already there.'

For about ten minutes I walked along the path, which was becoming less and less pathlike, until I was utterly convinced I had somehow missed them. There was no smell of burning, which I figured there had to be if a car had been set alight. But right then I emerged into a little clearing where sat the wreckage of Peter's tiny Toyota.

Nell was sitting under a tree, looking for all the world like an oversized garden gnome. Trill, in pony form, was stretched out beside her with her head in Nell's lap. Nell was braiding Trill's mane into thick seaweed plaits. Near them sat Anyan, who must have been able to smell my approach, as he was watching for me with ears pricked and tongue lolling happily. I waved at them, and Nell and Trill smiled at me in welcome. I'd never seen a pony smile before. Now I knew why. It was horrible.

Anyan, wagging his tail, got up when he saw me. He came toward me and I knelt down to scratch his ears, cooing, 'Who's a good puppy?' in baby talk. I absolutely loved dogs, and Anyan was quite a dog. Now that I wasn't under the influence of panic and adrenaline, I saw that he was just as huge as I remembered, but less fierce looking. I'm sure he *could* look fierce, but he didn't look much like a hellhound at the moment. The cool white light shed by the little luminescent balls scattered throughout the glen revealed that Anyan's coat was less black and more the dark reddish brown of wolves. He also had strange dark eyes that I thought were actually dusky gray. *They're oddly human*, I thought, as Anyan leaned forward to lap my cheek.

But our little moment was interrupted by Ryu's entrance. Anyan saw who it was and backed away from me. He sat down, watching Ryu intently.

'Good evening, Nell,' Ryu said, with a little bow toward the gnome. 'Nice to see you again, Trill,' he added, with the same courtly little bow. They both acknowledged him with a nod.

Then he turned toward Anyan and me. 'Anyan,' he said, his voice flat.

I giggled. That was the most serious meet-and-greet with a dog I'd ever seen.

But my laugh was cut short when Anyan, with a voice as rough as pebbles poured over gravel, growled back, 'Ryu.'

If he'd donned the top hat and tails of the Warner Brothers frog and sung 'Hello, My Baby' while tap dancing with a cane, I wouldn't have been any more shocked than I was at that moment.

'It's been a while,' Ryu commented, noncommittally.

'Yes, it has,' replied Anyan, sounding equally unmoved. He looked toward me. 'Why did you bring Jane?' he asked. 'These events do not involve her.'

'Why not?' Ryu's response had an undertone of heat to it. I was sensing these two had a history. 'She's one of us and therefore this does involve her.'

Anyan gave Ryu a hard look. 'You never did know how to separate business from pleasure,' he observed, his rough voice imbuing his accusation with a harsh note of finality.

Throughout their exchange I just stared, open-mouthed.
Part of me registered that I should be offended Anyan didn't
think I belonged there, but I was too surprised at the whole
talking-dog thing to focus on anything else. Finally, to put
an end to the conversation, Ryu changed track and said,
'Anyan, just release Jakes' car and I'll get to it. This shouldn't
take long and we'll be out of your fur.'

Anyan's hackles bristled almost imperceptibly, just for a
second, and I heard a faint *pop*. Something around the car
that looked like a force field from *Star Trek* sparkled then
died. The smell of burning rubber suddenly filled the little
glade. That must have been what Ryu had been talking about
when he said there was a 'protective spell' around it. But it
appeared that Anyan had been the one who set it, rather than
Nell. I'd already realized that he had somehow healed my
forehead that night at the cove, and now he was magicking
cars. *He must have been top of his class at obedience school*,
I thought at the same time that I remembered to be mad at
him. I glared at the dog. For his part, he did look decidedly
sheepish as he came toward me again.

Ryu started with the front of the car, examining under the
hood and then poking into the driver's seat.

'Why didn't you tell me you could talk?' I used the opportunity to hiss at Anyan.

'I'm sorry,' he said, his tail going down between his
legs. 'We didn't want to give you too many shocks in one
night.'

'Oh yes, it's a better plan to spread the shocks out so I
can embarrass myself as an added bonus,' I spat back.

I sat down on the ground, after putting my coat underneath
me to protect my good black trousers. The big dog lay down
in front of me and rolled over, exposing his belly to me in a
move of mock subservience. And I apparently spoke doggie,

because it worked. I felt my anger dissipate and I started scratching. Anyan sighed happily and shut his gray eyes.

'I thought you were just a hellhound, but you're obviously not. So what are you?'

'Barghest,' he rumbled, keeping his eyes closed. 'Do you know what that is?'

My scratching stopped and I looked at him, horrified. I knew what a barghest was, all right. I'd been obsessed with Roald Dahl as a child and had read *The Witches* about a hundred times. In fact, I'd just read it about a month ago. I read Dahl the way other people snuggle up to their old baby blanket.

In *The Witches*, the narrator's Norwegian grandmother explains to him that barghests are always male and that they are worse than witches. And the witches are bad because they make children disappear—

'Do you make children disappear?' I blurted out.

He opened one eye to stare at me curiously from upside down. 'No,' was his only reply. 'Why?'

'Oh, nothing,' I mumbled. I went back to scratching Anyan's belly, but warily this time.

At that moment, Ryu was just closing the backseat door of the car when it fell off with a loud crack. He grinned at me as he went to open the trunk, but narrowed his eyes when he saw what I was doing.

Before he could say whatever he was about to say, his expression grew startled. He looked at the trunk like it had bit him.

'There's a seal on this trunk,' he said.

Trill and Nell both snapped to attention. The two had looked like they were napping, but they were obviously just resting.

Trill raised her head so that Nell could stand up, and then

the pony lurched to her feet. Anyan, too, got up to go toward the car, so I went ahead and followed.

I stood behind them while they all stared at the Toyota like it might transform into a dragon at any second. 'Whoever placed that seal is strong,' Nell murmured, waving a chubby little hand like an antenna at the car. 'I can barely feel it is there.

'This will take a minute,' she said, grimly. Bracing her small feet and raising her arms, a look of intense concentration crossed her face. The others backed away to join me behind her.

There was no doubt that this time the surge of power I felt was real. If Ryu's glamouring had felt like a table fan blowing a waft of air past my skin, this felt like being caught up in a tempest. Power whipped around me, and I could see the others felt it as strongly as I did. I shivered, and Ryu took my hand while Anyan pressed himself against my leg reassuringly.

Nell was focused on the trunk, edging forward inch by inch until her hands were hovering right above the metal. She was fighting to close the last half-inch gap between her and the car, and the flux of power had become so powerful that it actually felt like a *real* wind. My hair whipped around my face and Ryu put his arm around my shoulder to help steady me as I nearly lost my balance. Even he looked strained by the effects of the energy unleashed around us.

Finally, just as the lashings of power were almost too much to bear, Nell cried out as she fell forward the slightest bit to breach the gap. She stood there, her hands against the trunk, gasping.

Trill went to her, nudging Nell with her slick little muzzle. Nell allowed the pony to support her as she went to collapse back under her tree.

Ryu let go of me and he and Anyan both stepped forward. Ryu put a hand on the trunk while Anyan crouched in readiness, hackles raised, a ferocious growl ripping through the grove. He was back to looking like a hellhound.

Ryu nodded at Anyan, and I saw that Ryu's fangs were extended. They glittered in the cold light and I realized that, at this moment, he was as frightening and inhuman as the slavering beast beside him.

I backed away another step, just as Ryu threw open the door of the trunk and then sprang back.

We all waited. Nothing happened.

Unless you consider the smell to be something. As the trunk lid had gone up, a smell like roasting meat wafted from inside. Check that: it was the smell of meat that had already gone rotten being roasted. I gagged, covering my mouth and nose with my arm.

Ryu and Anyan again exchanged looks and then both moved forward to peer inside the trunk. Then they swore together as if on cue.

I knew it was a bad idea, but I was too curious not to look. So I moved forward to stand next to Ryu, my arm still over my nose and mouth.

Inside the trunk was what looked like the half-burned body of an enormous gremlin. The half of its body that had been closest to the inside of the car was pretty charred, but the rest was still intact. Not that either side of the body was better than the other. The part that was charred was pretty horrible, but the untouched part was equally terrifying. The thing had mottled moss-green skin stretched tight over its bony frame. Large clawed hands with extremely long fingers were crossed beneath its awful head, which had long, pointed ears and a sharp, short muzzle filled with row upon row of razor-sharp teeth, like those of a shark. It had a piglike nose and, I saw, a pirate earring glinted in its left ear.

And from right under that ear extended the slash that had nearly decapitated it.

I stumbled away from the car, knowing it was too late. I crashed into the underbrush, spewing my lunch all over the vegetation. Somebody was holding my hair and patting me on the back while I threw up what felt like the majority of my organs.

When I was done, Trill turned me around and wiped my mouth off with her hand, which, to my dismay, she then wiped through her hair. *That was almost as gross as seeing the body*, I thought blearily, my stomach still churning.

She adjusted my clothes and hair and then put an arm around me to help me back into the grove. She sat me down next to Nell, who looked about as good as I felt. After handing me a bottle of water that she pulled out of Nell's bag, Trill went to help Ryu lift the body out of the car.

I turned my face away, toward Nell. I'd had enough nauseating sights for the evening. Nell patted my hand weakly and tried to smile at me. 'What was that . . . thing?' I asked her. 'Was it the murderer?'

'No,' she said, as her eyes closed. 'That was a lawyer.' And she was asleep.

CHAPTER NINE

When we were back in the Porsche and reversing toward the main road, Ryu turned the heat on and angled the vents toward me. I wasn't really cold, more in shock. But the warm air helped settle me, and after I'd rooted around in my bag to find a piece of gum, I closed my eyes and leaned back to enjoy it.

We'd spent about another twenty minutes in the little glen while Ryu and Anyan examined the remains of the thing in the trunk and then did another sweep of the car and the area. Finally, Ryu and Anyan had a brief, but intense, conversation and Ryu walked off to make a phone call on his cell. Trill helped Nell to her feet, and they said their goodbyes and ambled off into the forest. There was no fancy teleportation tonight, I noticed – Nell was still exhausted from breaking that seal on the trunk. Anyan followed them slowly, looking back at me as I waved goodbye. His big doggy face registered what looked like unhappiness, and I wondered if he had known the creature in Peter's car.

When I felt Ryu turn the Boxster back onto the main road and stop, I opened my eyes to meet his. He turned down the heat and smiled at me, gently brushing my cheek with the tips of his fingers. 'You okay?' he asked.

'Oh, just peachy.' I smiled at him. 'What was that thing?'

'A goblin,' he answered, distractedly. He reached over and picked up my hand to kiss the palm, like he had the night before. I felt a sharp throbbing in my lady bits while I sang the chorus to Sade's 'Smooth Operator' to myself.

'Nell said it was a lawyer.' I tried to keep my voice from trembling. 'Does she just enjoy making bad lawyer jokes?'

'No,' Ryu said, absently caressing my fingers with his own. *Sma-ooooth op-er-ate-ooor* . . . echoed through my head.

'His name was Martin Manx, and he was a lawyer, all right. Goblins often are. In fact, he was a very well-known lawyer. His firm works exclusively for the Alfar.'

'Alfar?' I asked, trying to concentrate on his words as he raised my hand to his lips to nibble on the tips of my fingers. The excitement of opening the trunk and finding the body had evidently had an entirely different effect on Ryu than it had on me.

'You might call them elves, but never, *ever*, let them hear you say it. They're the most powerful beings in our world,' he explained, between nibbles.

'Oh,' I said, not understanding a word he was saying as he turned my hand over to stroke his tongue gently over the old scars marring my wrist.

Right then my empty stomach made a noise like a strangled bear cub. Ryu started, then laughed, and the moment was over. I didn't know whether to curse my prodigious appetite or bless it.

'Hungry?' he asked, letting me pull my hand back to the safety of my lap.

'I shouldn't be,' I said, 'considering that I was just sick. But I am.' I rolled down my window and spat my gum out without thinking. Then I realized what I'd done and congratulated myself on my demonstration of refined elegance.

'Well,' Ryu said, 'how do you feel about a picnic at the beach?'

'That sounds amazing,' I answered truthfully. It did sound amazing – and very, very dangerous. I knew damned well that blankets on beaches at nighttime with handsome strangers usually meant one thing and one thing only: skinny-dipping.

Even if the water was too cold to go into all the way, any excuse for getting your partner naked was a good excuse. If she just *happened* to get so cold you just *had* to warm her up with your own body, well that was just the gentlemanly thing to do, right?

For a split second I wished I hadn't told Ryu I didn't feel the cold.

I was being very naughty. But at least my mother had never told me not to go swimming after a meal. Then again, she was apparently a seal.

You should also warn him about who you really are, my brain cut in. *He says he knows your history, but you can't assume you know what that means. So you'd better tell him now and get it over with. Rather than have him walk away after something serious has happened . . .*

My thoughts dampened my excitement, and we drove in silence out to the public beach by the cottage Ryu was renting. He pulled a blanket and a large basket out of the trunk, and I shot him a skeptical look. 'I was hoping you'd say yes,' he apologized, his eyes anything *but* apologetic.

We walked together down to the beach and I helped him spread out the blanket. Then I watched, marveling, as he made a gesture as if plucking an apple out of the sky and there suddenly appeared one of those glowing orbs of light. This one changed color from a bright white to a soft pink as he gently revolved it in his cupped hand.

'We call them mage lights,' he explained, leaving it

hanging just above where our heads would be when we sat down.

The picnic he had packed – or rather purchased from a very fancy deli in Eastport, I noticed – was absolutely marvelous. My dad and I are pretty dedicated foodies, mostly because we have nothing better to do but also because we both love to eat. And as Ryu unpacked his treats, I thought I'd died and gone to heaven.

Lobster rolls were the main course. Huge pieces of lightly mayonnaised lobster were nestled into the most delicious-looking buttery brioche, making me think guiltily about the talking lobster from my dreams. For side dishes, there was an amazing-looking panzanella – a colorful Italian salad made with toasted bread – and a Thai-style noodle salad with shrimp, vegetables, and crunchy peanuts. There was also fruit salad and a smooshy dollop of soft, sharp goat's cheese. For dessert, there were strawberries, both plain and chocolate covered, as well as two small *tartes aux citrons*. To drink, there was another bottle of champagne as well as a bottle of rich red Shiraz, 'for after dinner,' Ryu explained, with a toothy grin.

His expression, and his exposed canines, spoke volumes about his intentions for tonight, and I didn't know whether to run away or cover him with lobster filling and eat him up right then and there.

But first, I had something I needed to do.

'Um, yeah. About after dinner . . . well, I just want to make sure you know the truth about me. You said you knew my history, but I wanted to make sure you really knew it. I mean, knew me. Not that I am my history, or anything, but you need to know the truth about me.'

Ryu's expression softened and I saw that his fangs had retracted. Misreading these signs, I was unprepared for what he said next.

'Jane, honey, stop. I know everything I need to know. I know bits of your history, yes. And I know you've had a shitty life, in a lot of ways. But I also know you're brave, and funny, and that you've impressed some pretty impressive people with the way you've survived.'

I ducked my head, feeling embarrassed and confused. Ryu touched the fingers of my left hand, which had started fiddling nervously with my shoelaces. I stared at his lovely, strong hands, not sure how to react.

'I like you, Jane. Not despite your history, but because of it. And there's one other thing, something *I* think *you* should know.' Ryu paused for dramatic effect, and I finally raised my eyes to meet his.

'I am a breast man. And you, my darling, have an incredibly nice rack,' he concluded, causing me to blush and giggle. My mood thoroughly lifted, Ryu matched my laughs as he produced two champagne flutes from the bottom of the hamper, along with plates and cutlery. He turned the basket over to reveal its smooth underside; it made the perfect little table, which he set between us. *Does this guy shop at Pimps R Us?* my libido speculated, admiringly, as he popped the champagne and filled our glasses.

He handed me mine and we toasted. 'To you, Jane, and your entry into our society. I've no doubt you will have as great an impact on the others as you have had on me.' I flushed purple, and only barely managed a sip from my glass. If Ryu noticed my discomfiture, he didn't make a big deal of it. He simply passed me a plate, upon which he had sat one of the lobster rolls, and gestured toward the food to tell me to help myself.

Everything was perfect. What was supposed to be crunchy – like the bread in the panzanella and the toasted brioche rolls – was still crunchy, and nothing had gotten too cold despite its long wait in the trunk. I suspected that the same little shields that protect burned-out cars from prying eyes also made for handy picnic aids.

The champagne, again, went down like water and it was an unbelievably sensual experience eating all this delicious food while sitting across from a man who made my hands tremble every time he looked at me.

'Tell me about yourself,' I said, unable to bear being so close to him without saying – doing – something.

'What do you want to know?' he asked, grinning.

'I dunno, anything.' I shrugged. 'I feel so . . . comfortable with you,' I tried to explain. 'But I know nothing about you, it's ridiculous. Where do you live? What do you do?'

'Well,' he said, licking his fingers after he'd polished off his lobster roll. 'There's not much to tell. My base is in Boston and I live there most of the year, except for when I'm at our Compound. That's the seat of power for this Territory – it's about an hour outside of Québec. I'm an investigator, which means that I make sure that everything runs smoothly in my area. If anything untoward occurs, I deal with it and report back to the Compound. Or, if my services are needed by the Court, then I'm sent out to handle whatever has come up. That's how I ended up here.' He smiled at me, and my heart skipped about eight beats in a row. I was either falling hard for this guy or having palpitations.

He put down his plate and maneuvered himself around so he was sitting next to me. The palpitations were bordering on a coronary. I forced myself to breathe.

'As for what I *do*,' he said, helping himself to a strawberry. I knew without a doubt he was going to wind up feeding it to me.

Whoa, Nelly, my brain groaned, bracing itself.

Feeeeeeeeeeeed me, my body roared, like the plant in *Little Shop of Horrors*.

'I like music a lot, and going to the theater. I especially like opera but I'm not so much a fan of musicals. I love spending time around humans and I love their popular culture. Whatever is popular in the human world at any given time, I try to learn about it.'

He put the strawberry to my mouth, and I took my time fitting my lips about it. *Two can play at this game*, I thought, as I bit down ever so slowly. He smiled encouragingly, and I noticed his canines were a bit more pronounced. Then he put the strawberry to his own lips to finish it off, flicking away the leafy top.

'Right now I'm really into manga and new Brit pop,' he said. 'I know I'm late on the manga bus and that it's insanely nerdy, but I'm really enjoying it. I really liked *Appleseed* and I just ordered the sequel.' I had no idea what he was talking about, but smiled at him anyway. It was either that or ravish him.

Why am I having this reaction to this guy? I'm like a horny thirteen-year-old boy whose dad just gave him his first Playboy. *This is* ridiculous. *Get a grip on yourself, woman.* I seriously had no idea why I was so attracted to Ryu. I mean, he was absolutely and completely *gorgeous* but that didn't explain my almost entire lack of self-control or self-consciousness around him.

That's it, you know, my libido yawned, thoroughly bored with my second-thoughts and guilty deliberations. *You don't have to lie to Ryu. He already knows your biggest secret – the secret you couldn't even tell Jason – and to him it's perfectly normal. To him* you *are perfectly normal.*

Not for the first time since I'd met Ryu, I felt a flash of hope. *Maybe things can be different, maybe* I *can be different . . .*

To cover my confusion, I helped myself to some more fruit salad. I finished it off in silence. Ryu leaned back on his elbows beside me and I knew he was watching me.

When we finished the savory food – leaving dessert for later – we packed up the empty containers and plates and set them to the side. I'd tried not to eat too much, but it had been too tasty, and I was pretty full. I lay back, looking up at the stars and wishing I could undo my pants. *Or that someone would undo them for you,* I admitted to myself. I knew where this night was headed – had known since the moment Ryu said the word 'picnic'. And I knew I wanted what he wanted, if for different reasons. Maybe this was just another fling for someone like him, but it was *my* first chance to *have* a fling.

And man do I wanna get flung.

Ryu wiped off one of the plates with his napkin, setting it down above my head to place our freshly filled champagne glasses on it. Then he lay down next to me and placed a hand on my belly.

'The food baby's kicking,' I commented, nervously.

'Hmm?' he inquired. He had his head propped up on his hand, his weight on his elbow, so that he hovered above me disconcertingly. *You shouldn't have lain down*, my brain scolded. *Oh yes, you should*, my lady bits buzzed.

'My food baby. You know, when you eat too much . . .' My voice trailed off when I saw the look in his eyes. Ryu didn't want to hear about food babies. He wanted to kiss me. Which he proceeded to do.

His lips were hot against mine, but not as hot as the hand that had slipped under my thin knit sweater to stroke down my side. That hand gripped my hip, pulling me toward him, and his kiss deepened. His tongue flicked over my lips, seeking entry, and I felt a frisson as my own lips grazed a very sharp fang.

I froze, suddenly overcome by anxiety. I'd only been with one man in my life, and that had been years ago. Thinking of Jason, I felt my cold sliver shift inside of me. I'd wanted the opportunity to move on for so long. But now, confronted with a living, breathing – not to mention insanely hot – man who knew about my life and didn't run away, I felt my nerves as keenly as my lust. Not least because Ryu wasn't *actually* human; he was a vampire. Did vampires have sex like we did? Would he bite me? Did we need a condom? Or three, if we included his fangs?

Ryu's golden eyes opened, and he looked deep into mine. His hand emerged from underneath my sweater. He stroked it down to cover my belly and gave me one more gentle kiss before he asked, 'Jane, my lovely, what do you do to relax?'

I stared at him for a moment, slightly startled. 'I swim,' I answered finally.

He sighed. 'I thought you'd say that.' And then I knew what was coming. That old chestnut – skinny-dipping.

Ryu stood and stripped off quickly. I caught a glimpse of solidly muscled thighs and a high, tight derriere before he ran off down the beach, hollering, 'C'mon, Jane!' at the top of his lungs.

I knew that nudity on cold beaches led to gratuitous amounts of warming afterward, but it was too tempting to resist. Besides, the sea was *my* domain.

I pulled off my green Converse and matching sweater, and then off came the rest. Ryu was already splashing through the shallows when I caught up; then I flashed past him and out into the arms of my sea.

We swam for what felt like hours, although it must only have been about forty minutes. Not since my mother had left had I swum with another person the way I did that night. The sea was achingly cold and fairly rough, but Ryu could just about keep up with me. We splashed and played like otters: I'd let him catch me and kiss me, before I'd slip away again. When he looked like he was getting tired, I'd allow him to capture me for a little while longer, surreptitiously supporting him a bit while he took a breather. 'How can you swim so well?' I hollered at him at one point, the waves loud in our ears.

'We're strong,' he shouted back, running a hand over my backside. *That's not resting*, I thought, and dove away.

Adding to the excitement of tonight's swim was that I recognized, for the first time, what I was doing when I was in the ocean. That slight tingle, like static energy, I'd felt when the others had used their power was now coming from me. And for every burst of energy I used to hold Ryu up or to propel me away from him, the sea refilled it. I was drawing from her strength the way a fetus draws from its mother. Yet, conversely, I'd never felt so powerful, so in control, in my life.

When I could see that Ryu had had enough, I headed back toward the beach. I started walking to the blanket, still illuminated by the soft pink light, when I was picked up from behind. Ryu was carrying me, *like Rhett carried Scarlett*, I thought. *Except that Rhett and Scarlett weren't dripping wet and naked*.

I looked up at his handsome face as he smiled down hungrily at me, his fangs sparkling in the moonlight. I probably should have been freaked out by them, yet I felt entirely safe in his arms. His fangs marked him as different, making him closer to me somehow. We were both far from normal, and neither of us cared. This sense of security, coupled with the excitement of the evening and the feeling of power and authority I'd had swimming just now, wiped away all my previous doubts.

'Are you cold?' he murmured, as he lowered me to the blanket.

'No,' I whispered, all trace of anxiety gone.

'Well, I am,' he said, pulling me on top of him and wrapping us both in the blanket.

This time it was I who kissed him. I straddled his thighs, leaning down into his lips as his arms wrapped around me. I went into the kiss slowly, unsure of how to circumnavigate his prickly bits. But he was a good teacher, and pretty soon I was French kissing a vampire as if I'd been doing it all my life. Most of the basics seemed to translate. And when I sucked gently at his tongue as it entered my mouth, I heard him groan, and my heart thrilled at the sound. My lips trailed over his cheek, to his ear, where it explored a bit, and then traced down his jaw to his neck. He tasted like my sea, and I licked his skin ardently, loving the taste and texture of his salty clavicles under my tongue.

I also took a second to take a gander at his body. It was everything first impressions had promised. His shoulders were very broad and elegantly muscled, his hairless chesticles crowned by the sweetest looking little nipples. *Mmm, nipples*, my own body purred.

He moaned and tightened his arms around me as I worked my way down to one of those pretty pink nubbins. I sucked, gently at first, but more roughly as he responded by whispering my name. It all seemed a bit too much for him when I started to make my way over to his other nipple, and he only let me latch on for a split second before he buried his hands in my hair and pulled my face up toward his.

He held me to him to kiss me aggressively, his very extended fangs difficult to avoid, and I had a feeling my lips were going to be a bit sliced and diced when this was all over. There was no discomfort, however. Only the pleasure of his mouth on mine, transmitting to me his desire.

In the meantime, he'd had enough of being submissive. With preternatural strength, Ryu gently flipped us over so that he was on top. I felt something hot and hard against my thigh as he kissed me thoroughly, and I knew I'd had one question answered. Then his hands, and then his mouth, were at my breasts. His fingers massaged one while his lips locked on the other. I arched my back, my turn to moan, as his hand wandered from my breast to my stomach and down between my legs.

I spread my thighs as he shifted between them. I put one arm behind my head as a pillow and used the other to run my fingers through his hair as he began to kiss his way south, following the trail his hand had just blazed. I wasn't much good at map reading, but I knew when my own compass registered that he'd hit home. I couldn't help but press down on his head as his tongue lapped hungrily at the center of my pleasure, and he responded by squeezing my hips with his hands.

I nearly cried out with frustration when he moved back up my body to kiss me, letting me taste myself on his lips. Then he knelt upright between my thighs, holding onto my right hand. He put his thumb back on my sweet spot and looked me in the eyes while he gently licked at my wrist, kissing and nipping right where my pulse beat under my skin. Right over my old scars.

'I want to bite you, here, on your wrist,' he said, his voice husky with passion. 'I promise it won't hurt; that you'll enjoy it. Do you trust me, Jane?'

My stomach tensed as his clever fingers drove me toward orgasm and then stopped, backing off just enough to let me come down slightly before driving me forward again. Which was patently unfair, under such circumstances, since I would have agreed to just about anything he asked. That said, I also wanted him *as* a vampire. His swimming with me, like he did, had convinced me I wanted all of him, including those fangs. I nodded, incapable of speech, as I moaned my assent. He smiled, kissed my palm, and then went back to gently licking the rough skin of my wrist.

I could feel my pleasure building, and I put my fingers over his own to adjust the pace of his thumb. 'Ryu,' I warned, 'I'm coming,' just as I came. I cried out, arching my back, but his eyes never left mine.

And then he bit down, hard.

There was the slightest suggestion of pain, but it was quickly overwhelmed by both my powerful orgasm and a secondary sensation of pleasure coming from my wrist. It felt like my own climax, but somehow both fainter and edgier, and it pulsed with each powerful draw of his mouth. His teeth were only locked on my flesh for a minute before he let go, licking gently at the wound as the pain faded utterly.

'Wow,' I said, pulling my wrist down to look at it as he bent over to nuzzle my breasts. I inspected his handiwork; while my skin was still crisscrossed with ragged scars, they were nothing new. Ryu had completely healed me of his bite.

'Told you you'd be saying that often,' Ryu reminded my cleavage, before he kissed up my body to my mouth. His eyes bore into mine as his hands shifted my hips for better access.

I must have looked concerned, because he smiled. 'Don't worry,' he murmured. 'We don't need protection. My kind can't carry disease and neither can we procreate without intention. And procreation is *not* one of my many intentions for you tonight,' he explained, between kisses.

'Ummm, Ryu?' I retorted, intelligently, as he kissed down toward my cleavage again. It's just that I'd seen that made-for-

TV movie, and I knew better than to believe a man who said, 'Trust me, baby, my penis is harmless!'

'Hmmm?' he replied, nuzzling away at my boobs like a contented puppy. But when he saw that I still looked concerned, he smiled resignedly. 'I've got protection, if it makes you feel better,' he said. I nodded and he sighed, reaching for his trousers.

I knew he was probably telling me the truth and we didn't need the condom. Not to mention, I'd just handily violated every aspect of my blood-borne-pathogen training by letting him bite me. But I wasn't about to end up sitting in the free clinic, knocked up or with vampire crabs, so I gave Ryu's slightly martyred mug my best 'tough titty, McVitty' smile.

After he'd found a condom, I tried to mitigate his obvious disappointment by illustrating how applying latex could be fun for both parties, if approached with enthusiasm. And a little oral sex. Then, with one last parting caress to his under-carriage that left him cross-eyed, I lay back and opened myself to him. He followed me back down to the blanket, where, in one long, slow motion, he slid into me, leaving me gasping. *It's been too long*, I thought, reveling selfishly in my own pleasure. He moved inside of me, gently at first, letting me adjust to him as his lips toyed with mine. Then his kisses deepened, as did his thrusts, and soon we were going at it like two teenagers who had just discovered their apparently mismatched parts were actually wonderfully harmonized. I moved my hand between our bellies, placing my finger on my clit to help move things along, and he raised himself up on his hands to watch me touch myself.

'Oh, Jane,' he moaned, his hips starting to move errati-cally. My own pleasure was building fast, and seeing the lust on his face propelled everything even quicker. Calling my name, and burying his face in my neck, I felt him come just as my own orgasm washed over me, annihilating all conscious thought.

We lay there, kissing and cuddling for a few minutes, to catch our breath. I hadn't felt this good in a really long time. I knew there'd be hell to pay with my guilt the next day, but for right now I pushed everything out of my mind and just enjoyed the feel of Ryu's body pressed against mine.

When we had recovered a bit, he waggled his eyebrows at the ocean, and I laughed. Hand in hand, we walked down to the sea and scrubbed ourselves off in the shallows. Then we headed back to the blanket.

'Dessert?' he suggested, at the same moment that I shoved half of an entire *tarte au citron* into my mouth. 'I guess that answers my question.'

He chose to eat his tart off my thighs, which I think we both enjoyed.

CHAPTER TEN

If I'd thought a dead, nearly decapitated goblin was one of the worst things I'd ever seen, I only had to meet a living one to realize just how wrong I'd been.

When Ryu pulled up in front of the bookstore, I'd headed into the back to change and get ready for that evening. I still wasn't able to meet my own eyes in the mirror, so refreshing my minimal makeup was a slapdash affair. I took the opportunity to agonize, once again, over my behavior last night. I'd betrayed the memory of Jason with a bang, no pun intended, in the company of a man whose intentions were unclear to me. My attraction to Ryu was undeniably powerful, and apparently mutual. But in the cold light of day, the self-confidence I'd felt the night before was quickly eroding. What could someone like him want with somebody like me? He oozed confidence and authority; everything about him spoke of money, power, and status. Meanwhile, I didn't own a pair of panty hose. I was afraid to ask my hairdresser for a glass of water. And let's not forget the time Grizzie told me the fashion police were out to get me, on charges of banality, and I actually looked around to see where they were hiding.

Furthermore, Ryu is not Prince Charming, here to rescue

you from your enchanted slumber, my brain reminded me.
*You still have to live in Rockabill, taking care of the father
who won't move away and whom you wouldn't abandon even
if you could. All of which means that Ryu will go, and you
will remain.* I stared at myself, hard, in the mirror, finally
touching on the questions I couldn't answer.

What are you going to take from this? From him?

When I finally emerged from the bathroom, freshly
scrubbed and thoroughly flagellated by my self-doubts, Ryu
wasn't alone. Next to his Porsche was a large Audi sedan,
and arguing with him was what could only have been the
female version of that awful creature in Peter's trunk.

Ryu was obviously really angry, but the creature looked
entirely unimpressed. She just stood there, impassively, her
wicked-looking, long-fingered claws – painted a bold red, I
noted – wrapped around the handle of her expensive-looking
briefcase.

And she was *huge*, towering above Ryu by at least two
feet. Since the only goblin I'd ever seen had been shoved into
the trunk of a car, I had no idea they were so tall. Her bony,
mottled-green body was encased in a conservative gray business suit and her many-fanged mouth sported a lipstick that
perfectly matched her fire-engine-red nails. Her eyes glowed
a horrible piquant yellow and appeared to be dripping mucus,
but she did have lovely blond hair that was wrapped up in
an elaborate French twist. All in all, the contrasts added up
to one of the most repulsive sights I'd ever seen.

'Who is the suit arguing with your man?' Grizzie asked,
curiously. I couldn't believe she could see them, and I blinked
at her, confused. 'She's hot, in a corporate way. Maybe she's
a naughty secretary.' Grizzie leered, too busy pondering the
implications of 'naughty secretary' to notice that I was staring
at her with absolute disbelief.

Ah, the powers of glamour, I thought, as I mumbled something about not being sure who it was. Grizzie turned to me
and sighed when she saw what I was wearing. I thought I
looked nice in my sky-blue T and sexiest hipster jeans. My
shirt had three-quarter-length sleeves and was cut in a rather
deep V-neck. Because of the plunging neckline, and the fact
that it was pretty thin material, I wore a nice white chemise
under it. I was also wearing my boots again instead of my
Converse.

I looked down at my clothes, confused and a little hurt.
Grizzie came over and put an arm around me.

'You always look beautiful, Jane,' she said, apologetically.
'But you'd look even better in some leather. Or maybe hot
pants. Leather hot pants . . .' she finished, starting to look
decidedly predatory.

'Grizzie, it's November. Hot pants are not an option,' I
reminded her.

She looked at me as if I'd just cursed the memory of my
own mother. 'Hot pants, my dear, are *always* an option.'

I shook my head, put on my coat, and hugged her goodbye.
Ryu and the goblin were still arguing, but my curiosity was
getting the better of my apprehension. I wanted to know what
was going on.

Neither the bloodsucker nor the giant gremlin registered
my appearance at their side. Ryu was so angry he was nearly
spitting. No, he actually was spitting. His extended fangs
made talking difficult.

'You have no authority to take me off this case, Gretchen,'
he snarled. 'I was asked to investigate this matter, and that's
what I'm doing.'

'Yes, but Martin's death means the situation has changed,'
Gretchen the goblin replied impassively.

'How?' Ryu demanded. 'Manx's body was in Jakes's trunk:

ergo, his death is connected to Peter's murder and is therefore a part of *my* investigation.'

'But it's no longer your investigation.' Gretchen's voice betrayed not one iota of emotion as Ryu's hands clenched into fists and he had to visibly restrain himself. I took a step toward him. Whoever this goblin was, she was obviously in charge and Ryu would do himself no favors by attacking her. Plus, I had a feeling she'd kick his ass.

'You have been removed from this case and I have been given the authority to replace you.' The goblin rummaged in the outer pocket of her briefcase. 'Orin asked me to inform you that this is through no fault of your own. When a member of our firm is killed in action, our contract of service stipulates that *we* become responsible for the deceased agent's investigation.' The creature's yolk-yellow eyes flicked toward me for a split second, and I shuddered.

'This is horse shit,' Ryu spat, as she handed him a creamy white envelope.

'No, it's procedure.' The goblin zipped shut her briefcase's pocket and straightened her suit jacket. 'And procedure dictates that the firm itself is responsible for meting out justice for those who interfere with our agents. Alfar justice, however swift, is not goblin justice.'

Those awful yellow eyes remained emotionless throughout her speech, and I knew I never, ever, wanted to find out what goblin justice entailed.

Ryu, in the meantime, had ripped open the envelope and was reading the letter. He was still angry, but a look of resignation passed over his face as he finished, crumpling up the letter and its envelope decisively. 'Fine,' he said. 'The investigation is yours.' He visibly gathered himself, as if remembering his manners. 'I hope you find the murderer, and I am sorry for Manx's loss. He was a fine attorney.'

'Yes, he was,' the goblin intoned. 'Thank you for your understanding.' She paused as she got into her car, looking back at Ryu and me. 'Have no doubt: Martin's murderer *will* be punished,' Gretchen concluded, the finality in her voice sending a chill through my bones.

We watched in silence as she drove away. Ryu grumbled something incomprehensible, and then, balancing the crumpled ball of paper on the palm of his hand, I watched in awe as it went up in a little puff of bright-blue flame and smoke.

'Goblins,' he said sarcastically, finally turning around to acknowledge me. He drew me toward him, pouring his aggression into a feisty kiss before breaking away to tell me that I was a sight for sore eyes. He kissed me again, teasingly. 'And I *mean* sore. That red lipstick just did nothing for her complexion,' he murmured against my lips, and I burst out laughing.

When we were settled in his car, he sighed deeply and relaxed back against his headrest. 'Well, that threw a wrench into my plans,' he said, finally.

I had already thought about that. No murder investigation meant no reason for him to be in Rockabill. No reason for him to be in Rockabill meant Ryu would return to his normal life in Boston.

The thing that made me feel worst was how sad I was. I should never have gotten involved with Ryu in the first place, let alone *this* involved.

I didn't trust myself to speak, so I just sat quietly, my hands in my lap.

'Well, what's done is done.' He turned to me, putting a hand on my knee. 'I thought I'd have more time here, with you. But just because I have to leave sooner than I thought doesn't mean we can't enjoy ourselves. There's even a chance of thunderstorms tonight.' He arched a brow at me. 'And I bet your selkie half *loves* itself some storm.'

I laughed, swallowing my hurt. He was right; we had no reason not to enjoy our last night together. Besides, I'd known from the beginning that this was just a fling, and it's not like I could have fit anything more serious into my life. *And maybe you'll have more confidence from now on*, I told myself. *Maybe Ryu's just the beginning of a new life.*

We went to dinner at the Trough, again, and this time I hardly noticed the prying eyes of my nosy neighbors.

Amy was happy to see us, at least, and she asked if we'd be going to the Sty that night. When Ryu said yes, winking at me, she said she'd see us there.

I was happy knowing I would see Amy that night, and even happier when we pulled into the Sty and Stuart's SUV was nowhere to be seen. *He must be regaining his confidence by being an asshole in some other bar*, I thought. Ryu must also have been thinking about Stu, because he walked into the bar first, keeping me behind him while his eyes scanned the other patrons.

It was a Friday night, but still pretty early, so the bar half of the Sty was mostly empty. Sarah was serving food, but she flashed me a warm smile, as did Marcus when we approached the bar. We ordered drinks – red wine for Ryu, which I could see was totally not up to his standards when he tasted it, and a Jack and Coke for me. We toasted each other, but this time I took the lead. 'To your being in Rockabill. I've, um, really enjoyed your being here,' I stammered, embarrassed. But he looked so pleased I was glad I'd said it.

I excused myself to go to the bathroom, and when I came back Ryu was walking away from the jukebox. He met me halfway back to the bar and picked me up, twirling me around while the power of his glamour lifted the hairs on the back of my neck, just as Cheap Trick's cover of 'The Flame' came over the speakers.

'Cheeseball,' I murmured, leaning down to kiss him. He held me like that for what felt like forever, until I realized that our kiss had begun to wander into the realm of the X-rated, and I pulled back.

'You can put me down now,' I reminded him.

'I could,' he acknowledged, nipping at my breast so that lightning bolts zinged through my body.

'*Ryu*,' I scolded, looking around me. But our public display of affection went, of course, unnoticed. I was going to have to get used to this glamour thing.

'No one can see us,' he pointed out. 'Not even when I do this,' he said as he buried his face in my cleavage.

'No one but Sarah and Marcus,' I hissed, watching as the pair exchanged sly smiles.

Ryu set me down and leaned over to kiss me. 'You're so sexy when you're being human,' he growled.

And you're just sexy, I thought, as I took his hand and wrapped an arm around his waist, trying to distract him with dancing.

'Tell me about the goblin,' I said, to reinforce the distraction.

He took the bait, wrapping his arm around me and gently swaying to the beat before saying, 'Gretchen Kirschner is a senior partner in the firm Manx worked for, and even for a goblin she's a pain in the ass. But she's good. If she's involved, then that means something big is happening.' His expression clouded, just for a moment, and I could sense the wheels spinning.

'Our world is . . . complex,' he explained. 'Among us are beings who have lived for centuries, so you can't imagine how deep the intrigues delve. Gretchen's firm represents the big guns. They're only deployed by our most powerful beings under the most important circumstances. Why a member of that firm would be in Rockabill, of all places, investigating the death of a halfling is beyond me.' He frowned. 'And how Manx ended up in a halfling's trunk is even more worrisome. Jakes could never have killed a mature goblin, not without an army to back him up. But why either of them was here in the first place is the greater mystery. I already thought it was strange that the Alfar asked me to investigate Jakes's murder, and this is one plot twist I really don't like.'

The expression on Ryu's face, however, was not just troubled; there was also the faintest hint of enjoyment playing over his features as he contemplated the situation. *He loves this*, I realized. *Not the murders, obviously, but the intrigue, the complexity.*

'How old are you, Ryu?' I interrupted, curiously.

'Sorry?' he asked, as if waking from a dream. I repeated the question.

'Oh, in human years I'm very old, but for my kind I'm still an upstart,' he answered, smiling.

I waited until he answered my question. 'I've lived about 270 human years,' he said, watching for my reaction. 'Does that bother you?'

'It's strange,' I answered him truthfully, after a moment of thought. 'You've seen so much . . . done so much. It's intimidating,' I admitted. 'But sexy, too,' I clarified, trying to appear bold as I met his golden eyes.

It must have worked, because the next thing I knew he was bundling me into my jacket and into the Porsche. I barely had a chance to say goodbye to Sarah and Marcus and to ask them to tell Amy I was sorry we missed her. We abandoned our untouched drinks.

'Will you spend the night with me?' Ryu asked, as he

peeled out of the Sty's parking lot like he was going to put out a nursery fire. His fangs were already peeking out at me and I found the sight of them incredibly . . . stimulating. While I rummaged around my purse for my cell phone, I marveled at how quickly I'd gotten used to my vampire lover.

I had told my dad I wouldn't be there for dinner again that night, and I'd been almost offended by how pleased he seemed at that information. But I still felt incredibly awkward telling him I wouldn't be home at all that night. I don't know how much he had known about Jason and me, as the sex talk had been handled by Nick and Nan, and he'd made it clear when I turned eighteen that I was an adult and responsible for myself. But I was still his daughter and I didn't know how he'd react to my spending the night with Ryu.

He did take a deep breath when I told him I wouldn't be home until tomorrow. 'That's fine, Jane. Thanks for letting me know. Just . . . be careful,' he said, uncomfortably, 'and I'll see you in the morning. Do you have the weekend off?'

'Yes,' I said. 'I'll see you tomorrow.'

'Bye honey, I love you.'

'I love you too, Dad,' I said, and hung up my phone.

I gave Ryu the thumbs up, and if I'd thought he was driving fast before, now it felt like he was attempting to break the sound barrier. We must both have been determined to get as much from our little affair as we could.

His rental cottage was clean and simple, decorated in a vaguely Hamptons-esque style with lots of white paint and navy-blue accents. Not that I saw much of it before I was in the bedroom, Ryu hurtling us through the air to land on the mattress with a thump that rattled the bed.

He stripped off at the speed of light and had me nearly naked in equally record time. I was really turned on by his very evident need, but it was also pretty funny. Suddenly, as if just remembering something, he got up to fish around in his wallet. When he held up a condom, I nodded. He sighed, tossing it down next to my knee. I ignored his disappointment; until I had confirmation I couldn't end up with babies that had my eyes and Ryu's fangs, we were keeping things wrapped up.

He was back at my side in a flash, tearing off the rest of my clothes while I giggled. 'Honey, slow down. You're going to hurt yourself . . . we've got all night.'

'. . . not enough time,' he panted, finally wrestling off my recalcitrant underpants and then donning his latex armor. His body covered mine, his hand slipping between my legs. I gasped, both at his touch and at the slick proof of my own unmistakable excitement. 'Time later for more time,' he murmured, using his knees to prize my thighs apart while licking at my neck in what I had come to realize was the vampire version of fang foreplay. 'Time for many more times tonight,' he concluded, as he bit, taking me roughly at the same time. The pleasure was almost unbearable.

And he wasn't being coy. That night we had both world enough and time to roll around quite satisfactorily for many hours.

CHAPTER ELEVEN

'Tell me what happened to you,' Ryu said, his voice quiet in the dark. 'I want to hear it in your own words.'

I stiffened in his arms. Now was the time for cuddles, not the dropping of bombs.

'What?' I asked, hoping he meant something else.

'Tell me about your friend dying. And what happened to you after.'

I groaned internally. That was the last thing I wanted to talk about. It was more than a little weird telling the person you'd just had sex with about your very first – and only – lover. But it would be hell telling Ryu about Jason's death and what came after. Trying to put into words the depth of my grief was impossible. And I doubted if Ryu – who had compared humans to fireworks, after all – could ever understand what I was trying to get across to him.

I shifted, turning over to lie on my side away from him. But he wasn't letting me get away that easy.

'Tell me,' he commanded gently, as he shifted with me into spooning formation.

I closed my eyes and thought, until Ryu gently nipped my shoulder. So I sighed and started at the beginning, secretly hoping that I could make the beginning into the whole story. I started with my parents, and how they met. I told him about Nick and Nan, our amazing proto-hippy neighbors who had been like family to me. They had a son and daughter. The son was Stuart's dad and the daughter had fallen off the rails and gotten into drugs pretty heavily. She'd rather dramatically abandoned her little boy, Jason, in the train station in Chicago and his grandparents had taken him in. Obviously Jason was sad about his mother. But between my own parents and Nick and Nan, we were both as loved as two kids could be. And we'd come to love each other just as passionately. I don't know when it started; it was like we'd always been connected. We were everything to each other, and our relationship evolved with us. But as children we were like twins – so close you'd think we'd shared the same womb. And then when we were six my mother disappeared as well. At the time, Rockabill was a village where no one was divorced, or had a baby out of wedlock, or – gods forbid – abandoned their own flesh and blood. If Jason and I had been close before, now our attachment was almost preternatural.

'Jason and I understood each other, and we felt like it was us against the world,' I concluded, turning around so Ryu and I were nose to nose. He smiled at me encouragingly, but I took the opportunity to take his bottom lip between my teeth and give it a little nibble. Then I kissed him hard, opening my mouth to him as his tongue sought mine. Until he called my bluff and withdrew his lips with a determined shake of his head.

'I want the whole story,' he reminded me, his voice low and soft.

I shook an imaginary fist at him, gathering myself to begin.

'Jason and I shared everything,' I said, 'except for one secret.' Reminding myself to breathe, I continued. 'I never told him about my swimming. Because swimming is, in my family, as closely guarded a secret as incest, alcoholism, or infidelity are in others.' My voice broke, despite my attempt at levity.

The rest came out in a rush. 'So, really early one morning, I went to the beach for a swim. I left my clothes in my cove and I just dove right in. But Jason must have gone to the cove, too, or followed me from my house, or something. Anyway, he couldn't have known I would be okay. It was winter, the water was freezing, and there was a storm, so it was really rough. He must have thought I was drowning.' Fat tears rolled, scalding my cheeks. 'He must have been trying to rescue me.' My voice broke, and I couldn't continue. I shut my eyes. I felt Ryu's fingers brushing away my tears but I was miles away, reliving my awful memories.

I saw myself coming out of the water after a refreshing swim to find another set of clothes next to mine on the beach. I remembered how it felt when I knelt down to investigate, and what it felt like the moment I realized that it was Jason's Patriots sweatshirt with the distinctive maroon paint stains, Jason's battered old North Face jacket, and Jason's favorite pair of jeans. I'd never forget the emotion I felt at that moment, not that there was a name for it. I know that the German language makes new words by stringing together descriptive phrases until the required idea or emotion is properly expressed. If we did that in English, the word for what I felt while standing there clutching Jason's battered hiking socks would be a word made up of some terrible combination of total devastation, unholy terror, and the overwhelming need to find out that he was okay, that this was just a trick or a mistake.

'You know the rest of that story,' I said, my voice rough. I kept my eyes shut. 'I searched for hours for him, and then

I finally found him in the Sow. After a while he came to me. I thought that meant he was still alive and had swum. But he was cold and his eyes were staring.' I shuddered and Ryu's arms tightened around me protectively. 'I got us to the beach somehow. I was exhausted. I just collapsed with him and blacked out. Then I woke up to emergency services bundling me into an ambulance and Jason into the coroner's van. He was dead and I was nearly so.'

Ryu nodded, stroking a hand down my side. 'You used a tremendous amount of energy to pull him out of the Sow. Nell said everyone felt it for miles, but they had no idea what could have happened or who it could have been. They never figured it was you, since you were not supposed to have anywhere near that kind of capability. Your panic just brought it all out. When we lose control like that, it's very dangerous – releasing that much power can drain us to the point of death. You were lucky to have survived.'

My lips went tight and my gut clenched. 'Lucky?' I asked, oh so rhetorically. 'I don't think I was lucky. What I lived through after Jason's death nearly broke me.' Ryu frowned at me but I wouldn't let him interrupt.

'The drowning and near-drowning of two local teenagers was big news. We'd grown up around the ocean; we knew we had no business being in it when it was like that. Jason was dead and I was comatose for a few days, so everybody just went ahead and made up what happened. People said Jason and I had a suicide pact, or that it was an attempted murder-suicide, or suicide attempt and botched attempted rescue. Because Jason had been so perfect, and I was who I was, it was the last idea that people latched onto. Jason was too *alive* to want to kill himself, and he was certainly too good to want to kill me and then off himself. So, he must have stumbled across me mid-suicide attempt and tried to save me. And, in that ultimate ironic twist that is the stuff of great news ratings and terrible made-for-TV movies, I lived and Jason drowned. The media loved it,' I concluded, bitterly.

'Who would say such things?' Ryu marveled. 'Especially about children?'

I snorted derisively. 'Confronted with cameras, most people will say just about anything to be that little talking head on the news. And nobody ever liked me anyway. So the kids at school were more than happy to flesh out the motive for my attempted "suicide". Jason was beautiful, a star athlete, and really popular despite our relationship. No one had ever understood our connection. So people, namely this girl named Linda Allen and Jason's cousin, Stuart, told the media that Jason had outgrown me. That he was breaking whatever hold I had over him. That he only hung around with me because he pitied me.' My voice had grown frosty with rage and Ryu's eyes narrowed in sympathy.

'Linda even hinted that she and Jason had started going out and maybe that's what pushed me over the edge. As for why they did it, Linda's motivation was obvious. She'd always carried a torch for Jason and she is nearly as delusional as one of her romance-novel heroines. As for Stuart, he and Jason had *never* been close when Jason was alive. I think Stu used his cousin's death as an opportunity to cause drama because he just likes being an asshole. Especially to girls who can't beat him up for talking shit.

'Mercifully,' I said, trying to get my anger under control, 'I didn't actually have to see any of the news coverage at the time. I was lying in a hospital bed, with my arms and legs tied down so I couldn't "self harm". Not that people weren't keen to fill me in on what I had missed upon my eventual release back into polite society.'

Ryu shook his head, his face sad. 'What then?'

'Straight from the hospital, I was put into the loony bin for observation.' I smiled at him, a smile that didn't reach my eyes. 'If I hadn't been suicidal before, I most certainly was now. I couldn't imagine living without Jason; it was unthinkable. So I pandered right to their image of me: a dark soul bent on destroying herself and all she loved.

'Of course, it never occurred to me to tell the truth. That I had gone for a *swim*. That, after all our years spent bound up so close, the one secret I had from Jason was the fact that I somehow managed to survive the freezing cold water and the extreme tidal range of our little patch of the Western Passage to go *swimming*. Naked. Because of course I hadn't been wearing my wet suit the night Jason died, which fit in really well with my own mother's apocryphal public display of flesh. A TV-movie writer couldn't have come up with a more symbolic suicide attempt: abandoned daughter attempts to end her own life in a parody of her mother's scandalous appearance in their small town.'

I was pretty much ranting at this point, but Ryu just listened quietly.

'I remember one particularly bad day in the psych ward, after I'd given drowning myself in a toilet the good old college try, and I was strapped down and sedated. I woke up to my dad sitting next to me. He was crying. I whispered, "Just tell them." I was so tired of fighting and I think my barbiturate-addled brain thought that if we went ahead and told them I was swimming, they would let me out. And then I could finally kill myself in peace.

'My dad just squeezed my hand and I knew that nothing would ever be said. If I hadn't had a matching set of fuzzy cuffs binding me to the bed I would have knocked his block off. Of course, now I realize that my father telling people his crazy daughter wasn't really crazy because she actually swam

in the ocean, just like her mom had, would only have gotten
him his own vacation in the empty bed next to mine. But it
did take me a while to forgive my father his silence, and I
really regret that.'

I was annoyed to find I was crying again, thinking about
how much I had hurt my dad. He'd done the best he could
for me, and there was no 'right' way to act in a situation like
that. Not to mention that if I hadn't been in the hospital I
would have killed myself, without a doubt.

And just think, I told myself, *if I'd died, I would have
missed all the great things Rockabill had in store for me when
I got back.*

'That must have been terrible,' Ryu said, hugging me tight.
'I can't imagine being cooped up like that in some human
hospital. Especially when I knew I wasn't actually crazy.'

I laughed. 'Oh, that wasn't an issue. I *was* totally crazy. I
wasn't joking about the toilet, and that was only one of about
seven suicide attempts.' I raised my scarred wrists to him.
'These aren't football injuries.'

Ryu's eyes were sad as he traced my scars first with a
finger and then with his lips. 'How did you do these?' he
asked, finally. They were pretty jagged.

'I managed to sharpen a fork, believe it or not. But I was
on some serious medication, so I didn't feel it at all.' He
grimaced.

'And then there was my invisible friend,' I added.

'What friend?'

'At night, this mysterious stranger would come keep me
company. Not in a creepy, abusive-nurse way,' I added hastily,
seeing the look on his face. 'He couldn't have been real. He
wasn't on the ward and he didn't work there. He only came at
night – when the medication was extra strong.' I smiled; the
memories were oddly happy ones, despite the circumstances.

'Really,' Ryu said, his expression strange. 'What did this stranger look like?'

I shrugged. 'I dunno. Like I said, I was on some strong drugs. I know he was big and a man. I couldn't ever really see him, for some reason. When I'd try, everything would get fuzzy. Probably because he didn't actually exist,' I reminded Ryu.

'And what did he do when he was there?'

'Oh, he'd just hold my hand and tell me stories. They were amazing. Sort of like fairy tales but not any of the ones that I'd ever heard. I know this sounds crazy, since the guy was obviously just a barbiturate figment or something, but I swear he kept me from *really* going nuts. I would have been totally potty if he hadn't been there. Maybe he was the living embodiment of Prozac, come for to carry me home.' I laughed, but Ryu still looked somber. He'd wanted the truth, but maybe he hadn't expected me to admit to knitting with only one needle – which made me suddenly anxious.

'So, umm, you don't have to be scared or anything,' I told him, nervously.

'Sorry?' Ryu asked, his face gone from somber to confused.

'I'm fine now. You don't have to worry about me going off the deep end. No bunny boiling in my future, or anything. I promise not to impale both eyes on chop sticks if you take me out for Chinese food. Or jump out of a moving vehicle. Or steal your shoelaces to strangle—'

Ryu put his finger on my lips to stop my anxious patter.

'Jane, be easy. I don't think you're crazy. I think you were mad with grief. And I hate that you had to endure all of that, alone. You should have been better taken care of by our kind.'

I shook my head. 'I don't deserve pity,' I said. 'I'm the one that lied to Jason. He's the one who is dead. If you pity anybody, pity Jason. He should never have died that night.'

Ryu frowned. 'I suppose you've heard a million times that his death wasn't your fault?'

'If I had a nickel, etcetera,' I replied, my tone short.

'Well, his death wasn't your fault.'

'Yes, it really was. It would have taken me one sentence to tell him that I swam at night. Two to explain. Jason loved me no matter what, but I'd been taught that my swimming was such a big secret.' I said these words as if they were fact, but I was mercilessly hitting my own most sensitive nerve.

Because what if Jason hadn't accepted your swimming? I thought. *What if you feared the truth would be that last proverbial straw and would drive him away?*

'It doesn't matter, anyway,' I soldiered on. 'He's gone, and I've lived with his death for so long that it's like . . . a binding on my book. I need to move on. Even if I can't forgive myself, I need to move on.'

'Jane, honey, is that realistic? How can you move on from Jason if you still blame yourself for his death?'

I shook my head. 'I just have to, Ryu. I can't live like this any longer . . .' To my horror, my voice was breaking.

'Oh, Jane.' Ryu sighed, rolling me over so I was lying on top of him. He ran his hands through my hair. 'What am I going to do with you?'

Distract me, I thought, fiercely blinking back my tears. *Reinvent me. Get me out of my own head; rescue me from my life* . . . For a second, I pictured myself as Mina, and Ryu as Gary Oldman's Dracula. The young hot one, mind you, with the long hair, rather than the old guy with the weird boob wig.

'*Take me away from all this death*,' I'd say, as I slurped on his chest. But then I'd try to eat all my friends, who would have to burn my forehead with consecrated cookies. So that's not the best option . . . as well as the wrong definition of a vampire, apparently.

'So, what *are* my options?' I inquired, finally, peering up at him through my long bangs.

His suddenly hot eyes focused back on me as he pulled me up the hard length of his body so that I was within kissing range.

'I could abduct you in the night and lock you away in a tower until I have fondled away all traces of guilt and false accusations,' he said, punctuating his sentence with a gentle kiss to the frown that had riven my face.

'Or I could make love to you, here and now, with such vigor and intensity that you forget you even have a past, let alone remember the details of said past.' This time he kissed the eyebrow that had shot up at his boasting.

'Or I could do both, but include some whipped cream. And maybe those fuzzy handcuffs they sell,' he added, when I started to smile. 'A hamster or two?' he suggested, as the smile turned to a hesitant giggle.

'Hamsters it is, then,' he concluded, holding me tight for a proper kiss.

CHAPTER TWELVE

Ryu's BlackBerry cut through my dreams like a scythe. He was still awake; he'd been reading while drinking a glass of wine when I'd last opened my eyes. I was completely prepared to fall back to sleep when he answered it, but the tone of his voice startled me into awareness.

'Are you certain?' he asked, his voice dark.

'I'll be right there,' he said as he hung up, already pulling on his trousers.

'. . . whathebugger?' I mumbled, sitting up and rubbing my eyes blearily.

'That was Nell. It's Gretchen,' Ryu replied, grimly, digging around in our pile of shed clothes beside the bed for his shirt. 'She's dead.'

That little tidbit of information drove the last vestiges of sleep from my brain. 'Are you serious?' I asked, unable to comprehend what could have killed such a formidable creature. Or the fact that garden gnomes used telephones.

'Yes, and she was murdered in such a way as to get our attention.'

I scrambled out of bed as he threw me my shirt and jeans. I pulled on my clothes, not bothering with underwear, and shoved my feet in my shoes as Ryu held my coat out for me. 'Where are we going?' I asked, as we left the cottage but walked past the car.

'The bakery,' was Ryu's only response.

I had to trot to keep up with him, my short legs no match for his long strides. It was only about a five-minute walk from the cottages into the main square of town, but I was breathing hard by the time we got there. Surrounding Tanner's Bakery were a bunch of squad cars, a fire engine and a paramedic's van, and the coroner's hearse thingy. There were also quite a few Rockabill natives standing across the street, in various states of undress, watching the activity. I saw Marge and Bob Tanner, who owned the bakery, and my heart went out to them. They were nice folk, both as plump and soft as their famous potato buns, and Marge was sobbing into Bob's shoulder. They were wearing matching mauve bathrobes over striped pajamas.

Ryu was tense as we joined the crowd, and I knew it must be killing him not to be able to do anything. I didn't know how powerful glamours could be, but whammying a crowd, all of whom already had their whole attention fixed to a single situation, must have been too much even for him.

I took his hand as we watched them carry a figure wrapped in a black body bag out of the bakery and into the coroner's van. Ryu's fangs were extended and he gave a very catlike hiss as they drove away. Then he looked around as if searching for something and drew me away down the street into the alley that separated the Trough from our little local cinema.

It took my eyes a second to adjust to the gloom as we walked to the back of the alley and out behind the Trough's rear entrance, but then I saw Anyan waiting near the Dumpster.

He came toward us, his tail wagging as I went to greet him. But when he smelled me his hackles rose and he backed away. I didn't understand what had just happened, but it made me sad nevertheless.

'Anyan,' Ryu greeted him, perfunctorily. 'What the hell happened here tonight?'

Anyan's voice seemed even rougher than it had before, but he'd probably been woken up, just like us. He spoke to Ryu's midsection, not meeting his gaze, and I wondered again why they liked each other so little.

'Nell felt the goblin's death. Gretchen had some sort of emergency beacon that went off at the moment she died. Which means her firm will be aware of her passing as well, and are probably on their way here. But whoever killed her wanted to keep them busy. They put the body in that bakery oven so that it would be found by the humans. It is burned, but not so badly that it can't eventually be identified as inhuman. Whoever put it there knew that bakers start early, and that the body would be discovered before it was entirely incinerated—'

'Forcing us to scramble to recover it and any other evidence before her true nature can be sussed,' Ryu finished, and I could see the wheels were spinning once again.

Ryu looked at Anyan speculatively. 'Who is aware of your presence here in Rockabill?' he asked.

'No one besides Nell, Trill, and the other natives. But they are either circumspect or unaware of my history.'

'Good. Let's take advantage of that. Whoever did this thinks that we will have to wait for Gretchen's firm to take over, which will give the murderer time to escape. But I don't think that's what's at stake here. I think that Gretchen's murder is just a smoke screen to keep us distracted, and I'm starting to see the shape of things behind that cloud of smoke.' Ryu fell quiet, thinking, and Anyan kept his eyes on Ryu, ignoring me.

'Can you recover the body and its effects?' Ryu asked Anyan, finally. 'And I mean immediately.'

'Not a problem,' the dog answered, straight away. 'I've done it before.'

'Good. We'll tell Gretchen's firm we saw our chance and took it. They should accept that excuse, especially with your involvement. When you're finished, call me and we'll plan our next move.'

Anyan nodded his head sharply and set off, without once looking in my direction. I knew things were pretty tense at the moment, and that big stuff I didn't understand was going down, but I still thought his coldness toward me was uncalled for.

Ryu took my hand and we walked back toward his cottage as I pondered the evening's events. Then something occurred to me.

'Anyan said he has a "history". What did he mean by that?' I asked.

'Anyan was the leader of our covert ops during the last Great War of Succession. I served under him, actually. We owe a great victory to his cunning and strength, and he could have taken a high position in our Court. But instead he just disappeared.' Ryu shook his head. 'I knew he was out here somewhere, but I had no idea I would run into him carving out a little existence on the outskirts of Bumfuck.'

I wanted to tell Ryu that Rockabill wasn't all that bad, but I knew he wouldn't get it. I was getting a pretty clear picture of Ryu's priorities, and neither 'fresh country air' nor 'scenic views' made the list.

I pondered the implications of Anyan being a doggie general, just as another thought popped into my head. *How was a dog going to carry a body and its effects out of a morgue?*

But before I could ask Ryu, we were back inside the cottage and he was pulling my coat off me. And my shirt. And my jeans.

'Looks like I won't be leaving so soon,' he enlightened me, steering me toward the bedroom. 'Does that make you happy?'

'Oh yes,' I murmured, helping him undo his trousers. We fell onto the poor overworked bed, which creaked alarmingly. And for the next half hour I showed him exactly *how* happy the idea of his staying in Rockabill made me.

'Thanks for making breakfast,' my dad said, helping himself to another piece of whole-wheat toast.

'No problem.' I smiled at him. I'd made sure to be home that morning by nine, leaving Ryu fast asleep. I'd managed to snatch a few more hours of rest, which was all I really needed, so I felt fine despite our marathon evening of debauchery. When I woke up at eight, Ryu was out like a light but he'd left a note saying he'd pick me up that evening after sundown. Watching him sleep, I was once again hit by the fact that he wasn't human. I called what he was doing *sleeping*, but when I touched him he didn't respond at all. I shook him gently, thinking he'd want me to say goodbye, but it was like he'd flipped a switch and turned himself off. I knew that he could function during the day; we'd met during daytime hours. But he'd said his kind weren't at their most powerful during the daytime, so they must choose to take their rest during the hours the sun was up. *And when they rest, boy, do they ever*, I thought, poking him rather aggressively in the forehead about ten times in a row, just to check. He didn't even twitch an eyelid, and his breathing was only perceptible if I held my own breath, put my ear to his nose, and waited for what felt like ages. *No wonder people have thought they were the undead.*

'What are your plans for today?' my dad asked, interrupting my reverie.

'Well, I have lots to do around the house,' I said. 'And I'll make us dinner. Ryu's picking me up later.'

'That's great your friend's stayed so long,' my dad said. 'It's nice to see you busy.'

'You're just glad I'm out of your hair,' I teased.

'I'm serious, Jane. I'm happy when you're happy. And I know you feel responsible for me but I hate that I'm causing you to miss out on your life. Your mother and I had a child because we wanted to share our love with someone, not because we wanted a nurse to take care of us in our old age.'

I remained silent, feeling guilty because his sickness wasn't the real reason I hadn't had much of a social life.

As if he knew what I was thinking, my dad continued, 'And I know things haven't been easy for you since Jason died, and I know that certain things said about that night made it even more difficult. But you and I both know, even if no one else does, that Jason's death was an *accident*. A horrible accident and something that should never have happened because things like that just *shouldn't* happen. But it did, and it's not your fault. You have to understand that, somehow.'

I pushed my scrambled eggs around my plate. What Ryu had said that morning, what my father was saying now, it was a nice thought, but it was untrue. The fact is, if I'd just told him I swam, Jason never would have died. It would have taken less than ten seconds to utter those words, but I never did. And I'd live with that guilt for the rest of my life.

'Anyway,' my father concluded, recognizing my 'I don't want to talk about it' face from long experience, 'I'm just glad that you've got a . . . friend, and that you're going out like a woman your age should. It makes me happy. It's time you moved on.'

He was right. It *was* time I moved on, no matter what I still felt about Jason's death. So I smiled at my dad, acknowledging what he had said, while I took the opportunity to change the subject.

'What would you like for dinner, tonight, Dad? I'm feeling like steak. And maybe some creamed spinach . . .'

Ryu stayed for dinner that night, so I was glad we had decided on steak. I'd realized when I was checking over my neck and wrists for any signs of last night's activity why I was craving iron-rich food. But for my unusually large appetite, however, there were no outward signs that I was screwing a blood-sucking creature of the night. Except for the faintest, and I mean almost invisible, bruising on my neck and wrists, I was entirely unmarked by Ryu's and my affair.

I watched, happy to be quiet, as my dad and Ryu talked about poker. My dad loved poker and would even watch it on TV, which to me was the equivalent of watching paint dry. But for some reason, I was not at all surprised that Ryu was equally keen on the game. *I bet he's got himself quite a poker face*, I thought, just as he caught me watching him and gave me a toothy grin.

I smiled back, realizing, at that moment, just how happy I was that he hadn't had to leave Rockabill so soon. It felt like every minute I was with Ryu I was seeing a new Jane solidifying on the horizon. *Maybe*, I thought, *if he stays long enough, she'll get so solid you can just jump into her, and leave Old Jane behind*. I took a second to ponder the likelihood of being able to give New Jane thinner thighs . . .

When we were done eating, Ryu helped me load the dish-washer before we said good night to my dad. Then we were in his car and heading past Nick and Nan's old bed and breakfast – now a struggling boutique hotel run by Stuart's parents – and out into the wilds north of Rockabill.

We pulled up to a beautiful log cabin that was entirely wrapped around by a lovely verandah, or deck, or whatever the proper name for a log cabin porch was. Nell was on the porch rocking away in her little rocking chair, while Trill was playing frisbee with Anyan. I smiled at the sight, watching as the big dog made an enormous leap into the air to catch the frisbee. Trill had a powerful arm, and if Anyan hadn't caught it I think it might have taken off the top of a tree. Trill grinned at me and Anyan wagged his tail slowly, but didn't come over.

We headed up the porch to where Nell sat rocking. 'Good to see you again, child,' she greeted me, and then turned an appraising eye on Ryu. 'You look pleased with yourself, youngling,' she told him. He gave her a cheeky smile and his courtly little bow.

Moving inside the cabin, I admired its neat, homey interior. The first thing I noticed was the smell – it smelled deliciously of lemon wax and cardamom – and then I noticed all the art. There were amazing sculptures all over the place, tucked on top of and between various pieces of battered but attractive furniture. I hoped I'd get a chance to look at the sculptures up close, but now was not the time. I did, however, give as good a snoop as I could as we walked through to the seating area. The kitchen was surprisingly modern, with a state-of-the-art refrigerator and range. I assumed this was Nell's cabin, but I wasn't quite sure how she could reach the top of the stove. Which I didn't think was the most polite of questions, so I surreptitiously looked around for a footstool as Ryu and I settled onto the overstuffed leather sofa. Meanwhile, Trill sat down at my feet while Nell dragged her little rocking chair inside and sat down across from us. Anyan lay half in, half out the cabin's open front door, as far away from Ryu and me as he could get.

Nell nodded at Anyan and, causing the dog to flinch, said, 'While you two were amusing yourselves, Anyan has been very busy. The body is disposed of, and he's collected Gretchen's effects. Her briefcase was only slightly damaged by the fire, but her files and business planner had already been removed. Her killer overlooked her personal planner, but it contains very little information outside of her dental appointments. Goblins like to keep their teeth sharp,' Nell informed me, as an aside. I nodded gamely. 'Anyway, Ryu, you might be able to make something of its contents. Finally, Gus is on his way because Anyan was clever enough to remove *that*, as well,' Nell said, pointing to a large, jagged quartz rock sitting on a copy of *National Geographic* in the middle of the coffee table.

I blanched when I figured out what it was: the stone that had bashed in Peter's skull.

'Nice work,' Ryu said to Anyan, and for a second I got the impression he'd almost called Anyan 'sir'. *Maybe that's what this tension is about*, I thought. *Ryu used to be Anyan's underling, and now they're supposed to be equals. That can't be a comfortable situation.* I looked curiously between Ryu and the barghest, as if by comparing the two their secrets would be revealed.

Ryu took my hand just as we heard footsteps coming up the gravel drive, and Anyan whirled about to greet the new arrival. It was Gus, moving as slowly as ever, his eyes floating as if in space behind his glasses.

He gave us all a curt greeting, taking a moment to peer at Ryu and me, his enormous eyes blinking disconcertingly, before his attention was drawn to the stone sitting on the table. He walked toward it the way another person might walk toward an abused animal, before he gently picked it up and stood stroking it, humming to it like it might startle otherwise.

I shuddered. Gus's rapport with the stone was giving me the willies. Not only was it just weird, but I could see that the rock still had blood and, I imagined, wodges of brain goo on it. The rock was not something to be caressed; it was something to be Lysoled.

Ryu squeezed my hand. 'Gus, dear,' Nell admonished, gently. 'Can you tell us anything?'

Gus looked up and I could see that he was nearly crying. 'Oh, it's awful,' he said. 'She saw *everything*. She's still very upset.'

I couldn't help it, it was all too much. I let out a little snort of derision; it was either that, or run away screaming.

Gus abruptly turned toward me, the quickest movement I had ever seen him make. 'It's not funny,' he said, sharply. 'How would you like it if someone picked *you* up and used *you* to brain somebody?'

I looked at Ryu, helplessly. I think I was a little hysterical and it was taking everything I had in me, plus my literally biting my own tongue, not to burst out laughing.

Ryu took the situation in hand. 'Gus, Jane meant no offense. She is new to our world; be patient with her.' His words settled me, and I managed to give Gus a solemn nod. 'We need to know what the stone can tell you; does it have any idea who used it?'

Gus looked down at the rock for a long moment, his expression so compassionate I started to take him a little more seriously. 'I'm sorry,' he said, finally. 'She can't really tell humans apart.' Gus chose his next words with care. 'She just sees humans as ugly bags of water.'

Alarmed, I whispered to Ryu, 'Isn't that from a *Star Trek* episode?' but he shushed me.

'She would know the killer's scent, however. We stones have a very good sense of smell and wonderful memories,' Gus finished, giving a little sniff as if to punctuate his point.

I shuddered, imagining the rock walls of my cove smelling me every time I brushed past them . . .

'Thank you, Gus,' Nell said. 'That will be all.'

'May I take her with me?' Gus asked, pointing at the stone. Ryu interrupted then, to say, 'No, I'm sorry. We may have need of it later. But when this is all over, we'll be sure to return it . . . um, her, to you.'

Gus sighed, giving the rock a little hug and whispering to it before he set it back down on the *National Geographic*. He gave it a parting caress, then stumped back out the front door without saying goodbye.

I sat there, trying to wrap my head around what I'd just seen, while Ryu joined Anyan in the doorway. I watched as Anyan pointed his muzzle at a large paper bag sitting on the kitchen's granite-topped island, and Ryu went to collect it. Settling back down beside me, he began rooting around inside the bag. When I caught a strong smell of burning I realized it must be Gretchen's effects, and then I remembered Martin's body. I told my stomach in firm tones to *stay settled*, just as Ryu produced Gretchen's singed briefcase.

He went through the pockets, but it had indeed been cleaned out. There were a few receipts for dry cleaning and Starbucks, and a packet of tissues. *For dabbing at eye mucus*, I thought queasily, but then I shook myself. *Goblins probably think we're the hideous ones, with our smooth flesh and our fatty limbs. And she was murdered and stuck in an oven, which is not a nice way to go.*

Tucked away in an all but hidden back pocket of the briefcase, however, was a tiny pink planner that the killer must have overlooked. It was too small to be Gretchen's business planner, and it only contained personal appointments, so Nell was right in thinking that Gretchen probably had another planner for her professional dealings. Nevertheless, there might be something in there to give us a clue and Ryu was poring over it as if it were *War and Peace*.

'Hmph,' he grunted, suddenly. I had come to know Ryu's grunts, and that was a happy grunt. 'Look at this.'

Written in blue pen under the entry for today was 'Iris's, Eastport, 1:30.' There was a number scrawled underneath.

'Iris's is a boutique,' I told Ryu. 'It's really famous around here.' Ryu's eyes stayed on mine, expectantly, so I continued, 'The owner, Iris, does a really specialized personalized-shopping experience kind of thing. She has a store with regular stock in it, but she also brings in special stuff just for you if you're one of her clients. Who are mostly rich people with holiday homes. I've never actually been there. I've just heard about it. It's really expensive,' I added, lamely, well aware of my slightly shabby gray sweater. At this point in the week I was running out of 'good' clothes.

'Well,' Ryu said, taking his BlackBerry out of his pocket and dialing the number from the planner. 'Looks like you'll finally get your chance to visit Iris's boutique.' While it rang, he eyed me skeptically. 'And maybe,' he said, poking his finger through a small hole in the side of my top I hadn't noticed until then, 'she'll have something in your size.'

CHAPTER THIRTEEN

'Uh-oh,' Ryu said, as we pulled in front of Iris's elegantly understated boutique. There was an absolutely sublime black pants suit on the mannequin in the window, and a pyramid of handbags that probably cost a small fortune. And I mean individually, not just in formation.

'Huh?' I mumbled, practically salivating at the sight of a particularly enormous red leather bag that I could probably have fit myself into. And, boy, did I want to give it a go.

'There's a succubus in there. She's left her mark all over the place,' Ryu said, grimacing. I didn't think that was a very nice thing to say, and I told him so.

'I don't mean succubus in the wanton harlot sense,' he explained, patiently. 'I mean a real live succubus. They're what you might call cousins to vampires. But they don't feed off fear at all, just lust. And they can harvest essence from any bodily fluid, not just blood.'

'Oh,' I said, chewing my mental cud. And then everything came together. 'Oh, a *succubus*,' I said, remembering the exact details of my mythology. 'And *any* bodily fluid . . .' The thought was rather exciting, and I blinked. 'I gotcha.'

Ryu pulled me toward him for a lingering kiss. 'You're

almost too cute to fuck, Jane. But that just makes me want to fuck you even more.'

'Wow,' I murmured, as my libido kicked into high gear and I reached up to grab two fistfuls of his thick brown hair. Speaking of bodily fluids . . .

We pulled away from each other after a minute, panting. This was neither the time nor the place. Mostly because the stupid Porsche was too small to accommodate any horseplay. Foiled in my attempt to illustrate for Ryu what a true wanton harlot could do, and therefore rather frustrated, I was in no way prepared for what awaited us beyond the doors of Iris's boutique.

If I had thought Grizzie oozed sexuality, the vision that came to open the door for us was gushing sensuality in a torrent so palpable I actually stumbled over it. Softly manicured hands caught me, and I was face to face with the most perfect bosoms I'd ever seen. I'm no slouch in the boobies department, but these personalities were impeccable. 'Oh, honey,' came a voice like molasses. 'Are you all right?' The hands helped me straighten up, until I was gazing into the most beautiful blue eyes I'd ever seen in my entire life. They were like my sea during a storm or the sky on a summer's day. Or Nan's toilets when she'd used those cistern deodorizing-tablet jobbies—

'Ahem,' coughed Ryu, dryly, and I found the strength to detach myself from the vision.

'Iris, I presume?' Ryu continued, putting out one hand to shake the vision's while he used the other to haul me back to his side.

The vision turned the full weight of her attention onto Ryu, and I managed to straighten myself up. *Wow, that was intense*, I thought, trying to still my trembling hands.

'Yes,' came the butter-and-jam voice again. 'And you must be Ryu. It's a pleasure to meet you. Who is your friend?'

'Her name is Jane True,' Ryu said, stepping resolutely between Iris and me. 'Her mother is the selkie, Mari, who made her home in Rockabill for a time.'

'Of course, little Jane,' Iris said, circumventing Ryu and somehow getting her lovely mitts on me once again. She used one hand, placed dangerously low at the small of my back, to steer me into her boutique.

'I sold your mother a red wrap dress once,' she said. 'You were just a babe in arms, but I knew then you would be a beauty. Your mother certainly was. And look at you now.' She put her hand on my shoulder and spun me around, and then took a step back to get a good look at me. I was getting more and more flushed by the second and I looked back at Ryu for help. I could tell he didn't know whether to be irritated or to run and get a video camera.

'You have her hair, and her eyes,' Iris said, brushing my bangs away from my face. 'And her figure. She's built like a young Selma Hayek,' the succubus commented appreciatively to Ryu, who had stepped up to stand beside her. 'Like in *From Dusk Till Dawn*,' she continued, as they both ogled me. I could see that Ryu was showing some fang, and Iris's eyes had begun to glow eerily. For my part, I felt like I had FRESH MEAT painted on my chest.

'Thanks, Miss, um, Iris,' I interrupted. 'But we're actually here on business,' I said, giving Ryu what I hoped was a meaningful look.

'Hmm?' he queried, his eyes scanning back up my body, slowly. 'What? Oh yes, of course. Sorry.' He turned to Iris, professional once more. 'We're here because your name appeared in a diary belonging to Gretchen Kirschner, and we wanted to ask you what that appointment was regarding.'

Iris made a face. 'Oh, business, schmizness. I'll tell you all about Gretchen and what she wanted,' she said, giving me

the sweetest smile I've ever seen in my life. I took an involuntary step toward her before I realized what I was doing.
'*If* you let me dress up Jane. That sweater is simply not on,'
she finished, reaching out to touch it as if she thought it might
stain her fingers.

Ryu sighed. 'Fine, Iris. Whatever you like. Let's just get
to it.'

Iris gave a delighted little clap and raced off into the expensive bowels of her boutique. I gave Ryu a confused look and
he shrugged. 'Succubi aren't exactly what you'd call focused,'
he apologized. 'If we don't keep her happy, she'll never get
around to telling us what we need to know.' His eyes took
on a wicked glint. 'And you could use a new sweater,' he
teased. I was so mad I took it off and threw it at him.

'Ooh, you've started without me,' Iris murmured, giving
me a sexy smile. She was dragging behind her an entire
wheelie rack and I had no idea how she'd gotten around her
shop that fast.

'What are you, a six petite?' Iris asked, pulling me and the
rack over to the dressing room and handing me a pair of very
tiny-looking black trousers and a white blouse. 'Put these on
and we'll get to work.'

Once in the dressing room, I pulled off my old jeans and
began to pull on the pants. They were made of this really
stretchy material that hugged every curve. Or, more accurately, wrapped every curve in a death grip. They were long
and tight around my ankles, so I rolled them into cuffs,
thinking they'd need hemming. Then began the arduous
process of buttoning them up. After I'd sucked what felt like
my liver up into my lungs, I managed to get them buttoned
and zipped. Then I put on the white blouse, which I have to
admit was gorgeous. It was really soft fabric with just the
perfect amount of crispness. I had no idea who the hell would

iron it if I took it home, since I was a disaster at ironing, but for right now it looked amazing. I also had no idea what I actually looked like, because there was no mirror in the dressing room.

While I was changing, I could hear Ryu querying Iris. He wasn't having much luck, unfortunately. Every time he asked a question about Gretchen, Iris turned it around and asked a question about us: were we together? Were we serious? When did we meet? She was particularly curious about when he would be leaving Rockabill; I could tell Ryu was just about to lose it, so I chose that moment to step out of the dressing room.

Iris *tsk*ed when she saw me, and before I knew it she unrolled my pant legs and adjusted them so they settled around my lower calves and ankles with a sort of ruched effect. Then she straightened up and undid the two top buttons on the blouse, taking a moment to smooth the material down over my hips. And down over my backside, twice, while I tried to keep my face neutral. Then she pulled a wide, patent-leather red belt off of the rack and had it cinched tight, right underneath my boobs, before I could say 'help!' When she saw I was actually having trouble breathing, she undid the belt one notch, but upped the ante by slipping onto my feet the most badass, red patent-leather heels I'd ever seen in my life. 'They're Miu Miu,' she explained, and I nodded as if I understood her. 'New for this season. Mary Jane pumps are hot on the catwalks at the moment.'

I had no idea how the hell I was going to walk, but I managed to trundle over to the mirror. The black trousers fit like a glove, and the tight tapering legs actually made my short legs look long, especially since the pants fell about halfway down the enormous red heels. The positioning of the belt made my breasts look amazing, and I had shown off more cleavage in the ten seconds it had taken to check myself out in the mirror than I ever had in my life.

Iris stood behind me, looking at me in the mirror and making minor adjustments. I had just realized that most of the adjustments seemed to be located right around my breastal region, when Ryu said gently, 'Iris, we need to get back to business. Let Jane try on another outfit and we'll keep talking.'

I tottered back into the dressing room as Iris thrust a dress at me, rolling her eyes. 'Fine, if we *must*,' I heard her complain as I eased off the high heels with a sigh. 'The goblin called a few days ago, saying that she wanted to speak to me about Peter, but she never showed up for her appointment. So I can't tell you what Gretchen wanted, because I didn't actually meet her. So why don't we concentrate on Jane.' Her voice grew honeysuckle sweet. 'I have some fantastic lingerie in back—'

'As tempting as that is,' Ryu's dry voice cut in, 'I'm afraid we need to concentrate on what you just said about Peter. You knew Peter?' he asked. 'Do you know he's dead?'

I was inching my way out of the trousers, understanding what a snake felt like shedding its skin, when I heard Iris sigh. 'Yes,' she said. 'He was such a lovely man. He did this thing with his—'

'I'm sure he did,' Ryu interrupted her hastily, as I bit my tongue to keep from laughing. 'But someone murdered Peter. And now Gretchen, who came out to investigate Peter's death, has been murdered as well. All we know about Gretchen's investigation is that she was supposed to come see you, and we need to find out why.'

I slipped the dress Iris had given me over my head with pleasure. It was a silky material that felt like water caressing my skin, and it was the loveliest pattern. There were two shades of purple involved, a rich bright pink and a little white.

The pattern itself was vaguely geometric but some of the lines wobbled so that they lent an organic feel to the whole thing. There was an insanely long sash that I didn't know what to do with hanging from the waist, and if I'd shown off some cleavage before, I was practically an advertisement for it in this dress. Which was also very, very short.

There was a lull in conversation outside my dressing room, and I could tell that Ryu was trying to regroup. Iris definitely knew something she wasn't telling us; there was a slyness to her prevarications that spoke volumes. But I was getting the feeling that questioning Iris was like asking obedience of a golden retriever. You had to interject treats, ball throwing, and belly rubs as carrots, while the stick would get you nowhere. I'd also figured out that, under these circumstances, I seemed to make a suitable Milk-Bone.

I stepped out from the dressing room with a flourish. Iris gasped theatrically, clasping her hands together. Even given his annoyance, Ryu looked pretty pleased with the effect.

'It's a kimono mini-dress,' Iris explained, coming over to wrap the deep purple sash around my waist a bunch of times before tying it into a small knot in front. The 'mini' part was obvious, and the kimono part explained the huge sleeves. She pulled out another pair of enormous heels. This time they were the same lighter-purple shade of the dress and they had small triangular cut-outs coming up from the sole so that they were sort of tiger-striped, with the stripes being the little cut-out triangles. All the shoe's edges were lined in a thin etching of gold. 'Platform pumps by Christian Louboutin, as you can probably tell from the red soles,' she told me, slipping them on my feet.

When she swiveled me around, I had to admit I was quite a sight. The dress was gorgeous, and in the mirror, at least, I looked tall and elegant. In reality, I barely came up to Iris's chin and in those shoes I would probably walk like I'd just gotten off a horse, but if I kept still I made quite a satisfying illusion.

Iris was literally purring as she smoothed the material down over my hips. Then smoothed it again. And then again. I took my chance, and I struck.

'Iris?' I asked, quietly, not wanting to disturb her reverie.

'Yes?' she murmured, pulling the material covering my chest both slightly tighter and slightly apart, to up the boobage factor even more.

'Tell us about Peter,' I cajoled. 'Did he tell you why he was in Rockabill? He told me he was writing a book.'

Iris looked me in the eyes, and I took another little involuntary step forward. *This woman is dangerous*, my brain observed while my irrepressible libido merrily calculated the mechanics involved in catapulting myself into a lesbian affair.

The succubus laughed, and said, 'Oh, he *was* a naughty boy. He wasn't writing a book; he was investigating a halfling down in Rockabill. That's what he did. Well, that's all he could do really. He was practically human. He'd gotten almost none of his father's, an incubus's, gifts. But he could sense other halflings, for some reason.' She shrugged. 'You never know what you're going to get when you have a child with a human. Sometimes they're just like you, and sometimes they're just like the human parent. Sometimes they're like nothing else at all, and they come out entirely unique.'

Iris untied and re-tied the sash around my waist, slightly tighter and wider this time. I could see that Ryu was listening intently, but he was careful not to interrupt us.

'So, Peter was investigating a halfling?' I asked, already realizing what was coming. 'Was it me?'

Iris looked at me with confusion on her face. 'Oh, Jane,' she whispered. Her voice was like candied plums and it nearly broke my heart. 'I'm so sorry. I didn't even realize until you said that. It must have been you.'

I smiled at her and stroked her golden hair. It was softer than the fabric of the dress I was wearing. 'It's okay, Iris,' I murmured. 'You didn't know. And we don't know what he was doing, maybe it was innocent. Do you know what he was doing?'

'I only know that he investigated them to start a sort of . . . inventory of halflings. He said that his employer wanted to know about the halflings and who their parents were. And what their powers were if they had any. He said that he was making a sort of catalog . . . for future research.' I could tell that Iris's concentration was breaking up. She kept stopping and starting awkwardly. She looked genuinely distressed that I had been the halfling in question.

'Iris,' I interrupted her, getting out the carrot. 'Why don't I try on something else for you?'

She smiled like dawn breaking through the folds of night. 'Oh, yes. I have just the dress.'

She pulled a silver swathe of fabric from the rack, and her eyes were back to glowing slightly. 'I'll have to help you with this,' she informed me, doing a good job of keeping her buttered-rum voice professional.

I sighed. *In for a penny*, I thought, untying the sash around my waist and pulling the dress I was wearing over my head.

Iris took a moment to surreptitiously check me out before she held the silvery fabric over my head and pulled it down. She kept me faced toward her so that I couldn't see myself in the mirror, which was a nice touch. Between her sensuality and her obvious sales skills, I now knew why Iris's boutique did incredibly well despite its being so far off the beaten fashion track.

As she busied herself settling the dress where it was

supposed to be, I struck again. 'Iris? What Peter was doing doesn't sound very dangerous, and yet he was murdered. Did he say anything about feeling threatened?'

I couldn't tell if Ryu was concentrating harder on Iris's ministrations or my words, but he nodded at what I'd said. *I'm doing pretty well, for a sidekick*, I thought.

'There was something odd,' Iris said. 'Peter didn't want to talk about it, and we didn't really do much talking when we were together.' She smiled and reached around me to undo my bra as I stifled a gasp. She ran her hands down my arms to lower my bra straps and then took a firm hold of the material between my breasts, whisking my bra away so that it didn't interfere with the cut of the dress.

'But he said that there was something fishy going on. That something was happening to the halflings he was cataloging. He didn't say what, but it couldn't have been good because I could taste that he was scared when he said it.' I quivered at her casual use of the word 'taste' to explain how she sensed Peter's emotions, and at her stepping behind me to zip up the dress. She trailed the fingers of her free hand along my spine, causing me to stand up straight as she zipped. The dress was snug, but I think that's how it was supposed to be.

Ryu was gazing at me, fangs ahoy, while Iris stayed behind me adjusting the halter strap and then sweeping my hair up into a little ponytail to get it off my neck. The dress must have looked good because he was practically drooling.

Iris then slipped onto my feet *another* pair of red-soled ridiculous heels. I got the feeling she was insinuating I needed a little help in the height department. 'More Louboutin's,' she said. 'Slingback sandals.' They were black satin with a little peephole in the toe and these adorably large satin bows lounging across the top.

'He also said he thought he had seen somebody who

shouldn't be there, wherever he was investigating. He wasn't sure about any of this. He wasn't sure he'd seen who he'd seen and he seemed to find it hard to believe that whoever it was would be there,' she said, confusedly, as I tried to follow her train of thought. 'But he was almost certain, at the same time, that he was right.' Iris had stepped away to look me over appraisingly, and then stepped forward again to make a few minor adjustments to the dress.

'And he didn't admit it to me, but he was frightened. Especially toward the end,' Iris explained. She chose that moment to turn me toward the mirror, and even I gasped.

The dress was *incredible*. It had halter straps and a deep V-neckline that plunged downward toward its empire waist-line. There was a large, black, carved flower button thingy sort of visually joining together the waistline and the halter neck. The material was chiffon and there was tons of it floating around me. I'd never felt so gorgeous in my life. And the crowning glory was the shoes, which were just *sassy*. All thought of Peter fled as I turned around, getting the 360-degree angle from the three-sided mirror. *This isn't a dress*, I thought. *It's a gown.*

Ryu's voice was husky, when he finally spoke. 'Iris, all of this information is great. But do you have any idea *why* Peter was afraid?'

Iris turned to Ryu, and her expression was the most serious I'd seen all night. 'No, I don't, and I knew better than to ask. I've not gotten this far in life asking questions to which I know I don't want the answers. All I do know is Peter was genuinely afraid and that was enough for me.' Iris walked away from me, toward the elegant, ladylike little rolltop desk that was sitting against the wall near the mirror. She opened a bottom drawer with a key and took out a large accordion file.

I pulled the long skirt out, fanning the material and letting it fall, loving the feel of it against my legs. I just couldn't get over myself. *It can be yours if you kick off the heels and run*, I thought. *The succubus will probably catch you, but if you can get the keys to the Porsche you've got a fighting chance* . . . I told myself quite firmly to shut up.

'So, I haven't even looked at this,' Iris said, and I finally stopped admiring my image in the mirror. She handed the folder to Ryu, dusting off her hands as if glad to be rid of it. 'It's a copy of Peter's case file. He left it with me for safe keeping. He said if something happened to him to release it to the proper authorities.' She eyed Ryu speculatively. 'And I guess that's you. I just want it out of my shop.'

I could see Ryu was itching to get into the file, so I knew what I had to do. With a sigh, I reached behind me and tried to get a hold of the zipper to take off the gown. Iris saw what I was doing and came toward me to help.

As she zipped down the gown, she seemed to remember something. 'Oh, there is one other thing. Peter did tell me who he was working for.'

Ryu looked up quickly, his eyes as sharp and focused as a wolf's when confronted with a pound of sirloin.

'One of your kind,' she said, nodding at Ryu. 'Name of Nyx.'

I watched, fascinated, as Ryu turned about six different shades of purple. And then I watched, less pleased, as he swore like a trooper and tore my old gray sweater right in half. Which made it my turn to curse.

CHAPTER FOURTEEN

We drove out to Rockabill Bluffs, overlooking the Old Sow, so that Ryu could read the file and have a think.

The tiny trunk of the Porsche was filled with packages from Iris's, and I still felt a little weird about that fact. I hadn't wanted Ryu to buy me anything and I *certainly* wasn't comfortable accepting such expensive gifts. But he'd said that he was doing it as much for Iris's sake as mine – that he owed her as part of the information game they'd played and he'd bill it to the company anyway. So I let him buy me the pants outfit, the kimono dress, and their matching accessories, wandering away to look around the shop when she rang everything up so I didn't see what everything actually cost. I bet each pair of those red-soled shoes cost at least a hundred dollars. *So you needn't worry, my sweets*, I thought down at my battered old Converse. *Mommy will never replace you.* All joking aside, Ryu had even wanted to buy me the gown, but that's where I drew the line. I didn't need a gown in Rockabill, no matter how beautiful it was.

Iris had also thrown in the sweater I was currently wearing, since Ryu had laid waste to my own. It was a lovely cream-colored V-neck made of real cashmere. I'd tried to talk her out of it, but she was insistent. I could tell she felt really guilty about me being the subject of Peter's research, which was silly since she hadn't even known who I was.

When we got to the bluffs we parked a little way from the edge. Ryu rummaged around the packed trunk until he managed to extricate his picnic blanket and a bottle of wine. The mere sight of the blanket made me a little hot under the collar, but Ryu's face wasn't exhibiting any signs of erotic life. In fact, when he lit a little mage light that tagged along behind us like a faithful terrier, he still looked really pissed off.

'Ryu?' I asked hesitantly, as we spread the blanket and sat down. 'Who's Nyx?'

Ryu scowled. If I thought he'd looked angry before, he now looked positively apoplectic.

'Nyx is an absolute piece of shit,' he said, unhelpfully. Then he seemed to collect himself, and his voice took on the 'tour guide to the supernatural' tone I'd gotten so used to at this point. 'In our world, the Alfar rule,' he began. 'They're the oldest, and rarest, of our kind.' He stopped and thought for a minute, as if unsure how to continue. Finally, he started again. 'We don't study ourselves, the way humans do. We don't try to trace our origins or examine our past for the keys to our present. But some of us have our own theories as to how we came into being. We know that our kind has been around for a very long time – far longer than humans – and that in the beginning we were all the same. But, and this is just one theory, mind you, at some point we began to . . . interfere with ourselves.' At this point, Ryu paused to open up the bottle of wine. He took a swig and passed me the bottle.

'Basically, because of our access to the elements, we could force our own evolution. And that's what some of us think we did,' he continued. 'Different factions chose to pursue different strengths, admittedly making themselves vulnerable to certain weaknesses. For example, nahuals gave up most of their access to the elements in order to concentrate on developing their shape-shifting ability. Then humans came along, and they were impossible to get rid of.' I took another drink of the delicious red wine, choosing to ignore that bit about 'getting rid' of mankind. 'So we had to integrate them into our landscape, so to speak, and this led to further evolutionary engineering. Some of us, like vampires, succubi, and incubi, all evolved to harvest a concentrated form of power, what we call essence, straight from humans. After millennia had passed, these changes were occurring naturally rather than consciously, for by this time we'd lost the power to mutate ourselves directly.

'Are you following me?' he asked, and I nodded. I was getting the gist. 'The only creatures left who still resemble our origins are the Alfar. They remain the most powerful of us, and the longest living, but in some ways this has made them curiously weak.' He looked around, like he was betraying a secret, before he realized what he was doing. 'They are our leaders, and yet they are out of touch with reality. Their long lives mean they live in a world almost separate from ours. Yet at the same time their power allows them to rule over us—' He cut himself short, mentally veering back on course. 'Our current king and queen are Orin and Morrigan. They are of the fourth generation of Alfar, only three generations removed from the beings that first manipulated their own destinies. They are both tremendously old, but they have held their throne for only a short time – a little less than one hundred and fifty human years. When the former queen faded, there was a Great War of Succession. Luckily for those of us who fought with them, Orin and Morrigan won that battle.'

'Really? A war? Like a real war?'

'Yup, definitely a real war.'

'How did we not know?'

'You mean, how did humans not know?' Ryu asked, his lips quirking. I ignored his implication and waited for him to answer my question.

'Well,' he said, when he realized I wasn't to be baited, 'it was a long time ago, in terms of human advancement. There were less people, fewer ways to communicate, no cameras to avoid. Not all of us, after all, are as good at manipulating human technology or humans, in general, as my kind are. So it was close, and there were quite a few leaks. The fallen would sometimes turn up as murder victims, or battle sites would turn up as legends of hauntings. Neither side could risk exposure; both were weakened, forced into corners. So even though it was difficult to keep it secret from humans, we managed it.'

'Something you probably wouldn't be able to pull off, now. What with CCTV, global satellites, Google Maps—'

'No,' Ryu agreed. 'Another war would be too conspicuous to hide.'

I realized I'd polished off almost a quarter of the wine, so I passed it to Ryu who quaffed it nearly to the halfway mark with a look of relief. I lay down on my side, propping my head up on my hand, and waited for him to continue. He put the wine bottle down, nestling it into the blanket to keep it upright, and then lay down beside me, his eyes looking into mine. He ran a finger down my cheek gently and I smiled. He leaned toward me for a split second, but then seemed to recover himself.

He forged ahead, only his peeping fangs betraying his internal struggle to keep on task. 'Right, well, there have always been two philosophies, shall we say, regarding the relationship between our kind and humans. One says that we should live alongside humans – not entirely separate and not entirely equal – but peacefully. The other philosophy preaches a more "demon overlord" approach to the whole matter. To make an extremely long and complicated story short, Orin and Morrigan are of the former train of thought, as were those of us who fought with them. Whereas the party that lost thought we should enslave humanity and seize our rightful position as their natural leaders. The war was long – it lasted a few hundred years. Eventually, I was old enough to choose sides, and I chose Orin and Morrigan's. That's where we get to Nyx.'

Ryu turned over to lie on his back, his arms pillowed under his head. I snuggled up against him, placing my ear on his chest to hear his voice purring from the source.

'Nyx is my cousin, but she's older than me by a few hundred years. When the war started, she was firmly on the side of the "crush humanity" faction. Basically, she despises humans as anything but lunch. But she's also an extremely capable political animal, so when the tide started to turn in favor of Orin and Morrigan she did what any two-faced bitch worth her salt would do. She sold herself and her copious knowledge of the enemy to our side for the price of her life and a position in the new Court. Where, believe it or not, she's made quite a name for herself. People think that because they *know* she can't be trusted, they understand how to deal with her. Which totally underestimates the depths of her depravity and is eventually going to sink us all into some seriously profound doo-doo.

'So that's Nyx, in a nutshell,' he concluded, sighing. I could see that what he'd just told me meant that there was big trouble in little Rockabill. The disturbing nature of the idea that Jakes had been *cataloging* halflings was suddenly very evident, and for the first time that night, I confronted the idea that Peter had been collecting my own data for his little inventory. *Should have left the little shit in the Sow.*

'What do you think Nyx wants with Peter's catalog?' I asked.

Ryu exhaled noisily, scrubbing his hands through his hair in what I'd come to know was his gesture indicating extreme concentration. 'I have no idea,' he said, at last. 'But it can't be good.'

He rubbed a hand over his face and then sat up to take a mouthful of wine. He drank slowly, and then very deliberately corked the bottle and set it aside. I was lying on my back, mulling over everything I'd just been told. Ryu's world sounded incredibly complicated. And while I didn't know shit from Shinola, I feared that, because of Peter Jakes, I was involved whether I wanted to be or not.

Ryu had opened Peter's case file, and I sat up to see what was inside. In the pocket labeled 'Master List,' there was a register of names and places, about eighteen in all, with the first twelve of them crossed off. I shivered when I saw that 'Jane True – Rockabill, ME' was written underneath the last name that had been crossed off.

There were thirteen sections of the accordion file that had been labeled, and the names on the labels matched with the twelve names that had been crossed off, with one for me. Naturally, we started at mine.

Written in small, almost typewriter-perfect print was everything about me. There were my parents' names, their status – 'selkie' and 'human' – and their current whereabouts. I stifled my disappointment when I saw next to my mother's name the words 'location unknown'. There was my physical description, address, place of work, and even a list of my hobbies. Next to the heading 'Powers' was written 'Manipulation of water elements; strength as yet to be determined.'

Ryu and I exchanged a long look, and he put the contents of my personal file back into the folder. Then we took a brief look through the other files, but they all contained similar information. I was eager to snoop and see what the other halflings out there were like, so I took the file marked 'Gonzalez, Joe' and was poring over it while Ryu rummaged through the rest of the folder. Then he pulled out from the very back a sealed Ziploc baggie of newspaper clippings. It had been stuck in an unlabeled section and folded small so that you wouldn't see it if you just glanced at the folder.

I kept reading about Joe, who was the product of a male dryad and a female human. He was forty-eight years old, and lived in Shreveport, Louisiana. He had never met his father and had no idea of the man's true nature. He had very weak control over earth elements, his file read, but not enough for contact to have been necessary. Mr Gonzalez apparently just thought he had an unusually green thumb. I shook my head, putting the file back into the folder while Ryu mulled over the clippings. He appeared to be comparing them to the master list of halfling names.

'Shit,' he swore. 'This is *not* good.'

'What?' I asked, leaning toward him.

Ryu handed me the master list and the clippings. My heart froze when I saw that one of the clippings bore a headline about the murder of a local man, Joe Gonzalez. I picked it up, reading that the body of Mr Gonzalez, 48, native of Shreveport, Louisiana, had been found in his garden, a trowel buried in his skull. With trembling fingers I picked up the other clippings, all about murders, and compared them to the names surrounding Joe's on the list. They matched.

'They're all there,' he said. 'All twelve halflings that Peter had investigated are now dead. And all under suspicious circumstances.'

We sat in silence while I read the clippings. None of the victims had anything in common. They were all different sexes, races, ages, and were from all walks of life. They lived all over the country. Unless you knew they were halflings, you'd never know they had any connection to each other whatsoever. *But now they sure do*, my brain commented drily, as I felt a wave of nausea. Nearly all of the clippings mentioned the fact that whoever had killed the victim had sliced off a single ear, presumably as a trophy. And I'd been next on the list.

I stopped myself from going there; if I went there, I'd freak out. Instead, I mimicked calm as I put the clippings back into their bag, zipped it shut, and then put it back in the folder. Ryu wordlessly handed me the bottle of wine, watching as I pulled the cork out with my teeth and chugged another quarter of it down.

When I was finished, I took a deep breath. 'Do you think Peter murdered these people?' I asked, already knowing the answer. But I wanted to hear Ryu say it.

'No,' he said, confirming my suspicion. 'I think whoever murdered Peter, Martin, and Gretchen is the one responsible for these killings, as well.'

'Was Peter working *with* the killer, then? Tipping him off? Those clippings, the way they were hidden away like that – maybe he was hoarding them so he could get off on them at night, or maybe he was hiding them. He told Iris that something was going on, and she knew he was scared, but just because he was scared or in over his head doesn't mean he wasn't involved.'

Ryu shrugged helplessly. 'I wish I knew. Because if we knew what Peter's intentions were, we might catch a glimmer of *Nyx's* intentions in sending him out to create this catalog. Because that's the real question: why does she want to inventory halflings and what does the inventory have to do with the murders?'

'Which leads us to why Peter was murdered at all,' I interjected. 'Iris said he recognized someone – someone who shouldn't be around. Assuming that he was telling her the truth, and that he *was* innocent of any involvement with the killings, he presumably caught a few glimpses of somebody when he was out and about doing his investigations, and then, when he found out about the deaths, he put two and two together and figured out the identity of the murderer. And therefore became another victim.'

'But how the hell did Martin and his firm get involved?' Ryu asked. 'They do *not* answer to Nyx. They work exclusively for the Alfar, and that means our king and queen. And I figure Martin was probably murdered the same night as Peter, so Martin had to have been out here either investigating Peter or doing the same investigation *as* Peter.' Ryu growled with frustration, his hands back in his hair. 'We have lots of questions and no answers.'

I thought about that, and then I took a great leap. 'Why don't you just go ask them?' I asked. 'Nyx,' I clarified, 'and your Court thingy?'

Ryu looked at me like I'd gone gaga. He snorted, shaking his head disdainfully. Then the head shaking stopped, and then it turned into a slow nod, and then he was laughing.

'Oh, Jane.' He drew me toward him, burying his face in my hair. 'Why *don't* we just ask them?' he said, laughing. I tried not to shiver.

What you talkin' 'bout 'we' for, vampire? I thought. There was no way I was going anywhere near Ryu's Court. None whatsoever. Not a thing on earth could get me to . . .

And then Ryu was kissing me.

And then I was agreeing to everything he said.

Little rat bastard.

CHAPTER FIFTEEN

'Y ou have no business bringing Jane into the Compound,'
Anyan growled. I took an involuntary step backward, but Ryu
stood his ground. 'She is not ready for that place – not yet,
at least.'

'She is as ready to be introduced into our society as she'll
ever be,' Ryu responded, coolly. 'And she has every right to
go. She must come to know her mother's people.'

Anyan snorted contemptuously. 'The inhabitants of the
Compound are *not* her mother's people, anymore than the
inmates of an asylum are her father's,' he said.

'Just because you turned your back on Court life does not
mean that we all must follow suit.' Ryu's voice was dry but
his body was tense. Anyan snarled, hackles raised. You could
have spread the tension on a cracker and eaten it.

'Boys,' Nell interrupted calmly from the porch where she
was quietly rocking. 'Before you kill one another, why don't
you ask Jane what *she* wants to do?'

I quailed as two sets of eyes swiveled to meet mine. Ryu's
golden eyes watched me expectantly, believing they already
knew my answer. Anyan's gray gaze simply spoke of his
worry for me.

I knew it was crazy to be going off with a guy I barely knew, but there were so many reasons I wanted to that they outweighed the crazy. After all, how many chances would I get to meet my mother's people? To learn about my history? And it had been so long since I'd left Rockabill. The thought of being Jane True, Random Stranger, was too tempting to resist. Not to mention, part of me wondered if maybe, just maybe, my mother might even be there, at this Compound thing . . .

But the boys – well, vampire and giant talking dog – didn't need to know my innermost motivations.

'Um,' I began, clearing my throat nervously. 'I've already got the time off, and I'm all packed, so I think I'd rather just go ahead and get this over with.'

Lame, I know.

Yet my weak excuse caused Ryu to smile radiantly at me, even as he shot Anyan an obnoxiously triumphant look. The dog just shook his head and strode off to the cabin's porch, where he lay down like any other dog napping in a spot of sunlight. Since he hadn't bothered to speak to me since the night Gretchen died, I didn't really understand why he was so concerned. Then again, his attitude was probably more a product of contempt than concern. He most likely thought I was such a pathetic little halfling that I'd get eaten alive by the Alfar.

Will *I get eaten alive by the Alfar?* I worried, for about the fourth time that day.

Ryu and I had swung by the cabin to pick something up on our way to Québec, which was our current destination. Apparently things didn't really get going in this mysterious Compound till later in the week and Ryu wanted to have some time with me before we got there. So he'd asked me if I'd like to go to Québec first, which was on the way. I'd miss a week of work in total, so first thing that morning I'd gone by Read It and Weep to ask Grizzie and Tracy if they'd mind. Grizzie had said I could go if I promised to take pictures. Tracy had added, 'Of churches and things,' shooting Grizzie a baleful stare. To which Grizzie had responded, 'Fuck that, I meant of your man. Naked.' But in truth they were thrilled I was going off with Ryu and told me to take as much time as I wanted. And although I regretted the short notice, because I'd taken all of two days off my entire five years at Read It and Weep, I didn't feel that guilty.

Leaving my dad was another matter. I'd sat him down and told him all the reasons I shouldn't go with Ryu. He needed me: who would cook? Or do the shopping? Or clean? He would never remember his pills, etcetera. My dad had let me vent, and then he'd said, 'Go, Jane. I want you to go. I want you to stop worrying you'll abandon me. You're not your mother; you will come back. And everything will be fine. I'll eat and take my pills. I'm not as strong as I used to be but I'm not an invalid. Besides, the guys will swing by and give me a hand if I need anything.'

I'd sat there, shocked into silence by his mention of my mother. Was that *really* what I was afraid of? That something would take me away the way it had her? Deep down I knew my mother had loved both me and my father, and yet she'd still left. Did I think I'd disappear one day?

My dad had touched my hand and asked me if I was okay. I didn't know what to say, and I was afraid if I said anything serious I'd start crying. So I'd bravely confronted the real issues. 'You're *sure* you'll remember to take your pills?' I'd asked. He'd only squeezed my hand and nodded in response.

Packing, meanwhile, had been a cinch. I washed and packed my 'best' clothes, all of which Ryu had seen, thinking those would be okay for tourism in Québec. Then I used my dad's old garment bag to carefully pack the outfits that Ryu had bought me, hoping those would be appropriate for the Alfar Compound. I also packed my mother's red dress, smiling at the thought that she'd bought it from Iris, as well as a pair of low, black, sling-back heels I found in her closet. After that, it was just a matter of shoving my toiletries and makeup into my duffel bag and I was ready to go. I'd swum that morning for an extra long time, not knowing when I'd next get into the ocean, so I was pretty hyper. I could feel the power glowing under my skin, a little like the effect of about six shots of espresso. Not that I knew what to do with it.

Something to ask Ryu, I'd thought, looking forward to this weekend for so many reasons.

And as I began to daydream about those reasons, my brain touched on something that made me blush. Right before Ryu was due to pick me up, I'd run back upstairs with my duffel bag. I'd unzipped it and turned to my dirty drawer. Only this time I had made a withdrawal instead of a deposit.

I shifted uncomfortably, glancing over at my only other companion on the porch to check if he'd seen my suddenly flaming cheeks. Ryu had gone into the cabin with Nell, and I'd sat down on the stairs next to Anyan. But the big dog still seemed intent on ignoring me – which just made me more uncomfortable.

'Be careful, Jane,' he said, suddenly, without lifting his head. If he hadn't addressed me by name, I would have thought he was muttering to himself.

'I'm sorry?' I asked. I wasn't going to make his rude behavior any easier to get away with.

'Please, just be careful. The Alfar and their Court are dangerous. You have been raised as a human – their ways are not your ways.'

'Ryu will keep me safe,' I said, annoyed at how petulant my voice sounded.

'Ryu will do what is best for Ryu,' Anyan admonished, finally lifting his head from his paws. 'He would not hurt you, no. Nor would he willingly allow others to harm you. But he will not take *care* of you.' Anyan's voice, throughout our exchange, had been calm. But now he sounded sad.

I laid a hand on his head and scratched behind his ears, trying not to take it to heart when I felt him flinch. He was a complicated dog. *Never thought you'd say* that, *did you?* I thought.

'Thank you,' I told him. 'I will take care, I promise.' Then I let my hand drop. I could tell he didn't want me touching him.

Right then Ryu and Nell emerged from the door behind us, Ryu holding something heavy in a plastic shopping bag. He put the mystery item in the back of the car, where my own luggage was wedged. Ryu hadn't let me put anything in the trunk, for some reason. *I really hope there aren't any dead goblins riding along to Canada with us*, I thought, with a shudder.

We got in the car and sped off into the afternoon, Trill and Nell waving us goodbye. But when I looked around for the barghest, Anyan wasn't there.

The hotel in Québec was incredible. For our rare vacations, my dad and I always went camping. So the disparity between our old pup tents and Le Château Bonne Entente – which I think translates as 'Oui, We Take Kidneys' – was rather alarming. It wasn't a hotel so much as an *estate*, complete with pools and golf course and a spa and all of the other accoutrements of the rich and Botoxed.

I stood there, trying to fade into the background, as Ryu checked us in. He was, of course, a loyalty-program member, and all of the staff recognized him. I noticed that a few of the ladies seemed really to *recognize* him, and I stifled a wave of jealousy. For the first time since I'd met Ryu I began to appreciate the implications of his existence. He had to gather power from feeding off humans – although apparently halflings like me would do the trick – which meant that sex couldn't just be sex, could it? It was also sustenance, something he had to do regularly, no matter what the circumstances, in order to survive.

But the fact that these ladies might have been the equivalent of a Big Mac to Ryu didn't make their sultry glances at him any easier to bear. Nor did the appraising looks they sent winging my way. It was about an eight-hour journey from Rockabill to the hotel – although it had taken Ryu the Rocket about six – and I'd dressed to travel, not to impress the native *Québécoise*. I was wearing my kelly-green sweater and matching Converse – which I *had* cleaned up for the occasion – and my most comfortable jeans. But I knew I looked like a freshman in college just off to the library to study something geeky. At twenty-six, I was probably older than some of the women currently eyeballing me like they just *might* consider pulling out my hair, but they all looked eons older than me and oodles more sophisticated. Under the weight of their painted gazes, I suddenly had a tremendously powerful urge to do the running man. I don't know why.

If Ryu was at all aware of the tension his presence had created, he wasn't showing it. He just kept up his smooth patter – in French, no less – with first the receptionist and then the concierge. Then he came over to me, took my hand to kiss my palm, and led me off to the elevators, leaving our bags to be delivered up to our room. If he'd pulled out a sword and decapitated me, the various female employees who'd slowly congregated behind the desk would not have

looked any more horrified. I wouldn't be surprised if the next
day they all went out and bought themselves some Converse.

In the elevator, he pulled me toward him and kissed my
mouth hungrily. I felt grubby and tired after the long drive,
but my body still responded to Ryu's kisses. By the time our
elevator *pinged* to indicate we'd arrived at our floor, we were
both slightly disheveled.

'We're in here,' Ryu said, slipping his key card in the door.
I'd overheard the receptionist say that she had the Cocooning
Suite ready for us, whatever that meant. But despite the implications of the name, I was not at all ready for what greeted
me behind the door.

First off, my gaze was riveted by the enormous four-poster
bed. It was piled high with pillows and looked like it could
have fit half of Rockabill. Across from the bed was this
amazing sofa-lounger thingy that, with its ottoman flush
against it, made a big oval.

And then I saw the bathtub. Which was not in the bathroom, but sitting proud as a daisy right next to the four-poster
bed.

I gawped at the tub, and then looked around for the actual
bathroom. Was that the only place to bathe?

Of course not. There was an enormous state-of-the-art bathroom that had its own huge bath and shower. *The bedroom
bath is just for sex*, I realized. *Cripes!*

Ryu went into the room, taking out his wallet and keys to
place them on the nightstand. I was still standing in front of
the open door, marveling, when I heard the quiet sound of a
throat being cleared behind me. It was the bellhop with our
luggage. I let him through, moving into the room as if I
thought somebody might jump out at me, while Ryu tipped
him and gestured for our luggage to be set by the bed. I
flicked apart the heavy curtains to peer out the window.

We overlooked the Château's grounds, which looked absolutely magical, all lit up for the evening.

I heard the door close as the bellhop left, and the next sound I heard didn't really surprise me. It was the sound of water filling a bathtub. Then I heard Ryu open something, and a delicious smell filled the room – bubble bath. *He's done this before*, my virtue warned, at which my libido rolled its eyes.

Strong arms wrapped around my waist, and Ryu's teeth closed ever so gently on the nape of my neck. The gentle bite turned into a kiss that trailed over to my ear as his hands cupped my breasts. I turned around to meet his lips in a proper kiss as he pulled my sweater up over my head.

He led me to the bathtub – just in time to turn it off before it got too full – and the rest of our clothes joined my sweater in a heap on the floor. When I got in, the water was achingly hot and smelled like pears. The bath fit the two of us most comfortably. We proceeded to have the most fun in the tub that I'd had since I was a little girl, although my adult experience clashed with my childhood memories – there are indeed some bath toys more exciting than a rubber ducky.

The next three days were glorious. Everyone treated me with respect: there were no whispers or subtle glances between two gossips or hastily pointed fingers. Or, if there were, they were from women jealous of my relationship with Ryu, rather than because of my past.

While my lover slept, I spent the mornings swimming in the heated outside pool, and even though it was cold out nobody raised an eyebrow. I was just some girl who liked to swim so much she even did it in winter. That said, the pool didn't satisfy me like the ocean did, and I would have preferred it unheated. But I still enjoyed it thoroughly. Not least because I *could* enjoy it blanketed as I was in glorious anonymity.

Midafternoon, after Ryu emerged from his coma, we'd head into the city to do touristy things. I took loads of pictures and sent postcards to my father and to Grizzie and Tracy, and bought a few more to send on our return trip so that it looked like I'd spent the whole week in Québec rather than just half of it. Then we'd have dinner somewhere, go out for some drinks, and finally head back to the hotel for bath time. Boy, did I love bath time.

Our last day at the Château was the best yet, despite the knowledge that tomorrow we would be heading out to the Alfar Compound. We didn't even bother to be tourists that day. Upon his waking midafternoon, Ryu hustled me off to the Château's spa to get the full treatment: facial, manicure, pedicure, and this amazing massage that used hot rocks. I don't want to know how much it cost, but the fact that he got himself a manicure, shave, and a haircut made me feel a little better. I felt guilty about the pampering, but I have to admit I walked out of that spa feeling like I was made of rubber. Very content rubber, at that.

We dined in the hotel that evening, for which I wore my mother's red wrap dress. It was by Diane von Furstenberg, a name that even I knew, and it was the epitome of understated elegance. I was really careful with my makeup that evening, trying to do my own version of smoky eyes, which worked okay. They were more 'slightly hazy' than 'smoky', but it was still pretty. Ryu, dressed in a gorgeous charcoal-gray suit with a black shirt and no tie, had never looked so handsome. And that was saying something.

We lingered over dinner. First, we had raw oysters, one of my favorite treats. We sprinkled them with lemon juice and little slices of shallot soaked in vinegar. In my mouth, they tasted like the essence of the sea herself: briny and ozoney and scrumptious. Then we had a tasting platter of sashimi,

served with wasabi, soy, and ginger. I didn't have to be part
seal to enjoy the fish – it was all as fresh as could be and
absolutely mouthwatering. For our main course, we shared
an enormous Black Angus porterhouse steak – I figured that
should replenish my iron subsidies – and the taste of the very
rare meat was deliciously carnal. Just like the Wu-Tang Clan,
baby, I like it raw.

For dessert we had a selection of naughty little sweets the
menu listed as 'Sensual', a suggestion we needed like a hole
in the head. Underneath the table I'd had my bare foot on
Ryu's crotch since the waiter put down our steak, and by this
point in the evening he was reduced to stuttering, his fangs
were so long. Yet we were enjoying our tantalizing wait.
Knowing our bedroom was ready for us upstairs but that we
were going to hold off, just for now, was as much an aphro-
disiac as the oysters had been.

After we'd finished dessert, and our port, and each quaffed
our little demitasse of espresso, I very deliberately folded up
my napkin and slipped my foot back into my shoe. I stood,
Ryu watching me, and leaned over to whisper in his ear. He
nodded.

I left him there, in the restaurant, to go up to our room. I
very calmly pulled out my prize from where it waited, in
secret, in a pocket of my duffel bag. I shook it out, and then
draped it gently from a hanger. I took it into the bathroom
with me, hanging it so that the steam from my shower would
take out the few wrinkles it had collected during its stay in
my bag.

After I'd bathed and refreshed my makeup, I pulled the
red satin nightgown over my head. Looking at myself in the
mirror, I couldn't help but smile. Grizzie had done me more
than proud, she'd done me *fabulous*. The gown fit like a glove
in all the right places.

I brushed out my hair before opening the bathroom door. The lights were out in the main room, and it took my eyes a moment to adjust to the dark. But then my vision focused, and I could see Ryu sitting, still as a statue, on the sofa. He had kicked away the ottoman, so that it was up against the end of the bed. His hands were steepled in front of his face, but I could see he was watching me intently.

Without speaking, he held out his hand toward me.

I moved forward slowly, the pulse of my blood echoing in my ears. In the darkness of the luxurious hotel room, with Ryu so still and quiet, I was suddenly nervous. It was like this was the first night we'd spent together – everything that had become familiar felt new and strange.

Taking my hand, he pressed my palm to his lips, making me quiver with anticipation. Then he took my hips in his hands and leaned forward to inhale my scent, slowly raising his golden eyes to mine. I'd never seen anything so sexy in my life. *He's got more moves than MC Hammer*, my mordant inner voice observed.

He stroked his hands down my hips, enjoying the cool satin touch of the fabric as much as I did. Then he pulled me to him so that I lay on my back, over his thighs, with my bum fitted snugly in his lap as he cradled me in his strong arms.

He used his free hand to stroke my side – first down my ribs, and then over my breasts and along my stomach. His eyes followed his trailing fingers. When he finally spoke, his voice was husky with desire.

'This is how your life should be,' he said, his eyes gazing into mine. 'You should be dressed in satin . . .' He ran a finger over my lips, which parted under his touch. '. . . pampered . . .' he murmured, as I nibbled on his finger. '. . . loved,' he concluded, pulling me toward him for a kiss.

The emotions I felt hearing those words could not have been more conflicted if they'd been born on opposite sides of the Berlin Wall. Most brutal was the wave of guilt that swept over me. I *had* been loved in my life, and *really* loved, at that. What Jason and I had shared was far more profound than what I had with Ryu, no matter how sexually intense our relationship was. I never doubted that for a minute.

But on the heels of that guilt came a seductive voice that spoke to me of *circumstances*. I'd been so defined by the circumstances of my life – by my mother's disappearance, by my father's illness, by Jason's death.

Do you really *know what you want?* the voice whispered, ingratiating itself over the guilt.

I was deeply disturbed by that voice. I knew that the things that had happened to me were pretty extreme. I certainly resented how those things had impinged on my day-to-day existence. I hated how everybody disparaged my mother, how everybody thought I was crazy, and how we stayed in Rockabill despite everything. But I never doubted *myself*. I'd always felt I knew who I was and what I wanted, even if I knew that having those things meant I had to take shit from the likes of Linda and Stuart. Even discovering I was part seal hadn't really rocked my boat much.

But clasped in Ryu's arms, I began to question whether or not I had any clue about the things I'd taken for granted regarding myself, my life, and my motivations.

Maybe you just never knew what was really out there, available to you, the cunning voice whispered.

Be quiet! I thought, pushing the voice out of my head with an almost physical effort.

Helping me to silence the voice was Ryu, who seemed entirely unaware of my internal turmoil. He was busy exploring the exact parameters of my gown, running his hand up my bare leg where he had access through the nightgown's generous slit, then running his hand back down my other leg, over the soft fabric. *Even if you don't know what* you *want*, I observed, *he certainly does.*

And I want what he's having, my libido demanded, petulantly.

Stilling my chorus of inner voices, I raised my face to his lips. His kisses were deceptively gentle despite his flagrant desire.

I deepened my own kisses, letting him know I was as ready as he was. He adjusted his arm so that he could lift me up, single-handedly, using his preternatural strength to keep his other hand free. Not that it hadn't found something to keep itself occupied, to which my almost incessant moaning attested.

Ryu set me down on my knees on the ottoman, facing the bed. Standing behind me, he very slowly pulled my red nightgown over my head. He ran his hands down my arms, his lips suckling my ear lobe, to place my palms on the edge of the mattress. The air shivered about me as I waited, hearing him from behind me as he shed his own clothing. He took his time.

I heard rustling, and then a condom was floating in front of my face. I smiled, and nodded. Right on cue came Ryu's martyred sigh, but I heard him rip open the package.

When he was finished, he ran his hands down my body, from neck to knee, stopping gently to knead, then kiss, each round cheek of my bottom in its turn. Then I felt his body press against mine as he knelt behind me on the ottoman, wrapping his arms around me, his hands again finding my breasts.

I sighed, pressing back against him, his lips locked on the nape of my neck. He was breathing heavily and I could feel

him, hard and insistent, pushing between my legs. He let go
of my breasts to press one hand against my stomach, drawing
my hips nearer to his, while the fingers of his other hand
slipped inside of me. I hissed with pleasure as he stroked me
relentlessly; he wasn't playing around anymore. Just before
I came, he paused, withdrawing his hand to pull my upper
body around so that my neck was exposed. Then his fingers
were back where they belonged and, as my orgasm thundered
through me, I felt the sharp prick of his fangs. The pleasure
was so intense that everything went black for a split second.
When I swam back to full consciousness, Ryu had pushed
into me from behind, stoking the fires of my passion for a
second time.

Hours later, when we finally called it quits, we were both
too tired for one last bath. More's the pity, that.

CHAPTER SIXTEEN

'Is that it?' I asked, incredulously, staring up at the gigantic, but otherwise utterly banal, McMansion.

We'd left the hotel midafternoon that day and driven the few hours north to where the Alfar Compound was located. It was out in the middle of nowhere – we'd driven for about forty-five minutes without seeing a single sign of inhuman habitation before I caught my first glimpse of a very high privacy fence topped with both barbed wire *and* spikes. After what felt like an insanely long drive around the intimidating barrier, we'd finally pulled up to a heavy-duty security gate. Ryu had talked briefly into a camera, and the gates had creaked open. There was a long winding drive through heavily forested grounds before we pulled up in front of *this*: a house that, except for its gargantuan scale, could have been located in any recent suburban development.

Ryu looked at me like I was crazy, and then barked out his funny laugh.

'Oops,' he said. 'I forgot,' as he passed a hand in front of my eyes, muttering something under his breath.

My vision wobbled and I blinked. For a terrifying few

seconds my eyes simply wouldn't focus, but when my sight finally cleared, everything had changed.

In place of the McMansion stood a construction that looked like the product of a creative collaboration between Walt Disney, Tolkien, and M.C. Escher. The overwhelming effect of the building in front of me was one of *size*: it was both sprawling and very tall. But there was also something unreal about it – something about the angles, or the proportions, or how everything fit together that defied logic.

I shook my head, trying to focus on the details of the building. It consisted of dozens of variously sized towers that were connected by either large halls or open-air walkways. Overall, it was built of soft gray stone, although quite a few of the towers appeared pink in the midafternoon sun. The various roofs were, for the most part, the greenish bronze of aged copper or made up of clear panes of glass. But there were individual towers or halls that appeared to be slated or thatched. And there was one squat but very tall tower that looked like it was woven together of trees. Steep stone stairs led up to the main entrance, which was fronted by a formidable-looking pair of oak and iron doors.

I took a deep breath, feeling my brain quite literally adjusting to the vision in front of me. *I think it's giving me a headache*, I thought, *but it* is *beautiful*.

'There's a perpetual glamour on the Compound,' Ryu explained. 'Because you are so untrained, and it's so powerful, you were affected. But from now on you'll see everything truly.'

I had a feeling he was being optimistic, but I managed to smile at him nonetheless. I was extremely nervous, and my feet were already killing me. I was wearing the black trousers outfit Iris had picked for me – high heels, boobie belt, and all. I'd been practicing walking in the heels around the hotel, while Ryu slept, and I didn't think I was in danger of spontaneously tipping over anymore. But neither was I traipsing about like Sarah Jessica Parker.

Perhaps I will never learn to traipse, I'd decided.

'How can this exist out here?' I asked, trying to take in the sheer scale of the sight before me. 'How did they build it without anybody noticing?'

Ryu laughed again, putting an arm around my waist. 'This Compound has been here since before humans came to exist on earth, let alone in Canada,' he explained. 'Through human migrations, invasions, wars, and even urban sprawl it has endured, safe behind its walls. Not even Starbucks has been able to find it.'

Ryu smiled at me encouragingly and took my elbow to lead me up the stairs but I resisted. Before I went in, I needed to know something that had been lurking in the back of my mind since I'd first been chased by Anyan into my cove and found out the truth about my heritage.

'My mother?' I asked, my voice raw even to my own ears as I finally articulated the question that had been burning me up since Ryu had decided on this trip. 'Will I see her?'

Ryu paused, turning to face me. He brushed my bangs away from my eyes with gentle fingers.

'The chances are slim,' he admitted, unsure of how I would react. 'Selkies are not normally a part of Court life. Their world is the sea. We land lubbers only confuse them.'

My eyes closed as he said those words. If I was honest with myself, I didn't know if I felt relief or sadness. Part of me would give anything to see my mother again, and meeting Nell, Anyan, and Ryu – and learning the truth about myself – had made it seem like that might just be a possibility. But another part of me was still so *angry* with her – an anger I tried to deny, but was present nonetheless.

Ryu, bless him, merely waited quietly while I recovered myself. Opening my eyes, I tried to force a smile that wouldn't come.

'Well, I guess she couldn't have known I was going to be here,' I said, a bitter edge to my voice. 'After all, she's apparently been in bad reception areas for the past twenty years.'

Ryu pulled me toward him in a long hug, a gesture that found me suddenly fighting back tears. We stood like that for a good few minutes before his voice rumbled through his chest into my ear.

'Jane, I know your mother's leaving was incredibly difficult for you. And I know that nothing I say will change that. But the thing about selkies is that they need the sea as humans need sunlight.' He pulled back slightly, lifting my chin so I'd meet his eyes. 'A mere six years of having your mother with you was nowhere near enough time,' he continued, choosing his words with care. 'But for her to have lived six years outside of the ocean must have been a tremendous strain. I know that can't make your pain go away, or make her loss easier.' I'd never seen Ryu struggle for words, but he was struggling now. He shook his head, as if giving up. 'But she must have loved you and your father very much to have survived on land for that long, even with the sea right there. I want you to know that,' he finished awkwardly, waiting for my reply. I leaned my forehead against his chest, letting his strength support me for a minute while I digested what he'd said. Then I reached up to kiss the tender little indentation where his clavicles met, and I put my arm through his. Galvanized by his words, I was as ready as I'd ever be.

This time when he drew me toward the steep ascent separating us from the intricately decorated and incredibly imposing front entrance, I followed willingly. I reminded myself to breathe, as we climbed, glad that I'd had the foresight to swathe my heels in Band-Aids. If I survived this weekend in one piece it'd be a pleasant surprise; if my feet survived these shoes, it'd be a miracle.

The doors swept open before us as we walked into a beautiful front hall. I was trying to take everything in, but it was too much. There was so much *light* that it overwhelmed my first impressions. My eyes were dazzled; little flickering mage lights and enormous, man-sized candles vied with each other for dominance, while the vaulted ceiling itself appeared to be glowing as if, rather than a dreary November day, a brilliant summer sun was shining through the skylights. My vision was once again on the defensive, struggling to adjust, while Ryu led me forward into the depths of the Compound.

Another imposing set of doors – although these were more delicate, less obviously defensive – separated us from our goal. And now that my eyes had gotten used to the light, I could see why it was so blinding. The front hall of the Compound was built entirely of white marble and mirrors – there wasn't a single drop of color except for four brilliant mosaics. Two were on either side wall and two flanked the very grand interior doors on the central wall. One was a green leaf, one a bright lick of flame, one a quivering drop of water, and the last a cleverly composed gust of wind. *The four elements*, I thought, peering around to admire the artistry involved in their creation.

We hadn't yet seen a single soul. Nevertheless, I knew we were being watched. I could feel eyes on me as manifestly as if they were fingers brushing against my skin. My spine stiffened, pulling my small frame tight and pushing my shoulders back. My chin lifted defiantly and I saw Ryu glance at me approvingly, his golden eyes narrowed with anticipation.

As we strode the last few paces to the inner doors, they swung open and I caught my first glimpse of the Alfar Court.

All eyes were upon us as, to my surprise, our arrival was announced.

'Ryu Baobhan Sith, Investigator,' a sonorous voice intoned. 'Accompanied by Jane True.'

Ryu squeezed my elbow as I faltered, guiding me down the center of the long room toward what I could now see was a dais with two thrones. The beings sitting on those thrones pulsed with a power so tangible that I had to walk more purposefully – I was actually being physically repulsed by their strength.

In my peripheral vision, I caught glimpses of the other members of the Court. They were clustered about in small groups, some watching our procession with curiosity, others oblivious to anything except their own conversation. I couldn't let myself be distracted – I was really having to concentrate on moving forward – but it was difficult to ignore the dazzling suggestions of color, flesh, scales, and fur tempting my gaze.

And you were worried the belt was overkill, my brain snickered, as I caught a glimpse of a voluptuous female form clad in very revealing and vaguely belly dancer-esque garb. Her tummy wobbled invitingly as she giggled, and I nearly veered off our carpeted path toward her. *Something tells me that one is a succubus. And I wonder what else is here*, I thought, my mental voice colored with an admixture of apprehension and anticipation.

As we neared the dais, Ryu dropped into a low bow beside me. Unsure of what to do, I mimicked his bow. Sensing him straighten, I followed suit.

The beings before me were as cold, still, and perfect as marble. No one would ever mistake them for humans. But, except for their obvious beauty and preternatural calm, they weren't overtly odd. They were smaller than I had expected, although they were seated so it was hard to tell exactly how tall they were. I think I'd assumed they'd be giants.

We waited, their gaze heavy upon us, for what felt like forever. Finally, they spoke in unison, greeting first Ryu and then me. Their voices were low and I shivered at the power pulsing through their tone.

Ryu bowed again, so I went ahead and did the same, wondering if this was what church was like. The bowing made my belt cut into my stomach, so I hoped there wasn't going to be much more genuflection involved in tonight's activities.

I started, ever so slightly, as their heavy gaze swiveled from Ryu toward me. The woman spoke, alone, this time. 'Jane,' echoed her strange, grave voice. She held her hand out toward me and I stepped forward to take it in mine, having no idea what to do with it once it was in my grasp. To my surprise, she shook, and after a second I shook back. We stood there shaking hands for at least half a minute, like two executives closing a deal.

'Is this not correct human behavior for a greeting?' she asked, smiling at me kindly.

'Oh, right, um, yes. It is, actually, ma'am,' I stammered, totally at a loss for how to act.

She turned to her mate, unhurriedly. 'She is sweet, Orin. Do you not think so?'

The male version of the woman turned his pale silver-eyed gaze toward me and I only just managed to stop myself trembling. The queen still had a hold of my hand, after all, and shuddering at the sight of her man was probably not the most tactful response.

He looked me up and down, his expression unchanged. 'Lovely, my queen,' he responded, eventually. His head swiveled slowly back to its original position and I nearly smirked. *They're not what I'd call hasty,* I thought, as I

watched the queen take about five whole seconds to blink
her heavily lashed eyes.

She finally let go of my hand, and her eyes traveled
slowly back to Ryu. 'You have caught yourself a prize,
youngling,' she told him, her voice languorous. 'She is so
very human, and yet so open to the elements. You must be
feeding well.'

My eyes bulged as I frowned at Ryu, who looked suddenly
uncomfortable. His jaw worked as he tried to come up with
some sort of response, until he finally gave up and nodded.
'Yes, my queen.'

I'll give you a good feeding tonight, you turd, I thought,
furious at the queen's casual reference to my caloric value.
Am I just the supernatural version of an IHOP? I wondered.
Cheap, cheerful, and complete with a side of pancakes?

'We have given you your usual quarters,' the queen told
Ryu. 'Enjoy your time with us, Jane,' she said, her eyes again
meeting mine. 'We welcome you as family.'

'Thank you, ma'am,' I managed to respond, while I thought
something rude about the Addams Family.

Ryu and I bowed again, and he took my arm to lead me
away from the dais. It was only then that I noticed the figure
standing well behind the king and queen, partially hidden as
he was by the curtained alcove in which he stood. He had
the same silvery eyes as the Alfar monarchs, and the same
silvery hair. But whereas theirs was long, his was cut short
and combed forward like Caesar's. The way he stared at me
gave me a bad case of the screaming meemies. Unlike the
emotionless, almost unseeing, gaze of Orin, this creature
looked at me with eyes full of an emotion I knew well from
long experience: contempt. A shiver trailed up my spine and
I moved my hand to Ryu's, forgetting for a second that I was
miffed with him. His hand squeezed mine, encouragingly,

and I managed a modicum of dignity as we walked back towards the main entrance.

All in all, and except for Mister Crazy Eyes behind the throne, I think that went rather well, I thought, proud of myself for bearing up under the pressure of being introduced into this utterly foreign Court.

You're gonna get through this, I thought, suddenly feeling a wash of calm settle over me. *It's going to be okay.*

And so, of course, my feet chose that moment to get tangled on a little bump in the carpet. I tripped, hard, nearly wiping out. It was only the fact that Ryu threw himself in front of me to catch me that I stayed upright. He was on one knee, steadying me, and I was almost aloft in his powerful arms.

If we'd gotten only a smattering of attention on our walk in, all eyes were upon us now.

For a split second, I had the wild idea to tell Ryu to go ahead and hold me over his head, like Johnny does Baby in the climax of *Dirty Dancing*, but I managed to keep a lid on that suggestion.

With as much grace as I could muster, I withdrew from Ryu's grasp. He was trying with all his might not to voice his mirth, but laughter was sparkling in his eyes. I shot him a dirty look, which very obviously did nothing to quell his amusement, although he did manage to appear the slightest bit sheepish as he stood.

I held my head up high as we traversed the short distance between ourselves and the inner doors. Ryu managed to keep it together until they clanged shut, but then his sharp laugh boomed out into the empty entry hall.

'You are so in trouble, buddy,' I started, as he looked up at me.

He was laughing so hard he was nearly crying, and I

couldn't help it. I started giggling, and the next thing I knew I was doubled over, laughing as hard as he was.

'Oh, Jane,' he laughed, picking me up and carrying me toward one of the myriad stairways cutting through the hall. 'You really are precious.' He was still laughing, but there was the slightest hint of fang showing.

I nestled against his chest, suddenly tired. I yawned and he looked down at me.

'Wake up, Jane,' he gently admonished. 'The night's hardly even begun.'

I'd had a funny feeling he was going to say that. I sighed, and tried to gather up my strength for the rest of the evening.

You can handle anything they throw at you, Jane True, I told myself.

As long as you take off those stupid fucking shoes.

CHAPTER SEVENTEEN

A dryad did my makeup, and all I can say is Bobbi Brown, watch out. I looked *hot*. I'd asked if she could do smoky eyes, and if I'd managed 'slightly hazy' she achieved 'smoke, wind, and fire'.

That I was asking a creature I'd heretofore only studied in Mythology 101 to give me smoky eyes didn't really faze me. I had discovered that instead of being shocked or afraid of Ryu's world, I reveled in the weird. I was suddenly an utterly average wall flower in an imaginarium of the bizarre. It was a wholly satisfying treat for me to feel suddenly . . . banal.

'You look lovely, Jane,' Elspeth breathed, as she adjusted my bangs slightly. Elspeth had been introduced to me as my 'personal attendant', which *was* something I couldn't get over. I was more fazed to have a maid than I was that she was a dryad. I wasn't really sure if I was in fairy land or turn-of-the-century New York. I felt like Lily Bart, and I wondered if I would have to tip Elspeth with my winnings from that evening's bridge. But considering this lady's maid lived in a tree, I doubted her personal expenses were very large.

I was dressed, again, in the red wrap dress. Luckily, I'd managed not to drool on it at dinner last night. I wanted to save my kimono dress for tomorrow, and from there I'd figure out what to wear on our last evening in the Compound. I hoped that the supernatural folk did things like humans and that Thursday would be slightly less dressy than Friday, although that left formal attire for Saturday. But for all I knew they would have a Hawaiian-style luau on Saturday, complete with leis and roasted pig. Picturing the king in a Hawaiian shirt over some swim trunks made me giggle. And then I pictured him as a Speedos man and all laughter ceased.

Elspeth stood me up to adjust the wrap's sash and led me to the mirror. My jaw dropped, my mouth curling into a silent 'o' at the sight of the woman reflected back at me. I was gorgeous. And it wasn't just the makeup or the dress – it was like that new Jane I'd always dreamed about was suddenly staring back at me. This Jane stood tall and proud, no longer hiding. Elspeth had put my hair up in a twist, and I'd let her trim my bangs a bit. So nothing concealed my eyes, something I would normally have been horribly self-conscious about. But this Jane's dark gaze looked sexy and exotic, not weird or crazy.

For a second, I nearly panicked. *This isn't me*, I thought, staring at the confident young woman in the mirror.

Exactly, I realized. *This isn't you. And it's fucking awesome . . . So suck it up and* enjoy *yourself.*

I had just turned around to check out my own ass when Ryu walked in. He was also wearing the same suit he'd worn the other night, and he looked just as handsome.

'Great minds, and all that.' He grinned, watching as Elspeth finished fussing. She smiled at me and whispered, 'Go forth, with pride,' which I assumed was a tree's way of saying, 'Knock 'em dead.' I appreciated her kind words, as well as her efforts, and gave her a little hug.

She left, leaving Ryu and me to stare at each other. He was looking *pretty* foxy so I wasn't really able to be too angry with him, but the Queen's words had still stung.

'Jane,' he said, eventually. 'About what Morrigan said—'

'About me being the equivalent of a power bar?' I finished, dryly.

'Yes,' he said, coming over to put his hands on my hips. He looked down into my eyes, pulling his sincerest face. 'I have to admit you are quite a mouthful,' he said, and it was such a sexy thing to say that part of me was actively promoting I give him a mouthful right then and there, while the other part of me was totally pissed off for being so easily manipulated. 'But,' he continued, 'that's just it. You *are* everything your blood promises. Throughout our time together you have been strong, adaptive, and heady; your presence fills a room, invades my thoughts.' I saw some fang as he leaned down to kiss me, punctuating his sentence. 'You're already amazing and my mind reels at your potential. I see you as an example of our kind's future and to me that is as exciting as your blood, your body,' he finished, running his hands up my arms to cup my face, his kiss deepening.

I sank into his arms, cooing happily, until we were interrupted by the sound of my stomach booming its protest through the room like a clap of thunder. The vampire started and I sighed, drooping in Ryu's embrace. I have an exceptional talent for the ruining of moments.

My lover straightened up, looking both amused and slightly miffed. 'Hungry?' he inquired.

'Of course.' I grinned at him, ruefully. 'Do you have to ask?'

'Well, let's go down and get you something to eat. I need to keep my little power bar packed with nutrients.'

I considered threatening him with a good spanking for

that comment. But I was fairly certain that he'd say yes, meaning I'd never get dinner. And I, too, have my priorities.

Luckily, we went in a side door this time – I could not have borne another walk of shame down that long aisle. A few beings smiled when they saw me, but overall everyone was being very circumspect about my near face-plant, for which I was grateful.

We had come in through a door that emerged about midway through the throne room, and Ryu took a moment to look around, as if planning his next move. I took advantage of my chance to rubberneck, and man, did I get an eyeful. The room itself was relatively plain. There was the dreaded central aisle, carpeted by its rich red runner, but the rest of the floor and the walls were all the same gray stone. Many huge pillars supported the cathedral-like ceiling, which was made of glass. There were no other windows in the great hall.

If the room was unadorned, however, its inhabitants more than made up for that. To our right, and nearest to the throne, there seemed to be quite a few beings similar to the king and queen. They all exhibited the same uncanny tranquility and were equally colorless, vibrating with power at the same time that they displayed a curious lack of vitality. I assumed they were all Alfar.

Intermixed with the Alfar were some creatures I recognized, or at least thought I recognized, and others that were a complete mystery to me. The succubi and their male counterparts, the incubi, were easy. They were the ones that made me reach to undo my wrap the minute they looked at me. But other than their extreme powers of seduction, they came in all shapes and sizes. Iris was admittedly gorgeous, but not all the rest of her kin were so stunning. In fact, some were downright average in appearance. And yet they were all captivating. They bore themselves with such confidence, exuding an air of sexual frankness, that it almost transcended charisma. And I had the feeling that their powers of attraction could only partially be attributed to magic.

I was, however, mystified by the apparent predilection for vaguely piratical mustachios among the incubi, but I guess there is no accounting for taste. I do enjoy a good 'mustache ride' joke, however, and the naughty half of my brain was merrily riffing away.

Meanwhile, towering over everyone else, their mucus-weeping eyes coldly assessing those around them, were goblins galore. 'Why all the goblins?' I asked Ryu, on the down low.

'They're sort of our community's version of white-collar workers: doctors, lawyers, accountants, and stockbrokers. They're tremendously intelligent and curious beings, and they're especially good at understanding the intricacies of human society. I think it's that they appreciate a good bureaucracy. Give a goblin a thick sheaf of paperwork, to be completed in triplicate, and you've made yourself a friend for life.'

'And are they giants?' I hissed, nodding behind us toward an absolutely enormous and incredibly ugly pair of creatures that were guarding the doors we were standing in front of, and, I now noticed, seemed to be on guard duty throughout the room.

'No,' Ryu said, his eyes surreptitiously still roving around the room as he patently overacted engaging in conversation with me. He was really scanning the crowd, looking for someone. 'Giants are extinct. They were killed off by humans, believe it or not.' He nodded when I made a 'huh?' face. 'Giants traded all of their offensive powers for their huge size and a few strong defensive shields to block elemental attacks.

They never thought they'd have to contend with teeny-tiny spears. Early hominids hunted giants as they later did mammoths.' He shook his head, sadly. 'It was a lesson for us all.'

'So, what are those big guard thingies?' I prompted him. They were enormous and sort of *knotty*. If I hadn't already met a dryad and discovered her to be almost human outside of her strange suppleness, I would have thought that the guards were tree spirits. But on further consideration, maybe they were more knobbly than knotty. They were fleshy and incredibly ugly – kind of the way I would imagine a troll to be.

Careful, Jane, I thought. *Or you'll offend an actual troll. They're bound to be here, somewhere.*

'Spriggans,' Ryu informed me. 'They're mercenaries, really. But some are loyal to the Alfar – or so they claim. They're rumored to be the only surviving progeny of giants, but I think that's just PR. Oh, and watch your handbag and jewelry around them. They're compulsive thieves, like magpies. Only spriggans will chop your head off if you try to get your stuff back. Whereas magpies just squawk.'

I giggled, but pressed on. 'Are there any trolls?'

'Nah, they stick to their caves, luckily. Since they bathe in their own feces.'

I gave Ryu a horrified look, and it was his turn to giggle, only his giggle sounded like a Pomeranian choking. Which only set me off again.

When we'd composed ourselves, he turned to me and ran his hands over my hips, smoothing down my dress. He took a moment to fidget with the front of my wrap, sneaking a caress of my breasts. I leaned into his touch and was rewarded with a little fang. Ryu came toward me, not kissing me, just pressing his forehead against mine and taking a deep breath. Then he straightened, and I could tell he was preparing to move.

'Are you ready to mingle?' he asked.

'No,' I said, completely serious.

'Good. Just follow me and do what I do. And no shaking hands. Don't touch *anybody* unless I say it's okay.'

I grimaced internally. I was more than happy remaining on the periphery of the great hall, but Ryu was not a peripheral sort of guy. Slipping my arm through his, he led me into the room, exchanging greetings with various creatures as we passed.

The good thing about moving forward was that now I could see we were heading toward another set of doors on the opposite side of the hall, through which I caught a glimpse of heavily laden dining tables. My stomach had long since resorted to a quiet war of attrition, eating away at itself rather painfully, but it wakened with a new fury when I caught a glimpse of the food.

Dinner, however, would have to wait. Ryu was walking across the room at a very stately pace, exchanging greetings with various beings. They all greeted him using the full title with which he'd been introduced. I wondered if he used Baobhan Sith all the time as his last name, and I asked as much when I had the chance.

'No. For formal identification we go by our first name and our faction. I don't mind being called a vampire, but it pisses some of us off. As for last names, we don't use them, usually. For those of us who live among humans, like I said, we have made-up ones. Goblins have gotten rather attached to theirs since it makes filing easier. But otherwise we just use our factions.' He thought for a moment. 'Last names are a very human thing, when you think about it. They imply possession, ownership, property rights, all of that. We don't own each other, even when we're bonded, nor do we own our children if we're lucky enough to have any. And in our world, if

you can't defend what is yours, someone takes it from you.'
He shrugged, a *c'est la vie* sort of gesture.

I frowned, again struck by the paradoxes of his society. On
the one hand, there were aspects of this world that I was coming
to admire. There was an openness, a lack of embarrassment or
amour propre, that I appreciated. But there was this constant
undertone of brutality that made me shudder to contemplate.

*As if humans are really any different. Nasty, brutish, short,
and all that jazz*, I thought.

But at least we try, I argued with myself.

*Who tries? You try, your dad tries, average people try. And
for their attempts at goodness, average people are mugged
by strangers, molested by predatory uncles, massacred by
their own governments. At least here there's no pretense.*

I was so wrapped up in my own thoughts that I didn't
realize Ryu had introduced me to somebody until he covertly
elbowed me in the ribs. I looked up to see this absolutely
gorgeous being in front of me. He reminded me of David
Bowie in his Ziggy Stardust days: slender and androgynous.
An enormous, fiery coiffure swept up to a point about a foot
and a half above his head, and he was clad in what looked
like flames. His eyes were auburn and slitted like a cat's. He
was beautiful, and I reached out a hand without even thinking.

Ryu grabbed my wrist with a hiss, and I saw a look of
genuine fear on his face. The being had sprung back, out of
my reach, and I blinked. *Oh yeah*, I remembered, *I'm not
supposed to touch*. And then I realized why.

The hair that looked so fiery and the clothing that looked
like flames were actually just that – the being was swathed
in a molten sheath of fire.

'Chester is an ifrit, darling.' Ryu's voice was calm despite
the scare I'd given him. 'He's a fire elemental. No handshakes
allowed.'

The being gave me a wry smile. 'More's the pity,' he said, looking me up and down. I blushed, suddenly shy.

'Yes, well, it was good to see you again, Chester. I hope your stock portfolio recovers.' Ryu paused, and I could tell he was struggling to contain something. He lost. 'Don't get burned again,' he quipped, chuckling helplessly. Both the ifrit and I rolled our eyes, and the being bowed slightly to me and stalked off.

'I don't know what's worse – your joke or the fact that that amazing creature is named Chester.'

Ryu sighed. 'I can't help it. Ifrits are too easy. And I thought my joke was on fire.' He chortled, and I just shook my head.

'Right, sorry.' He kissed my palm. '*You*, meanwhile, don't get to touch. I like my women like I like my steak – nice and rare. So try not to flambé yourself this weekend.'

I nodded solemnly, as I caught sight of an adorable fat man. He had a shaved head and his Buddha-like cheeks were split by an endearing grin. He had no shirt and was wearing pantaloons and curly-toed shoes. My eyes widened, and I pointed. Before I could speak, Ryu sighed.

'Yes, that's a djinn, or a genie. But they're not what you think.' He steered me carefully away from the little group clustered around the djinn. I noticed they were all incubi and succubi. 'Wally only grants one kind of wish, and although that wish does involve some rubbing, it's not of his lamp. Which is rumored to be more of the standing floor than the desk variety.'

I grinned. 'So the enormous pantaloons—'

'Are as practical as they are fashion forward,' Ryu confirmed.

We were getting close to the doors separating us from the food, and my stomach urged me on with as much finesse as a jockey whipping his mount through the final furlongs of the race.

I had crept into the lead, trying to hasten our arrival at the dining hall, when I felt Ryu halt. I groaned inwardly but turned around, forcing a cordial smile. That smile was wiped from my face when I saw who had slowed our progress: the pale creature that had been standing behind the king and queen. And if I thought he was bad, the being currently lurking behind *him* made my skin crawl.

Ryu was introducing me, and I only just managed to contain my urge to step behind him for protection. While the short-haired Alfar wasn't oozing contempt as he had been before, I had long experience with interpreting various gradations of loathing. On a scale of one to ten, what lurked in his eyes was a definite eight and three-quarters. Maybe a nine.

'Jane, this is Jarl, Orin and Morrigan's second. Jarl, this is Jane True.'

'Enchanted,' Jarl said, lying his face off.

Fibber, I thought. 'Likewise,' I said.

My eyes flicked to the creature standing behind Jarl. It wasn't his personal style that alarmed me, although that was certainly intended to shock. He was dressed all in leather and shredded denim, with a towering blue Mohawk. He also sported a piercing in virtually every available inch of skin. His ears and eyebrows were lined with them, and he had what appeared to be steel tusks sprouting from above each lip. His cheeks sported three small spikes apiece, and there was another line of small spikes dotting his forehead, along with a very heavy-looking bull ring through his nose. His neck was laced with safety pins, like the kind worn by the evil guy in *Highlander*. But this dude wasn't trying to disguise any scars; he'd just poked dozens of holes in his neck for the hell of it.

One thing I would have expected to be pierced, yet wasn't, was the man's tongue. But that's because he didn't have a human's tongue – his was that of a snake, cloven tip and all. I nearly hollered when it flicked out at me.

And yet not even the tongue really bothered me – what got to me were his eyes. They were *dead* – pale as a corpse's and equally lifeless. They flicked over me and I shuddered. Any discomfort or trepidation I'd felt at seeing the other denizens of the Alfar Court vanished when this thing's eyes finally met mine. He didn't make me nervous, he scared the *shit* out of me.

I could swear I've seen him before, I thought, my mind racing. But that was stupid. I'd never fail to recognize somebody as markedly distinctive as this guy. *He'd stand out, just a bit, in Rockabill.*

Jarl watched me take in his companion, and I saw that he thoroughly enjoyed the fear I was doubtlessly radiating. Ryu was tense beside me, and I couldn't help but take a step closer to him, pressing myself to his side.

'Jimmu,' Jarl said, and I noticed that his voice was high and whiney, which made me feel slightly less terrified. For about two seconds, until I realized that 'Jimmu' was Mr Dead Eyes and that Jarl was attempting to introduce us. Personally, I'd rather be introduced to the four horseman of the apocalypse, all at once, at a swinger's party.

'. . . meet Jane,' Jarl finished, a small smirk playing at the corners of his lips.

He's a nasty piece of work, I observed, as Jimmu glided forward toward me.

And this one makes Jeffrey Dahmer seem like Mr Rogers, my brain concluded, as Jimmu bowed with a sinuous grace that made him that much creepier.

'Jimmu likes nothing better than to meet halflings,' Jarl droned. 'Don't you Jimmu?' Jimmu blinked lethargically and Jarl chuckled, running a hand over Jimmu's scalp under where the thick Mohawk began. I felt my stomach flip-flop, so freaked out that it forgot to be hungry.

Ryu put a protective arm about my shoulder. 'Well, it's always a pleasure, Jarl,' he said, briskly. 'But if you'll excuse us . . .' Ryu inclined his head toward the pair, and steered me away. I looked back over my shoulder, a choice I quickly regretted. Jarl was whispering something into Jimmu's ear, while the latter's eyes finally exhibited some emotion. The emotion was pure, unadulterated hatred. I quickened my pace, whipping my head around to stare sternly ahead.

'What was that *thing*?' I hissed, when we were safely through the dining hall doors.

'Which thing?' Ryu asked, balefully. '"Thing" accurately describes either of that pair.'

I shuddered, starting to tremble as my brain replayed the look Jimmu had given me. He made Stuart look like the president of my fan club.

'Either, both, whichever,' I babbled.

Ryu chafed his hands up and down my upper arms, as if to bolster my strength. 'Jimmu is a naga; they're two-formeds. Their second form is, appropriately enough, a serpent.' I nodded – that made sense. 'Jarl raised Jimmu and his nest-mates from the egg.' I pulled a face, but Ryu was clearly not joking. 'Jimmu was the first to hatch, so he's the strongest as well as the most bonded to Jarl. Nagas are like really deadly chickens – they bond to the first person they see when they emerge from their eggs. Anyway, Jarl claims to love his nagas like a father, but they're really his puppets. They do whatever he commands.' Ryu's voice was grim.

'As for Jarl, he is, as I said, Orin and Morrigan's second-in-command. He is Orin's brother – older by a few hundred years but less potent in strength.'

'And he obviously doesn't like me,' I added.

Ryu blanched. 'Jarl possesses little tolerance for humans,' Ryu explained in what I had a feeling was the understatement of the decade. 'And even less for halflings, I'm afraid.' He took a deep breath, as if preparing himself for something. 'Jane, there are beings in our world who resent halflings – some even hate them.' I tried not to roll my eyes. *No shit, Sherlock*, I thought, recalling the feel of Jimmu's and Jarl's eyes on me.

'Most of us will accept you, and many, like me, feel that you are as necessary for our survival as you are, quite simply, good for our existence.' He paused, thinking. 'Our kind need . . . shaking up. We need new blood, new ideas, new voices.' He smiled at me, running a finger across my cheek and over my lips. 'Especially when those voices come from lips as sweet as yours,' he finished, leaning forward for a kiss.

I knew he was trying to distract me, and it worked. I had a funny feeling this wouldn't be the last time the subject of my halfling status came up, but for now I let it drop. I was used to being despised and I was *hungry*. My stomach had recovered from its introduction to the Creepy Twins, and it had started doing something I can only compare to kicking me in the spine. My eyes looked appealingly at the food spread out only feet from us.

Ryu laughed, following my gaze. 'C'mon, Jane. I don't want you to starve to death,' he sighed. 'I think you only like me because I feed you.'

I had already grabbed a plate and was piling it high. But I spared a moment to turn back to him. 'Actually, I like you because you play my kiki like Jimi Hendrix played his guitar.' I grinned lasciviously at the shocked look he gave me, then laughed as his fangs ran out, warp speed. He reached a hand out for me, but I danced away, grabbing a drumstick as I moved.

I left him there, shaking his head, while I finished filling my plate. I knew I'd pay for that comment later, when we were alone.

At least I certainly hoped so.

CHAPTER EIGHTEEN

After I ate, I could barely keep my eyes open. We'd found an out of the way corner to chow down, and between the food and the stresses of the day I was nodding off like a narcoleptic. I was propped up against Ryu, who had a far-away look in his eyes. I think he was going over everything he'd seen today. I let him mull, until a particularly fierce yawn nearly popped my jaw off.

Ryu narrowed his eyes at me. 'You need to swim,' he declared.

'Hmm?' I asked, sleepily.

'You need to swim. Your reserves are low; you need access to water.'

What he said made sense. Instead of my normal four or five hours of sleep, I'd slept about seven the past two nights. Yet here I was, dead on my feet and it was only nine o'clock.

'There's a pool out back. It's like an artificial ocean, for when water elementals visit the Compound. The Alfar keep it charged. We can go now, if you like.'

I leaned my head against his shoulder, and he smoothed a hand over my hair. Part of me was enjoying just sitting here, supernatural-people watching. I had a full belly, a chair on which to rest my still-sore feet, and a handsome man massaging my neck. But the thought of water was *very* tempting, and after a minute more of soaking up Ryu's ministrations, I clambered to my feet.

'Are you sure there's nothing else you need to get done here tonight?' I asked.

Ryu frowned. 'No. Nyx doesn't seem to be in attendance, and I don't want to tip her off by asking about her. Nobody moves a muscle in this Compound without everybody else knowing. So we'll see if she's here tomorrow night, and if she's not we'll change plans.' He shrugged. 'In the meantime, we may as well enjoy ourselves.' He ostentatiously flexed his fingers. 'I need to get some practice time in, after all,' he said, arching an eyebrow at me. I felt a flush of heat in my groin at the same time as I managed a little laugh.

When he took my hand, I was more than happy to follow.

We took another side door and were greeted by a long passage strewn with variously sized and shaped doorways. Now that I was a little less dazed by the sheer magnitude of everything around me, I was soaking up more of the details. That said, if asked, I don't know if I could actually describe what I saw, since the décor in the Compound was unlike anything I'd ever seen. I can only describe it as what you'd get if you imagined time-traveling sorcerers with a penchant for antiquing trying to achieve a modernist look that incorporated natural materials. So basically, it was a complete hodge-podge of styles and yet it *was*, itself, a coherent style. It reminded me a little bit of the steampunk aesthetic of movies like *The League of Extraordinary Gentlemen* or *The Golden Compass*, rather than the cathedral-like elven cities of Peter Jackson's *Lord of the Rings* or the sleek minimalism of the vampire hidey-holes in *Blade*. And yet, although it was beautiful, there was a practical and lived-in feel to the Compound.

It certainly wasn't a human municipal building, and it was luxurious. Nonetheless, it was obviously designed to work for the creatures inhabiting it.

After walking for what felt like forever, we finally emerged into a beautifully cobbled courtyard. Large conifers lined the walls, and the cobblestones were different colors, forming a mosaic of a tree whose branches intertwined with its own roots. I recognized the symbol: a Celtic tree of life. *Who influenced whom?* I thought. *Did humans just forage ideas and symbols from the supes, or have humans had their own impact?* Thinking about the king and queen, and their paradoxical combination of power and lethargy, I was starting to understand how the latter was a distinct possibility.

We exited the courtyard through an ornate iron gate in one wall, and before us stretched a large faux-lagoon thingy, complete with waterfall. It was surrounded by lush vegetation, and there were various little nooks and crannies, some partially hidden, where there were shallow places to sit or lie down in the water. Suddenly, I realized what I was looking at.

'Ew, is this a sex grotto?' I asked Ryu. ''Cause that is so Hugh Hefner.' I wrinkled my nose. 'Gross.'

Ryu looked at me, feigning dignity. 'We do not have *sex grottos*,' he sniffed. 'This is a love lagoon. Or a petting pool. Or a fornication fountain. But never a *sex grotto*.'

I giggled, just as Ryu reached out and, with a flick of his nimble fingers, undid my wrap.

'Yowza,' I mumbled, as it fell open. He pushed my dress down off my shoulders, at the same time pulling me toward him for a kiss. In the next ten seconds my panties were around my ankles and my bra was unhooked. *This guy is good*, I admitted to myself, begrudgingly.

But so am I, I thought, as I wiggled free of both my clothes and his grasp to dive into the pool. *Catch me if you can!*

As soon as I hit the water, I gasped. If swimming in my ocean made me feel like I'd had a few espressos, this was the equivalent of shooting heroin. Power surged into me, erasing my weariness and sending heady waves of energy through my limbs. I also sucked in a mouthful of water, some of which went right down my windpipe.

I came up spluttering, gasping for air. Ryu was with me in a flash, holding me up till I could breathe.

'. . . so sorry,' he murmured. 'I should have warned you.'

I hacked and wheezed for another thirty seconds, and then everything went wonky as the world spun. Between my momentary lack of oxygen and the fact that the water's unnatural power was literally flooding my brain, I felt faint. No wonder I hadn't been drawn to the pool like I was to the ocean – this force was totally abnormal and insanely strong. Ryu carried me to the side of the pool and sat me down on the edge. Standing between my legs, he held me upright until the dizziness passed.

When I could finally open my eyes without seeing four of him, I leaned into Ryu. 'Wow,' I mumbled, still feeling the power arching up from my legs where my calves dangled in the water. '*That* is some good shit.'

Ryu laughed, holding me tight. 'Glad you're enjoying it,' he murmured into my ear.

'Now I know why people do crack,' I said, pulling back to look at him, wide-eyed. The pool was making me feel more than a little tipsy. 'I always thought, "Who does crack?" I mean, seriously, who wakes up and is like, "Hmm, I think today I'll try me some crack." I get why people do other drugs. But crack? Who does crack?' I looked at him, not blinking. 'This pool explains why people do crack. This pool *is* crack.' I finally blinked, hard, feeling like the top of my head was being lifted off and my brain replaced with ambrosia salad.

Ryu looked distinctly worried. 'Okay, Jane, I think you've had enough.' I giggled at him. Ryu was funny.

I admired him as he jumped out of the pool to my side. 'You're still wearing your clothes!' I informed him, in case he hadn't noticed. He'd taken off his jacket and shoes, but he was still wearing his trousers, shirt, and socks. His thin black shirt clung to his muscular chest. I craned my neck back to get a better look as he put his hands under my armpits to haul me upright and out of the water. Then he turned me around to hug me tight, as my feet dangled at his shins.

'You're *hot*, Ryu,' I murmured, as I stared into his lovely face. 'Seriously hot. And so I am going to tell you a secret.'

'A secret, huh?'

'Mm-hmm. I'm not really me right now, but don't tell anyone. Shhhh! It's just between the two of us . . .' I trailed off as I realized I was no longer in that amazing pool.

'I know, baby. It's the water. You'll feel better soon.'

That wasn't what I had meant, so I told him so. 'No, silly, I'm *really* not me. I'm the *other* Jane,' I whispered, conspiratorially. 'But she's way more fun than the real Jane, so we're going to roll with it.'

Ryu looked concerned for a second, but I'd moved on.

'Ryu, why aren't we swimming? Can't I swim a little more?' I cajoled. 'I like swimming.' Ryu set me gently on my feet, but the second he let go, I pinwheeled backward, nearly falling into the pool.

'Wheeeeeeeeeeeeeeeeeee!' I cried, as he lunged forward to grab me.

'You're strong, too,' I said, relaxing back into his arms. 'I like strong.'

'Yes, dear.' He grinned, pulling me forward so that I was on my own two feet, but he was careful still to support me. 'I'm sure you do.'

'I really do!' I declared, petulantly. 'And I like swimming. Why aren't we swimming?'

'I think you've had about enough swimming, for tonight,' he said, gently.

I thought hard. 'We can have sex in the pool,' I wheedled. 'Lots of sex!'

Ryu laughed. 'I know we can, darling.' He kissed my forehead. 'But for right now,' he said, picking me up to carry me toward the Compound, 'we're going upstairs to sleep.'

'Oh, poo,' I said. 'You're no fun. I bet the genie would take me swimming.'

'Now, you're just being naughty,' Ryu said, sticking his tongue out at me. I tried to grab it.

He laughed and gathered me even closer. I wound my arms around his neck and pressed my cheek to his. 'I like you, vampire man,' I whispered in his ear.

'I like you too, Jane True,' Ryu said, his voice husky.

I'd just gone in to give his edible little ear a nibble when a sharp voice cut through our intimacy like a scythe.

'Aww, how sweet. My cousin has himself a little pet.'

Ryu tensed, his grip around me tightening almost painfully.

'Ryu,' the nasal voice continued, 'put down your halfling and say hello.'

I winched my head around, trying to find the speaker. Her voice was mean and I didn't like being called a pet. *I'll give you a pet*, my ambrosia salad threatened.

'Nyx.' Ryu's voice was low. 'As always, a pleasure.'

I giggled. He was being sarcastic.

'What *did* you do to the girl?' Nyx asked. I had finally found her and was trying to get a good look. But she was upside down. No, I was upside down. No, I was looking at her from upside down. My head hurt.

'I didn't know you were so hard up that you had to drug them these days.'

'You're hilarious, *cousin*. Jane is just fine.'

'Yes,' I clarified. 'I'm *fine*.' Then I lowered my voice to hiss, 'Put me down' at Ryu.

'Are you sure?' he murmured. I nodded.

He set me gently on my feet, keeping a protective arm around my waist. I looked down.

Oh shit! 'I'm naked,' I whispered to him.

He nodded, the slightest smile breaking through his grim expression. But his eyes were still cold.

'It's so small,' the voice said, disparagingly. 'Like a little doll. I know you're barely past adolescence but I did think you were done playing with dolls, Ryu.'

I bristled, assessing the creature spouting off in front of me. She was tall – taller than Ryu by a few inches – and she had the rangy, muscular build of an aerobics instructor or modern dancer. Her features were small and sharp and her lips were thin, made thinner by being compressed into a tight little grimace that I think passed for a smile in her world. Her light-brown hair was short-cropped like Ryu's, but that was their only family resemblance. She was wearing a tight black minidress with black knee-high fuck-me boots. I guess she was good-looking, in a Gap model sort of way, but her attitude spoiled it.

'She's a total bitch,' I observed. *Did I just say that out loud?* my ambrosia salad speculated.

Ryu snorted, and the bitch looked at me sharply.

'What did you say, halfling?'

I thought for a moment. 'I just called you a bitch,' I eventually clarified.

She sputtered, staring.

'Because you really are,' I advised. 'You might want to work on that.'

Nyx was stalking toward us, and I realized she wasn't happy.

'I was just trying to be helpful,' I told Ryu, defensively. 'Nobody likes bitches.'

He put a hand firmly over my mouth and pushed me behind him. I shrugged and looked around for my dress.

'Nyx,' he warned, 'calm down and back off. We've got things to discuss.'

'Like how much I'm going to enjoy ripping off that little shit's head?'

I straightened up, but before I could open my mouth Ryu's hand was clamped back over my lips. I bit him. He winced, but he left his hand where it was.

'No one is ripping off any heads,' Ryu said, dryly. 'Leave Jane be; she's not herself.' He paused. 'And she's right, anyway. You are a bitch and you know it.'

Nyx's thin lips stretched as she deigned to laugh. 'What you call "bitch", I call "natural leader with a flair for intrigue". Maybe someday you'll understand that, *investigator*.'

Ryu had let me go and I'd spotted my dress. I tottered over to it, and wrapped it around me. The sash gave me some trouble, but I managed to beat it into submission and knot it securely.

I picked up my shoes, underpants, and bra and waited where I was for Ryu to finish questioning Nyx. I think I was starting to sober up. Either that or I was just too stoned to move.

'Yes, well,' Ryu persevered through his obvious irritation. 'That reminds me of why I'm so happy to see you. I wanted to ask you about something.' His voice was level, but his eyes gleamed with anticipation.

'Peter Jakes,' he said, finally, with the air of someone dropping a bomb.

We both waited.

The bomb fizzled, unexploded.

Nyx just smiled. 'Oh, you mean the halfling. He served me.' Ryu looked startled – he'd obviously been expecting some kind of subterfuge from Nyx. 'What do you want to know about him?' she queried, innocently.

Ryu recovered swiftly. 'Did you know he is dead?'

'Oh, yes, I'd heard through the grapevine. It's too bad, he had his uses. He was practically human and absolutely terrified of me, so he'd do in a pinch for a feeding.' Nyx looked over at me. 'You know how it's handy to always carry a packed lunch,' she said, eyeing me venomously.

I tried giving her the finger, but accidentally gave her three.

Ryu wasn't giving up, asking Nyx what Peter had been working on when he died.

'Oh,' she said, sweetly. 'I don't know. I'd loaned him to the Alfar. They asked to borrow his services and I'm nothing if not helpful.'

'What would the Alfar want with Jakes?' Ryu's voice betrayed his concern.

'Jarl has Orin convinced that there's something to studying halflings, and Jakes could identify halflings.' Nyx shrugged. 'Some of the higher-ups are growing concerned about our falling birth rates – they've apparently hit an all new low. I think that just means more opportunities for the rest of us, but some still bear a sentimental attachment to the young.'

'So, Jakes wasn't working for you, he was working for the Alfar,' Ryu clarified, and Nyx nodded.

'I don't know what they were doing, but yes, that's my story.' She smiled sweetly. 'And I'm sticking to it.'

Ryu frowned. I could tell he was disturbed by what Nyx had just told him. The female vampire stretched languidly, her muscles rippling under the tight fabric of her clothes.

'Well, it's my time to hunt,' she said. 'There's a hillbilly bar an hour from here that I enjoy terrorizing, if you want to leave your baby doll and come along for a real meal. Or maybe we could compromise and chase her around the Compound. She doesn't look very fast, but we could give her a head start.'

Ryu shook his head. 'You'll never change, Nyx. I realize that, even if no one else does.' He walked away from her, toward me. The ambrosia salad was about halfway converted back to brain matter, and it recognized that Nyx had been completely serious about hunting me. Which it didn't appreciate.

Ryu took my free hand, the one without the underwear and shoes, and led me back toward the gate.

'Is that a no, cousin?' Nyx called out behind us. 'Well, good night anyway. Enjoy your little mongrel girlfriend. Although how she can satisfy you is beyond me. I guess some of us have more sophisticated palates than others.'

We both ignored her. If there had been any doubts in my mind as to the status of halflings, Nyx had clarified them for me.

Her nasal voice echoed behind us as we walked across the little courtyard and into the Compound. Neither of us spoke until we were safe behind the doors of our shared rooms.

'I'm sorry,' Ryu murmured, pulling me close the minute the lock shot home.

'I know,' I said. 'It's not your fault.'

'But still, that was totally uncalled for. Which I guess is the definition of Nyx, really – "uncalled for".'

'Don't worry about it,' I said while shedding my wrap for the final time that night. I climbed into bed, my brain still buzzing but my body suddenly exhausted. 'I'm used to uncalled for,' I finished, thinking of Linda and Stuart.

Ryu stripped off his wet clothes and slipped into bed beside me. His skin was chilly, and I gasped as he wrapped himself around me for warmth.

'Sorry,' he mumbled. I forgave him.

I turned over so I was facing him, our noses nearly touching. 'That Jakes wasn't working for Nyx, it's not good, is it?' I asked, quietly.

Ryu's eyes closed. When they reopened, he sighed. 'No, it's not.'

I thought of my name on Peter's master list, underneath the others that had been crossed off. I turned back around, pressing myself up against Ryu's chest. He tightened his arms around me.

'Jane?' he asked, eventually.

'Yeah?'

'What did you mean when you said you weren't really you? That there were two Janes?'

I gulped. *Way to sound schizo, genius.*

'Oh, that? Nothing. Who knows what I meant.'

Ryu didn't push it, but his body, stiff behind mine, told me he wasn't happy with my response. So I snuggled back against him, pulling his hands up from my waist to cup my breasts.

'You'll stay here with me?' I murmured. 'Till I'm asleep?'

'Of course,' he murmured, relaxing against me as he kissed the nape of my neck.

Sleep came quickly that night, despite all that had happened – all that I'd seen. But my dreams were dark and I knew that, on the morrow, I would face an even greater challenge.

For I had no doubt the dawn would bring more Alfar intrigue and – worse yet – another pair of Iris's dreaded high heels.

CHAPTER NINETEEN

Standing on the very edge, I eyed the swimming pool with trepidation. I did *not* want a repeat of last night's performance. Starring as a crack whore for one night was enough. *Did I really offer Ryu sex for swimming?* I wondered, again. *Thank god I never tried drugs. I'm a public service announcement waiting to happen.*

I stretched my leg forward, balancing on the other, and started to dip my toe in before reconsidering: a toe might be too much. Instead, I sat down on the side of the pool, legs crossed beneath me. I cautiously extended my right hand toward the water. I'd start with a finger.

I'd fallen asleep for a few hours the night before, and then at about three in the morning my eyes had *pinged* open. If I'd been afraid of being hungover from my crack-pool experience, I needn't have been. I was completely awake and I felt like the Energizer bunny hooked up to a nuclear reactor. Luckily, Ryu was up reading and we managed to find ways to amuse ourselves. He was particularly keen to imitate my behavior after my dip in the Alfar pool, for which I had to discipline him thoroughly. Around six, he switched himself off and succumbed to catatonia, leaving me to fend for myself.

I read Ryu's book – Dostoevsky's *Notes from Underground* translated by Pevear and Volokhonsky. It's one of my all-time favorite reads and the translation was amazing, but my attention was so insanely focused I read it in half the time it should have taken me. Having exhausted Dostoevsky, I took a very long time in the bathroom, mud-masking and shaving and exfoliating and basically trying to kill as much time as possible. Which was difficult, since I was so energetic I was moving at light speed.

When I did emerge from my morning toilette, I was relieved to find Elspeth waiting for me in our little sitting room. She took me down to breakfast and showed me how to get to the swimming pool. My buzzing nerves appreciated the reprieve that her calm presence granted.

Eventually we'd ended up back at my room, and Elspeth had excused herself. I'd decided to put on my swimsuit and try out the crack-pool again, but carefully this time. And here I was.

My index finger hovered right above the surface of the water until, very slowly, I dipped it down so that the water came up to just above my nail. It was like jamming my finger in a light socket – power surged up from the pool, into my arm, and then coursed through my body. I withdrew my hand, feeling like I'd been struck by lightning in reverse. And kind of liking it.

I dipped my finger in again, then a third time. I laughed, feeling the slightest bit giddy but also enjoying the sensation the water gave me even though I had no idea what the feeling meant. I got how everything worked when I was swimming: the ocean filled me with power and I used that power to help me manipulate the ocean. There was a direct relational exchange I understood. But could I use that power outside of the water? I didn't see why not, in a theoretical sense, but imagining myself producing mage lights or whammying my friends and neighbors with a glamour struck me as ridiculous. I still thought of myself as, fundamentally, the same Jane True that had gone to work over a week ago not knowing anything about the world whose edge I was currently skirting.

Yet so much had happened so quickly and I knew I was not confronting any of it. I was just trying to bluff my way through without contemplating how my life was changing. Because I didn't want to think about that aspect of this past week – the fact that my life *would* be changed, but not in any way I could anticipate or control.

But what if it doesn't? my cynical self queried. *You're going back to Rockabill when this is over, to your dad and your friends and your life. And you know damned well that Ryu isn't going to give up the excitement of his life in Boston or here at Court to join you. So maybe you'll just go back home and nothing will have changed. You'll know this stuff is out here, somewhere, and you'll feel a little closer to Amy and a little more welcome at the Sty – but what happens if that's all you get? No membership card to a secret society or special access to a world of excitement, danger, and romance – just memories and some cute, but incredibly impractical, shoes.*

I thought about what I'd said to Ryu about there being two Janes. Was that how I imagined the rest of my life? One Jane for Rockabill, and one Jane for outside Rockabill? 'Cause *that* strategy sure as hell wasn't going to solve anything.

I frowned down at my reflection rippling on the surface of the water. *Here's an idea . . . don't go there*, I thought, as my body used my mental distraction to help itself to a fourth finger dip. My spine vibrated with energy.

I sighed. I really wanted to swim – to feel water on my limbs and to bury my worries in the monotony of physical exertion. But I knew I'd be back to reeling around like a drunken sailor if I dared get in that pool. So instead I stood up and wrapped my towel around my waist. I'd have to find something else to do for the next few hours.

I turned to go back through the little gate separating the pool from the courtyard, and I heard a rustling behind me. *Ryu?* I wondered, although he hadn't had enough downtime yet to be awake. *Probably Elspeth doing something considerate, like bringing me my clothes or a robe*, I decided. The dryad was like a mind reader – I'd not only woken up to find her waiting for me, but somehow she'd gotten ahold of what we'd worn last night and had it all cleaned. *I wonder who does the dry cleaning in this place? Magic brooms?* I turned to greet her.

But it wasn't Elspeth. Instead of the somewhat woody friendliness of my personal tree spirit, there loomed Jimmu. He stood silently across the pool from me, having emerged from what I could now see was a little path bisecting the dense tropical vegetation surrounding the grotto. He was only wearing a pair of black board shorts and he must have been working out. He glistened with sweat and piercings, including quite a few more that his shirtless state revealed. His Mohawk had fallen down to drip greasily around his face.

Let's not forget the sword he's carrying, my inner voice interrupted. At the sight of that sword, I wanted to flee but I found myself rooted to the spot.

We stood like that, staring at one another, for at least thirty seconds. I think he was as surprised to see me as I was to see him. The sword was sheathed, thank goodness, or there's a distinct possibility I would have wet myself. All I know about swords I learned from watching *Highlander*, and this one definitely looked designed for decapitation.

My legs were finally working, and I made the mistake of

taking a step back. *Never show fear*, I recalled, too late. Jimmu's cold eyes narrowed, and he came toward me.

The pool was between us, so he had to skirt around it. I had more than enough time to run away: to hightail it out of the gate behind me and back to the Compound and safety. But I was motionless, hypnotized by Jimmu's sinuous movements. He kept his eyes on me as he approached, and I finally understood Kipling's descriptions of Rikki-tikki-tavi's battle with the cobras Nag and Nagaina. Jimmu's emotionless eyes held me captive, his serpentine physicality lulling my reflexes. I had no doubt that he intended to kill me – and yet I stood there, frozen, as if waiting for my lover rather than my murderer.

That's not to say I wasn't panicked. Fear was flooding through my system, and every voice rattling around in my head was screaming at me to move, to flee, to get the hell out of there. But those voices were overwhelmed by the weight of Jimmu's gaze.

Suddenly there was another sound, straight ahead of me, from the hidden path Jimmu had just vacated. Jimmu halted his sinuous progress and then his tongue flickered between his lips. But he kept his eyes on me, holding me still.

He's tasting the air, I realized, shuddering.

I couldn't see my savior, although something was definitely there, crashing about in the vegetation. Jimmu's eyes narrowed, and then he looked toward the sound, finally breaking his contact with me. My breath escaped with a whoosh as I was released from whatever spell I'd been under.

As I whisked around to run toward the gate to the Compound and away from the power of Jimmu's gaze, I caught a glimpse of the naga unsheathing his sword and heading back the way he came. He was pursuing whoever had ruined his murderous intentions for me, and as I ran through the gate and flew through the courtyard I thanked my mystery rescuer with every ounce of my being. I knew it hadn't just been a rabbit; the look on Jimmu's face when he turned toward the noise was one of recognition and anger. And I couldn't imagine Ryu hiding like that, so I had no idea who it was. I just hoped that whoever it had been knew what he or she was getting into, waking the wrath of Jimmu like that.

By this point I was well into the Compound, but I didn't stop running till I saw my first creature. A passing cougar – which I hoped was a nahual and not the real deal – paused to look at me curiously, before shrugging its shoulders and shaking its head as it continued on its way. There were a few other beings flitting about the end of the large room I'd found myself in – some sort of music space, it looked like, from the instruments lining the walls – so I took the opportunity to double over, gasping for air. I had a terrific stitch in my side, and I seemed to have dropped my towel by the side of the pool. I was also covered with sweat, mostly from my shattered nerves, and shaking. In other words, I looked as good as I felt.

I also didn't know what to do. I knew I needed to get back to Ryu; he was the one being I trusted in this Compound. And I had to tell him what had passed between Jimmu and me, not least because I didn't think I was safe left alone.

There was no doubt in my mind that Jimmu's intentions had not been to shake my hand and ask me about New England's chances in the Super Bowl that year. He'd definitely wanted to commit some atrocious act of violence on my person, but *why*?

Just because I'm a halfling? I wondered. *Or is there more to it?*

I really hoped Jimmu wanted to kill me for a better reason

than my genetic heritage, although I knew that humans were more than happy to massacre one another for that very reason. But if halflings like me were so hated that killing us was considered sporting by some of the supernatural community, then I would *never* be safe in my mother's world.

And no longer entirely at home in your father's . . .

I shook myself – now was not the time for reckoning with my future. Right now, I had to get to the safety of my room and Ryu without being hacked to death by snake-men. No small feat, I might add, since I had no idea where the fuck I was.

They really need to provide visitors with maps, I thought, looking around while trying to figure out which way to go. I normally had a really good sense of direction, but this place baffled my navigational systems.

I knew I didn't want to return the way I came, in case Jimmu had finished chopping to bits whatever had interrupted us, so I went forward toward a large set of double doors. I felt foolish in my faded old swimsuit, but nobody paid me any attention. Which was good, since I was pretty convinced by Jimmu's behavior that *anybody* could be out to kill me just because I was what I was. Not a nice feeling, I might add.

I quietly opened one of the big doors and slipped through. Shutting it gently, I turned around to find myself face to face with the Alfar queen, Morrigan.

Oh, crap, I thought, as I managed a particularly graceless little bow.

The queen nodded her head regally toward me. Standing, she was probably about five foot six but the power pulsing from her made me take a step back. Two lovely attendants stood slightly behind her, protectively, but when they saw who it was and what I was wearing, they backed away.

I'm not much of a threat, am I? I thought, wishing they'd share that opinion with Jimmu.

'Jane,' the queen's heavy voice intoned, as she smiled slowly. 'What a pleasure to see you.'

'Thank you, ma'am,' I replied.

'Did you rest well?'

'Yes, ma'am.'

'Did you enjoy our pool?'

'Oh, yes, thank you,' I said. *For putting drugs in it*, my inner crack fiend added. 'It's very strong,' I finished.

'Yes, it would be, for you.' Her eyes met mine and for the first time since we'd met I felt like she was really *looking* at me. 'You live in Nell Gnome's territory, no?' she asked. I tried not to giggle.

'Um, yes, I think so. Nell Gnome's.' *Say* that *twelve times fast.*

The queen eyed me appraisingly. 'She'll have to train you. I'll be in touch with her. We cannot leave you defenseless.'

No, we certainly can't, I thought, recalling my paralysis in Jimmu's presence.

'In the meantime, how are you enjoying your time in our Compound?' The queen took my arm, and I relaxed. Jimmu wasn't going to get to me through Morrigan, and I doubted if the queen would let a houseguest get her head whacked off in front of her, even if I was just a halfling.

'Oh, it's really lovely,' I said. *Except for the threats of violence, my nearly engulfing myself in flames, and the fact that I'm always lost the minute I leave my room.*

'It must be very strange for you, after spending all of your life among humans.'

'Yes, well, there are many things here that I find . . . challenging.' I figured that was diplomatic enough. 'But it's also very beautiful and very exciting.'

The queen inclined her beautiful head toward me and I thought I heard the faintest of laughs come from her lips. 'It's not often we Alfar are called *exciting*, although I suppose that, taken as a whole and with everything being so new to you, the Compound would seem intriguing.' She paused, briefly. 'And our younger factions do race around so; they still enjoy such activities.'

And the Alfar don't? I thought, skeptically. I'd seen the way Jarl looked at me, and his introducing me to Jimmu the way he did was definitely the first roll of the dice in some little game he was playing. Not that I knew what the game was, or how I fit into it.

Morrigan had led me back into the room with the instruments and then out a side door to the left. We walked down a few stone stairs into the first of a series of kitchens and other domestic areas. If I'd been expecting brooms sweeping by themselves, like in *Fantasia*, or pots stirred by unmanned spoons, like in *Harry Potter*, I was disappointed. There were many creatures at work here, although the nature of the creatures themselves was more than entertaining. There was a room full of washing machines being loaded by a particularly disgruntled looking orangutan, and I saw what had to be an ifrit lazily painting her nails as she sat beneath a large spit upon which an entire pig turned, roasting. A particularly voluptuous succubus waddled past us carrying a bucket of cleaning products, and I would have given my right eye to see her scrubbing something, anything, on her hands and knees. *How* do *they get any work done?* I wondered.

The queen was still talking about 'the younger factions', by which I assumed she meant all the other types of supernatural beings that were not Alfar. I knew she didn't mean *young* as in newborn, since basically everyone I'd met since I'd learned about this world had mentioned the fertility problem thing. At the same time, the Compound was very large and seemed relatively crowded. If there were other Compounds like this throughout the country and all over the world, then the supernatural population – especially considering their long lives – must be quite large.

'. . . coordinated tonight's entertainment,' Morrigan was saying. 'So it should be amusing. She's very original.'

I had no idea what she was talking about, but I pursed my lips and gave a considered nod: my *how een-teresting* pose.

'My, um, lady?' I asked awkwardly, working up my nerve. 'How many of you are there? Do you know?'

Morrigan frowned, and for a moment the air around us crackled with that signature of power I couldn't quite get used to. But then her smooth features settled back into her usual bland expression.

'There are five Territories dividing what humans would call North and Central America. The rest of the world is divided up into similar proportions. Each Territory supports a variety of beings, all of whom are ruled by an Alfar monarchy, which leads from its own Compound. As for population, it depends on the location of the Territory as to how many and what sorts of beings it can support. Some areas are more populated than others and the variety of different factions differ from place to place. Succubi and incubi no longer fare very well in the Middle East, for example, and the ifrit don't enjoy rain forests. But exact numbers are unknown, not least because our border lands – the areas between Territories – tend to be wild, uncontrolled places that resist Alfar intervention. We do know, however, that our numbers are most assuredly shrinking.'

Morrigan looked at me questioningly, as if to ascertain whether or not I was following her. I nodded, and she continued, 'I'm sure you have heard that our birth rates

are dropping.' I nodded again. 'Procreation has never been
easy for us – we cannot breed without intention.' Ryu had
said the same thing, the first time we'd made love, and I'd
never asked him for details, although I'd understood the gist.
But I was more than a little intrigued when Morrigan
explained. 'We do not have natural cycles the way humans
and other animals do. We do not produce an egg or sperm
automatically; we have to consciously create the capacity for
life within ourselves. It takes months of concentration and
large amounts of energy. So it has always been a challenge,
but one that could be met.' Here, Morrigan frowned again.
'In the last few hundred years, however, it has become
increasingly difficult, at least when both partners are
elemental. For some reason, our ability to procreate with
humans has been less troubled, although that issue is, in
itself, a contentious one.'

What the queen was saying was fascinating on a number
of levels, and I had so many questions I wanted to ask. To
my horror, however, my libido muscled its way to the front
of the queue, demanding answers.

'So,' I heard myself say, 'when someone, um, let's say a
baobhan sith, tells you that they can't get you pregnant or
give you any . . . umm, other gifts, they're telling the truth?'

For a split second, Morrigan grinned, and it was the first
really *human* response I'd seen from her. But a second later
the grin was gone, and her face had settled back into her
usual flat expression.

'Yes, child, all of what you have been told is true. Our
elemental powers purge us of disease, and we are infertile
unless we choose to be otherwise. And that choice is a difficult process to embark upon. So we are safe to breed with
humans, even when they are half-breeds.'

Morrigan fell into an awkward silence, as if remembering

to whom she was talking. I gave her a benign smile, to tell her that I wasn't offended.

We'd emerged back into a main hallway of the Compound, and I was beginning to recognize things. I think the queen was taking me back to my rooms.

'But we are not like humans,' Morrigan continued, her smooth features radiating calm once more. 'We do not throw teams of, what do you call them? Scientists?' I nodded. 'We do not throw teams of scientists to vex nature and solve our problems. We are as long-lived as mountains, and we have faith that our problems will work themselves out. A few hundred years in the life of an Alfar is but a blink of an eye. Soon, we will wake up to a new dawn in which all of our concerns have resolved themselves.'

She smiled beatifically as I worked hard to keep my eyebrows from shaking follicles with my hair line. *What is she talking about? I wondered. She acts like the Alfar are all that's out there. What about the nahuals? Ryu said that Russ was old, at four-hundred-something years. He, for one, doesn't have the lifespan of mountain ranges to wait around hoping for offspring.*

Besides which, even if they do live forever, that just gives them more time to obsess. Look at what short-lived human couples are willing to do to have a baby. And while I get it that the Alfar aren't exactly brimming with emotion, Ryu, for one, is passionate and Iris is definitely *emotional. Even Morrigan betrayed a hint of feeling when she started talking about this subject, before she got all weird and Vulcan about it. Not everybody can be as cool with not having babies as the Alfar make out to be – if they really are them-selves.*

We'd walked the last few minutes in silence – I had no idea where to begin after what Morrigan had just told me, and she seemed content to be quiet. When we got to my door, she stopped to say goodbye.

'Take care, Jane,' she said, her eyes expressionless. 'We will see you at tonight's feast.'

I attempted another bow, this time with a bit more refinement. 'Thank you, queen, er, lady,' I finished. *I really gotta ask Ryu what to call these folks*, I thought. My 'royal etiquette' was really not up to snuff.

She smiled, unfazed by my discombobulation, and I slipped into our room.

I shook Ryu like a can of whipping cream but he was out like a light. So – after checking, double-checking, then triple-checking that both our outer door and our bedroom door were locked – I decided to take another shower. I felt gross after my encounter with Jimmu; his eyes had been like clammy hands all over my skin. I shed my swimsuit and started the water.

I had so much to think about that I barely knew where to start. First of all, my run-in with the queen had meant that I hadn't really processed what had happened beside the pool. And there'd been no way I was going to tell *her* about it, considering Jimmu was the foster son of the guy who was both her brother-in-law *and* her own second-in-command. Despite the fact I knew damned well that even if Jimmu hadn't actually been intending to kill me, he was definitely going to do *something* unpleasant. But who would believe me besides Ryu?

Jimmu really does hate you, my brain reminded me, unhelpfully. And I still couldn't shake the feeling that I'd seen him before. But it was *impossible* – how many six-foot-tall men with blue Mohawks and steel tusks had I seen that I failed to notice one more? *Unless he glamoured you*, I thought, suddenly. *But then why would I remember not remembering?*

My brain ached at that thought – going down that path was like watching one of those shows about time traveling where you knew if you concentrated on the plot for even a second it would rip to shreds. *Let's just say you would remember not remembering, and leave it at that*, I thought, clinging to my sanity with an iron grip.

And what the hell is up with the Alfar? The other half of my brain interrupted. *They are so powerful, but so* complacent. *There's no way everybody else is fine with not procreating. Otherwise, they wouldn't be so scared of halflings. You only hate what you secretly envy or desire*, I thought, with a nod to freshman psych.

If they're having problems procreating, why not do *something about it? I get it that humans 'vex' nature and what not – you don't have to quote Bacon to make me realize we have some fundamental flaws as a species. But not to do anything, and especially when you have such power?* I snorted, lathering up a wash cloth to scrub away all vestigial Jimmu eye-traces.

I get it that they cultivate this cool façade, but it's gotta be pissing off members of their community. Who I bet wouldn't mind if the Alfar invested their copious resources on some 'teams of scientists' of their own.

Teams of scientists, I thought. *Teams of scientists . . .*

That's it, I wondered, as my wash cloth dropped with a *splat*.

Teams of scientists . . .

I turned off the water, calmly, although I was roiling on the inside.

I wasn't crazy; I *had* seen Jimmu before. And now I remembered where.

CHAPTER TWENTY

Wake up, wake up, wake up, wake up, I thought at Ryu, trying to bore a hole in his forehead with my brain waves.

I'd tickled him, shaken him, scratched him, pinched him, thrown a glass of water on him, kissed him – I'd even flicked his testicles with a fair amount of force. He hadn't budged.

So now I was lying with my face right above his, trying to wake him through the power of my focused will. I didn't think it was working.

Wake up, wake up, wake up, wake up, I thought, getting so frustrated I was ready to scream. *Did his eyelid just flicker?* I wondered, not daring to hope. *WAKE UP!*

Ryu's eyes flickered again; he was definitely switching on. Suddenly, he was fully awake, staring at me with a fair amount of surprise registering on his face.

'Good morning, Jane,' he mumbled. 'What the hell are you doing?'

I had so much to tell him that it got jumbled on the way out, and all that emerged from my mouth was an inarticulate 'aaaaargh' sound.

'Oh, really? That's great. Is there coffee?' Ryu pushed me

gently away so he could sit up. He made a funny face and his hand went to his crotch. 'Ow, must have slept funny.' He eyed me suspiciously. 'Why is my pillow wet?'

'Ryu,' I said, swiftly changing the subject. 'Jimmu was at the bookstore the day you came, and was at the Sty the first night we were there. He was with all these academics so I didn't recognize him at first but I *know* it was him.'

Ryu was looking at me like I was speaking in tongues. 'Jane, what are you talking about?'

'I know you're going to say it's impossible but it's not. He was totally going to kill me this morning but something was in the bushes and he like *hypnotized* me, so I couldn't move, and he had a *sword* . . .' I was definitely babbling at this point, so I tried to rein it in. 'But I got away, and then I saw Morrigan, and she mentioned "teams of scientists", and I *knew* I'd seen Jimmu and then I realized where.' I took a deep breath. 'At Read It and Weep.'

'Why would Jimmu be with a bunch of academics?' he asked, rubbing his eyes.

'Well, he must not have actually been *with* them, but just used them as cover, or something. I don't know. I didn't ask him, obviously.'

Ryu was unconvinced. He shook his head and ran a hand through his hair. 'I'll be back in a minute, honey, and then we'll talk about it.'

He went to the bathroom and I took the opportunity to organize my thoughts. I needed to tell him exactly what had happened, from the beginning and in a way that actually made sense. I knew I was *not* crazy – I could see that greasy academic sitting there staring at me, and I knew that without his piercings, and with his hair combed back, and with those big glasses on, Jimmu *was that academic*.

Ryu emerged, now dressed in pajama bottoms. He gestured

for me to follow him into the sitting room, and then he called down for coffee and food to be brought up while I settled myself onto our little sofa.

'I know it's hard to believe, but you've got to hear me out,' I started, before he had even put down the phone. I kept talking while he sat down next to me. 'The day you first came to Rockabill, that morning a bunch of academics came in on a bus to see the Old Sow. One of them totally gave me the willies because he was staring at me. Then we saw him again, that night at the Sty. After the thing with Stuart, when you went out to check that the parking lot was clear, I was waiting by the door and I saw him hidden in the far corner. He was watching me again.'

Ryu was listening, as I'd asked him to, but he didn't look convinced.

I forged ahead, anyway. 'When we got here and I met Jimmu, I could swear I recognized him, but I just figured I was crazy because obviously I would remember someone who looked like him, right? But then this morning, I went out to the pool. Jimmu surprised me, with a sword. I think he must have been practicing, because I don't think he was expecting me. But he scared the shit out of me, and he was coming toward me when something distracted him. Anyway, his Mohawk had fallen and he looked even *more* familiar.' Ryu was staring intently at me – he could tell that I believed what I was saying, if nothing else.

'I ran away into the Compound where I bumped into Morrigan. We were talking, and she mentioned the fertility problem thing, and she was talking about teams of scientists. Later, thinking about what she had said, I realized that if you took out Jimmu's piercings and dressed him in conservative clothes with some big geeky glasses, he'd be the guy from the store.'

Ryu sat quietly for a moment, and I could tell the wheels were spinning.

'Ryu,' I continued, 'I think Jimmu's the one behind the murders. Why else would he be in Rockabill? And it would explain why he's exhibited such animosity toward me. I was next on his list.'

Ryu shook his head, as if to clear it of what I'd just said. 'Jane, if what you're saying is true, then everything just got seriously complicated. Jimmu does nothing without Jarl's consent, and Jarl does nothing without the knowledge of Orin and Morrigan.'

He watched me, waiting for his words to sink in. 'So if Jimmu *were* the murderer, I can't see how he acted on his own,' he concluded. 'Which would mean that the Alfar are directly responsible for these killings.'

'Fine,' I said, my mind racing. 'Maybe he's *not* the murderer. Maybe he was following Jakes for some other reason, maybe to check up on him for the Alfar. But he was *definitely* in Rockabill. I *know* it was Jimmu I saw that day. Despite his disguise.'

'I just can't believe it, Jane.' Ryu shook his head. 'I'm sorry, I know that you believe what you're saying, but I can't believe it was Jimmu. I don't *want* to believe you – it would mean too many incredibly bad things if what you're saying is true.'

I stared at him, never more frustrated with anyone in my life. *What part of 'I know it was Jimmu' don't you comprehend?* I wanted to scream. But deep down I understood his fear – because I could see that what I'd said implied that something was rotten to the core of Alfar society.

At that moment there was a light tap on the door, and Elspeth came in with coffee and breakfast for two. We sat in silence as she arranged the trays. *How can I get you to believe me?* I thought, staring at Ryu.

And then I remembered my Edith Wharton. The servants know everything in those books.

'Elspeth,' I said, my voice tense. 'Can I ask you something?'

She nodded, smiling benevolently. 'It's about Jimmu,' I started, then paused. I didn't know where to begin. 'I saw him this morning,' I continued, trying to stall till I could figure out how to ask her what we needed to know. 'He'd been working out. Those piercings are really something.'

'Yes, they are.' Elspeth's smile was gone, and she shuddered. 'Every time he does it, he makes me help. It's awful.'

Ryu's eyes narrowed and he inhaled sharply. 'What do you mean, every time?' he asked, his voice low.

'Oh, Jimmu is always leaving the Compound. When he does, he takes his piercings out, and then he has to re-pierce himself since he heals so quickly.' She looked at me, and I tried to keep my expression from betraying my excitement. 'He makes me help him do the piercings.' She shuddered again. '*All* of them.'

I got what she was insinuating and gave her a sympathetic grimace. 'And the Mohawk?' I asked. 'Is that new?'

'Yes.' She was surprised. 'It is actually. He's only had it for a few days. Since he got back from his latest adventure. He doubled the piercings and gave himself a Mohawk. You'd think he was in disguise.' She laughed, as if to imply how ridiculous that notion was. Ryu and I exchanged looks.

'He left them in this time, though.'

'What?' Ryu and I asked, simultaneously.

'Jimmu left the Compound about a half hour ago. He's not coming back until tomorrow, apparently. But thankfully he didn't take out his piercings this time.'

'Do you know where Jimmu went?' Ryu asked nonchalantly.

'Oh, no, of course not. We never know where he goes. Only Jarl can keep tabs on Jimmu.' Elspeth smiled again. 'Well, enjoy breakfast. Shall I come round tonight to help you get ready, Jane?'

'Thanks, Elspeth, I'd appreciate it,' I said, getting up to usher her out the door. Ryu and I definitely needed to talk, pronto.

When we'd exchanged goodbyes and she'd left, I shut the door behind her after taking a quick look around the hallway to make sure nobody was lurking about to hear our conversation. I was getting paranoid.

Just because you're paranoid doesn't mean they aren't out to get you, I reminded myself as I shut and locked the door.

'Well?' I asked Ryu, returning to my place on the sofa.

He leaned back and closed his eyes. When he opened them again he looked rueful. 'Okay, maybe Jimmu could have been in Rockabill. But *why*?'

'I don't know, Ryu. Iris said that Jakes recognized someone who made him afraid. Maybe Jakes realized that Jimmu must have been the murderer all along.'

'Or maybe Jimmu was following Jakes,' Ryu interjected, 'but it's because he knew *Jakes* had gone rogue and was killing the halflings. Which would also explain why Jakes was scared.'

I frowned. 'I can't believe that Iris could sense, or taste, or whatever, that Jakes was scared but not also be able to sense that he was a serial killer. But you would know better than me about that.'

Ryu poured us each a cup of coffee, and I reached for a croissant even though I'd already had breakfast. *No point in going hungry, after all*, my stomach sighed, contentedly.

'I don't know what to say,' he answered, finally. 'Jakes could have hidden something like that from Iris, especially if he was such a psychopath that he genuinely didn't rate murder a big deal. But I've met Jakes, and he wasn't a psychopath that I could tell. Although I guess that psychopaths don't usually advertise themselves as such.' He shrugged. 'But my gut instinct is that you're right, and that Jakes didn't kill the halflings. Especially since he was also murdered and that Gretchen and Martin were murdered after him.' He sipped his coffee slowly, as if drawing strength from his cup. 'I just really don't want to contemplate the idea that Jimmu is the one who murdered them all.'

'Well,' I said, 'there's no point in thinking about the repercussions of Jimmu being the murderer if we don't even know whether we're right or not. What we need to do is figure out how we prove whether it was Jimmu, and then we can take it from there.'

We drank our coffee in silence. I helped myself to another croissant.

'Lucky Jimmu went out today, isn't it?' I commented, as Ryu poured himself another cup. He blanched at me.

'I knew I should have packed my cat-burglar clothes,' he said, quaffing his coffee before standing up. 'After all, I do look pretty hot in a ski mask.'

The lock clicked open with a *snick*, and we held our breath. When no one yelled at us from inside the room, we exhaled. I took another surreptitious look around the hallway as Ryu pushed open the door to Jimmu's quarters.

We crept inside, closing the door after ourselves. Ryu turned on the lights and we looked around to get our bearings. Jimmu's rooms were just like the ones shared by Ryu and me: a small bedroom with en suite bathroom and a small sitting room. And despite the fact that these rooms served as Jimmu's only home, they were equally as impersonal as ours.

'Where'd you learn to pick locks?' I hissed at Ryu. 'And why doesn't Jimmu have better security? He doesn't look the trusting sort.'

'I'm Nosferatu, remember?' Ryu grinned. He was loving this, I could tell. Since we'd left our rooms he'd radiated happiness. He might not like the exact circumstances, but he was definitely a man who loved action. 'What kind of a night-walker can't pick a lock? And as for security, this is a public compound. Servants need to get in and out of these rooms, as do cleaners or maintenance. What you gain in overall security living in the Compound, you lose in privacy.' He pointed to the bedroom. 'You look in there, I'll look in here.'

I poked my head into Jimmu's bedroom, making sure he wasn't napping before I walked in. Something told me he *always* got up on the wrong side of the bed. But the room was as empty and anonymous as the sitting room. I started with the bathroom, which, except for an industrial-sized bottle of hair gel and a sliver of soap lying in the dish, was completely empty.

The bedroom wasn't much more interesting. There were a few pairs of underpants, mismatched dark socks, and some wife-beaters in one drawer of the bureau. In the closet hung a few pairs of ripped-up jeans and a few T-shirts. I started to close the door, when I noticed that there was something on the top shelf.

I pulled the little armchair from the corner of the room over to the closet and stood on it to get a closer look. On the highest shelf, in the very far corner, I caught a glimpse of the edge of a steel box. I stretched out my hand, unsure whether or not I'd even be able to reach, and nearly grazed the lid. But just as I was about to make contact, I felt that tiny unmistakable frisson of power. I hesitated, deciding not to risk it.

'Ryu,' I called. 'I might have something.'

He came in, dusting off his hands. 'Nothing in there,' he said. 'Jimmu doesn't even own a magazine. He's quite an exciting guy. What do you have in here?'

'I don't know,' I answered. 'There's a box up on this shelf, but I didn't want to touch it. I think it's whammied.'

Ryu grinned. 'Whammied?'

'You know, magicked. I could feel the tingle.'

Ryu got up beside me and peered into the closet. He hissed, his fangs suddenly extended.

'Jane, get off the chair.'

I got down without hesitation. I took commands well, when they sounded like that.

Ryu's hands hovered on either side of the box as he concentrated. I felt the hairs on the back of my nape rise, and my bangs twitched slightly as the power swirled around him.

Finally, after what felt like hours but was probably about thirty seconds, he chuckled, sounding very pleased with himself.

'Whammy, indeed.' He grinned, lifting the box off the shelf and jumping down from the chair.

'You're a clever clogs, not touching that,' he said, as he set the box down on Jimmu's bed. 'If you had, you would have blown up not only yourself but a substantial section of this part of the Compound.'

'Great,' I said, dryly. 'Thanks for telling me. So how did you open it?'

'Boxes are my specialty,' he said, grinning lecherously. 'I'm good at opening things.'

And I'm living proof, I thought, not taking the bait. 'What's in it?'

'Let's find out,' he said, undoing the little latch at the front of the box.

We both peered inside. 'Oh, crap,' said Ryu. I gagged.

Inside the box was a Ziploc bag. At first I thought it contained dead mice. Then I thought it was dead hairless mice. Then I realized what it was.

The bag was full of ears.

Protected as they'd been by Jimmu's shield, they were untouched by decay. They'd also been sliced off cleanly, with surgical precision. Neither detail, however, made them any less grotesque. Mashed up together in a bloody heap, they struck me as so vulnerably, individually *human* – from the slightly thickened helix of one to the prim little pearl earring bejeweling another. I think I would have preferred them rotten and unidentifiable.

I sat down on the bed, heavily, my stomach heaving. Ryu shut the box and then got back on the chair to replace it. I watched, taking deep breaths, as he wiggled his fingers in front of the box's clasp. When he was finished, he put the chair back where it was supposed to be, and then took my hand and led me to the door. We walked out of Jimmu's rooms, after Ryu checked to make certain no one was in the hallway, before frog-marching me back to our own quarters. Where I bolted for the bathroom, just barely making it to the toilet before I spewed up both croissants and my coffee.

Ryu held my hair out of my face with one hand, stroking my back with the other. He murmured to me quietly, as if settling a horse. I couldn't stop retching – every time I felt a little better I'd think of Joe Gonzalez from Shreveport. One of those ears had been his. All he'd ever done was grow really nice tomatoes, and for that his ear was in a Ziploc bag while he moldered in the ground.

Eventually I got control of myself, and I sat back into Ryu's arms. He held me, still whispering a steady stream of calming nonsense into my ear. I stood, with his help, and went over to the sink where I brushed my teeth and splashed cold water on my face.

We curled up together on our big bed, with me clinging to Ryu I was so scared. It had all seemed like this cool mystery before, while the names of the deceased were just that: names printed on slips of paper. But seeing those ears, I knew this was real. Those names represented real people – all dead – and I'd been face-to-face with their murderer that very morning.

I'd been next on the list.

I pressed my eyes shut and I felt myself trembling. Ryu held me tightly, gently kissing my face, whispering to me to come back to him. But if coming back to him meant taking part in his fucked-up Court, I'd rather stay out here in la-la land, thank you very much.

'Does it help if I tell you that you were right?' he asked, when I'd finally stopped trembling.

I thought about that one – it was tempting. 'Maybe,' I answered, eventually.

'Well, you were right.'

I opened one eye, meeting his golden gaze. 'How right was I?'

'Totally, completely, and utterly correct,' he said, mock-seriously.

As usual in my world, humor worked where nothing else could. Not that I was capable yet of laughter.

'What are we going to *do*?' I asked, opening both eyes.

He frowned. 'I have no idea,' he replied. 'This is too big for either of us, especially since we still don't really know what is going on.' He thought. 'Let's just get through tonight. I'll make some discreet enquiries at dinner, and tomorrow we can start fresh. But for tonight, I think we've both had enough.'

I thoroughly agreed – I'd *definitely* had enough for one

night. Or for the rest of my life, really. I was beginning to see the downside of my mother's world, to say the least.

Ryu looked at his watch. 'It's two now. So we have about six hours until dinner. Elspeth will be here around five to help you get ready.' He pressed himself up to me. 'What should we do?' he asked, his fangs leering at me.

He cannot be serious, I thought, as he ran a hand across my stomach up toward my northern territories.

I guess he is. Then it occurred to me.

'I know what we can do,' I said, swinging my legs over the side of the bed to stand.

He watched me with interest as I rummaged in my bag till I found what I was looking for. I pulled out the pair of purple heels. 'You can help me figure out how to walk in these things,' I said, grinning.

I don't think it was what he had in mind, but it was about all I could handle at that point. And he turned out to be quite a dab hand at walking in heels, which was one of those things I placed firmly under my 'don't ask' policy.

Somehow we got through dinner that night. It was a more formal affair than the smorgasbord from the night before, with all of us sitting down for a proper meal. We sat with Chester, the ifrit, and a few nahuals. They kept talking about their stock portfolios, which once I got over how bizarre that was struck me as incredibly boring. So I smiled and nodded, concentrating on keeping my ass covered by my short dress. Ryu asked as many questions as he thought was safe, but didn't seem to discover anything. As Elspeth had said, no one knew anything about Jimmu's recent activities.

During dinner there was also some entertainment. An Alfar singer warbled an incredibly long and monotonous ditty that sounded like what Enya might dream up while in a Nyquil-induced hypnogogic state. Then there were some ifrit fire jugglers and some acrobatic nahuals that would shift shape midway through their tumbles. Under any other circumstances I would have been riveted, but considering what we'd learned that day I just wanted to crawl underneath my bed and stay there till I could go home.

We begged off early, thank heavens, and snuck back to the safety of our room. The only thing that made the otherwise nightmarish day I'd had worth it was the look on Ryu's face when he held up a condom and I shook my head no, remembering Morrigan's assurances. After we'd had gloriously infertile, crabs-free, bareback sex – much to Ryu's delight – and when it was time for me to sleep, Ryu kissed me good night and got out of bed. But he didn't leave. Instead, he took his book and sat with his back to the door. I knew he'd stay there like that all night, protecting me until I was awake and it was his turn to shut down and rest. I was mentally and emotionally exhausted, but I'd been convinced I would never get to sleep. Instead, I curled up and was out like a light, hardly able to believe it myself.

CHAPTER TWENTY-ONE

In the end, I decided to go to breakfast. Part of me wanted to stay holed up with Ryu till he woke, but my stomach was in no way agreeing with that idea. Every time I picked up the phone to try to call down for food, I ended up getting yelled at by a male voice speaking what I think was Arabic. So, by that point in the morning, I was starving. In fact, my stomach was growling so loudly that I thought it might wake even the vampire up, and since Jimmu was supposed to be in absentia, I figured I was fairly safe. Then again, I threatened, if my stomach got my head chopped off, I'd never feed it again.

As I'd discovered yesterday, with Elspeth, breakfast was a haphazard affair at the Compound. The dining tables were again set up buffet style, and various beings came and went, either loading up a plate and sitting down at a free table or just grabbing a pastry or piece of fruit and going about their unearthly business.

Today when I entered the dining room, I could tell that something was up. Groups of people were talking in low voices, and there was an obvious air of excitement in the room. I saw Elspeth talking to a few other creatures in a corner, and so I went over to see what was going on.

'. . . unbelievable that such a thing could happen,' one of the group – an incubus – was saying.

Elspeth nodded at the speaker, and then turned to greet me. She introduced me to the others, all of whom were Compound servants.

'What's going on?' I asked, curiously.

Elspeth shook her head, as if in disbelief, looking at me with wide eyes. 'Oh, Jane, I don't even know where to begin,' she said. When she didn't continue, I realized she was serious.

'The beginning?' I suggested, patiently.

'Right, yes.' The dryad took a deep breath. 'Well, it turns out there have been a series of murders all over the Territory and in other Territories as well – of halflings.'

My stomach clenched, but I managed to keep my features neutral.

'None of us were aware this was happening – the Alfar were investigating in secret. But then their investigators were *both* murdered. One of the investigators was a halfling himself, and the other was a goblin. And when the goblin's manager went out to assess the situation, she was murdered as well.' Elspeth looked very upset, and my heart went out to her. *Yeah, it's lucky she wasn't there*, my brain commented sarcastically. *The charred goblins were pretty gross.*

Elspeth continued, her voice lowering. 'Jarl was so concerned about what happened that he sent out the nagas – all nine nestmates. They've been scouring the territory for the murderer, even getting access to neighboring territories.' She said this last bit with particular emphasis, and I got the impression that it was a big deal for cross-territorial cooperation like that. Personally, I was getting quite a good dose of astonishment myself. Ryu was insistent that Jarl would have to know that Jimmu was the murderer, but Elspeth was claiming that Jarl was shocked and appalled by the murders. Either Jarl was playing the Compound or Jimmu was less dependent than everybody thought. I prayed it was the latter.

'This morning Jarl gathered together the heads of the factions here at the Compound and told them what had been happening. He told us about the murders but also the good news – that the murderer has been apprehended.' My eyes widened. Had his own nestmates discovered Jimmu's deeds and turned on him?

'That's why Jimmu left in such a hurry,' she continued. I nearly clapped I was so excited. *Ryu and I are safe, and this nightmare is over*, I thought. *Thank heavens . . .*

'Apparently Jimmu's nestmates discovered the true identity of the killer – a human – and Jimmu was sent to exact justice.'

Oh shit balls, I thought. That was *not* how I wanted Elspeth's story to end.

'How could a *human* kill two goblins?' the incubus was asking, his mustache waving hello at me. I was in such shock I barely wanted to make out with him when he said it.

The ifrit shrugged, her halo of fire swooping dangerously close to my own hair. I backed away a step. 'We all have our vulnerabilities,' she said. 'Remember the giants.' The various beings nodded their heads somberly and I got the impression that particular quotation was the supernatural version of 'Remember the Alamo'.

'Oh, well,' the incubus said, breaking the mood. 'At least it means we get to have a party.' He turned to beam his sex rays at me. 'Did you bring your party clothes?' he asked. I mumbled something inarticulate, moving toward him powerlessly, but luckily Elspeth came to my aid.

'Let's take you to the pool, Jane,' she said, glaring at the incubus.

'Pool, yes, mmm,' I burbled, as she steered my reluctant little legs away and out toward the courtyard.

Being Elspeth, she had the good sense to grab some fruit, pastries, and coffee on the way out. Once I'd recovered from the incubus juju I gave her a hand, sticking the bananas in the waistband of my jeans like pistols and taking the coffees.

We ate in the grotto. I would have preferred to have sat in an outhouse, but since I didn't want to get into why I was no longer a big fan of the pool, I kept mum. Elspeth was telling me about the festivities planned for that night, and even though the majority of my mind was wrapped up with mulling over what she'd meant when she said that Jimmu was expected to 'exact justice' for the murders, there was still a small part of my brain that was worried about what I was going to wear.

You are such a girl, I criticized myself, wearily.

And you are Captain Obvious, my brain replied, irritatingly smug.

When I'd finished eating, I stuck a finger into the pool a couple of times, still listening to Elspeth babble. Then I went back to where she was sitting and we had a good chat. She wanted to know how I'd met Ryu, but I didn't want to inform her that either of us had anything to do with the halfling murders. So, I just told her that we'd met in the course of one of his investigations, but didn't specify which. She didn't press the issue; she just wanted to get to the juicy bits about how we got together and stuff. I felt like a bit of a skank, admitting that we'd barely known each other before everything het up, but she seemed to think it was all very romantic. And sitting there, telling her about our first date, and the night at the beach with the picnic and stuff, I realized it *was* pretty damned sexy.

Even if you are still a hootchie, my virtue asserted.

You shut your pie hole, the libido warned.

I asked Elspeth about her life at the Compound and she told me everything, and I mean *everything*. She was a tree, after all, and she had very little appreciation for what humans might find interesting. *Or even half-humans, at that*, I thought. But despite her inability to edit, Elspeth's stories were fascinating. After all, I still knew so little about this world that even hearing about their arguments over whether the nahuals who preferred cat shapes should be given litter boxes or expected to use the toilets 'like everybody else' was still informative. I kept thinking about Jonathan Swift's famous poem about how 'Celia, Celia, Celia shits!' in which the narrator discovers proof that the love of his life – the angelic Celia – goes to the bathroom just like everybody else. In movies or books, you never saw Dracula leave off chasing the virginal heroine to have a wee. But here I was learning that, just like Celia, the supernatural community does – indeed – shit. I found it strangely comforting.

So I sat with Elspeth for hours, listening to her stories and relaxing in the weak November sunlight. A few beings came out and swam in the pool, but they seemed unaffected by its power. I guess unless you were like me, a water elemental or whatever the hell I was, it was just a pool. And not uncut heroin.

When it was time for lunch, we wandered back into the Compound. I was surprised to see Ryu there, already awake, until I realized it was after three o'clock. He was sitting with Wally, the djinn, and I waggled my eyebrows at him as we approached. Ryu managed to keep a straight face, excused himself, and came toward me.

'Not so fast, you little minx,' he said, pulling me into a hard embrace.

'Aww.' I grinned. 'I wanted to meet your friend.'

'I'm sure you do, darling. And Wally would love to meet you, too. He'd meet you right up against the wall if you gave him a chance. But you're all mine,' he finished, giving my lower lip a predatory nip that nearly sent my body plummeting to the floor and my libido crashing through the roof.

I actually whimpered, and Ryu chuckled. Then his face grew more serious as he whispered into my ear. 'Did you hear what happened?'

'Yes,' I said, all traces of lust suddenly wiped from my system. 'Elspeth told me this morning, at breakfast. I thought at first she was telling me that they knew it was Jimmu who'd done it, but no such luck.'

Ryu frowned, his expression troubled.

'What are we going to do?' I asked.

'I've got no fucking clue,' he replied, shaking his head. 'The game's afoot, obviously. The problem is, we have no idea what the game is, or who's playing it, or what the stakes are.' He was mixing his metaphors, but I didn't think he'd appreciate being confronted on that one, so I just nodded.

'We need more information,' I said. 'And I need lunch.'

Ryu rolled his eyes. 'I'm going to hook you up to an IV and roll it around with you. You *never* stop eating.'

'Hey, you eat during sex and you don't hear me complaining.'

He blinked at me before he burst out laughing. When he finally stopped, his pupils were dilated and he was flashing me some full-frontal canines.

'You're not complaining because you're usually shouting my name.' He smirked. 'Or calling out to God. But don't feel bad – it's a mistake many women make.'

I gave him the hairy eyeball. 'It's because every time we make love I'm dreaming of sandwiches. Grilled cheese –

cheddar, of course – with bacon. And just a little chopped up tomato sprinkled between the cheese and the bacon.'

Ryu pulled away to meet my eyes appraisingly. 'You're not serious, are you?' he asked.

I considered telling him that I was, just to get him back for the 'all the other women' comment, but decided against it.

'No,' I said. 'It's really because you rock my casbah.' I stretched up on my tiptoes to kiss the frown from his lips.

'Can lunch wait?' he asked, when I let him up for air.

No! my stomach grumbled. But there was a resounding vote of *yes!* coming from down below my belt. The below-the-belt party won, and I took Ryu's hand to lead him up to our room. 'But you have to order us some sandwiches,' I said as we trotted up the stairs. 'Grilled cheese. With bacon and tomatoes.' He nodded, and both parties cheered. It was a win-win situation.

Hours later, lying intertwined with Ryu with the remains of my sandwich clinging to my lips in the form of a few stray crumbs, I groaned. But this time it was with trepidation and not pleasure.

'What's wrong?' he murmured.

'Elspeth is going to be here soon and I have no idea what to wear. I'll have to borrow something. Or wear that red dress again. Is that dressy enough, do you think?'

Ryu's grin widened. I stared at him, but he didn't spill. We were at an impasse.

'Okay,' I said, breaking under the pressure. 'What's the dealio?'

'Go look in my closet, top shelf. You'll need a chair.'

I had a feeling I knew what was coming, but it was way too *Pretty Woman* for me to believe. I got up out of the bed and dragged our little armchair over to Ryu's closet. I tried not to let it remind me of the last time I looked in the top shelf of a closet. But this time instead of a metal box full of ears that was set to blow up at a strange touch, there was a large white box wrapped in silver cord. It had a sticker labeling it as being from Iris's boutique. I liked this box much better.

'Oh, Ryu,' I whispered. 'You didn't.'

'Of course I did,' he said from the bed. 'As soon as we decided to come out here, I had Iris wrap it up. You might not get a chance to dress up in Rockabill, but you certainly will here.'

I finally found the strength to pull the box down from the shelf. It was very large and unwieldy, and I wondered where he'd had it stashed. *Duh*, I thought, *of course.*

'I thought you had the goblin bodies stuffed back there!' I exclaimed, getting off the chair and climbing back into bed next to Ryu, clutching the big box to my chest. I felt like a little girl at Christmas.

'Huh?' Ryu asked, confused.

'In the trunk of your car,' I clarified. 'When you wouldn't let me put my stuff in there, I figured you had the bodies back there.'

'Why would I have goblin bodies in the back of my Porsche?' he asked, like that was the craziest thing he'd ever heard.

I looked at him, levelly. 'Ryu, I'm still getting over the fact that there *are* goblin bodies out there, period. Whether or not it's reasonable to shove them into the trunk of your car is really beside the point.'

He laughed and leaned forward to kiss me. 'Good point,' he conceded. Then he teasingly shook the box. 'Open it,' he commanded, gently.

I undid the silver cord and lifted off the box cover. Underneath a thin wrapping of tissue paper lay the silvery dress and the pair of heels with the black bows.

'Oh, Ryu,' I breathed. 'I feel just like Julia Roberts. Only without the hooker aspect. Thank you so much.'

'You're welcome, Miss True,' he said, leaning back against the headboard. 'And this one is from me. No company expense accounts were harmed in the purchasing of this present.'

I'd stood up, held the dress in front of me, and looked at myself in the mirror. It was just as perfect as I'd remembered it. Although what I was going to do with my boobs was beyond me – hopefully Elspeth had some magic spell for keeping boobs and dresses in their proper places. I turned to Ryu, grinning like a jack-o'-lantern. For the moment, all traces of anxiety were gone.

'Amazing sex, beautiful clothes, *and* a grilled cheese when-ever I ask – I could get used to this life,' I joked, turning back to the mirror and trying to balance the dress against me and hold up my hair at the same time.

Suddenly Ryu was behind me, wrapping his arms around my waist, underneath the dress. He nuzzled into my neck, inhaling deeply. 'That's the plan, Jane,' he murmured, before meeting my gaze in the mirror.

For a split second I thought he was serious. Then my brain kicked in. *Get over yourself*, it advised, remembering all the women at the hotel. *He does this for a living . . . literally.*

Laughter burbled up from my lips and I turned around in his arms, the dress pressed between us.

'So that's why the Alfar put crack in their pool. Get me addicted, and I'll never leave!'

Ryu returned the laugh and took the dress from me. He hung it up, ever so gently, then pushed me toward the bath-room as he started getting dressed.

'Go get ready for Elspeth, sweetness. I'll meet you back here when it's time for dinner.' I nodded. 'And Jane,' he said, his tone suddenly serious. 'Be on your toes tonight. I have no idea what is going to happen. But if anything bad kicks off, you run – get out of the main hall and try to make it back to our rooms. When you get here, lock the doors, and don't open them for anyone but me, okay?'

I was again plunged into worry about this evening. Which was good; I should never have let myself get lulled into a false sense of security.

He smiled at me, but his expression was tight. 'I'll keep you safe,' he said. 'I swear. But don't trust anyone else. Just run and I'll find you.'

'Okay,' I said, giving him an equally unhappy smile. He kissed me on the cheek and then took a suit bag out of the closet as well as the shopping bag he'd picked up from Nell and Anyan's cabin.

'I'm meeting Wally,' he said. 'Then I'll find somewhere else to change. I don't want to get in Elspeth's way.' He kissed me goodbye, giving my hand an encouraging little squeeze before he left.

When Ryu was gone I took a deep breath. I felt totally unprepared for tonight. I was like a mouse that had found herself invited to the neighborhood cats' spring fling. I should be donning armor and stashing semi-automatic weapons about my person, not worrying about whether I should wear my hair up or down that evening.

Which reminded me . . . *Should I wear my hair up? Or down?* I sighed, betrayed by my vanity at a time when I most needed to be strong and cynical. I decided I'd let Elspeth choose, and went to get in the shower. If I was going to my death that evening, I could at least go out looking my best. *Which means you should wear underpants*, I thought. I looked at the beautifully flimsy dress hanging in the closet.

Nah.

CHAPTER TWENTY-TWO

Even I had to admit that I looked pretty hot. But Ryu, he was almost out of this world. 'Gee whillikers,' I breathed, when he came in to the sitting room where I sat waiting. He was wearing the most beautiful tux I'd ever seen – not that I'd seen many – and he looked *gorgeous*. We just stood there, looking at one another for a few seconds.

'You look fantastic, Jane,' he said, finally. I stood up and gave him a little twirl. How could I *not* look fantastic in this dress? Even Elspeth had been impressed when I'd taken it out of the closet.

My hair was, once again, up in a little twist. As for the boobs, those had been taken care of the old-fashioned way. When I explained to Elspeth my concerns – that I couldn't wear any of the bras I had with me and going commando was not an option – she'd said that would be no problem. I'd thought she was going to do some magic – a spell to keep everything in place and perky. But no: to my horror, she'd pulled a roll of duct tape out of her little bag.

'All is fair in love and fashion,' she said, the tape ripping ominously as she unrolled a piece. So, underneath my dress I was trussed up like a heating duct, but nobody had to know that except for me. And the emergency medical team that I planned on calling to get the shit off.

Ryu and I fussed over each other for a few more minutes, and then I took his arm and we went down to dinner. I was very careful to pick up my feet so I didn't trip over anything, and Ryu wasn't taking any chances either. He had his other hand wrapped over mine like a vice, which I appreciated. Balletic grace and I were not on speaking terms.

The hall was beautifully decorated that evening – bedecked with flowers and other natural elements. Instead of using the dining room, tables were set up in the main hall on either side of the central aisle. The main dais had also been elevated, and the thrones replaced with a head table. Underneath that dais was a new secondary dais, which was empty and meant to be a stage, I figured.

Ryu had planned our entrance to be fashionably late, of course, and the room was quite crowded when we arrived. Over the three days we'd been in the Compound, it had slowly grown from mostly empty on Thursday to what looked to be about full capacity on Saturday. Obviously the weekend was *the* time for the supes to hit their Court, and I wondered how often they had these kinds of parties. Ryu rolled his eyes when I asked him.

'They somehow find an excuse to have something like this just about every weekend,' he said. 'The Alfar have the resources, and everyone else gets bored, so it's something to do. As you've noticed, the Compound is as much a family home – albeit a dysfunctional family home – as it is a seat of power. The servants who live here are less employees and more inhabitants who make sure that the upper echelon are properly taken care of. The Alfar, in turn, keep everyone safe and they circulate their power about – feeding the land, the pools, and all that. Even the air we breathe is charged, for those who have access to air elementals. But all of this also means the Compound has to be out of the way, away from humans and the excitement of human life. So the beings that live here year-round come up with stuff to lure the city types in on weekends. Of course, it *is* also the seat of power, so anyone who has any important Territorial business to conduct tends to do it here. But no matter what the occasion, everybody likes a party.'

As befitting the circumstances, all and sundry in attendance looked resplendent. There were lots of designer clothes flashing about, but also a lot of stuff that looked like costumes from some kind of sci-fi or fantasy movie. Except some of the costumes, I realized, were actually shape-shifter tricks. One woman had a luxuriant feather bikini, like a Las Vegas showgirl, but a closer look revealed that the feathers were actually growing from her flesh. A few other people appeared to be hybrids: there was a cat-woman and cat-man couple, who I don't think were wearing costumes, and I spotted what looked like a minotaur in a corner. Ryu nodded when I asked him if that was a nahual.

'They like to play with their appearance,' he said. I was getting an insight into human mythology that just about blew me away. Archetypes my foot; humans had just been the victims of tricky shape-shifters. The likes of Carl Jung and Joseph Campbell were in trouble.

Ryu and I wandered about, him conversing with various beings while I smiled and tried not to stare. He seemed to know everyone and was treated with quite a bit of deference by many. Nyx had seemed to be making fun of him when she called him an 'investigator', but I got the impression that he was actually well respected.

Speak of the devil, I sighed, as a familiar form came toward us.

'Cousin,' Nyx greeted Ryu, ignoring me.

'Nyx,' Ryu said. She was wearing a tight white sheath dress that left nothing, and I mean *nothing*, to the imagination. If she'd had any pubic hairs, I could have counted them. I also noticed that she had a very befuddled-looking man standing behind her. He was huge – bulging with muscles but presenting to the world a slack-jawed expression that emitted a zero on the personality scale. He was dressed in a suit, but it didn't look like it fit him very well. And then I noticed his neck.

What I'd first thought were love bites were actually just bites. All over his neck raw-looking wounds glistened angrily- in the low light of the hall. *He's human*, I realized. *Nyx just gave a whole new meaning to the expression BYOB.*

'I see you brought your own dinner, as well.' Nyx's voice echoed my own thoughts, and then I registered that she was talking about me. Ryu's jaw clenched and I squeezed his hand. After the provocations I'd endured in my life, Nyx was no more annoying than a mosquito buzzing around my face. If I could ignore her, so could he.

Ryu's voice oozed contempt. 'You never cease to impress me with your refinement, cousin,' he said. 'Remember to leave this one alive; I wouldn't want to have to run you in for improperly disposing of your garbage. Again.'

Nyx smiled sweetly. 'That was just an accident, Ryu. Can I help it if I'm simply too much for them? But this one looks strong, doesn't he? He should go the distance.' She shrugged, as if to indicate it didn't *really* bother her if he didn't. 'And then I'll put him back where I got him, with only a few night- mares to remind him of our time together.' She gave me a predatory look. 'No harm, no foul,' she sneered, her tone rubbing my nose in her words.

I watched in horror as a flicker of what looked like fear

crept over the big man's features, before a sweep of Nyx's hand over his eyes ironed out his expression so that it was as bland and lifeless as before. I turned to Ryu but he hadn't noticed the man's discomfiture.

Ryu shook his head and gave Nyx a mocking little salute, before leading me away. When we were out of earshot I stopped him. 'You've got to do something for that man,' I said. 'He shouldn't be here, not with her. Did you see his *neck*?' I finished, my hands going to my own throat.

Ryu sneered. 'She likes to leave them unhealed, so that they freak out when they wake up. It causes no amount of trouble for the rest of us, but nothing we do can stop her. For some reason she has Morrigan's favor and she's allowed her little games.' Ryu was angry, but I could tell that he was more irritated that Nyx got special consideration rather than that she had enslaved some poor human who she was clearly abusing.

'Ryu,' I said, trying to keep calm. 'What about the man?'

He looked down at me, as if suddenly realizing what I was talking about. 'Oh, he'll be fine. She doesn't dare kill this one, not after what happened the last time. And he must have gone to her willingly enough to begin with, otherwise she couldn't have enthralled him so thoroughly.'

'So he was asking for it?' I said, contemptuously. I couldn't believe what I was hearing.

'Look, Jane, it doesn't make me any happier to see him like that than it does you. You know I don't do things the way that Nyx does. I find her . . . predilections equally distasteful.' I sensed a *but* coming.

'But,' he continued, affirming my suspicions, 'I have no authority to tell her how to conduct her affairs. As long as she doesn't bring undue attention to our community, my hands are tied.'

I closed my eyes, trying to get my emotions under control. I was so angry I could spit, but I didn't know who pissed me off more. Obviously, Nyx's behavior made her a strong contender, but I wasn't having sex with Nyx. Hearing the man who – just hours ago – had made love to me talk about the murder of some human as an *inconvenience* to his own kind made my skin crawl.

Ryu took my hand to kiss my palm, and for the first time in our short relationship feeling the touch of his lips did nothing for me.

'I'm sorry,' he said, registering my coldness. 'I wish you hadn't been confronted with all this. Not yet, at least.' He searched for the right words. 'Our ways are not human ways,' he said, after a while. 'Some of us are more . . . considerate in the use of our powers than others. Some of us are, quite simply, what humans would deem monstrous. But you can't judge us by human standards, and eventually you'll come to understand that. You're one of us, Jane, whether you like everything about our community or not.'

I stared at him, unable – unwilling – to process what he was saying.

'In the meantime,' he continued, uncomfortably, 'we do have a system of checks and balances to make sure nobody gets too out of control. And I'm part of that system. So please don't look at me like that.'

He sounded so apprehensive that I blinked, shaken out of my appalled reverie. I looked deep into his golden eyes, as if I could find the answers I wanted written on his corneas. But all I got for my trouble was a flash of memory – the moment I realized his eyes must be hazel when we first met. I grasped that memory, attaching to it like a leech.

'Oh, Ryu,' I said, reaching for him. He folded me in his arms. 'I want to go home.' And I really did, I realized.

Rockabill, and the word *home*, had taken on a whole new significance for me.

'I know, baby,' he whispered into my ear. 'I'll take you home when this is all over. I promise.'

Let's hope it's not in a body bag, I thought, thinking of that poor man's neck.

He held me for another minute, as I recovered my equilibrium. We were interrupted by the loud clang of a gong sounding from the edge of the raised dais.

'Dinner time,' Ryu said. 'You okay?'

I nodded, shaking myself mentally. Ryu took my hand and led us to our table. We were sitting in the first row, near the dais, with Wally. Ryu was careful to keep himself and a few other beings between me and the djinn. Wally and Ryu exchanged covert little nods, and I knew they had something up their sleeves. Even if the genie wasn't actually wearing any.

After we took our seats, the Alfar high table filed in and took their places. Morrigan and Orin were seated at the center of the table in the fanciest chairs, naturally, and Jarl was seated next to Orin. He looked particularly threatening in a high-collared royal-blue robe that made him look like he'd raided a Martian overlord's closet. I also saw, with a start, that Nyx was seated at the very end of the high table. Her hunk of human man-meat sat disconsolately on the edge of the dais, at her feet. He looked lost and my heart went out to him.

Then the entertainment began. There was another singer, but this time he was unmistakably a kelpie. Like Trill, the man had grayish-green skin and seaweed hair. He was also unabashedly naked, although whereas Trill was relatively smooth and hairless, this guy looked like he had a coral reef extending down his chest to his groin, mostly covering his genitals. I leaned back into my seat to enjoy the sound of his singing. His voice spoke to me of the sea, and I closed my eyes. Through his words, I felt the ocean on my skin, tasted her salty tang, and thrilled to the echo of her waves in my ears.

For the first time since walking into the great hall I relaxed just a fraction. And when I felt Ryu's slippered foot glide up my calf I smiled, my eyes still shut tight. Until I remembered that Ryu wasn't wearing slippers, and my lids snapped open. Wally gave me his Buddha-riffic grin from across the table, and I sat up straight, carefully withdrawing my leg. Ryu hadn't noticed his friend's infraction, so I kept mum, shooting the genie a dirty look. He shrugged at me, looking for all the world as peaceable and harmless as a castrated monk.

But I was finally beginning to understand that nothing was as it appeared, here in the Alfar court.

After the singer, we were entertained by a group of incubi and succubi who danced like Cossacks trained by whirling dervishes. They spun like tops, kicking high their legs and tossing each other gracefully up in the air. Ryu put both hands on my knees, to remind my suddenly totally aroused body that it had to stay in its seat and not get itself a little tossing of its own.

I breathed a sigh of relief when they were finished. Dancing sexpots were all a little too much for my human half. Finally, dinner was served, and I dug in. Rather than individual plates, we were given large platters of food to share among the table. Everything was, of course, delicious. About the only thing I could unreservedly say was good about the Alfar was that they sure knew how to keep a body fed. I'd never eaten so well in my life, and my dad and I are both pretty dab hands in the kitchen.

During dinner there was a band. One person played an

electric guitar, another a bodhran, and a third the panpipes, but they were the only instruments I recognized. After the meal, the musicians all cleared away, and another group of succubi – this time all dressed in belly-dancing clothes – stood up to take their place.

Oh no, I groaned inwardly. *Not again.*

But just as the little group jiggled merrily into position, Jarl stood. He'd been oddly unfocused for the majority of the meal, his eyes turned inward as if he were in a trance. I'd kept an eye on him throughout the evening, trying not to feel like a fly caught in a web.

Everyone's attention was riveted on Jarl. The succubi wordlessly cleared the stage.

'They've returned!' Jarl's voice rang out, just as the double doors at the end of the hall flew open. Everyone stood. After exchanging concerned looks, Ryu and I joined them on our feet.

For a moment no one appeared. And then for another moment, I was too short to see what was happening. I cursed my midget-hood, although when I finally did get a glimpse of what was coming up the aisle, I wished I hadn't.

Jimmu was in the lead, and flanking him was an honor guard of eight nagas – four on each side, consisting of all nine nestmates in total. They glided down the central aisle with the same serpentine grace and they looked like siblings, not least as they were all dressed in the same punk style. Except that each of them carried on their backs a sheathed sword, and they weren't for decoration. *Not even the Ramones went in for swords*, I thought, not liking where tonight was going. Nine Jimmu clones, all armed, did not bode well for my safety.

They strode soundlessly down the aisle, and all in attendance shrank back as they passed. I was clearly not alone in being scared witless by the nagas. As they neared our table, Jimmu's cold eyes flicked to mine and it was like his hand had reached around my throat. I gasped, fighting to breathe, until his dry eyes swept back to gaze ahead. Ryu placed a protective hand on the small of my back to remind me he was there.

That was when I saw the sack. As they passed, I noticed that Jimmu carried a large burlap bag, soaked with red stains, over his shoulder. I shuddered at the sight, my brain taking a moment to catch up to what I'd instinctively recognized.

Jimmu and the other nagas had reached the first dais by this time. They mounted it in one smooth motion, fanning out into formation and dropping down onto one knee apiece, heads bowed. Jarl watched them with obvious pride, returning their obeisance with a slight inclination of his head.

'Report!' his voice rang out. Jimmu stood.

'Justice has been served,' he said, his snake tongue flickering between his lips. I'd never heard him speak before now, and his voice was just like his eyes – cold and dead.

I put a hand protectively over my stomach as I watched Jimmu swing the sack down from off his shoulder. I had a pretty good idea of what he was carrying, and my only goal at this point was not to barf on the table.

'The murderer was apprehended,' Jimmu continued, pulling a rolled up piece of paper from his leather jacket's breast pocket. 'And a confession extracted,' he said, as he passed the paper to Jarl. Jarl didn't even bother to open it, passing it wordlessly to Orin and Morrigan. They read it in silence, nodding once when they'd finished.

'And you took action?' Orin asked, his voice dispassionate.

'Of course, my king,' Jimmu said, as he opened the sack.

I braced myself as I watched the naga upend his bloody burden. It felt like it took eons; time had slowed in the way it tends to when you're about to experience something that will change you forever. I'll never forget the sound that the naked, gore-encrusted limbs made as they smacked against the wood floor of the dais. First an arm, and then a piece of torso, and then the rest of the various bits that make up a whole human being fell out of the sack with a dizzying array of crunches and splats. I tasted bile as I looked around me. But instead of sympathetic looks of horror, no one looked particularly bothered except for Ryu. Who knew, as well as I did, that whoever was in that sack was not the killer but some innocent victim of the nagas' deadly games.

When Jimmu bent down to pick up the head, holding it aloft by the hair so that all could see, my world shrank as everything went wonky. The dead man's eyes were rolled into the back of his head, and I saw that he had a beard. It was well groomed. The beard, believe it or not, was what pushed me over the edge. It's not that I recognized the body; he was a stranger. But seeing that carefully trimmed beard – a symbol of the man's everyday existence – brought home to me his humanity and his vulnerability. I swayed on my feet, dizzily reaching for the table as I nearly went down. From a very great distance, I heard someone shout 'Nooo!' in an anguished voice. 'It's all a lie,' the voice continued, panicked. It was a very loud voice, I thought, as my stomach continued to heave. And very close. Very, very close, in fact.

That's when I realized that the voice was mine.

And all eyes of the Alfar Court were on me.

I should have worn the underpants, I thought, as my brain began to understand the implications of what my mouth had just done. *Because I am so going to die*.

CHAPTER TWENTY-THREE

All eyes were on me: some curious and some clearly shocked. Ryu's eyes expressed the latter sentiment – he was staring at me like he'd never seen me before in his life.

I blinked, still unable to believe that I had been the one who spoke.

Crawl under the table! Now! my brain was shouting, but my feet were rooted to the floor.

It was only when Jimmu began to move toward me that Ryu seemed to recover. He moved in front of me, toward the central dais.

'May I approach, my king? My queen?' he requested, his voice strong and clear. Orin and Morrigan nodded slowly in unison, and Jimmu halted.

'Please forgive my companion's outburst,' he said, moving out into the center of the aisle but still leaving quite a bit of distance between him and the nine nagas. 'She did not mean to say that our esteemed colleagues are lying. Rather, she was voicing our shared opinion that there must be a deeper mystery to these murders.'

There was a murmur of voices from all around us, as various beings whispered back and forth. They were probably placing bets on how long Ryu and I would live, and I had a pretty good idea that the odds were *not* in our favor.

'After all,' Ryu continued, smooth and confident as a silk bustier. 'How could a mere *human* take on two full-grown goblins?' He paused for effect, and I saw a number of heads nodding. He was playing his audience like a fiddle.

'It's not that I doubt the nagas' word,' he said, ever so earnestly. 'I know how loyal Jimmu and his nestmates are to their master, but perhaps – just *perhaps* – this human only played a peripheral role in the murders.' I enjoyed Ryu's little jibe at Jarl but I didn't like him giving *any* credence to Jimmu's slaughter of an innocent. Meanwhile, I could see that the nagas had tensed slightly and had shifted their positions so that they were *just* that much more defensive. Their snake tongues were furiously sampling the air, tasting the crowd's reactions to Ryu's words and trying to anticipate what would happen.

Orin and Morrigan were looking into each other's eyes and I got the feeling they were silently communing. Jarl took the opportunity to butt in, and I caught the slightest edge of desperation to his voice as he tried to regain control of the situation.

'What is the meaning of this disturbance, Ryu Baobhan Sith?' Jarl interjected. 'Your words are a clear provocation against my foster sons and daughters who have served our community so loyally. You say that you mean no slight, and yet you imply that they are, indeed, deceitful. I appreciate neither your spoken words nor their unstated implications.'

Ryu's hazel eyes had widened, expressing his – entirely feigned – disbelief at Jarl's words.

'My Lord,' Ryu said, appearing aggrieved. 'I am very sorry if I have given the impression that I doubt the nagas' loyalty. I am absolutely certain that they performed their duty faithfully.

Undoubtedly, this human was somehow involved in these murders.' I took a deep breath and counted to ten. Ryu had to do what he had to do.

'I am simply voicing the view that many of us have expressed since hearing of these dreadful crimes – that a *human* cannot have been wholly responsible for these murders.' Many heads were now nodding, and the murmur of the crowd increased but Ryu pressed on, his voice rising in volume to combat the din.

'But there is, of course, a fairly simple way of proving or disproving this theory.' With these words the room went silent.

For a split second I saw a flash of concern cross Jarl's face, although the nagas remained as impassive as statues.

Morrigan's eyebrow arched elegantly. 'Continue, investigator,' she commanded.

Ryu's voice betrayed not a single note of triumph, but I knew him well enough at this point to sense that was what he was feeling. The set of his shoulders, the slight uplift of his chin – everything about his posture said 'check, and mate'.

'My queen.' He bowed. 'Knowing that Jarl had set his most trusted servants the task of discovering the murderer, and knowing that they would perform their duty tirelessly, I thought it wise to bring with me a piece of evidence from my *own* investigation of these crimes that might be helpful in ascertaining the true guilt of the murderer.'

Throughout the room glances were being exchanged – no one had known that Ryu had any role in the investigation. A few shot me curious looks – his showing up at the Compound with a halfling in tow probably made a lot more sense.

Ryu, meanwhile, had nodded toward Wally who stood up and began fishing around in his enormous pantaloons. Finally, he pulled out the shopping bag that Ryu had picked up from Nell and Anyan's cabin. Wally waddled over to give it to

Ryu, who gave the djinn a tight grin and a curt nod. Wally returned Ryu's smile benignly, but I caught a glimpse of his eyes. They gleamed with anticipation and aggression. I quailed internally, noting that the genie did not return to his seat but instead backed to the edge of the aisle, remaining close to Ryu.

'I have in this bag the weapon that was used to kill Peter Jakes,' Ryu explained, pulling out the bloody stone and holding it aloft. 'A stone spirit has already confirmed that this rock can identify who wielded it.' Ryu paused, letting his words sink in before nodding to his king and queen. 'My Lord,' he said. 'You have the power to ask the stone to identify the being who saturated it with Jakes's blood. I sincerely hope that it will justify the actions of Jimmu and his nestmates. But in case there is an element of this investigation that they have *accidentally* missed, then that, too, will be revealed.'

The entire hall held its collective breath as the Alfar lord and his lady again silently communicated. After what felt like hours, they turned to face their Court.

'It will be done,' Orin's aloof voice rang out, as he stood. 'Hold the stone aloft.'

Ryu raised his arm, carefully balancing the stone on his open palm. The nagas were tense, and I saw one of them casually reach behind her to adjust the hilt of her sword. They were preparing for action. I started looking around for exits.

Orin raised an arm, and I felt the stirring of a power even more intense than that unleashed the night Nell opened the trunk of Peter's car. The air was crackling around me and my hair escaped from its updo to whip around my face. I had to hold onto the table, until suddenly the power seemed to solidify and focus on Ryu. Everything went quiet, although the air was pulsing with energy. I knew now what people meant when they spoke of the calm at the eye of the storm.

All eyes were focused on the stone, which was now floating just above the reach of Ryu's outstretched palm. It spun frenetically in the air, occasionally darting this way and that only to return to its starting position above Ryu's head where it hovered uncertainly. Orin's features sharpened as he concentrated, and the stone suddenly stopped spinning. Everyone held their breath, except for me. I took the opportunity to take off my shoes. I knew what was coming.

There was a sharp gasp from the nahual next to me as the stone suddenly shot toward the central dais as if it had been fired from a cannon. There was another, more universal, exclamation as the stone whizzed straight over the pile of man parts, darting unerringly through the air and straight toward Jimmu's head. The naga's serpentine reflexes whipped his hand up and he caught the stone gracefully, its weight smacking resoundingly against the flesh of his palm.

'*No!*' Jarl cried, a look of absolute anguish disfiguring his features, his hand clutching at his breast. 'Jimmu . . .' he whispered, reaching out his other hand toward his favorite servant.

The naga shook his head fiercely, dropping the stone and reaching for the hilt of his sword. It hissed its release, the sound echoing through the hall as the other nagas all unsheathed their own weapons.

'You do not control me, Jarl,' the snake man broke in, to Jarl's evident surprise. After a split second, the Alfar second-in-command seemed to recover himself.

'Jimmu?' he repeated, only this time his voice was questioning.

'Jimmu and his nestmates act on their own,' the naga said, firmly. My eyes narrowed. *I think the Christian just threw himself to the lions.*

Morrigan's voice was still low and heavy, but there was

an element of tension to her tone. 'Are you admitting to your guilt?' she asked.

'Yes. I killed the halflings and the goblins.' Jimmu's voice was as indifferent as if he were ordering coffee.

'Why, Jimmu?' Jarl asked. I wondered if he were asking why Jimmu was sacrificing himself or if maybe – just maybe – he had genuinely been in the dark about Jimmu's actions. I hoped that was the case, but something told me not to get too attached to that idea.

'Halflings are abominations,' the naga replied without hesitation. 'They are defilements, corruptions. They deserve to die, as their very existence makes a mockery of our society.'

Don't hold back, now, I thought. *Let us know how you really feel . . .*

I needn't have been concerned; sharing his feelings about half-humans was something that Jimmu was, apparently, quite happy to do. 'I thought your interest in the halflings brought shame upon us. I thought you were intending to invite them into our society. The idea disgusted me, and so I followed Jakes and did away with his subjects one by one. Until he began to suspect me – then he was just one more halfling stain to be blotted out. The goblins, well . . .' He shrugged. 'They got in the way.'

There were hisses behind me, and more than a few goblins – towering above most of the other creatures in the hall – bared their multitudinous fangs. I took a firm grip on my beautiful shoes and inched away from the table.

'Is this all you have to say on the matter?' Orin asked, his expression still bizarrely calm, as if he were inquiring about the weather. 'Are these your justifications for your actions?'

Jimmu's shoulders eased up and down in a graceful shrug. 'My only justification is the existence of such things as *that*,' he said, turning around to point at me. I groaned inwardly at the same time I gave an automatic, if entirely inappropriate, little wave. *Why the fuck did I just do that?* I thought, as Jimmu continued his diatribe. 'Halflings are a disease that must be purged from our society,' he intoned. 'Any of you who cannot see that are disgracing yourselves and our people.'

The hall was silent. I looked about, and although most beings around me looked angry at Jimmu's words, there were quite a few that I thought didn't look entirely displeased. I also noticed that quite a few beings were eyeballing me right back, and I quickly averted my eyes.

Finally, Orin's and Morrigan's voices rang out. They spoke as one, their words throbbing with authority.

'Jimmu Naga and nestmates: you have committed serious crimes against our community, to which our halfling brethren resolutely belong. You have risked bringing undue attention to our existence with your actions. And you have spoken falsely to your king and queen, and to their Court. For these crimes, which amount to acts of treason, your lives are forfeit. Kneel and accept our justice, as is our right.'

Rather unsurprisingly, none of the nagas knelt. Instead they formed a circle around Jimmu, their firstborn brother and natural leader.

'So be it,' the nagas spoke together – as if to prove that they, too, could speak in stereo. As one, they raised their swords in front of them, all of which had begun to glow blue as if sheathed in the eerie fire that Ryu had used to burn the goblin letter so many days ago.

That evening there'd been a lot of noises, like the sounds made by what came out of Jimmu's sack, that I'd never heard before and never wanted to hear again. But the next noise to echo through the hall was one I was pretty sure I recognized.

It was the unmistakable sound of the shit hitting the fan.

With a fierce cry, Jimmu launched himself from his position among the nagas straight toward Ryu.

But my lover was nothing if not prepared. In a flash, Ryu shrugged out of his jacket while Wally pulled two scimitars out of his pantaloons. The djinn threw one wickedly curved blade to Ryu, while they both took defensive stances. I watched in disbelief as Ryu responded to Jimmu's charge with Neo's beckoning gesture from *The Matrix*.

The tiny portion of my brain that had a modicum of control shook its head, while wondering what the hell else Wally had in his pants. *Maybe a way out?* I thought, as Jimmu's sword met Ryu's with a resounding crash. With that sound, the rest of the nagas were aloft, attacking various points in the room. In response, creatures were pulling cudgels and edged weapons from underneath skirts, from inside coats, even from out of thin air. The nahuals all turned into lions, tigers, or bears (*oh my!*) while the Alfar created either little mage-light-looking things that they launched like projectiles at the nagas or lightsaber-looking shafts of light.

Meanwhile, the nagas – who I had to remind myself only numbered nine in total – appeared to be everywhere at once. Three had transformed into enormous black snakes. They were *huge*: long as RVs and thick as three WWE wrestlers grappling together. Their fangs looked as long as my body, and they had cobralike hoods that were scaled in red on the inside.

Somehow, the six that had remained in human form were no less scary than their serpentine brethren. They moved as swiftly and inexorably as water poured from a glass, cutting a swathe before them with their burning swords. I watched in horror as a naga female cut down a nahual in the shape of a tiger. The big cat had leapt from a table behind the snake woman, but she had spun around like a top and suddenly the cat was in two pieces, neither of which was moving.

Similar scenes of carnage were taking place throughout the room, but my attention quickly went back to Jimmu and Ryu, still locked in single combat. Their swords were moving so quickly they blurred and I had no idea who was winning. I wanted desperately to help my lover, but I didn't see how I could get near. I thought about throwing my chair, but I imagined accidentally tripping Ryu and I shuddered. I had never felt more powerless in my life.

A feeling that was exacerbated when someone used the opportunity provided by the ensuing fracas to goose me. I jumped, and turned to find that Wally had somehow gotten behind me. He smiled at me, his eyes flashing, and I backed away a step. *Trust no one*, Ryu's words echoed through my memory.

But Wally wasn't there to hurt me. 'Get out of here, halfling,' he said. 'Your bedmate is busy and it's about to get nasty.'

Bedmate? I thought, incredulously. *And what the hell do you mean, it's about to get nasty?*

But I took Wally's advice. With a last, and very pained, look toward where Ryu was battling with Jimmu, I grabbed my shoes, turned tail, and fled.

Suddenly an explosion rocked the hall. The king and queen had finally taken action, aiming two large orbs of energy at one of the snake-formed nagas. Both orbs hit like torpedoes, blasting off the snake's head. Its body swayed, pumping blood up into the air like red oil, before crashing down to the ground, pinning a shocked incubus under its weight. The Alfar monarchs calmly began creating new missiles, blasting energy into small balls that grew slowly in their palms.

I had been knocked off my feet by the reverberations of the blast, and it took me a moment to clamber back up. The part of me that wasn't shitting itself was amused that I was still clutching my shoes. Like I said, I had my priorities. My earlier scouting had revealed an exit immediately to the side of our table, which only required a short sprint to reach. The way was also relatively clear, as most of the action was currently located in the center-front of the hall. Still crouching, I gritted my teeth and focused on my goal, preparing to make a run for it, when my steps faltered. I'd caught a glimpse of the human whom Nyx had brought – he was still sitting on the edge of the head table, apparently oblivious to the chaos around him. I couldn't just leave him there, and his kidnapper was too busy to keep him safe. Nyx was currently clinging to the back of one of the snake-formed nagas' hood, yelling bloody murder with one of her arms stuck into the creature's eyeball up to her elbow. She looked happy as a pig in shit.

I swore, changing direction. There was another exit immediately behind where the man was sitting, which was as good a door as the one I was heading toward, and I could grab the man on my way out. I crouched down to make myself as small a target as possible, and scuttled toward the front of the hall, trying to balance skirting around the action with getting to my destination as quickly as possible.

When I got to one of the hall's thick pillars, I leaned against it for a moment to release the breath I'd been holding since I started off. There had been two more Alfar grenades lobbed, one of which had punched a nasty-looking hole in one of the remaining snakes' hood, leaving it reeling. Orin's, however, had gone wide, landing with horrific consequences among a little knot of Compound servants. Forcing my gaze away from the bloodbath, I prayed that Elspeth wasn't among them. When I caught a fleeting glimpse of Ryu, still alive but also still fencing with Jimmu, I took a deep breath and worked up the courage to leave my pillar. Not least because coming toward me was a slowly moving bundle of activity that seemed to consist of two spriggan bodyguards and the other naga female. It looked like all three were trying to club each other to death, and I remembered what Ryu had said about the spriggans being mercenaries. One of the big brutes didn't seem to know *quite* which side it was on.

I used the pillar to help propel myself into the melee, running as fast as I could toward the man and the door behind him. I yelped as an arm landed with a thud in front of me. To my horror, I recognized the golden circlet encompassing the fat bicep – it was Wally's. Just then the djinn was there, kneeling to pick up his amputated limb. He rolled his eyes at me like he'd dropped his wallet and stuck his arm back on, where it knitted smoothly back into position. Pulling *another* weapon from his pants – this time a cruel-looking mace – he launched himself back into the fray, smiling as if he were handing out candy rather than concussions.

I shook my head and sprinted off, again, until I finally made it to my destination. When I reached him, the man was still sitting as if he were on his sofa at home rather than planted at the edge of a battlefield. I grabbed his arm and pulled him toward the door, but he didn't budge. I pulled harder and harder, until I was leaning over so far I practically made a forty-five-degree angle.

I stood up and let go. Turning to him I surveyed his face. There wasn't a hint of activity going on behind his glazed eyes. So I called upon every iota of womanly instinct I had and pulled back my open hand to let fly a resounding *slap*. I think I might have given him whiplash.

The slap worked. His eyes blinked once, then again, as he suddenly seemed to come alive. I grabbed him by the shoulders to focus his attention on me – it wouldn't do either of us any good if he chose that moment to panic. The Alfar had sped up their barrage, and smaller explosions were detonating all over the hall. We had to get out of there, tout suite.

'Hey, buddy,' I said, loud enough so he could hear me over the noise but trying to keep my voice calm at the same time. 'What's your name?'

'Ed,' he said, nonplussed. 'Where am I?'

He started to look around but I put my hand to his cheek to keep his gaze on mine. 'Ed,' I advised. 'We're somewhere neither of us wants to be. So let's get out of here, okay?' I took his hand and tried to pull him up, but he *still* wasn't moving.

'There was a woman,' he started to say.

'Yes,' I interrupted. 'There was a woman but she's gone now. You're safe as long as we get moving. Like now,' I added, my voice starting to crack from stress. A flurry of activity had started up to our right and creatures were launching themselves out of the way. Something was coming.

I pulled harder on his hand, and he looked into my face. As if sensing my anxiety, he started to get up. I backed away, signaling for him to hurry. He nodded as if he'd made a decision and got to his feet resolutely, leaping away from the dais to land behind me. He nodded at the door. 'Get going,' he said, and I had just started to turn when I felt something wet splatter against my cheek. The man's expression changed, very slowly, from one of determination to one of confusion. We both looked down, equally astonished at the sight of the blazing sword protruding from his chest. The light died from his eyes as he crumpled to his knees. I realized I was screaming.

A movement from behind the man's body drew my eyes. It was Jimmu. He'd thrown the sword – either at me and the man had gotten in the way or at the man to get him out of Jimmu's path. Either way, there was now nothing standing between me and the naga's murderous rage.

I backed away, fighting Jimmu's paralyzing gaze and wishing I'd had the chance to call my father. I hadn't even thought of it – I'd been too swept up in events to put my affairs in order. But I guess people in their twenties don't normally think in terms of ordering their affairs. A mistake I wouldn't make again – quite literally.

And just think, a few days ago you were worried about living forever, I thought, as Jimmu's snarling face came to within an inch of mine. He obviously wanted to look me in the eyes when he killed me.

But before the dagger Jimmu was holding could reach my throat, Ryu was upon him. My lover was bleeding profusely from a terrible gash on his cheek, and he seemed to be favoring his left leg, but he still managed to propel Jimmu to the ground and away from me. The dagger was knocked aside and Ryu took that opportunity to begin pulverizing Jimmu's face with his fists. Knowing that I was still not exactly safe, and not wanting to see anyone ground into a bloody pulp no matter how much I disliked them, I left Ryu to it. With one last look at the dead human I'd tried to save but ended up killing, I fled through the door.

I found myself in another of the Alfar Compound's interminable hallways. This one was narrow and lined with dark stone, and only a few doorways appeared to interrupt its flow. I gave my eyes a moment to adjust to the lack of light before I set off down the hall. After a few seconds I heard a noise that gave me pause, until I realized that the sound was one of my own making. I was crying – all of tonight's various shocks reverberating uncontrollably through my system. But as long as I kept walking, I decided not to worry about the tears.

Which meant I never heard my attacker's footsteps. One minute I was walking forward, the next I was pinned up against the wall, a hand around my throat crushing the breath from me.

Oh nuts, I thought, as everything went gray. *I should have seen that coming.*

CHAPTER TWENTY-FOUR

Jarl was definitely not happy with me.

'You bitch,' Jarl hissed, his face broken with grief. 'You stupid half-breed bitch. You've ruined *everything*.' He was almost sobbing.

He really loved them, my analytical self observed. *Ryu was wrong. Jarl genuinely considered the nagas his children. And Ryu and I are responsible for their deaths.*

Overwhelming my analysis of tonight's events, however, was my body's response to the fact that it was about to die. Jarl was not content with merely suffocating me; he was slowly increasing the pressure on my windpipe, watching my eyes as he approached the point where he crushed the life from my body. He was going to enjoy every second of my death.

My vision was fading as the pain in my throat increased. I wish I could say that my life flashed before my eyes, or that I saw a vision of our maker, or that I had some other kind of epiphany about the meaning of life. Perversity, however, seems to be my middle name, and all I could think of was *how* exactly Wally had kept all that stuff in his pants. Especially the swords. Surely that was dangerous.

Just before everything went black, a shadow flashed in my

peripheral vision and Jarl suddenly released me. I sat down with a *whoosh*, as oxygen flooded my system. Breathing through my crushed throat was agony, but pain wasn't going to quell my body's need for air. I felt myself slide down the wall, till I was lying on my side. I could see Jarl's booted feet and huge paws dancing around in front of me as my vision came and went. One second everything was black, and then the lights went up and the boots were dangerously near my face, before everything went black again. Then the paws were between me and the boots, then they were shimmering, and everything went black. Suddenly there were two pairs of feet, one pair booted and the other bare, until darkness again whisked me away. A flurry of sound brought back the light, and I thought I saw Jarl flying through the air to land with a resounding crash against the wall. Then everything was black again, but I could feel someone easing me up to a seated position. Hands were at my throat, but gently this time, and a voice that sounded like it was underwater was telling me to hold still, that he'd make it better. Warmth suffused my system, and my vision returned enough for me to register a blurry face in front of mine. I closed my eyes in relief as my agony receded, my brain scrambling to catch up with events.

Jarl, it reminded me, with a kick, and I looked over to where the Alfar was still lying against the wall. I blinked and whimpered when I saw his huddled form twitch.

'Shit,' the voice cursed, obviously seeing what I was seeing. Where the stranger's hands were as gentle as a mother's, his voice was as rough as a dog's growl. 'We're going to have to finish this later, Jane. Let's get you somewhere safe.'

Strong arms picked me up and flung me over a wide shoulder. I struggled, finally registering that I had no idea who this man was. I thought I recognized the voice, but what I thought I recognized wasn't possible.

'Keep still,' the man growled, gently. 'Until we get you out of here.'

I know you, an eighth of my brain argued, while another eighth told me I was nuts. The last three-quarters were still reeling from my near-death experience.

Suddenly, my addled mind comprehended that the guy holding me was completely naked and, with the way he was carrying me, I had a good view of a rather splendid back-side. He'd picked up the pace till he was trotting, and we were bumping through the Compound at an impressive speed. Which meant that I'd slipped down, somewhat, so he was holding my thighs tight over his shoulder and I'd come nose to cheek with a single formidable buttock.

Trust no one, Ryu's voice again reminded me, just as we went through a set of doors and into the cold air of the night. The evening's chill and the burst of fresh oxygen crashed through my system, enflaming my senses and putting my own consciousness firmly back into the driver's seat.

I began to struggle in earnest, still unsure of the intent of the buck-naked stranger. He'd saved me from Jarl, but for what purpose? Why hadn't he put me down, or brought me back to Ryu? Panic rose as my body managed to dredge up another burst of adrenaline from somewhere. Staring at the muscles rippling in front of my face, I made a spur-of-the-moment decision. I wanted down, and I wanted down *now*. So I bit, hard, at the first thing my teeth found – which was, of course, the vulnerable keister of my captor.

The man roared, and I slipped precipitously toward the ground. I could see from the Celtic mosaic that we were in the little courtyard right beside the grotto. Swearing like a sailor, the man caught me just before I crashed into the very painful-looking cobblestones. Strong arms pulled my legs down his chest, till he could get his hands around my waist.

He pulled me off his shoulder and sat me down against a wall, where I stared up at him mutinously. He was standing with his back to me, twisted around so that he could peer at his own backside. Where I saw, to my pleasure, a rather perfect set of teeth indented in his smooth flesh. A dentist could have taken a molding from his ass, I'd bitten him so hard.

'Jesus, Jane,' the gravelly voice swore, as he rubbed at the bite marks with his hand. 'You nearly broke the skin.' His stormy gray eyes met mine. 'And human bites are the *worst*,' he said as my brain went into overdrive.

'You *bastard*,' I choked, finally. Talking hurt but I was so angry I didn't care. 'You're supposed to be a *dog*.'

Anyan looked at me, apparently as confused as I was. 'You knew what I was,' he said, defensively. 'I told you I was a barghest.'

My eyes nearly rolled out of my head. 'What am I, a supernatural encyclopedia?' I coughed, the effort of speaking finally getting the better of me. But I was so angry I forced myself to continue. 'I thought,' I started, but it was too much. My throat up and quit on me as I was racked with pain.

Anyan knelt beside me in a flash, his large hands again enfolding my neck. 'Shush, you,' he murmured. 'Keep still. Let me heal you properly. Your windpipe was nearly crushed.'

I gave him my most baleful stare, even as I felt his hands again emit that gentle warmth that I knew meant a release from pain. He was carefully stroking his thumbs over my windpipe, examining me. Finally satisfied that I wasn't going to keel over and die, he deigned to meet my hostile gaze. But when I saw the concern in his eyes, my anger melted away.

He was still healing me and I couldn't yet talk, so I had a chance to study him. He looked somehow familiar, but not in the anxiety-inducing way Jimmu had. In his human form,

Anyan was like someone I'd known in a dream. It was a strange sensation, but it wasn't uncomfortable. I examined his face, so close to mine. His hair was the same color as his fur had been, and equally wild and long. It poofed out in loose, wiry curls that fell just past his high cheekbones. His features were very strong – a long, prominent nose that was quite crooked, a wide mouth with full lips, and an angular jaw. His eyes were large and expressive, but that description fit every bit of him. If he'd been a big dog, he was a huge man. He must be well over six feet tall, and his hands met easily around my neck. He could have crushed my head like a grape.

I know you, I thought at him. For a second, I thought I knew where from, but then the memory faded again. I concentrated, staring intently into his gray eyes.

'I'm sorry,' he said, finally. 'I didn't mean to deceive you. You seemed to know what I meant when I told you I was a barghest.'

I smiled at him, ruefully. 'Roald Dahl,' I eventually managed to wheeze.

He stared at me for a second, before comprehension dawned on his face. *'The Witches?'* he asked, with a laugh. 'My god, woman. No wonder you looked worried.' He chuckled – a rich, dark sound – and his laugh reverberated through his hands and into my body. 'Don't worry, that's not an accurate description.'

I raised my eyebrow, and he smiled, understanding me. 'We're two-formeds, like your mother. Human-formed and dog-formed, obviously. But with extra big teeth and paws,' he said, smiling at me to reveal slightly elongated canines. He didn't show me his hands, but I was very much aware of how big those were, considering they were wrapped around my throat.

We sat in silence for a few more seconds until he slowly released my neck. In the meantime, I was being very careful to keep my eyes away from his crotch. I couldn't deal with checking out a guy whose adorable fuzzy ears I had been scratching just a few days before.

'How does it feel?' he asked. I cleared my throat experimentally, feeling only the slightest tickle. I extended my experiment to a cough, happy when there was no pain.

'Much better,' I said, finally. My voice was raw, but that was about the only evidence left over of my run-in with Jarl. That and utter exhaustion. I felt like I'd run five marathons in a row and I knew I was minutes away from total systems failure. I think I was also in shock.

'Good,' he said, his hand going to my chin so that he could study my face. I studied him right back, my memory dancing forward and back, teasing me.

'Ryu should never have brought you here,' he said, his rough voice mournful. 'It was too soon.'

I was exhausted, on edge, and now Anyan had reminded me that I was still worried about Ryu's safety. Hearing those words meant I had two choices: I was either going to flip out or start crying hysterically. I chose the former.

'I am *not* a child, you big mutt,' I said rancorously, all of tonight's frustration aimed squarely at Anyan's hairy chest. 'Just because I'm a halfling doesn't mean I'm weak, or unworthy, or stupid. I have handled everything your fucked-up Court has thrown at me, and I've survived.' I reconsidered that statement. 'Barely,' I admitted, 'but I *did* survive. So stop treating me like some lower species. Dog breath.' I added, after a moment, rather lowering the tone of my spur-of-the-moment speech.

My words obviously stole his thunder, and he sat down next to me heavily. He didn't speak, at a loss for words.

'I never meant that,' he said, eventually. 'I've *never* thought you were pathetic and I don't consider you half of anything.' His voice was sad, the tone so familiar yet unidentifiable that I wanted to scream. 'You're Jane,' he concluded, 'and that's enough.' He looked over at me, his face shadowed but his eyes still visible.

Of course . . .

'You were my invisible friend,' I heard myself say.

He frowned, looking guilty.

'When I was in the hospital, after Jason died. You came to me. We talked and you told me everything would be all right. You told me stories and held my hand while I slept.' Once I said those words, I knew I was right. And his expression proved it, no matter how crazy I sounded.

'I visited you,' he admitted. 'I couldn't leave you alone in that place. We – Nell and I – felt guilty about Jason's death.' He thought about his next words before continuing. 'That cove, it's ours, you know. We keep it hidden for our own use, otherwise it would just be taken over by local kids, but you saw through our glamour. We didn't make it strong enough. You brought Jason there and we knew we should have sealed it up. But you were both so young and so innocent, and you'd been through such hard times. So we let you use it, and you were comfortable there. Too comfortable,' he added, remorsefully. 'If we hadn't let you use that cove, you would have been more circumspect about your swimming. And if you'd been more wary, Jason would be alive.' He shook his head, sadly. 'I'm sorry, Jane. It's our fault he died.'

There was no doubt in my mind: what he was saying was ridiculous.

'Anyan,' I heard myself say. 'That's not true. Jason's death, it was . . .'

My voice trailed off. I was about to say that his death had been an accident.

My entire world wobbled, and I took a few deep breaths.

'So I would visit you,' he persisted. 'You were so . . . broken. And you should never have been in that hospital. We should have intervened. But I probably made things worse, didn't I?' His voice was so low I could barely make out what he was saying.

'No,' I said, automatically, not realizing that I felt that way before I'd said it. 'You're the reason I got through. I mean, I didn't know you were real, and I did think you were proof I was crazy at times. But when things got really bad, when I thought I couldn't get through another day, you'd be there and I didn't feel so alone.'

With those words we were both struck dumb. Tonight had been way too intense – too many revelations, too much violence, too many painful memories. *Too much pain, period*, I thought wryly, rubbing a hand over my throat.

'Were you the one by the pool that day, with Jimmu?' I asked, finally breaking the silence. He only nodded.

'Thank you,' I said. 'You saved my life, twice.' I took a deep breath. 'And I apologize for calling you dog breath. Your breath actually smells like toothpaste. Which makes a lot more sense now that I know you have thumbs.' He gave me a slow smile that I returned, although my brain was still agitated. 'So, why did Jarl attack me?'

Beside me, Anyan sighed. 'I think Jarl knew what Jimmu was doing and I believe that Jimmu was working on his orders. But perhaps Jarl was telling the truth and he knew nothing.' I felt Anyan's powerful shoulders shift as he shrugged. 'Who knows what motivates the Alfar in general, and Jarl in particular. But he's always despised half-humans.'

'Well,' I said, 'Ryu will definitely have something to say

about the fact that I was attacked . . .' My voice trailed off as Anyan turned to look at me. He made a little gesture and a tiny mage light flickered into life next to our heads.

He stared into my eyes so intently I thought he was going to fall forward and head-butt me. 'Jane,' he said, his harsh voice choked with emotion. 'There are forces at work here that neither of us can understand. You are new to this world and I have been out of the loop for too long.' He shook his shaggy head, angrily. 'I have let us both down, and I am sorry. But you must listen to me. You must tell *no one* about what passed here tonight between you and Jarl. Not even Ryu.' I started to protest, but he placed a single finger over my lips.

'Ryu cares for you, I know that,' he said, reluctantly. 'But you must understand that his position and his ambition make him . . .' He paused. 'Not untrustworthy, in the sense that he would intentionally harm you. But dangerous, nonetheless. Until we know what Jarl's attack means, we must keep it to ourselves. Please, you *must* trust me.'

Our faces were inches apart, and his eyes were so earnest that I paused. Mentally, however, I was scrambling, ready to come to my man's defense. Of *course* I had to tell Ryu what had happened here, tonight. He was *Ryu*, fercrissakes.

But before I could articulate my feelings, we were interrupted.

'Oh my gods, Jane,' barked a familiar voice, and my heart lurched. I pushed myself up against the wall, rising painfully to my feet. 'Thank heavens you're all right,' Ryu babbled happily, till his eyes lit on Anyan. He stopped dead in his tracks.

'Ryu,' I sobbed, suddenly more than ready to have that good cry I'd been verging on earlier. I managed to stand and made my way over to him, where he folded me in his arms.

I buried my face in his chest and breathed him in, clinging to him like a barnacle. He did smell a bit foul, actually – but underneath the blood and the sweat was the familiar scent of Ryu.

He caressed the back of my neck and his lips pressed against my forehead. 'What happened?' he asked. 'Why is Anyan Barghest here?'

I opened my mouth, ready to tell him everything. About Wally and his arm, about the spriggans and their possible treachery, about Nyx and the eyeball, and, most important, about Jarl and his attack on me.

But for some reason I paused, just for a moment, and looked back. Anyan had stood up and moved away from us. He was nearly out of the little gate that led to the pool. I met his eyes, recalling the sound of human body parts hitting the floor as they were dumped from a sack. I shuddered, finally understanding what he'd been trying to tell me. I trusted Ryu, I really did. And I knew that he wouldn't stand to see me hurt.

I turned back to my lover, who was watching the barghest with a decidedly unfriendly expression. I noticed Ryu's cheek was already healed. 'I don't really know,' I said, finally. 'I must have gotten hit on the head, or something. When I woke up I was out here, with Anyan. He healed me,' I added, lamely, as I heard the soft *snick* of a gate closing behind me.

Ryu looked into my eyes, frowning. At long last, he shook his head and said, 'Okay, Jane. As long as you're safe, I'm happy.' His arms were back around me and I relaxed into his hard embrace. Better late than never, I understood Anyan's words. Ryu cared for me, and he took his job seriously. If I told him what Jarl had done, he'd investigate. *And right now, with no evidence beside a half-human's testimony, Jarl would squash Ryu like a bug*, I thought, as I wiped my nose on

his shirt. I was snotty from crying and he was already filthy.
It wasn't ideal but he was holding me so tight I couldn't move
my arms.

'Did you just wipe your nose on me?' he asked, finally.
His voice was tight with various emotions, but 'oh no you
didn't' had clawed its way to the top of the list.

'Maybe,' I mumbled, peering up at him.

'Oh Jane,' he said, pulling a handkerchief from his back
pocket. With which he wiped his already filthy shirt and *then*
my nose. 'What am I going to do with you?'

'Take me home?' I suggested, hopefully.

'Of course,' he said, although his eyes were sad. 'I promised, didn't I? But first, I'll take you to bed.' After wiping
my nose again to be on the safe side, he picked me up to
carry me inside. Holding me tight to his chest, he covered
my face with butterfly kisses. He was still limping slightly
but I figured if he could handle my weight I'd let him. I
wasn't in too good shape at this point, either. 'I was so scared
when I couldn't find you,' he said, eventually.

'I was scared, too,' I said, very truthfully.

'I'm sorry everything turned out the way it has. This was
not how I imagined introducing you to Alfar society.'

'I know, Ryu. I know.' Then I remembered something. 'Did
you kill Jimmu?' I asked, rather surprised at how matter of
fact I sounded.

'Oh, yes,' Ryu said, grinning at me fang-tastically. 'But he
was being very obstreperous about it,' he added. 'He just
wouldn't cooperate and die.'

'Hmm. Well, that's good. That Jimmu's dead, I mean. Oh,
and you should have seen what I saw Wally do,' I added,
starting in on an edited version of my evening's surprises.
Just because I couldn't tell him *everything* didn't mean I
couldn't tell him some things.

When I was done telling him about Wally's arm, and what I'd seen Nyx do to the naga, we were back at our room. I had to give Nyx credit. She might be a bitch, but she was definitely hard core.

We didn't talk much after that, at least not verbally. Despite everything that had happened, or probably *because* of everything that had happened, I found my body had a lot more to say than I thought it would. Despite its exhaustion, it wanted to converse about life, and mortality, and fear, and pain, and love, and pleasure. Especially pleasure.

Luckily for me, Ryu's body was more than happy to join with mine in a dialogue that lasted until we were both too tired to speak, either literally or figuratively.

If I'd known discourse could be this fun, I thought, as I fell asleep in Ryu's arms, *I would have joined the debate team* . . .

CHAPTER TWENTY-FIVE

'Daddy!' I shouted, racing to hug him.

That he was surprised to see me getting out of the back of a Mercedes was an understatement. Equally surprising was the vehemence with which I greeted him.

'Are you all right, Jane?' he asked, his voice concerned. 'What happened?'

I choked back my overwhelming sense of relief at seeing my dad, and my home, setting a bright smile in its place. 'Oh, everything is fine, Dad,' I said, when I could finally trust myself to speak. The driver had removed my bags from the back of the car, setting them on our front porch, before quietly motoring off.

'Why didn't Ryu drive you back?' he asked, his voice suspicious.

'Oh, something came up. But don't worry, Ryu was great. The trip was great.' I paused, collecting myself. 'Seriously, Dad, everything was fine and Ryu could not have treated me any better, honestly. But he had to stay in Québec for business so he sent me home in a car. This ride was more comfortable than his, anyway.'

My father kept staring at me, as if he wanted to ask me

more, until it was my turn to grow suspicious. *How much did he know about my mother and her world?* I wondered. He must have known *something* was up, but I didn't know just how much *something* entailed.

'Dad?' I asked, gently. 'Is there anything you want to ask me?'

He started, drawing away from me. He began to say something, and his jaw worked helplessly for a few seconds before he stopped. This happened again a few moments later.

Then he shook his head. 'No, Jane,' he said, finally. 'There's nothing I want to ask you.'

I couldn't help but feel disappointed. I certainly hadn't planned on confronting my father with the truth of my mother's existence, but now that I had the chance I realized I wished that I could tell him. But if he didn't want to know, I didn't want to force the truth upon him. My father had already suffered his share of betrayal.

I rummaged around and eventually found a smile for him. He returned it, relieved. 'So, what did I miss?' I asked, changing the subject. He took the bait, and started telling me what had happened while I was away. Which wasn't much. But, being my dad and me, we made it into enough to get us through.

After we'd caught up and had an early dinner, I went upstairs to unpack. But first I lay down on my childhood bed, never so happy to be home in my life. *I love you, Rockabill*, I thought, surprised at how profoundly I meant it. Stuart and Linda would never look so scary again, ever. Not after twenty-foot snake people, minotaurs, and everything else I'd seen that weekend.

The morning after the battle had been horrible. Luckily, everyone I'd come to know in the Compound – except for Jimmu, obviously – was safe. Wally was apparently impervious to most forms of death, so he was fine. And Orin and Morrigan had never been in any real danger, as none of their people had let anything get close to them. As for Elspeth, she'd not even been in the main hall at the time – she'd absconded with one of the nahual acrobats that had performed at the previous evening's dinner. They'd all been exceptionally bendy, and I reckoned she was a lucky woman – or tree – on a number of levels. *Then again*, I thought, thinking of Elspeth's strange suppleness, *maybe the nahual was the lucky one – she is awfully limber for timber.* Then I laughed at my own joke, because I'm a dork.

But my friends' safety was about the only good news. The death toll was frighteningly high, especially considering how there were so few young ones to take their parents' places in the community. Besides the nine nagas, there had been twenty-three creatures hurt too badly to be saved. I gathered from people's reactions that it was a tremendous blow to the Territory, and it obviously took a huge personal toll on the loved ones of those who died.

More worrying, a few of the beings killed had been fighting *with* the nagas, rather than against them. The battle had revealed a deeper schism in the community than anyone had ever thought existed, and that schism revolved around the issue of halflings like me. In his role as an investigator, Ryu was going to be very busy for the next few months sorting out the bad apples. And because of my role as the 'stupid half-breed bitch' who started the whole thing, I had to get the hell out of Dodge.

So Ryu had apologized profusely and stuck me in a hired car. I totally didn't mind the hasty retreat. Indeed, I'd never thought I could be that happy to get back to Rockabill. But now, safe in my own bed, I almost wept with relief.

Eventually, I got up to unpack. I hung up what was still

clean and piled everything else in my hamper. Finally, I was left with the large white box and its contents.

I'd lost the shoes, in the end. Apparently, nearly getting choked to death was what it took to separate me from designer heels. But they'd miraculously shown up the next morning, laid in front of our external door. The shoes I took out of the box and put in my closet. Then I pulled out the dress.

Unbelievably, considering how delicate it was and what I'd been through, it was entirely intact. Except that it was covered in blood. I knew whose it was; it was Ed's, the human that Nyx had kidnapped and who had died because he'd been standing between me and Jimmu.

I sat, cross-legged, on my bed holding the dress. It was so beautiful, I should have it cleaned. But instead I carefully folded it back up, blood and all, and stowed it back in the box. The gore encrusting it would serve to remind me of everything I needed to remember: that underneath the glamour and excitement of my mother's world skulked a dark reality. Human life meant nothing to the Alfar and their Court. We were merely an expendable nuisance for the majority of beings in that society.

And, for better or worse, I was half human – something I could never forget. Beings like Nyx or Jarl would never *let* me forget it, but neither did I want to. I'd quite obviously taken being human for granted until very recently, but now I clung to it like a badge of honor.

After I'd unpacked and put in a load of laundry, I did as Ryu asked and called him to tell him I was home safe. We talked only briefly. He sounded exhausted and we'd just seen each other that morning. But he promised to visit as soon as everything quietened down and said that he'd phone me next week. Meanwhile, I should call him if I needed anything. I felt all warm and fuzzy after I spoke to him, not least because

I kept having flashbacks of him sword fighting. I know you're not supposed to get horny for violence, but I couldn't help it. I got horny for violence.

Then I called Grizzie and Tracy. I told them all about Québec, exaggerating everything slightly so it seemed as if that part of the trip had taken the entire week. I promised to show them pictures at work tomorrow. I was very excited to see my friends; I'd missed them very much.

When Grizzie hung up to get their dinner out of the oven, Tracy asked me when I would next see Ryu.

'I'm not really sure,' I answered truthfully. 'I know he really likes me, but something came up when we were gone that's going to mean he's crazy busy for a while. So, we'll see what happens.'

'And you're sure you're okay with everything?' Tracy asked.

'No,' I told her unexpectedly, startling even myself. I'd known I would eventually have to deal with everything that I experienced last week, but I hadn't expected it to hit me in the gut like a karate chop. 'I've got a lot of stuff to think through, Trace. But it's not because of Ryu. He was great.' I was suddenly tired. 'Look, I gotta go. I'll see you tomorrow.'

She said goodbye, her voice expressing her concern for me.

After the last vestiges of sunlight vanished from the sky, I left for the cove. When Tracy had asked me if I was okay, my first reaction had been to say 'yes'. But for the last eight years, I had told myself that I wasn't *ever* supposed to be okay again. *Oh, Jason*, I thought, as I entered our secret world where we'd laughed and made love and discovered ourselves in a way I knew few people ever did. Because of Jason, I knew what love was, and because I knew what love was I knew who *I* was.

I knelt down in the sand, facing the ocean. I hadn't thought about Jason all week and I'd been *alive*. Even with all the fucked-up things that had happened, I knew that there were moments during my trip with Ryu when I'd been the happiest I'd been since the night Jason died. Admitting that, the sliver of me that had frozen up that terrible night in the Sow made itself known and I felt like I'd killed him all over again.

My tears dripped hot and heavy down my face. I'd wanted so desperately to move on, and last week had begun breaking a trail for me, if only I was brave enough to follow. And yet all I could think about, right now, was everything I would have to leave behind and everything I would have to confront. I opened myself, half unwilling, to everything I tried every day not to remember. My hands flexed convulsively in our sand as memories of Jason flooded through me: our using the cove to play Prince and Princess, when he would 'rescue' me from the huge old driftwood log we used as a bench when it wasn't serving as a convenient villain; the first time we kissed in a way that didn't feel like brother and sister; how those first, fumbling kisses evolved into an intimacy that shouldn't have been possible in two people so young; how we clung together throughout our griefs, and our hurts; and how we realized that what brought us together was our shared knowledge that life bore no guarantees and no consolation prizes. But despite our own losses, I'd never foreseen that *he* could be taken away. That had never been a possibility, until it happened.

I was so desolate that I didn't stir, or even attempt to stop my weeping, when I heard large paws padding through the sand behind me. I was just happy my visitor had come as a dog. I found him easier to deal with that way.

Anyan sat down in the sand next to me. He let me be, not touching me or interfering in any way, until I'd cried myself out. After the last shuddering gasp was torn from my chest and my tears had ceased, he finally spoke.

'He'd want you to live,' was all the big dog said. 'If he loved you the way you know he did, he would want you to live.'

My throat closed as tightly as when Jarl's fist was around it. I'd been told versions of that line about a million times by my dad, by Grizzie, by Tracy, by doctors, by nurses, by shrinks, and even by the occasional stranger. But hearing it from Anyan – the matter of fact way he said it – broke through my carefully erected barriers.

I thought of how much I'd loved Jason. I'd loved him not just for what he gave me, or what I thought we would build together, but because Jason was Jason. I loved him because he was kind, and generous, and he knew how to live in a way that drew others into his happiness. If I had died, and Jason had survived, I would not have wanted him to change. I would want him to be happy. Because he was a good man, and because I loved him.

I knew Anyan was right. Jason *would* want me to live, because he was Jason.

I was crying again, but this time with a sense of release. I finally admitted to myself that, while some people in Rockabill hadn't made things easier, they weren't the ones who had kept me bound to my grief, imprisoned in my own past. I'd done that to myself.

I would *always* love Jason, and I would forever regret the part I had unwittingly played in his death. But at that moment, staring at my hands buried in the sand of our cove where we had loved each other with such unerring force, and hearing the soft susurrations of my sea whispering to me of forgiveness, I finally appreciated the depth of what our love had meant.

Be at peace, my beloved. It's time for us both to rest . . .

Anyan leaned down, his soft tongue grazing my knuckles. I managed to smile into his big doggie face, until the impulse took me to throw my arms around his neck. I sank my nose into the thick fur of his ruff, inhaling his scent of warm, clean dog spiced with an undertone of cardamom. He obligingly allowed me to cling to him for a minute, before withdrawing slightly to lick the last of my tears from my cheek with quick strokes of his able tongue. I met his gray gaze with my black, and for the first time in a very long while, I smiled with my whole being.

'Go swim, Jane,' his rough voice commanded, as he used his broad head to nudge me toward the water. 'Nell will begin your training tomorrow and you'll need all the energy you can get.'

A startled thrill of anticipation shivered through me at his unexpected words. I hadn't thought things would move so quickly. *My training*, I thought. *Tomorrow I'm going to start training*. What exactly I was going to learn was a mystery to me, but the thought of being able to use the power I could – even now – feel pulsing under my skin floored me.

I thought about the tricks I'd seen Ryu and the others do: the mage lights, the glamours, the swords of fire that cut tigers in half. I had no desire to cut a tiger in half, but still. The idea that I might one day do even a quarter of those things thrilled me and I couldn't *wait* to see what I was capable of.

'Wow,' I breathed, imagining that the next time Ryu took me to a beach to seduce me with naked swimming and sexy finger foods *I*, Jane True, would be the one to light the mage light. Maybe I could even make it a disco ball.

Boom chicka boom boom, my libido chimed in, doing its best imitation of a seventies porn soundtrack.

And maybe the next time an evil elf grabs you by the throat you can rescue your own damned self, I thought, putting a different spin on my excitement.

I pulled off my Converse and socks and stood up to undo my pants. It was only after I'd gotten as far as unbuttoning them halfway down that I remembered.

Anyan's stormy gray eyes met mine, wide and innocent as my sea.

'Bad dog,' I scolded. 'Shoo.'

He rumbled a growling laugh that did no justice to my memory of the rich chuckle he'd sent through my body when he'd been in his man form. He stood up, shaking the sand out of his fur.

'I'll be around, Jane. Practice hard and do as Nell tells you.' He gave me a long look, and I suddenly felt uncomfortable.

'Yes, boss,' I said to break the tension. He chuckled again, in response, and disappeared through the gap in the cove walls.

I stripped off the rest of the way quick as could be, then raced into my sea. She reared up to greet me, pulling me in and filling me with her cold power. I roiled in her waves, played in her currents, and drank deep of her strength.

Let them come for me, I thought of Jarl and Nyx and the others like them, who assumed I would be weak. *Because next time I'll be ready.*

Acknowledgments

There are so many people I have to thank for *Tempest Rising*.

First of all, to my family. Everything that I've accomplished is because of you. To my parents: you have given me the luxury of time and space to become what I am. To my brother, Chris: you'll always be my hero. To Lisa: you are an inspiration. Much of Jane's strength and warmth I first saw in you. To Abbie and Wyatt: your Aunt Nikki loves you very much. You are amazing individuals and I am very proud of both of you.

I can't begin to express my gratitude to my Alpha Readers, Dr James Clawson and Christie Ko. You treated me like a real author when I still thought the whole thing would turn out to be a joke. I would also like to thank Judy Bunch, for coming in at the end and walloping my grammar. You are a true teacher, and I continue to learn from you every day. In that vein, I'd like to thank all my teachers. Who'd a thunk it would culminate in comic hor-mance? I owe you all so much.

I would also like to thank the people who were there to watch the circus unfold. To all of my friends and colleagues from Edinburgh, thank you for your time, support, and never telling me to shut up. Special thanks to the staff at Bean

Scene, in Leith, who let me use their cafe as my 'office', and extra special thanks to Jamal Abdul Nasir, who had to live with me living in a corner of our flat, muttering to myself.

I owe eternal gratitude to Rebecca Strauss, and everyone else at McIntosh & Otis, for believing in someone who came so far out of left field. To Devi Pillai, thank you for seeing the potential in Jane and for taking a chance on me. Thanks to Alex Lencicki and Jennifer Flax for putting up with my endless questions. I hope to do all of you at Orbit proud. Not least because Lauren Panepinto found the amazing artist Sharon Tancredi to bring Jane to such beautiful life. I can't wait to see the next cover.

Huge thanks have to go to everyone at LSU in Shreveport for continuing to support a new hire who suddenly became an urban fantasist, and to all of my students who continually inspire, challenge, and entertain me.

Finally, thanks to everyone at the League of Reluctant Adults and to all of the other writers who have been so obliging to the newbie. I feel so blessed to have been welcomed into such an amazing fraternity.

extras

www.orbitbooks.net

about the author

Nicole D. Peeler is off on another adventure! This time, she's moving to Pittsburgh to teach in Seton Hill's MFA in Popular Fiction. Yes, folks, she'll be mentoring up and coming urban fantasists as they try to break into the publishing world. Or, as she likes to call it, 'infecting them with her madness'. In the meantime, she's still taking pleasure in what means most to her: family, friends, food, and travel.

Find about more about Nicole Peeler and other Orbit authors by registering for the free monthly newsletter at www.orbitbooks.net

interview

***How did you come up with the idea for* Tempest Rising?**
It was all very quick, and I sound very hippie-dippie when I
talk about it. But I first had Jane's essence; it all started with
the idea of someone like Jane getting stuck in an urban fantasy
world. Jane is an amalgamation of all these really strong, inde-
pendent women that I know, like my sister-in-law. These women
do amazing things, and they just get it done. If I did the stuff
they did, I'd make a T-shirt praising myself. And yet, it's all
just one more day for them. That said, these women are human-
woman strong, not warrior-woman strong. They are nurses, and
activists, and teachers; not Amazonian predators with
broadswords. So I wanted Jane to be human, but be supernatural. Which left me at an impasse, until it hit me to make her
a selkie. Then I thought that full selkie had limitations, but if I
made her *half* selkie, I was golden. Jane could be magic; she
could be human; she could have some kick-ass adventures.

***What was it about selkies that appealed to you? Since you're
writing about selkies, will Orbit pay for you to fly to Scotland
and do research?***
I'm sure that Orbit will definitely spring for me to take many
trips to Scotland, especially as I plan on setting the last book
of the series in Edinburgh. I'm sure they'll also pay for me to
stay at the Balmoral every time. Right guys?

Seriously, though, the selkie myth was perfect for my
purposes, and it was what really made Jane real for me.

I'd always been fascinated by the selkie stories, and especially those where a mortal man finds and takes home a seal skin, in total innocence. In some of the stories, the men trick the seal-women, but I always liked the innocent guys. The tragedy of such myths, when the seal-woman finds her skin (usually it's found and given to her by one of her children) and then leaves, really affected me. I think it was that idea of being so driven that one is forced to make outrageous sacrifices. I'm a very driven person, so it's probably all Freudian. But using this myth allowed me to have a very magical heroine who wasn't the more typical Urban Fantasy warrior-woman. Nobody expects a seal to pick up nunchucks and start whaling on people. I wanted Jane vulnerable, but to face danger *despite* her vulnerabilities. Having a vulnerable, but brave, heroine was very important to me.

Have you put any of your own personality traits or interests in your heroine? Or is she completely different from you?
I'd like to think I was like Jane, and I definitely gave her my warped sense of humor, but she's a lot braver and a lot nicer than me. She's also way cuter than me, although I did make her a nerdy English literature person, which was pure self-indulgence on my part.

If you could have chosen any other career instead of being an author, what would you have been?
Actually, writing is my second career. I'm a full-time assistant professor of English literature at Louisiana State University in Shreveport. I've been really blessed, in that I've gotten to do both of the things I've wanted to do. I wouldn't give up either job for the world, and I really do have to pinch myself sometimes, when I contemplate how everything has fallen into place for me. That said, I would never be where I am without the support of my family. They've given me everything, and I can't begin to express my gratitude.

***How much research do you do on your subject matter? Do
you find it helps inspire, gives you a launching point? Or does
it bog you down?***

I have very strong feelings on this subject. As an academic,
I research the hell out of everything before I do it. And I
approached writing this book the way I approached everything else in my life: with research. The first thing I did when
I thought, 'I'm going to write a book,' was to Google 'how
many words is an average book'. And I never got a straight
answer. The reply talked about average YA books, average
Epic Fantasy books, average Romance. But when confronted
by these diverse non-answers, I had to make my *own* decisions. Did I want a long book, like something by Robert
Jordan? Did I want a really quick read, like *The Curious
Incident of the Dog in the Night-Time*? I decided I wanted a
beach read, something that is about 90,000 words, and that a
reader can ingest in one day if they feel like it. In other words,
while researching what *other* people did, I narrowed down
what *I* wanted to do. My other example regarding the import-
ance of research is the Old Sow. Everyone who has read
Tempest Rising has told me I was a genius making up the Old
Sow. Well, I'm not, because I didn't make it up; it's real. I
knew what Rockabill would be like, and I knew Jane would
swim. But then I'm Googling Maine and I find there's a
whirlpool called the Old Sow. I could never have made that
up. Who would think to name a whirlpool after a pig? Then
I thought of the implications for Rockabill, and suddenly I
had the Trough, and the Pig Sty, et cetera. And I had an
instantaneous vision of Jane out-maneuvering a piglet, an even
more dramatic representation of how Jane's swimming was
not normal swimming than what I had before. Then came a
vision of her finding the body in the Sow itself. My point is
that the Old Sow enhanced the novel immeasurably, and I
couldn't have invented it. So my advice to every writer is to
do research. You'll always find something to inspire you.

How old you were when you first thought about writing a book, and were you drawn to Urban Fantasy at a young age – or did you just read anything and everything?

I started reading when I was very young, and I read very adult books, very young. I did a book report on *The Clan of the Cave Bear* in third grade. The teacher nearly had a heart attack. Anyway, I always wanted to be a writer, but outside of taking two elective creative writing courses – one in high school and one in college – I never actively pursued it. But I always loved fantasy, and I loved urban fantasy before it was even called Urban Fantasy. One of my favorite authors as a child was Mercedes Lackey, especially her series with Vanyel about Valdemar. Then I read her series with Diana Tregarde, which was definitely Urban Fantasy, but I don't know if people even called it that, back then. Anyway, it had a vampire love interest, and I was hooked. I felt the same way about Charles de Lint. His use of mythology floored me, and the book *Greenmantle* had an especially huge impact on me. I think I was probably ten when I read it, and I've read it probably twenty-five times since. Its depiction of the supernatural world was so ambivalent, and the possibilities for violence very frightening. I loved it, naturally. But I also read everything else I could get my little mitts on.

What is the most important ingredient in:
  a) your life
  My friends and family, for sure.
  b) your food
  That would have to be cheese or sour cream. I'm a dairy person. Hence my girlish figure.
  c) your writing
  I think I owe my writing to all my reading. That's why it kills me when people tell me they want to be a writer but they don't read.

d) your drink
Bourbon, baby. Bourbon all the way.

What can you tell us about the next novel?

I'm really excited by *Tracking the Tempest*. It's faster-paced than *Tempest Rising*, and you really see how much Jane has changed in the four-month span between the two books. It's also set in Boston, which is very exciting, as Boston University is my alma mater. The plot of *Tracking the Tempest* has Jane pursued by a maniac Ifrit-Halfling, and a whole new group of *very* creepy baddies sent by Jarl. There's oodles of Ryu at his metrosexual best, but I'm also giving you a whole lot more Anyan. Sweet, sweet Anyan. It all culminates with Jane rather dramatically saving the day, and making some major decisions that may surprise you. I'm really, really pleased at how *Tracking* turned out, not least because I had some major performance anxieties. I never thought I'd write a book, and out popped Jane. It was this weird, semi-mystical experience, even for me, and I was the one getting up at four in the morning and writing all day in my nightgown. So I really didn't know if I could pull it off a second time. But I think this book is even stronger than the first. That said, my Alpha Readers, the whole team at Orbit, and my amazing agent have been there for me every step of the way. Thanks, guys!

if you enjoyed
TEMPEST RISING

look out for

RED-HEADED STEPCHILD

book one of the Sabina Kane novels
by

Jaye Wells

1.

Digging graves is hell on a manicure, but I was taught good vampires clean up after every meal. So I ignored the chipped onyx polish. I ignored the dirt caked under my nails. I ignored my palms, rubbed raw and blistering. And when a snapping twig announced David's arrival, I ignored him too.

He said nothing, just stood off behind a thicket of trees waiting for me to acknowledge him. Despite his silence, I could feel hot waves of disapproval flying in my direction.

At last, the final scoop of earth fell onto the grave. Stalling, I leaned on the shovel handle and restored order to my hair. Next I brushed flecks of dirt from my cashmere sweater. Not the first choice of digging attire for some, but I always believed manual labor was no excuse for sloppiness. Besides, the sweater was black, so it went well with the haphazard funerary rites.

The Harvest Moon, a glowing orange sphere, still loomed in the sky. Plenty of time before sunrise. In the distance, traffic hummed like white noise in the City of Angels. I took a moment to appreciate the calm.

Memory of the phone call from my grandmother intruded. When she told me the target of my latest assignment, an icy chill spread through my veins. I'd almost hung up, unable to believe what she was asking me to do. But when she told me David was working with Clovis Trakiya, white-hot anger replaced the chill. I called up that anger now to spur my resolve. I clenched my teeth and ignored the cold stone sitting in my stomach. My own feelings about David were irrelevant now. The minute he decided to work with one of the Dominae's enemies – a glorified cult leader who wanted to overthrow their power – he'd signed his death warrant.

Unable to put it off any longer, I turned to him. 'What's up?'

David stalked out of his hiding place, a frown marring the perfect planes of his face. 'Do you want to tell me why you're burying a body?'

'Who, me?' I asked, tossing the shovel to the ground. My palms were already healing. I wish I could say the same for my guilty conscience. If David thought I should apologize for feeding from a human, I didn't want to know what he was going to say in about five minutes.

'Cut the shit, Sabina. You've been hunting again.' His eyes glowed with accusation. 'What happened to the synthetic blood I gave you?'

'That stuff tastes like shit,' I said. 'It's like nonalcoholic beer. What's the point?'

'Regardless, it's wrong to feed from humans.'

It's also wrong to betray your race, I thought. If there was one thing about David that always got my back up, it was his holier-than-thou attitude. Where were his morals when he made the decision to sell out?

Keep it together, Sabina. It will all be over in a few minutes.

'Oh, come on. It was just a stupid drug dealer,' I said, forcing myself to keep up the banter. 'If it makes you feel any better, he was selling to kids.'

David crossed his arms and said nothing.

'Though I have to say nothing beats Type O mixed with a little cannabis.'

A muscle worked in David's jaw. 'You're stoned?'

'Not really,' I said. 'Though I do have a strange craving for pizza. Extra garlic.'

He took a deep breath. 'What am I going to do with you?' His lips quirked despite his harsh tone.

'First of all, no more lectures. We're vampires, David. Mortal codes of good and evil don't apply to us.'

He arched a brow. 'Don't they?'

'Whatever,' I said. 'Can we just skip the philosophical debates for once?'

He shook his head. 'Okay then, why don't you tell me why we're meeting way out here?'

Heaving a deep sigh, I pulled my weapon. David's eyes widened as I aimed the custom-made pistol between them.

His eyes pivoted from the gun to me. I hoped he didn't notice the slight tremor in my hands.

'I should have known when you called me,' he said. 'You never do that.'

'Aren't you going to ask me why?' His calm unsettled me.

'I know why.' He crossed his arms and regarded me closely. 'The question is, do you?'

My eye twitched. 'I know enough. How could you betray the Dominae?'

He didn't flinch. 'One of these days your blind obedience to the Dominae is going to be your downfall.'

I rolled my eyes. 'Don't waste your final words on another lecture.'

He lunged before the last word left my lips. He plowed into me, knocking the breath out of my chest and the gun from my hand. We landed in a tangle of limbs on the fresh grave. Dirt and fists flew as we each struggled to gain advantage. He grabbed my hair and whacked my head into the dirt. Soil tunneled up my nose and rage blurred my vision.

My hands curled into claws and dug into his eyes. Distracted by pain, he covered them with his palms.

Gaining the advantage fueled my adrenaline as I flipped him onto his back. My knees straddled his hips, and I belted him in the nose with the base of my hand. Blood spurted from his nostrils, streaking his lips and chin.

'Bitch!' Like an animal, he sank his fangs into the fleshy part of my palm. I shrieked, backhanding him across the cheek with my uninjured hand. He growled and shoved me. I flew back several feet, landing on my ass with a thud.

Before I could catch my breath, his weight pinned me down again. Only this time, my gun stared back at me with its unblinking eye.

'How does it feel, Sabina?' His face was close to mine as he whispered. His breath stunk of blood and fury. 'How does it feel to be on the other end of the gun?'

'It sucks, actually.' Despite my tough talk, my heart hammered against my ribs. I glanced to the right and saw the shovel I'd used earlier lying about five feet away. 'Listen—'

'Shut up.' His eyes were wild. 'You know what the worst part is? I came here tonight to come clean with you. Was going to warn you about the Dominae and Clovis—'

'Warn me?'

David jammed the cold steel into my skull – tattooing me with his rage. 'That's the irony isn't it? Do you even know what's at stake here?' He cocked the hammer. Obviously, the question had been rhetorical.

One second, two, ticked by before the sound of flapping wings and a loud hoot filled the clearing. David glanced away, distracted. I punched him in the throat. He fell back, gasping and sputtering. I hauled ass to the shovel.

Time slowed. Spinning, I slashed the shovel in a wide arc. A bullet ricocheted off the metal, causing a spark. David pulled himself up to shoot again but I lunged forward, swinging like Babe Ruth. The metal hit David's skull with a sickening thud. He collapsed in a heap.

He wouldn't stay down long. I grabbed the gun from his limp hand and aimed it at his chest.

I was about to pull the trigger when his eyes crept open. 'Sabina.'

He lay on the ground, covered in blood and dirt. The goose egg on his forehead was already losing its mass. Knowledge of the inevitable filled his gaze. I paused, watching him.

At one time, I'd looked up to this male, counted him as a friend. And now he'd betrayed everything I held sacred by selling out to the enemy. I hated him for his treachery. I hated the Dominae for choosing me as executioner. But most of all, I hated myself for what I was about to do.

He raised a hand toward me – imploring me to listen. My insides felt coated in acid as I watched him struggle to sit up.

'Don't trust—'

His final words were lost in the gun's blast. David's body exploded into flames, caused by the metaphysical friction of his soul leaving his flesh.

My whole body spasmed. The heat from the fire couldn't stop the shaking in my limbs. Collapsing to the dirt, I wiped a quivering hand down my face.

The gun felt like a branding iron in my hand. I dropped it, but my hand still throbbed. A moment later, I changed my mind and picked it up again. Pulling out the clip, I removed one of the bullets. Holding one up for inspection, I wondered what David felt when the casing exploded and a dose of the toxic juice robbed him of his immortality.

I glanced over at the smoldering pile that was once my friend. Had he suffered? Or did death bring instant relief from the burdens of immortality? Or had I just damned his soul to a worse fate? I shook myself. His work here was done. Mine wasn't.

My shirt was caked with smears of soot, dirt, and drying blood – David's blood mixed with mine. I sucked in a lungful of air, hoping to ease the tightness in my chest.

The fire had died, leaving a charred, smoking mass of ash and bone. Great, I thought, now I have to dig another grave.

I used the shovel to pull myself up. A blur of white flew through the clearing. The owl called out again before flying over the trees. I stilled, wondering if I was hearing things. It called again and this time I was sure it screeched, 'Sabina.'

Maybe the smoke and fatigue were playing tricks on me. Maybe it had really said my name. I wasn't sure, but I didn't have time to worry about that. I had a body to bury.

As I dug in, my eyes started to sting. I tried to convince myself it was merely a reaction to the smoke, but a voice in my head whispered 'guilt'. With ruthless determination, I shoved my conscience down, compressing it into a tiny knot and shoving it into a dark corner of myself. Maybe later I'd pull it out and examine it. Or maybe not.

Good assassins dispose of problems without remorse. Even if the problem was a friend.